CAN A YOUNG WAR PROTESTER FIND HAPPINESS IN A SHELL-SHOCKED WORLD?

Ludwig had everything he'd ever dreamed of at his fingertips.

All he had to do was sell out and let himself be drafted.

His career, his family, and his love were all at stake.

But his principles and the prospect of martyrdom seemed a much more rational—and exciting—choice of action . . .

AN ACCIDENTAL MAN

An Extraordinary Novel by the Author of *The Sandcastle, An Unofficial Rose* and *The Flight from the Enchanter*

IRIS MURDOCH

Since *Under the Net* in 1954, IRIS MURDOCH has published a new novel almost every twelve months. Before starting this, her fourteenth, she paused for a year for other work.

IRIS MURDOCH

An Accidental Man

WARNER

PAPERBACK LIBRARY
NEW YORK

WARNER PAPERBACK LIBRARY EDITION
First Printing: January, 1973

Copyright © 1971 by Iris Murdoch
All rights reserved

Library of Congress Catalog Card Number: 79-171893

This Warner Paperback Library Edition is published by arrangement with The Viking Press, Inc.

Cover illustration by Paul Bacon

Warner Paperback Library is a division of Warner Books, Inc., 315 Park Avenue South, New York, N.Y. 10010.

TO KREISEL

An Accidental Man

An Accidental Man

"Gracie darling, will you marry me?"

"Yes."

"What?"

"Yes."

Ludwig Leferrier stared down into the small calm radiant unsmiling face of Gracie Tisbourne. Was it conceivable that the girl was joking? It was. Oh Lord.

"Look, Gracie, are you serious?"

"Yes."

"But I mean—"

"Of course if you want to back out of it—"

"Gracie! But—but—Gracie, do you love me?"

"Can you not infer that from what I said just now?"

"I don't want inferred love."

"I love you."

"It's impossible!"

"This is becoming a rather stupid argument."

"Gracie. I can't believe it!"

"Why are you so surprised?" said Gracie. "Surely the situation has been clear for some time. It has been to all my friends and relations."

"Oh damn your friends and relations—I mean—Gracie, you do really mean it? I love you so dreadfully much—"

"Don't be so *silly,* Ludwig," said Gracie. "Sometimes you're just a very *silly* man. I love you, and I've done so ever since you kissed me behind that tomb thing in the British Museum. I never thought I'd be so lucky."

"But you expected this?"

"I expected it now."

11

"I didn't."

"So are you now dismayed?"

"No! I've loved you for ages. But you're so sort of grand. Everyone's after you."

"I'm not grand. And that's a very vulgar way of putting it."

"Sorry—"

"I'm small and ignorant, whereas you know everything."

"As if that—! I thought I was one of hundreds."

"Well, you're one of one."

"You've been so calm!"

"A girl has her pride. Shall we now go hand in hand and tell my parents?"

"No, please— I say, will they mind?"

"They'll be delighted."

"I somehow thought they wanted you to marry that guy Sebastian."

"They want what I want."

"They won't mind my being American?"

"Why should they? Especially as you aren't going back to America any more."

"You said once they wanted you to marry an Englishman."

"Only because anyone else might take me away. But you won't. We'll be living in Oxford."

"I don't know about Oxford. Oh Jesus, Gracie, I can't believe it, I'm so happy— Darling, please—"

Gracie's divan bed, on which they were sitting, was very narrow and fitted in beneath a long white shelf. Small fat cushions, which Ludwig hated, and which Gracie referred to as her "pussy cats," further reduced the sitting or lying area. Ludwig banged his head on the shelf. One hand burrowed under Gracie's warm thigh. His head sank and he felt the roughness of his cheek against the smoothness of her taut dress. Crushed close together, two hearts battered in their cages. No screen of calm now. Ludwig groaned. He had never made love to her. The thing was anguish.

"Mind the table!"

He began to fall off, twisting a rubbery leg to avoid a

crash, and subsided embracing the coffee pot while Gracie above him stifled laughter. "Ssh, Ludwig!"

The Tisbournes' house in Kensington, pretentiously called Pitt's Lodge, was a narrow poky little gentleman's residence cluttered with elegant knick-knacks masquerading as furniture. Ludwig had already broken two chairs. Behind the papery walls of the small rooms Gracie's parents were omnipresent. Now just outside the door Clara Tisbourne was calling down to her husband, "Pinkie darling, the Odmores want us for the *second* weekend." It was an impossible situation even if Gracie had been willing. He could not take Gracie to his own apartment because Gracie disliked Mitzi Ricardo. Mitzi also disliked Gracie and referred to her as "little Madam" until she realized that Ludwig loved her. Perhaps it would have to be the British Museum again.

"Whatever shall we do?" he said to Gracie.

"About what?"

They had never discussed sex. He had no idea whether Gracie was a virgin. Must he now tell her about his campus amours? Oh Christ.

"Here. Yes, I know. Dear Ludwig, just sit quietly and hold my hand."

He looked into the mysterious guileless eyes of the girl to whom he had committed himself, his life, his future, his thoughts, his feelings, his whole spiritual being. She was so fantastically young. He felt centuries older than this opening flower. He felt coarse, gross, ancient, dirty. At the same moment it occurred to him that she was almost totally a stranger. He loved, he was engaged to be married to, a complete stranger.

"Gracie, you are so pure, so true."

"That's your *silly* talk."

"You're so young!"

"I'm nineteen. You're only twenty-two."

"When shall we get married? How quickly can one get married in England?"

"We've only just got engaged. *Please*, Ludwig. You know the way Mama bounces in."

13

"What's the use of being engaged? I want—"

"It's nice being engaged. We shall be a long time married. Let's enjoy our engagement. It's such a special time. I've so much liked the first five minutes of it."

"But, Gracie, how are we going to—"

"Besides, Mama will insist on a big white wedding and those things take ages to organize."

"Surely we don't have to have all that crap? Gracie, you know you can always get what you want—"

"Well, I want it too. It will be such fun. I'll have Karen Arbuthnot as a bridesmaid—"

"Gracie, have a heart—"

"We couldn't get married now anyway with Grandmama so ill. Supposing she were to die on our wedding day?"

"Is she very ill?"

"Aunt Charlotte says she's dying. But that may be wishful thinking."

"I feel so terribly afraid I'll lose you."

"Don't be idiotic. Here's my hand here, feel it."

"Gracie, poppet, are you sure you don't mind—"

"What? Ludwig, you're *trembling*."

"It's all so sudden. I've been in such a state these last weeks."

"About little me?"

"Yes, about you. And about— Yes. Gracie, you're sure you don't mind what I've done? I mean my not going back ever, my not going to fight, you know—"

"Why should I mind your not wanting to fight in a wicked war? Why should I mind your choosing to live here in England with me and become English?"

"Later on you might want to go to America and we couldn't, I guess."

"I don't want to go to America. You are my America."

"Dear Gracie! But—you don't think it's dishonourable?"

"How can it be dishonourable to do the right thing?"

How indeed.

They were sitting side by side, precariously, as if they were on a boat. Ludwig held her right hand tightly in his. His left arm was stretched round her shoulder. His bony

14

tweedy knees were pressed against her sleek knees, pale brown and shiny through openwork tights. She smelt of young flesh and toilet soap and pollen. Oh God, if they could only take their clothes off! Outside it was raining. Warm early summer rain playfully caressed the window. A bright subdued light showed the small pink and white houses opposite against a dark grey sky which shone like illuminated metal. There would be a rainbow somewhere above the park. Elsewhere that war was going on, high explosive and napalm and people killed and maimed. There were people out there who had been at war all their lives.

The crucial date had passed. He had torn up his draft card some time ago. But until lately there had been a way out. Now there was none. He had taken a carefully considered step and with it had chosen exile. He had no regrets, except about his parents. He was their only child. It had been the achievement of their lives to make him what they could never be, genuinely American. They would never understand.

"Have some more elevenses," said Gracie. "Have some Tennis Court Cake. I know you like marzipan. Have some Russian gateau."

Her little bedroom, which she called her sitting-room, and in which indeed they had so far done nothing but sit, was cosy and prim. Its formality and order were those of a child. This schoolroom neatness, this bitty folky flowery charm, represented, Ludwig suspected, not only Gracie's unformed taste but also some vanished era in the taste of her parents. He had once heard Gracie resisting Clara's enthusiastic ideas about redecorating it. A growing miscellany of pictures now fought with the sprigged wallpaper: small Impressionist reproductions, engravings of hawks and parrots, photos of the Acropolis and Windsor Castle and the Taj Mahal. Yet Gracie knew nothing about architecture, nothing about birds, and constantly mixed Van Gogh up with Cézanne. Indeed she appeared to know very little about anything, having firmly left school early and refused any further education. What on earth is one to do, he had once thought, with a girl who has no idea

15

who Charlemagne was and who doesn't care? Later he admired her nerve and came to prize her calm ignorance. She was without the pretensions and ambitions which powered his own life. Her simplicity, her gaiety, even her silliness lightened his Puritan sadness. Yet he also knew that she was no mere kitten, this almost-child. There was a formidable will crushed up inside this unfolding bud.

"No thanks, no cake."

"Have a jelly baby."

"No. I'm still feeling kicked in the stomach."

"Well, I'm *hungry*."

Gracie was a great eater, but remained slim. She was a pale miniature-looking girl with a small well-formed head and a small eager face. She had glowing powdery flesh, very light blue eyes, and wispy half-long silvery-golden hair. When she was petulant she looked like a terrier. When she was self-satisfied, which was often, she looked Oriental. She was not coquettish, yet she was very conscious of herself as a young and pretty girl. Her tiny mouth was aware, thoughtful, stubborn. She seemed to Ludwig like a precious relic, an heirloom of vanished feminine refinement, something almost Victorian.

"Do you think you'll get the Oxford thing?"

"Gee, I hope so. I try not to think about it. It matters so much."

"I'd like to live in Oxford. It's such a pretty place. And you can get into the country."

"You won't mind being the wife of a stuffy old ancient history don?"

"Don't be absurd, Ludwig. Do you think I want to marry an astronaut or something? I only wish I wasn't such an ignoramus. I'll just have to keep quiet and smile. I suppose there are wives like that in Oxford. Still, the rest of the family will make a show. Papa was a Senior Wrangler and Mama was at Bedford and of course Patrick—"

Anxiety about the Oxford job had contributed to his torment, he wanted that job so dreadfully. Oxford had in these months grown huge and wide and magnetic in his consciousness. This too was a kind of being in love. He pictured himself there like a man picturing paradise. He feared disappointment like a man fearing hell. Of course whatever happened now he would stay on in England after his London scholarship year was over. Athena had here sufficiently seized him by the locks. All the elements of his case were clear to him and he had no more doubt about the rightness of his decision. The war was a piece of absolute wickedness in which he would take no part. He would not fight for the United States of America in that war. But neither was it his task to make politics, to shout and speechify and martyr himself. I am not a political animal, he told himself repeatedly. He was a scholar. He would not waste his talents. He would stay in England, where by a pure and felicitous accident he had been born, and take part in the long old conversation of Europe. To regret that his role was in so many ways an easy one was purely sentimental.

The analysis was clear and the decision was made. Only his Protestant conscience, like a huge primitive clumsy processing machine, obsolete yet still operational, continued to give him trouble. If only he could take that awful uncomprehending misery away from his parents. He dreaded their letters in which, in language which both offended and touched him, they begged him to come home and get himself "straightened out." Did they really think he must be mad? He dreaded their confused reproaches, their fear. Old European terrors, inherited from generations of wandering ancestors, coursed in their blood and made them shudder from breaking the laws of the United States and evading its decrees. And there was their dreadful wrong-headed pride. Grief at his absence, fear of bureaucracy, what the neighbours thought, it was all jumbled together.

His father's family were devout Protestants from Alsace. His mother's family were Lutherans from Bavaria. His maternal grandfather, who disappeared during the war and was thought to have died in a concentration camp, had been a minister. A strong and rigid disapproval of Hitler had led both families to migrate westward, and Ludwig's parents had met soon after the war in Mont-de-Marson,

17

where Ludwig's father had been working as an electrical engineer. They soon decided to emigrate to America, but while waiting for their visas went first on a brief visit to England so as to improve their English. Here, with what now seemed an intelligent prescience, young Ludwig had achieved an English birth, and with it the right to British nationality, although before his first birthday he was already in the U.S.A. He grew up happily enough, normally enough, as an American child, his parents' joy. Yet in his blood too, old European things lived and waited, and as he became an adult and an intellectual he found himself an unidentified person, a changeling. He inherited the physical awkwardness of his parents and their deep conscientious anxiety. He grew up into problems which they had hoped to leave behind. He was uneasy with his hybrid name. He felt ashamed of being an Aryan German and yet also ashamed of having ceased to be one. His parents, perfectly bilingual in French and German, spoke only English at home, laboriously conversing even when they were alone together in this language which they never fully mastered. Ludwig learnt his French and German at school. His parents were grateful to America, and the glow of that gratitude was shed over his childhood.

When he came at last to Europe no blood relations awaited him. All had died or scattered. What mainly confronted him was the ghost of Hitler. This and many other things needed to be exorcised. As a historian and as a man he needed somehow in thought to undergo the whole passion of recent history, but he could not do it. Faced with what he had so significantly missed, his intellect became hazy and faint. He remained outside it all and yet burdened by it as by something heavy forever trailing behind him, a part of himself which he could never properly see. In America he felt European, in France he felt German, in Germany American. Only in England, which he found in some ways most alien of all, could he somehow forget or postpone the problem of who he was. The company of other historians suited him, Oxford and Cambridge scholars, joky unexcited men who just took him for granted and assumed quietly that of course he would stay and become British. He was so grateful for that.

There will be a time, he thought, beyond all this, when I shall work calmly on remote important things, and when all this anguish will be over. Meanwhile he knew, engaging his conscience with his reason as if these were independent sovereigns, that he did not feel guilty only because he was disappointing his parents. He felt guilty exactly as they did because he was disappointing the U.S.A., because he was breaking the law, because he had decided not to return, because he feared death and would not be a soldier, because he was behaving as cowards and traitors behave. He accepted the guilt with a kind of calm as if it were not an admonition but a mere phenomenon, an experience, a punishment: a punishment for what was happening right now in the little white house in Vermont where his parents brooded over the incomprehensible doom which their son had pronounced.

The decision was made, completed like a long journey, but still strange to him, and rediscovered every morning with a painful lurid surprise. Of course it was no accident that he had mismanaged the whole thing so horribly. This particular muddle he recognized as, for himself, characteristic. If he had elected to be British much earlier he would never have been drafted. He had, he bitterly put it to himself, hoped to get away with it, hoped to have without drama the best of both his worlds. His drafting had been deferred and deferred again. He had thought and thought but without ever quite bringing himself to make up his mind. There was so much involved, so much at stake. He knew he could stick if he had to, and also he knew himself as in some ways an instinctively timid man, a quiet man who was unwilling to raise his voice, unwilling to be stared at. The final summons came unexpectedly. And now he could not defy it with impunity. As far as the United States was concerned he was in bad trouble. Scurrying now for the bolt hole of another nationality would not save him from the automatic retribution of the country which he was so precipitately abandoning. This aspect of the matter, once he did decide to stick, he deliberately refrained from examining in detail. It seemed that at least fifteen years must pass before he could return without facing immediate arrest. With his claim for British nationality pending it was, he had been advised, unthinkable that he should be extradited as a deserter. But as an American he was now done for.

How much, apart from his distress for his parents, this would really hurt, he had not yet been able to estimate. He was quite certain that he was acting rightly. But this did not make it burn less. He suffered his pangs of guilt and fear and loss and waited for these sufferings to pass. There would be a time for reconciliation and quiet work and the treasure caves of Europe, a time, oh God, for Gracie. He had told her these things, but only in a cool and abstract way. He did not know whether he was glad or sorry that she had accepted them without puzzlement, without profound questioning. With how much of the real tangle and torment would it be fair to burden her; and if he was to marry her would it be right to burden her with less than all?

Her little strong right hand was gripping his. "What a pity Patrick is too old to be a page."

"A page? Oh sure. I can't see Patrick as a page! I hope *he*'ll approve?"

"Oh yes," said Gracie, licking her fingers and still holding his hand, so that he felt her tongue on his palm. "He said you were the only genuine intellectual among my swains."

Patrick was Gracie's younger brother. He was still at boarding school. He was bookish and ambitious.

"Will your parents come over for the wedding?"

Would they? Would they want to? So many things were happening so fast, creating new worlds in which old instinctive ways of acting were no good any more.

The rain suddenly pattered on the window like a handful of pebbles, then grew quiet again. The room brightened with a vivid dark golden light.

"I don't know."

"Who will you have as your best man?"

"Must I have a best man? Well, I guess I'd have Garth

if he were over here by then, you know, Garth Gibson Grey."

Ludwig felt a faint electrical shock. Guilt again possibly. He had thought a good deal less about Garth in recent weeks, though when he had first arrived eight months ago the return of Garth had been the thing to which he had most looked forward. He had made Garth's acquaintance when they were both students at Harvard. Garth, a graduate of Cambridge, England, had been his first close English friend. Garth was studying philosophy. They had immediately started an argument which went on for days, weeks, months. The Harvard philosophers did not think highly of Garth. But Ludwig decided he was one of the most remarkable men he had ever met. He longed for Garth to come back so that they could experience England, Europe, together. He had made all his great decisions since their last talk. He had mentioned them in letters, but without emotion. Garth had replied laconically "Good," then written about other things, then stopped writing altogether. He was due home in July, but July was still a long way off. And now there was Gracie.

Ludwig recognized the little guilty shock as a realization that when Garth came he would no longer be alone. He would no longer be waiting. I am surrendering my aloneness forever, he thought, clutching Gracie's hand. What would Garth think about his *engagement*? Garth and Gracie, whose families were acquainted, had known each other slightly since childhood. It was through Garth, or more immediately through Garth's father, Austin Gibson Grey, that Ludwig had met the Tisbournes, Charlotte Ledgard, Mitzi Ricardo, Mavis Argyll, and many other of those fearfully English English with whom he now felt so surprisingly at home. Garth had suggested to Ludwig, who was to precede him to England by a year, that he should look up Austin. "You may be able to help my father," he said cryptically. Austin had certainly helped Ludwig, finding him digs at Mitzi's place, introducing him to people, setting him on the path to Gracie. Had Ludwig helped Austin? Austin was not easy to help. "Austin is hopeless," George Tisbourne used to say. "Elder brother

21

trouble of course." Austin's elder brother Matthew was a horribly successful diplomat. Austin was not so good at coping. Ludwig rather liked Austin's hopelessness. It relaxed his nerves to see Austin flounder. Of course poor Austin had serious troubles, but for some reason one could never take them too gravely. How surprised Austin would be about Ludwig and Gracie! "Not a chance," Austin had judged when Ludwig told his love. And what would Garth say? Garth would say nothing. Garth the lone wolf. But Garth would be in some way disappointed. He would feel that Ludwig had been absorbed into ordinariness. They don't like each other, Garth and Gracie, Ludwig had earlier intuited from Gracie's chatter. He could see why. And he felt now with a kind of sadness and a kind of pride what it was like to be responsible for the being of another.

"Do you find that your ears stick to your head at night?"

"I don't know, poppet."

"Mine do, it does feel funny. You've got such nice sleek animal ears. Some men have such coarse ears. Ludwig, do do something for me. Cut your hair very short, the way it used to be. I love it furry."

"Okay, honey. But it looks so sort of grey when it's short."

"I like it nice and grey."

He had begun to grow his hair, it occurred to him guiltily, to please another girl.

"And another thing, Ludwig darling."

"What, angel?"

"Don't go to see Dorina like that any more."

Feminine intuition.

"Why not, sweetheart? You know it's not—"

"I know it's not. I know it's for Austin. But I hate your being a sort of emotional go-between for them."

Dorina was Mrs. Austin Gibson Grey. Something had happened to poor Austin's second marriage. But what had happened no one could make out, least of all perhaps Austin and Dorina.

"Austin trusts me. I can help."

22

"Austin must unravel all that muddle for himself. Please keep out of it. Don't go to Valmorana."

Valmorana was a sort of hostel for distressed girls which was run by Dorina's elder sister Mavis Argyll. Mavis was a social worker and generally agreed to be "wonderful," one of those dedicated single women on whom society so much depends. Dorina, fleeing for reasons unknown from her husband, had taken refuge there.

"You see, at present Dorina just wants to be by herself, but they each want to know how the other——"

"Yes, yes, Ludwig, I understand. It's not that I'm against Dorina, one couldn't be. She's so touching and sort of caught. And with Austin as a husband—— It's that it's all such a *mess* and you can't really help them, no one can, and you'll just get pulled into it too——"

"Don't get excited, sweetie——"

"Your going there is like secret police or something. It's not very important to you, seeing Dorina, is it?"

"I guess not—— But how can I—— I'm supposed to be going there tomorrow. What will they think?"

"One mustn't worry about what people think. You said that to me once. Make some excuse."

"But poor old Austin, he hasn't got anyone——"

"Austin gives me the creeps."

"But why—is it his funny hand?"

"No, of course not, I don't mind his funny hand. He finds me attractive."

"How do you know? God, he never made a pass at you, did he?"

"No, but a woman knows. A young girl always knows."

"So what? I guess everyone finds you attractive. It's not a crime, poppet darling."

"I find him repulsive—no, that's too strong. He's old. I hate it when old people find me attractive."

"He's not fifty!"

"His face creams and mantles like a standing pond."

"I think he's got a very nice face."

"He's so unfortunate."

"That's not a crime either!"

"It is in him. Bad luck is a sort of wickedness in some

23

people. No, I don't mean that either. I hate his soupy sort of emotions, the way he looks at life. Sorry. I just don't want you to go to Valmorana. If you do you'll get involved in their *thing*. I don't want you to be *interested* in them and in their horrible messy world of quarreling and forgiving. Please. Do you see?"

Ludwig felt distress. How could he hurt Austin and Dorina, who had both been so kind to him? And why shouldn't he be interested and try to help? He was about to argue when he realized: she is jealous of Dorina. He felt touched, tender, delighted, grateful.

"All right, honeybun, anything you like. Say, do you think your parents have gone out? I can't hear a thing."

"No, I can hear Papa typing. Please, Ludwig. Oh darling, I'm suddenly so frightened. We will be all right, won't we? Oh let us be all right forever. There are such terrible things in the world."

❈❈❈❈❈

"Recession. Yes," said Austin Gibson Grey. He was not sure what recession meant, but he knew what Mr. Bransome meant.

"It is a matter of computerization."

"Indeed."

"There is nothing personal involved."

"Quite."

"The management consultants who were here last month—"

"I thought they were interior decorators."

"Possibly they were so described."

"They were."

24

"It was a matter of being tactful."

"I see."

"Recommended a thoroughgoing streamlining of staff ratios."

"Ah yes."

"You appreciate that we have been losing money."

"I do."

"Our situation, I say in confidence, is difficult."

"I am sorry."

"We shall pay you of course for the entire month."

"Thank you."

"But I trust you will feel free to leave at any time."

"How kind."

"I expect you will wish to find another post."

"I will."

"I am sure you will have no difficulty in doing so."

"I hope you are right."

"And in fact your successor here—"

"I thought I didn't have a successor. I thought that was the point."

"Well, just a graduate trainee— I will provide you with excellent references."

"About my pension—"

"I thought you would ask that."

"Can I take it in a lump sum?"

"You were enrolled among our temporary nonpensionable staff."

"That was a long time ago."

"Time does not alter such things, Mr. Gibson Grey."

"But I distinctly remember—"

"You joined a voluntary pension scheme."

"What will that bring me now?"

"I am afraid nothing."

"Nothing?"

"You become eligible for benefits at the age of sixty-five."

"Sixty-five!"

"You opted for scheme F-Four with smaller premiums."

"I see!"

"Here is your signature."

25

"But I haven't any money," said Austin, "I haven't a penny. I've saved nothing."

"That is not our affair, Mr. Gibson Grey."

Was Mr. Bransome going to turn nasty? Was Austin going to burst into tears?

"I mean, I think it's a bit unfair to sack me suddenly after all these years without warning."

"Temporary nonpensionable staff are always subject to this hazard. This was made clear in your terms of appointment. Would you care to see your terms of appointment? They are here on the file."

"No, thank you."

"We want to make things easy for you, Mr. Gibson Grey."

"Thank you."

"I have here a draft letter of resignation. Miss Waterhouse has just typed it."

"You mean *my* resignation?"

"Yes."

"I'll sign it."

"Don't you want to read it?"

"No, thanks."

Austin signed the letter with his left hand. His right hand had been stiff since boyhood.

"And here is a little mark of our appreciation."

"What is it?"

"A book token. The contributors have listed their names."

"So all these people knew I was going and I didn't?"

"We wanted it to be a nice surprise."

"How charming."

"Well, I think that is all, Mr. Gibson Grey."

"Can I leave at once?"

"At once? Certainly if—"

"I don't think I want to meet my successor."

"I would hardly—"

"And I've got my book token."

"Then it remains to wish you good luck."

"And good luck to you, my dear Mr. Bransome."

Miss Waterhouse and the Junior watched with ecstasy as Austin cleared out his desk. It was not every day that they witnessed a sacking. Miss Waterhouse lent Austin a carrier bag. The Junior chewed gum, which Austin had forbidden him to do in the office. At the bottom of one of the drawers Austin found a photograph of Betty. He tore it up and dropped it into the wastepaper basket.

I cannot and will not rise upon my humiliations to higher things, thought Austin. He was sitting in the pub. It was raining. He started to eat a pickled onion and bit his tongue. He always bit his tongue in moments of crisis. Perhaps he had an abnormally large tongue? How did the tongue survive anyway, leading its dangerous life inside a semicircular guillotine? When he came to think about it, it was like something out of Edgar Allan Poe.

It flickers, he thought, it flickers. Behind the visible world, always just upon the threshold of some possible mode of perception, there was another and more terrible reality. He stared till his eyes grew hazy, till they watered not with ordinary tears. Was it like this for others? No. The world of the happy is not the world of the unhappy, as some idiot philosopher had said. Why was he not a successful ordinary man pulling girls' tights off in the backs of cars? How to overcome anxiety. He once wrote for a book called that. It was all about diaphragmatic breathing. It did no good.

Looking-glass man, he thought, trying vainly for the millionth time to flex the fingers of his right hand. If only I could turn myself inside out and made the fantasy real, the real fantasy. But the trouble was that there were no good dreams any more, nothing good or holy or truly desirable any more even in dreams, only that awful thing behind the flickering screen. Dorina had been a good dream. There had seemed to be another place where Dorina walked barefoot in the dew with her hair undone. Altogether elsewhere there were cool meadows and flowers and healing waters. That had been the meaning of Dorina. Could he ever reach that place? Oh softness of fantasy life which nothing resists.

Garth and Dorina must not know that he had been sacked. But someone in the office would tell someone who would tell the Tisbournes and they would send the news around. The Tisbournes always found out everything. How pleased they would be. How intrusively anxious to help. How delighted all his enemies would be. By his enemies of course Austin meant his friends. How he despised himself for caring what the Tisbournes thought. Even from that petty servitude he was unable to free himself. Thank God Garth was in America. Thank God Matthew was abroad, elsewhere forever, and that they had stopped writing to each other. The Tisbournes' sympathy would torment him. Matthew's sympathy might kill him.

Perhaps it was providential after all that Dorina was still at Valmorana. O my little caged bird, how painful it is to think of you and yet how sweet! Dorina was to have been a fresh start, a stepping-stone into some sort of elegant life. Her innocence had been so important to him, his capture of it such an achievement. How he had loved her dependence, even her ghost-haunted weakness. Would he ever live with her again in blameless ordinariness? That was his only significant goal. But now everything they did seemed to hurt each other. How had it come to be like that? And how had it all become so *public*, with everyone endlissly interfering and trying to run his affairs? Why could he not keep his trouble to himself like other people did? Sister Mavis had carried Dorina away into her never never land, her fairy domain of false light. But Dorina was the real princess. Mavis was just a smart Bloomsbury Catholic with a failed life. I'll get another job, he thought, and get Dorina back. For the present it's just as well she's with Mavis. She's safe there, they can't get at her there, she's protected and shut in. Later on I'll take her away. I was in a rut at that stupid office, that was part of the trouble. Need I despise myself forever because of a fat boy in a football jersey?

What a pity Dorina had turned out not to have any money after all. The world of the pecunious is not the world of the impecunious. If there is nothing in the bank any more what happens, what does one do? What happens

28

when a human life just irretrievably breaks down? Now he had debts and no income. Whom could he borrow from? Charlotte? I'll let the flat and move in with Mitzi Ricardo, he suddenly thought. What a good idea. I can make a bit on the letting. Mitzi had suggested this once before when he was broke, after Betty's death, before Dorina. Mitzi loved him. He knew that Mitzi had suffered at his second marriage and had quietly rejoiced at his troubles. Mitzi was a big powerful girl, a big blonde with a big face and a loud voice, who had been quite a famous athlete before she wrecked her ankle. He liked Mitzi and her tough defeated acceptance of the mediocre. Mitzi thought Dorina thought her "common," but of course Dorina couldn't even think a word like that. Mitzi would be sweet and gentle with him, yes, that was what he needed now, gentleness and a healing of bruises, the gentleness of lame people. Mitzi would ask nothing and expect nothing. What a relief. And he need not discuss things with her. One hated outsiders and confidants in the end.

Ludwig Leferrier was there too, whom Austin trusted. An American friend of Garth's had seemed the last thing that Austin could do with. But he had got on amazingly well with Ludwig. He could talk about Garth to Ludwig without pain. Perhaps because the big slow American boy conceived of no horrors here. Ludwig's admiration for Garth both touched and exasperated Austin. Ludwig thought of Austin as a fond father proud of his clever son, as if such a relationship somehow covered and accounted for everything. Of course Austin was a fond proud father. Yet was Garth really so remarkable? Austin feared his son's judgement, but that was another thing. There were indeed many other things. He was grateful to Ludwig too because Ludwig, while being friendly, loyal and discreet, could make neither head nor tail of the Dorina business, and did not, as everyone else did, pretend to understand it better than Austin did himself.

What did I do with that photo of Betty, he thought, as he lifted his steel-rimmed specs out of a pool of beer. Austin was vain about his appearance and resented the glasses, which were newcomers in his life. He began to ferret about in Miss Waterhouse's carrier bag. Then he remembered that he had torn the photo up and thrown it away. Why had he done that? Why was he always doing things that he didn't mean to or want to? The pub was closing and he would have to go back to the flat. He would take some aspirins and lie down. But then the demon asthma would come and bind his breast in a hoop of steel. It had been his constant companion, forbidding rest, ever since the accident with the gas. And afternoon repose was hell anyway, as he knew from terrible Saturdays and Sundays when his body and his mind ached with twitching boredom and fatigue and fear. Quietness came to him now only when he was unconscious.

Suppose he were to go to the National Gallery. Would Titian or Rembrandt or Piero work a wonder for him, as they had once done? No. All books, even the greatest, became exhausted if read often enough and all pictures lose their power to charm. Only youth preserves some illusion of radiance because the ability to be surprised has not yet worn away. And when he felt wistfully that his own life had once had the clarity of art, he was merely remembering his boyhood, the bright time before he fell down that rivulet of stone while the fat boy laughed and laughed.

When he was ten he had had to learn to write with his left hand. Every nerve of his being resisted this. He had fallen through the looking-glass and could never get back. Even now when he was tired he formed his letters the wrong way round and the old weak penetrating feeling of impotence swept over him again. His Quaker parents had told him to make of his physical disability a spiritual advantage but he could not and would not. For him the Inner Light was early quenched. He detested his parents' complacent seriousness. But he had never made it out of their rotten milieu as Matthew had.

That was all long ago and even poor Bet was dead long since and the miseries she had caused him were spectres which the years had wasted and the fat boy in the football jersey was an elderly Buddha, an ambassador, a "Sir." "Oh, are you Sir Matthew's brother?" people would say with ill-concealed amaze. Let Matthew now stay away

30

from him forever, let him end his days in an Eastern monastery, as he once said he would, and let the world know him no more. Indeed, Austin had already come to believe that Matthew was dead, for only so could his own heart be at rest.

✠✠✠✠✠

"Grace Leferrier. It's a nice name. Yes, very nice."

"You aren't too sorry about Sebastian Odmore?"

"I knew Gracie would never marry Sebastian."

"I think you're making the best of a—"

"No, I'm not, Pinkie. I think it's lovely."

George and Clara Tisbourne were drinking after-luncheon coffee in their tiny dining-room. George was a civil servant working on Millbank and came home to lunch most days. The rain had stopped and a faint steam arose from the wet cement in the tiny garden-yard. There was a lake about the drain, which was blocked again.

"And it all happened this morning?"

"Yes, about eleven o'clock, Gracie said."

"Was she calm?"

"No. She pretended to be. But she was all of a tremble. So am I. Let's have some cognac."

"Gracie engaged!" said George Tisbourne. "It's certainly a significant moment." He fetched the brandy. "Or will she change her mind?"

"She loves him. She's all hazy."

"She's often hazy. Better wait a bit before announcing it."

"I did want an Englishman," said Clara, "but I suppose an American is next best, and he is a very nice American.

31

I must say when Americans are sweet they're very very sweet."

"And he's definitely staying here?"

"Oh yes. He's the expatriate type. Detests his homeland. Besides, he was born here."

"Good. He seems to be a clever chap. I wish Gracie had condescended to have a bit more education."

"Gracie knows what's best for herself. She's a very sure-footed animal. She will make her life work."

"Yes, she's always known best, she never really depended on us, even as a child."

The parents contemplated in silence the awe-inspiring mystery of their daughter.

"He's quite good-looking too," said Clara. "That wide smile and those nice square teeth. Even being prematurely grey rather suits him. Only I wish he didn't speak so slowly, sometimes one's concentration fails in the middle of a sentence."

"Who are his people? What does his father do?"

"Naturally I asked Gracie at once. She didn't know!"

"I suppose his parents aren't rich?"

"I somehow think not. And I couldn't ask Gracie that when she was in such an interesting spiritual condition."

"Hmm. Speaking of—do you think?"

"No. But I think the sooner we have that weekend with the Odmores the better."

"Clara!"

"Oh Pinkie, I do hope it will all work, I couldn't bear it if Gracie wasn't happily married. Think of the torment. Will they communicate all the time like we do? I shall never be able to talk enough to you between now and the end of the world."

"If they don't talk it needn't matter. Every marriage is an individual."

"I think Saint Mary Abbots, or whatever it calls itself, don't you?"

"You mean for the wedding? Why not Saint George's, Hanover Square!"

"Well, we are Barkers people, you know, not Harrods people, and it is our local church."

"I suppose the parson won't mind? We never turn up. I haven't been since Patrick's christening."

"I know the parson, he belongs to Penny Sayce's bridge circus."

"I say, have you told Alison?"

"I never talk to poor Mama now on the telephone, it's too painful. I rang Char and Char will tell her."

"What was Charlotte's reaction?"

"Dry. Surprised Gracie had that much sense. Poor old Char, she's always resentful and trying to score."

"She tries to put us down a bit, but that's natural. Of course she loves us, but she's got to defend herself. An elder sister always has ambiguous feelings about a younger one, especially when the younger one is happily married and she's single."

"And especially when the younger one has married the man she wanted!"

"If Charlotte ever wanted me those wants are past and gone long ago."

"I'm not so sure. Charlotte is deep. She's distinguished and weird and proud. What goes on in my dear sister's mind I wonder?"

"Nothing mysterious, Clara."

"All minds are mysterious. What goes on in your mind, Pinkie, if it comes to that? We talk ceaselessly and without a shred of concealment and yet the real quality of being you is utterly hidden from me."

They looked at each other. George had no sentimental secrets from his wife, but there was one thing he had never told her. He had studied mathematics and intended to be a mathematician. But before those cold Himalayas of the spirit his courage had fainted, and he had turned early away to the world of the warm, the lucrative, and the easy. He was a clever man and an able civil servant, but these were simple skills which he exercised, and he often felt his mind sluggish and cheated of greatness. He never talked to his wife about these matters or told her that he despised himself eternally for this failure. Yet perhaps now it did not matter too much, that pusillanimous choice,

33

because as one grew older and saw death in the distance nothing mattered too much any more, even virtue.

"You can read my mind as if it were all cast on a screen over my head," said George, and drank some brandy.

"Poor Char. I wonder how often she has regretted answering the call of duty and looking after Mama. I don't think she knew when she started how much of her life was being asked of her."

"It's been a long time."

"I know you used to think Mama was a *malade imaginaire*."

"She began as one. I think she was amazed when she found she was really ill."

"Well, Char got stuck long before that. Does one regret having been dutiful, I wonder?"

"I think sometimes one regrets that most of all. Charlotte was trapped. It wasn't just duty."

"I know. Some people just miss the bus. Poor Char has had no sort of life."

"You're wrong. She plays a very special role. The role that some unmarried people play in the lives of their married friends. Married people need unmarried people. There's a kind of priestly efficacy."

"You mean Char's always available? She isn't, you know. She hates it all. She's not a kindly minister."

"That's not necessary. The thing is partly symbolic. She's *there*."

"Like the family cat!"

"How is your mother, by the way?"

"Sinking. I suppose she might go on sinking for years. You remember that crisis ages ago, and she recovered. I think all the same we won't have this house redecorated."

"You think this time next year we'll be in the Villa?" The Villa was the family name for Clara's mother's house in Chelsea.

"I don't know. You won't mind Char being there too? Mama did say she was leaving the place to us jointly. We can convert the basement into a nice flat for Char."

"If we move in Charlotte will move out."

"Oh God. Well, let's not worry about it now. I must say

34

the Villa is a stunning house. And it'll be marvellous to have some more space, after this shoe box. And some more money. Aren't I being hardhearted and worldly?"

"You used to say you enjoyed making economies. You used to say you'd hate to be rich."

"I'm growing old, Pinkie. I've changed my mind."

Clara's mother, Alison Ledgard, had married an ineffectual solicitor who had wanted to be a poet but had written few verses after his marriage. Alison's own family, however, were Ulster linen merchants and Alison had been a considerable heiress.

'You ought to see Alison more often," said George.

"I know I ought to. But it's so terribly painful seeing her so frail and not herself any more and some days she can't even speak. And all that fearful energy isn't gone, you know, it's just pent up inside, her eyes can *glow*, it's terrible. And somehow one feels her life was so wasted just because she was a woman. She ought to have been galloping across the steppes at the head of some horde."

"Has she met Ludwig?"

"No. I somehow don't think she'll care now. When she got really ill she stopped being interested in the children. They are so bumptiously young."

"The terrible solipsism of youth can offend the old. Patrick has been quite good with her lately."

"Yes, Patrick is a bit quieter and more gentlemanly. I suspect it's the influence of Ralph Odmore."

"Charles says Ralph has stopped being a dandy and has become a hippie."

"Oh dear. Still, Patrick will look adorable with long hair."

"Gracie must take Ludwig to see Alison all the same. Gracie hasn't been near her for ages."

"I know. I have chid her, or does one say chided. She just says, 'Shut up, Ma.' I do wish she wouldn't call me 'Ma,' she does it on purpose."

"I remember Gracie saying that Alison's awful energy wore her out!"

"I know what she means. Well, of course she must take Ludwig. A September wedding, don't you think? I wonder if we shall have the Villa by then. I wish Ludwig wasn't lodging with that ghastly gin-swilling Amazon."

"You mean what's-her-name, Mitzi Ricardo?"

"Austin says she ought to have been a boxer. I wonder if she ever gave him a straight left? He'd like that."

"One does feel sorry for her."

"I think I'm going to give up being sorry for people, Pinkie, it does no good. What with poor Charlotte and poor Mitzi and poor Penny and poor Austin and poor Dorina—"

"Oh Clara, I quite forgot a bit of news that I heard this morning. Austin has just lost his job."

"You mean got the sack?"

"Yes."

"Il ne manquait que ça. Of course it was sure to happen. Like when he was in the army and just gassed himself as quickly as possible. What was he doing there?"

"Clerical work."

"Poor Austin is no genius, but we must rally round. You can find him something, Pinkie. He must get a job before Garth comes home. Think of the loss of face."

"Garth would be censorious?"

"Yes. I can't stand children who judge their parents. Thank God ours don't."

"How do you know?"

"Well, they keep quiet about it. Garth used to be a little monster."

"It's not so easy to help Austin, he's so damn touchy."

"Let's ask him for a drink."

"He won't come."

"He's as bad as Char. I wonder what poor little Dorina will think of her husband's latest."

"I suspect Austin won't tell her. And Clara darling, we mustn't tell her."

"You still think we should keep clear of the Valmorana set-up? I must say I'm suffering agonies of curiosity. Of course it serves Austin right for marrying into that sort of arty Catholic family. It's an alien tribe. Do you understand what's going on?"

"No. I think we can't understand and we're better at a

distance. Mavis doesn't want us round there sightseeing. And Austin would hardly welcome our advice!"

"I remember he went for you once when you said something helpful. You were quite white!"

"He suddenly became ferocious."

"He's a bit of a Jekyll and Hyde, our Austin. I think Dorina is afraid of him. You know, I suspect Austin originally thought Dorina had money. She's the sort of girl who ought to have money, only it happens she hasn't. Of course she's socially one up from Betty, but just as poor. So Austin was unlucky again. Aren't I cynical?"

"Any man could marry Dorina for love. She's enchanting."

"I am jealous. Yes, I know she is. She's one of those fey charmers. But what has happened to that marriage? Austin can't bear anyone to go near Dorina, yet he doesn't go himself."

"Well, don't you go. Let them sort it out."

"Not that I can take Valmorana really. You know the place is empty?"

"Empty?"

"Mavis has cleared out all her naughty girls and is having it redecorated."

"Is she going to chuck the hostel? I can't think how she stood it."

"I don't know. There's some change. Anyway she and Dorina are alone in that huge house, like a couple of Burne-Jones saints in a stained-glass window. Mavis makes everything so fairies-at-the-bottom-of-the-garden, you know what I mean. And she's so peculiar about Dorina, half possessive and half pleased it's all turned out a mess."

"There's no contradiction there!"

"Perhaps Austin married Dorina because Matthew failed to marry Mavis."

"The Matthew-Mavis thing is a figment of your imagination, my dear, like the Matthew-Betty thing."

"By the way, Hester Odmore phoned this morning. She's still down with Mollie at the Mill House. They've got poor Penny staying. They want to change the date again. I

37

suspect they've had a grander invitation! She said Charles had met Matthew at that Conference in Tokyo."

"News of Matthew is rare. What of him?"

"Charles says he's all right except that he's got terribly fat and lost his looks."

"Did he ever have any?"

"Yes, in a Henry Jamesy sort of way. But he looks quite old now. Whereas Austin seems to get younger and younger in spite of his misfortunes."

"Geoffrey Arbuthnot says Matthew has made a packet speculating in Hong Kong."

"Good old Matthew. Socialism and mysticism have not precluded capitalism."

"He's not due to retire yet, is he? I suppose he'll settle in the East. I'm sorry we've lost Matthew."

"So am I, Pinkie. Somehow Matthew is fun. Like Austin."

"Good God, is Austin fun?"

"Well, you know. You think Matthew won't come home?"

"No. After all that power. Here he'd just be an elderly diplomat writing his memoirs. In the East he can keep some mystery in his life. Matthew needs mystery."

"In the East he can keep some servants in his life. Matthew needs comfort. He is a bit of a hedonist."

"But only a bit."

"You're envious, Pinkie. Possibly even jealous. You remember how awfully keen Gracie was on Matthew when she was a child?"

"I say, did you tell Hester Odmore about Ludwig and Gracie?"

"No. I hadn't heard the great news when she rang. Oh dear, oh dear. You know I am the tiniest bit sad about Sebastian. He would have been the perfect son-in-law."

Mitzi Ricardo laid down her magazine and lifted the telephone. "Secombe-Hughes photographic studio, good afternoon."

"I say, Mitzi, it's me, Austin."

"Austin! How lovely. Long time no see." Mitzi was blushing. She was very pale-skinned and given to blushes and freckles.

"Can I come round and see you?"

"You mean now?"

"Yes. Is old Secombe-Hughes there?"

"No. He's out at the— He's out on a job." Loyalty forbade her to disclose that her employer was at the betting shop. Business was not good.

"Hooray. I'll come round in a taxi."

The Secombe-Hughes photographic studio was a semi-basement in Hammersmith, with a damp wooden stair down to it from the street, and a well of bricked-in garden at the back full of docks and nettles and suckering elder bushes. Lurid green moss grew upon the brick walls and wafted its spores into the house, where little lines of greenery appeared around windows and along wainscots. The studio was not designed for dwelling, having no kitchen or bathroom and only an outdoor lavatory shed whose arrangements had long since ceased to function. However, since the latest decay of business Mr. Secombe-Hughes had been living at the studio, though he still feebly affected to conceal this from Mitzi by covering the camp bed with newspapers and pretending to arrive in the mornings. For a longer time he had been using the garden as a lavatory and had indeed almost entirely used it up, creating a special lingering foxy stench which even the summer rain, now liberally falling out of what appeared to be a blue sky, could never, with its pure celestial freshness, quite defeat.

Mr. O. Secombe-Hughes—the O. stood for Owen, a name which he had vainly and without optimism implored Mitzi to employ—was a Welshman suffering in exile. His age was uncertain. He wore a bowed Druidic persona, would like to have had a beard only it would not grow, and had once won a small prize at an eisteddfod. He had been a fairly successful photographer. Photos of younger versions of some well-known faces adorned the albums. But drink and ill luck and betting and Mr. Secombe-Hughes's own special Welsh devil and, he occasionally hinted, women had done for him somehow. He had a few faithful clients. But there was no denying business was rotten. Mitzi rang the betting shop or the pub if anyone turned up.

Mitzi had come to typing late in life. She had never managed to master shorthand, she was a poor typist, and she could not spell. She and Mr. Secombe-Hughes seemed made for each other. He paid her modestly for her modest services and, as she guessed, liked her because he saw her as another piece of wreckage and in no position to judge him. Her mediocrity calmed his nerves. Later she noticed with some anxiety a tendency towards the sentimental. Mr. Secombe-Hughes might have been good-looking once. His eyes were still as grey and glittering as a slate quarry in the rain. But his face was podgy and crawled over by tiny scarlet veins and his longish greasy hair looked soaking wet. He had always been given to tossing his hair and peering, and it took Mitzi some time to realize that he was ogling her.

She found him physically horrible but she liked him and could not be cold. Some muddle might soon have developed had it not providentially come about that Mr. Secombe-Hughes began to owe Mitzi money. With much hair-tossing he explained one day that he was not in a position to pay all her wages and would she accept half and an IOU? She now had several IOUs. A time would come, Mr. Secombe-Hughes mysteriously asseverated, when all would be well and she would get her money. How this time was to come, unless perhaps borne by a swift horse, was unclear to Mitzi, and she kept intending to leave and then deciding not to, because of pity, because she doubted whether she would find another job, and because she thought that if she hung on she would get some money whereas if she went away she would get none. Meanwhile Welsh honour forbade the continuation of attentions to a lady to whom money was owed, and ogling ceased.

Mitzi had saved a little money from the time when she had been a successful athlete, and she had a house, also in Hammersmith, in a melancholy road off Brook Green, of which she owned the freehold and where she usually took in one or two lodgers. Mitzi Ricardo was thirty-five. It was now ten years since the unspeakable accident which had changed her from a goddess into a wreck who could not frighten even Mr. Secombe-Hughes. Her parents, now dead, had been in a poor way in the clothing trade. They were Christianized Jews and they had but one child, a strong radiant little sprite whom they christened Margaret. Mitzi was her father's nickname for her. This child had wings. A perceptive schoolteacher paid for her to have ballet lessons. She won a scholarship. She began to be a little success, then at the age of fourteen a six-foot-high success, as supple as Proteus and as lithe as an Etruscan Aphrodite. She was a phenomenon. Why she had ever left the world of ballet for the world of sport she later wondered. Any other path would not have led through a million entwining contingencies to that hideous tennis-court moment when she sprang over the net, tripped, fell, and through some utterly improbable complex of injuries destroyed her ankle forever. She had had bad advisers. She was too tall. There were so many temptations. She wanted to play at Wimbledon. She had not the nerve or the courage to give her life over to the austere disciplines of art. She wanted money. She wanted fun.

She achieved her ambitions. She played several times at

Wimbledon. Innumerable tennis balls rose before her, dazzling cubes of which with terrific force she hit the upper surface. She competed in the Pentathlon at the Olympic Games. She was a good skier, coming up to championship standard. She wrote regularly for the sporting pages of the papers, at least she signed her name under things which other people wrote. She drank champagne on jet aeroplanes. Southern suns bleached her hair and gave her freckles. She declined charming proposals of marriage. She no longer minded being six foot one. Then suddenly in a clap of thunder it was all over.

At the end of a diminishing vista of hope, after consultations, operations, therapy, doctors, quack doctors, even prayer, she limped away alone. A newspaper offered her a job as a sports journalist, but she refused it. Tears would have prevented her from seeing the Centre Court now. Why should she suffer the endless consequences of a single moment? Her life had been wrecked by a momentary absurdity which it should be possible to delete. She raged only briefly against fate. She was glad that people quickly forgot her. Sympathy was the last thing she wanted. She had to become another person so as not to die of grief. She took a secretarial training. She tried to take up religion. She tried to become resigned. She lived quietly and squalidly in the mess of her emotions. The person who helped her most, though he was far too self-absorbed even to notice it, was Austin.

She first met Austin when, after Betty died and while Garth was still at school, he took rooms in the same lodgings as herself in Holland Park. This was before she had decided to use her capital to buy a house. Austin had just sold his and was looking for a flat. He was in a state of black misery. His gloom cheered her up, as the gloom of others often quite automatically cheers. Here was someone who seemed even more miserable than herself. Then there was his stiff hand, she liked that. He promised to tell her how it happened, but never did. They met a lot in pubs. Mitzi was beginning to need alcohol and Austin had been needing it for some time. At home, however, they scarcely visited each other's rooms. This was partly because Austin's evident bereavement made him untouchable. It was also because Mitzi was going through a long crisis in her relationship to her body. She had so triumphantly been her body. Now it was no longer a soaring flame of weightless incarnate soul, but a stump of clay, a thick heavy object, separate from herself, which she had to trundle slowly about, sometimes with pain. And with lameness and obscurity there was also the loss of youth. Alcohol and lack of exercise did their part. Mitzi began to get fat. She felt gross. So it was that although she found Austin attractive she did not expect him to touch her.

He took an intelligent interest in her which, though it was largely politeness, was a novelty to Mitzi. And he helped her not only by being more unfortunate than herself. He also, without noticing it, educated her. He talked to her occasionally about books, pictures, music. Dimly she learnt one of the most important of all lessons, how art can console. She read fewer magazines and more books. More even than this perhaps, and more unconsciously still, Austin helped Mitzi by a revelation of how it was possible to live simply by egoism. Austin, with nothing particular to boast of, never seemed to doubt his own absolute importance. Just because he was himself the world owed him everything, and even though the world paid him very little, he remained a sturdy and vociferous creditor. Misery could not crush Austin. Simply being Austin enabled him to carry on.

When Mitzi bought the house off Brook Green she offered Austin the best rooms, but he declined, having just found the little flat in Bayswater which he inhabited still. They continued to meet in pubs. Mitzi did not get any thinner. Soon she would have to go to the Outsize Shop. People turned and stared after her in the street. However she was just beginning to inhabit herself again when Austin went off into a daze about Dorina. Austin had known Dorina for a long time. His brother and Dorina's sister had been friends. Mitzi had met Dorina once or twice and thought her frail and affected and a bit unreal. She could see that Dorina was sorry for Austin, and Mitzi even resented this slightly on his behalf, though of course she was sorry for Austin too. Then Austin announced his second marriage. Mitzi was faint with jealousy and remorse. Why had she never really tried, why had she not conceived that he might be in the mood for marriage? But her own egoism was tougher now. She had made dull quiet friends and expected little of life. She persuaded herself that her love for Austin had never been anything really personal, had never really filled her and become *her* love for Austin. It had been just a vague yearning, an ideal, something like what she felt when she came out of the cinema. Later, however, she was cheered by news of Austin's troubles and woke every morning to a small glow which was the knowledge that Austin was unhappy. When she saw him very occasionally for a drink they behaved like old friends.

"What a shame! After all those years!"

"I could sue them I expect," said Austin. "But one can't be small-minded. One has one's dignity."

"Of course one has! Let them see that you reject them!"

"That's right. I reject them."

"What a shame! And you came straight round here. I'm so glad."

"You can help me, Mitzi," said Austin.

"You know I'd help you any way I could!"

Austin was drinking powdered coffee in Mitzi's little office. Although it was so early in the summer he contrived to look sunburnt. He had a long doggy nose and longish hair the colour of milk chocolate which he tucked back behind his ears. He wore a serene majestic expression and his steel-rimmed spectacles gleamed with a fine consciousness. "Mitzi, I won't beat about the bush. I'm broke."

Let me lend you something was on the tip of Mitzi's tongue but she recalled that she was broke too. "I'm so sorry."

"I shall soon get another job, of course."

"Of course! A much better one."

"A much better one. But meanwhile I'm in a fix. I thought I could manage if I let my flat. You can get big rents now."

"Jolly good idea."

"But then I'd need to live somewhere else, wouldn't I."

"Come and live with me," said Mitzi.

"Oh. Do you think I could? You did so kindly suggest it once before. I know you need to let the big rooms. But perhaps I could just sleep in the attic."

"Certainly not," said Mitzi. "You can have one of the big rooms, one's just gone empty."

"But, Mitzi, I couldn't pay you enough."

"You can have it free. Don't be silly, Austin, we're old friends."

"*Could* I, Mitzi, honestly?"

Ten guineas a week gone bang, she thought, and Secombe-Hughes offering another IOU. Still, Austin in her house! "You could pay me something later."

"When I get a good job. Of course it may be difficult. I don't want to take just anything. It may take time. I can't promise, you know. I'd really rather—I mean, I could sleep just anywhere."

"Austin, don't worry about the money. You can have the room for nothing."

"You're a friend in need, Mitzi old girl." He clasped her hand, squeezed it, dropped it, looked relieved, and reached for his coffee.

Mitzi felt an old amicable exasperated pity for him and a momentary desire to hit him. She laid her fingers spread wide upon his chest, touching the material of his jacket rather than him, an incoherent gesture such as an awkward affectionate animal might have made.

Austin patted her arm briskly and rose. "Can I come this evening?"

"Yes, yes." Austin in her house. She felt protective, huge. Austin there at night, every night, like in the old days. "You can have the front room on the second floor. Oh, by the way, guess who's engaged?"

"Engaged?"

"Engaged to be married."

"Who?"

"Ludwig. And guess who to?"

"I don't know," said Austin, looking worried.

"Gracie Tisbourne."

"Oh. How do you know?"

"He rang me just before lunch."

"Oh. I wouldn't have thought of that match, would you? I wonder if it will work?"

Mitzi felt a vague thoughtless interest in Ludwig's engagement, not pleasure since she did not like Gracie, but not displeasure either. Now seeing Austin's annoyance she felt sad herself. She was fond of Ludwig. And she knew that Austin was fond of Gracie. He liked Ludwig too. But the spectacle of the young people's happiness clearly gave him no joy.

The sunny sky was producing rain again. Austin said, "I'll go and pee if you don't mind." He went through the studio and out into the ragged garden. Mitzi followed and watched him. He went over by the wall with his back to her. As the sky slowly darkened he looked like Mr. Secombe-Hughes, standing there sturdily with his feet apart. The smell of male urine was wafted on the damp air. I hate men, she thought. I just hate men. I hate them.

"Clara, is that you? This is Charlotte. I think she's going."

"Oh God. We're dining with the Arbuthnots."

Charlotte was silent for a moment. "Well, do as you like. I'm just reporting."

"Are you sure?"

"Yes. The doctor says— Yes, I'm sure."

"All right. We'll come round."

Charlotte replaced the telephone.

Dr. Seldon was putting on his coat.

"Please, doctor, don't go. Please don't go."

The doctor took his coat off again, controlling a look of annoyance. "There is nothing more I can do, Miss Ledgard."

"She may have one of those awful seizures and you said if she did you would give her a shot—you know—to send her off quickly."

"Close the door, please, nurse," said the doctor.

Nurse Mahoney closed the door of Alison's room. As the door closed Charlotte saw Alison looking at her. Only one of Alison's eyes was open, but such a fierce consciousness was collected in it that Charlotte felt as if a dart had pierced her. Why had she spoken like that almost in Alison's presence? She would not have done so this morning. As the day went on she had come to see her mother as remote, a ship moving slowly away. How much could that fading mind still perceive?

"Sorry. She couldn't have heard and understood, could she?"

"I don't know," said the doctor. "I don't think it will be necessary to help her on. She will go very soon."

"Will she go peacefully?" I couldn't bear it if she fights, thought Charlotte.

"I think so."

"But suppose she doesn't? Please stay."

"The nurse can do all that is needed."

"You mean the nurse can give her the shot to—help her on?" Charlotte used the doctor's phrase. It sounded strange, more like birth than death. Death can be a struggle, an achievement, too.

"No," said the doctor.

"No?"

"It will not be necessary," he repeated.

"Please sit down in here. Can I bring you anything? Wait a little while. She'll go soon, you said so, it will be such a comfort. Please wait until my sister and brother-in-law come. My brother-in-law wants to ask you something." Charlotte invented that. Men attended to what other men wanted.

"All right. I'll wait."

"Can I give you tea, a drink?"

"Some tea perhaps."

"Nurse, would you make some tea for the doctor? I'll sit with her a while."

Charlotte had opened the door again. Nurse Mahoney got up from the bedside. She said, "Could I make a telephone call, please, Miss Ledgard?"

"Yes, certainly."

The nurse went out. She was red-haired and Irish, broad-faced with golden eyes, very young, utterly untouched by the drama in which she was taking part. Next week it would be another one. She was kind and efficient, but her thoughts never engaged with these people, they were all, except the doctor, unreal to her.

Charlotte took the nurse's chair and stared at Alison. Alison's face was villainously contracted with what seemed already a pain of the spirit rather than of the body. Spirit too travailed. Perhaps it finally travailed most of all. Or did it mercifully perish first? One eye was tightly closed, the other hugely wide, moist as with unshed tears and full of consciousness, Charlotte thought. Yesterday there had been tears, and they had been terrible. Today none. Had Alison overheard that conversation? Even with the door shut Charlotte could hear Nurse Mahoney talking on the telephone to her boy friend. She was telling him that she would be free tomorrow. And I too, thought Charlotte, I too shall be free tomorrow.

Today had been so busy, so awful. This is the first moment I've had to sit down, thought Charlotte. Now everything is fixed, everything is arranged for. Alison must do the rest. There had been turmoil. Now at last there was silence. Alison was looking at her. The single eye stared, not with love or hate or even fear—there had been such dreadful fear—but just with a sort of pure consciousness. As with a small child now perhaps consciousness had become an end in itself. She sees me, thought Charlotte, purely at last, and then knew that this was nonsense. Alison saw nothing, knew nothing, in all probability. "How is it with you, Mother?" said Charlotte. Even the language had become strange, estranged.

48

Alison stared, then murmured something, a word. She had murmured the same word once before. It sounded like "trees."

Charlotte looked at the window. The window was full of light blue evening sky. The two lime trees in the front garden had been cut down. Alison had wished it, Charlotte had arranged it. Later on Alison had regretted it and spoken of "My dear trees. My poor trees. I killed them." Charlotte had been harsh with such sentimentality. There were so many other real things to regret.

"It's better without the trees," said Charlotte. "More light."

Her mother murmured the word again.

"More light, mother. Better."

Oh let me not pity her now, thought Charlotte, later, not now. Go, go in peace, she prayed. Poor poor mother. She's had a good life, she thought. But what did that matter now, and was it even true?

"Are you comfy?" said Charlotte. She touched the pillows, touched her mother's dull dry grey hair, always now undone and straying, which sometimes in a dim light made her look like a girl. There was nothing more to be done. She did not try to adjust the pillows. Though it was evening time there was no point in feeding Alison again. That was a strange thought. Alison would need no more food. That life-long rhythm had ended though consciousness itself was not yet at an end. There was nothing more to be done, in the many years long task. It was strange, as after an examination when suddenly books that have been a part of daily life are set aside forever. Oh let me not pity her, not yet.

"Would you like some tea, Miss Ledgard?"

"No, thank you, nurse. I think there's someone at the door. Could you sit with my mother?"

Charlotte went out into the hall. The doctor had opened the door and George and Clara were coming in, followed by Gracie.

Charlotte was irritated that Gracie had come. Gracie would be a spectator with alien thoughts.

"Oh Char darling!" said Clara in a loud whisper. Clara had been crying.

"My dear," said George. He gripped Charlotte's arm, pressed it hard and let it go. He touched her cheek with his hand.

"How is she?" whispered Clara.

"Take your things off," said Charlotte in her ordinary voice. She felt stiff with something, embarrassment, hatred, grief, or perhaps the pity for her mother which she had been fighting off all day. How dare Clara cry.

George and Clara put their coats on the settee in the hall. They were in evening dress, George very formal, Clara in long green silk with black embroidery, Oriental. Gracie, who was wearing a white mackintosh, dug her hands into her pockets and leaned back against the hall door.

"Pretty dress," said Charlotte to Clara mechanically.

"Thank you, dear Charlotte."

The old litany.

"You wanted to see me, I believe," said the doctor to George.

"Oh er yes," said George, responding instinctively to the doctor's important male manner. "How er— Nothing unexpected, I suppose? Is she likely to pull round again this time? I remember last time—"

"I'm afraid not," said the doctor. He and George went into the drawing-room. The dining-room was Alison's bedroom. Charlotte took her meals in the basement. There were no living-in servants. There had been a maid called Pearl, but Alison sacked her because she thought she had taken a Georgian spoon which later turned up inside the sofa. Charlotte did most of the work of the house.

"Dear Char, has it been awful?" said Clara in a low voice.

"Not particularly. Come in and see her. She won't know you."

Gracie pushed past them into the drawing-room, following her father.

Charlotte opened the door again and there was Alison still there, propped up in what looked like a little shrine.

50

The nurse had turned on the bedside lamp. Bottles glinted on the side table like offerings, there were flowers, too many flowers. It was like a Hindu temple Charlotte had once seen in a picture.

"Clara to see you, Mother."

"My darling," said Clara. She had never said that to her mother before in her life.

"Don't upset her," said Charlotte.

Clara advanced and took the chair which the nurse was offering. She took hold of Alison's hand and then relinquished it quickly. Charlotte knew why. The hand felt dead already.

Alison slowly turned her head. She had to turn it so as to see Clara out of her one eye. Her lips moved, muttering something.

"What's she saying?" said Clara. " 'Release'? Oh my darling—"

"Don't cry, Clara. You can stop those tears."

"I'm sorry, Char. You are always so strong. I'm not sure that I can bear this."

"Then go away," said Charlotte. "You told me to tell you. Now say good-bye and go."

"I can't—say good-bye—"

"Clara!"

"Sorry—"

The single eye regarded Clara with intensity, the weak drooping lips moved.

" 'Trees,' " said Charlotte. " 'Trees,' she's saying. You know."

"I don't think so. What is it, Mama? Tell Clara."

"May I come?" said George. "Dear Alison, hello, it's George."

The doctor entered and stood beside the nurse at the door. George was behind his wife, leaning over her, looking into the old crooked face with a kind of curiosity. A handsome pair, thought Charlotte. George's copious hair was greying into a pleasant peppery salty brown. He could not help looking youthful and calm and debonair. Now he was full of concern, but soon he would be thinking about stocks and shares. Clara looked beautiful, older, her

51

face made keen by anxiety and pain, the light of cheerful self-satisfaction withdrawn. Only her unconscious hair, dyed to a rich dark chestnut and carefully done for the evening, curled with a light casual art about her head, waiting for gaiety to return.

Alison was trying, terribly, trying, the closed eye twitching.

"What's she saying?" said Clara. "What's that she's saying?"

" 'Priest,' " said George.

"No!" said Charlotte.

"Oh dear," said Clara, "do you think we'd better—"

"Doctor, what do you think?" said George. "Is she conscious enough to—?"

"Quite possibly," said the doctor. "It's hard to tell."

"Who shall we—oh dear—" said Clara.

"Don't be silly," said Charlotte. "She can't have said 'priest.' Mother would never use that word."

"You know she had that Roman Catholic phase," said George.

"She never had a Roman Catholic phase," said Charlotte. "She abominates Catholicism. Mother, you don't want a priest, do you? You don't want a *priest* surely?"

The eye turned on Charlotte and the lips moved and the face was very lightly convulsed as with some huge inner effort which could find only a tiny tiny outward expression. Charlotte made herself stiff, controlling sudden choking emotion.

"I think she does," said George. "There was that priest she had talks with."

"That wasn't a religious thing, it was about charity."

"We can't know, Char," said Clara. "We'd better be on the safe side. Hadn't we better call him? What was his name—Father Mennell—"

"I will not have a Roman priest in this house," said Charlotte.

There was silence.

"But if she wants—" said George. "Don't you agree, doctor?" He was standing back now, responsible, serious.

Why did I say that, thought Charlotte. It's not what I

52

meant. I just meant—I must protect her—we can't have all that mummery here—we can't have a priest mumbling over her and scattering holy water— It's a matter of dignity—We must let her go in peace.

"Has she some customary spiritual adviser?" said the doctor.

"No," said Charlotte. "She was brought up a Methodist, but she hasn't been near a Methodist church or any other church for years."

"There's that nice man, the local parson chap," said George. "Mr. Enstone. What about him?"

"She didn't say 'priest'!" said Charlotte.

"Hadn't we better ring up Mr. Enstone?" said Clara. "He knows her quite well, he sometimes came here, didn't he—and it's better to be on the safe side, isn't it? After all she may last for hours or days or—"

"Charlotte?" said George.

"Do what you like," said Charlotte. Now she must concentrate on feeling nothing.

George left the room. As he brushed by Charlotte she smelt whisky on his breath. The doctor was looking at his watch. The nurse was surreptitiously looking at herself in the mirror and patting her hair. George was telephoning in the hall.

Charlotte turned and left the room. She went into the drawing-room. A decanter and two glasses stood on the table where George and the doctor had been treating themselves. Gracie was sitting on the sofa, her long legs stiff in front of her, her hands stiffly clasped, not looking up. Clara and the doctor came in.

"I think I'll have a drink too," said Clara. "Doctor, will you have a little more?"

"Thank you. Then I must run."

"Char?"

"No, thanks."

"Gracie, anything?"

"No."

Like the nurse, Charlotte looked into the mirror and automatically patted her hair. Rarely now did she give more than a quick glance at a looking-glass, more rarely still did she look intently into her own eyes, as young people do. What could she see therein but things better not avowed? She gazed now at her distinguished narrow face and coiled-up pale grey hair and big violety blue eyes. Her life was on the change. Would there be a time when it was not pain to regard herself so? How delicate and yet how steely had been the bonds of her servitude. She had the head of a Victorian bluestocking. She should have spent her life fighting for something, education perhaps. As it was it was spent, spent, and she had not even fought for what she had too late come to regard as her rights. It had been given for what she had too late realized were not even her principles. And now she was very nearly old. Yet tomorrow she would be free and rich. And when she had said, surprising herself, "I will not have a Roman priest in this house" she had meant "in my house." Alison had told her that the Villa would be Charlotte's. Had she told Clara? The sisters never spoke of such things.

"He isn't there," said George from the door. "I left a message. We've done all we can."

"We mustn't leave her alone," said Clara. She had taken a good dose of neat whisky. "Hadn't we better do something—I don't know—read the Bible to her or something? It's so awful not being able to communicate."

"You go in and see her, Gracie," said George.

"I don't want to," said Gracie.

"Charlotte, read something to her, we must, since we can't talk to her. We can't just sit and stare at her. She used to care about the Bible."

"It's impertinent," said Charlotte. "Why should we force religion on her now?"

"It could do no harm to read a psalm," said Clara. "That's not really religion. I'm sure she *did* say 'priest' anyway."

"It'll sound so final. We might as well read the burial service."

"Don't be silly, Char. We *must* sit with her, and—"

"Well, you read a psalm if you want to," said Charlotte. "Anything's better than squabbling in here."

"I couldn't read," said Clara, "it would sound awful. You read, George."

"We don't know any psalms," said George.

"Read 'The Lord is my shepherd.' What number is it? It's somewhere near the beginning. Is there a Bible, Char?"

"Yes. Here." There was a Bible. Alison had even asked for it once. But not lately.

Gracie was talking on the telephone to someone who was presumably Ludwig Leferrier. "Darling, I can't—I'll ring you again about eleven— We don't know, but probably— Yes, I hope so—"

"What number is that psalm, Pinkie, can you remember?"

"I think I really must go," said the doctor.

"*Please* stay," said Charlotte. "Have another drink."

Someone was ringing the front-door bell.

"That'll be Mr. Enstone," said George.

Charlotte went. It was the man next door asking if anyone visiting the house had left their car blocking his garage. Charlotte said no. He asked after Mrs. Ledgard and Charlotte said she was as usual. She looked over his head at the beautiful perky ordinary selfish material world of motor-cars and evening appointments and she closed the door. She had been surprised to see the darkness outside.

"Gracie, do go in and see Grandmama," said Clara, "while Papa is finding the psalm."

"I'll go in with all of you," said Gracie. "She doesn't want to see me alone. We never know what to talk about."

"She can't talk now anyway."

"Then it's even more pointless."

"Here it is," said George.

"Come, Char, please."

"I really must go," said the doctor.

"Please stay, something may happen."

"I'm sorry, Miss Ledgard. There should be no more complications. Everything will be quite plain sailing from now on."

"Can the nurse—"

"Everything that's necessary. There is no need to telephone me until tomorrow morning."

"You mean whatever happens? Well, thank you, doctor."

"Not at all. Good night, good night."

"Come, Char. Come, Gracie."

The doors of the shrine were opened and they all went in. The nurse drew back. Clara turned on another lamp.

Alison was regarding them with that terrible urgent one-eyed stare, so meaningful yet so ambiguous, divorced in its extremity from the ordinary conventions of the human face. Did this travailing look express entreaty, question, fear, anger, surprise, grief? The liquid eye bulged with will. The limp hands crawled slightly, the lips moved. Yesterday there had been a little communication. Today there was none, only that look and that murmur. But the huge caged power of the personality, still dreadfully alive, stirred in its prison.

"Dearest Mama," said Clara. "George is going to read to you. Just you rest now."

She sat down beside the bed and George drew up a chair on the other side. Clara, better for her whisky, captured one of the creeping hand and held it firmly. Charlotte and the nurse stood by the fireplace. Gracie, looking both scared and embarrassed, stood just inside the door.

George said "My dear!" and then began to read. "The Lord is my shepherd, I shall not want. He maketh me to lie down in green pastures. He leadeth me beside the still waters. He restoreth my soul. . . ."

Charlotte turned her back to the room and closed her eyes. In some appalling way George and Clara had been right, as so often in some appalling way they were. The old words, whatever they meant, were filled with an irresistible authority. The words were at home in this scene. They had been here before. Gently they took charge, silencing all voices but their own, soothing the place into something ancient and formal and calm, making of it the temple of a mystery, the perennial mystery which was

56

about to be enacted. Charlotte looked back at them all now and saw how each face had become stilled and blank. Tears were swelling out of Clara's eyes. Only Alison, still trying to utter her sound, seemed separate from them all, raised like a god above the offered litany.

Someone was ringing the front-door bell.

George stopped reading. Clara mopped her eyes.

"Perhaps that's Mr. Enstone now," said Clara.

Charlotte went to the door.

It was Mr. Enstone.

"I am so sorry," said Mr. Enstone. "I was at the Youth Club, it's Ping-pong night, and somebody came over with a rather garbled message. Did Mrs. Ledgard want to see me?"

"She is at the end," said Charlotte. It was an odd phrase, but Mr. Enstone understood and changed his expression.

"I am very sorry. Can I help, talk to her?"

"She can't talk," said Charlotte.

"We think that she asked for a minister," said George, who had come out followed by Clara. "We were just reading to her from the Bible."

"Well, do please go on," said Mr. Enstone.

"No, I think you should do that," said George, holding out the Bible.

"No, please," said Mr. Enstone.

"Perhaps you could talk to her a little," said Clara. "You do know my husband, don't you, Mr. Enstone?"

"Yes, indeed, how do you do."

That dolt cannot speak about ultimate things, thought Charlotte. Better to go on reading. To go on and on and on.

"I'm afraid I don't know her very well," said Mr. Enstone. "But I will if you think that's what she wants."

They all trooped back into the bedroom. The nurse jumped up again. Gracie was standing at the bottom of the bed.

"She keeps trying to say something," said Gracie.

"You know our daughter Gracie."

"How do you do."

57

"Do sit here, Mr. Enstone."

"Mrs. Ledgard, forgive me, I know that I am half a stranger to you, but your children have asked me to come here in case there are any words of comfort which I can utter. Can you understand me, Mrs. Ledgard, may I take your hand? At this time we know, what we ought always to know, that we are mortal beings with but a short span of days and that our end as our beginning belongs to God. We see the vanity of earthly things, the hollowness of selfish wishes, we see now that nothing matters or is truly real except God, that sun of Goodness which has shone, however clouded by sin, upon our lives, which at our best we have loved, and which at our end we know to be the only thing which is worthy of our desire. Let humble desire for God and knowledge of His reality and His love fill your heart, Mrs. Ledgard, and do not resist the Power which draws you now to Himself. In moving towards God we move from shadow to light, from false to true, from sham to real, and into that great peace which passeth all understanding. Now will you all please join me in prayer—"

"She's saying that word again," said Gracie. "I think it's 'lease.' "

"Is it not 'peace'?" said Mr. Enstone.

" 'Lease'?" said Clara. "She must mean the lease of the house."

"Where is the lease of the house?" said George.

"I'm not sure," said Charlotte. "It used to be in the drawing-room bureau. Shall I look?"

"I'll come too," said Clara. The two sisters left the room.

"I can't see it."

"Does it matter if it's lost?"

"I wonder if there's some snag."

"Oh God, you mean legally—"

"Have you found it?" said George from the door.

"Char thinks there's some legal snag."

"Have you ever seen the lease?"

"No, but— Here it is."

"Let me look."

"No, let George look."

"Supposing there's some snag?"

"How long has it got to run?"

"Better give it to her."

"But she's in no state to—"

"You give it to her, Char."

"Perhaps she wants to show us—"

"God, I hope it's sound."

"Better open it out so she can—"

"I'm so sorry, Mr. Enstone," said George. "I don't think she wanted a priest after all. But we're very glad you came. Please don't go."

"Here, Mother," said Charlotte. "The lease. The lease of the Villa. Was that what you wanted?" She put the unfolded document onto the bed, working it in under the palm of the limp hand. But Alison did not look at it and made no attempt to grasp it and in a moment it fell to the floor. George picked it up and began to examine it eagerly.

Alison Ledgard stared up at her eldest daughter. Visibly concentrating all her power she whispered and at last Charlotte understood. What Alison was saying was "Treece." Treece was the family solicitor. Oh God, thought Charlotte, she wants to change her will. She hates me, she has always hated me, she will disinherit me. Could she, would she, at this last hour, do so? Yes. Hatred was pure now. Charlotte hesitated.

"I can't understand what she's saying, can you?" said Clara. "It can't have been—"

"She's saying 'Treece,' " said Charlotte.

"Of course that's it!" said George.

"What is that?" said Mr. Enstone.

"Our solicitor," said George.

"I'll telephone him at once," said Charlotte. She turned to go. Then she turned back. "Don't worry, Mother. I'll get Treece. He'll come at once. I'm sure he will. Don't you worry, dear."

The great staring eye closed and tears suddenly washed down Alison's cheek.

Tears came to Charlotte too. She went out and began to dial Treece's number. The number started ringing but there was no reply. She heard it ring and ring as she turned her head about, trying to toss the flooding tears from her. There was a strange sound from the bedroom like the cry of an unfamiliar bird.

"There's no answer," said Charlotte.

She returned to the doorway. Alison was lying sideways now, her head drooping towards the edge of the bed, the eye open and fixed in a kind of surprise. Clara was sobbing. Gracie pushed past Charlotte in the hall. "She is with God," said Mr. Enstone.

※※※※

Austin Gibson Grey put the telephone down. Ludwig had just rung to say that old Mrs. Ledgard had died and that he and Mitzi would be waiting up for Austin with a bottle of whisky. Austin felt no regret about old Mrs. Ledgard. Clara once, thinking he would not mind, had gaily told him, "Mama says you're a buffoon!" He did mind. So the old woman was gone. Good, Charlotte would be rich and would lend him money. Charlotte had a feeling for him, one always knew. And Ludwig and Mitzi were waiting. And the whisky. That was good too.

Then he recalled with pain that Ludwig was now engaged to Gracie. Why had just that had to happen to just those two? Everyone was going away from him and entering into a conspiracy with everyone else against him. It was always like that in the end, he could never keep anybody. Betty. And Mavis had taken Dorina, everybody

60

had taken her. Ludwig had been his shield against more things than could be told. Gracie he had always adored. She was the only being he had loved simply from childhood. Only now of course it was not so simple, now that he could sense so sweetly in her eyes, in her whole maidenly body, her intimate knowledge of his desire. That was his secret with her. To Ludwig he had entrusted everything in the sure faith not only that nothing would be judged, but that nothing would be understood. There were sometimes wonderful people of whom one could be sure in this way. But now Ludwig and Gracie would discuss him. There would be complicity and betrayal.

He stood alone in the middle of the sitting-room panting a little. It would be an asthma night. It was late now, after eleven o'clock. Two cases which he had packed stood by the door. He would get a taxi. He would go to Mitzi for whisky and a kiss. My life is on the change, he thought, what will be? Whatever will be I must survive it and go on believing in the other side where everything will be all right. The flat was full of toylike knick-knacks which he had bought to please Dorina, she was so easy to please, any little thing delighted her. At one time he had brought her home a present every day, a china cat, an electric torch, anything. The pureness of these pleasures sometimes amazed him, they smelt of spring, of all that had once seemed lost. Dorina was renewal of life, his innocence, his youth. And yet she was also something old, ghost-haunted, touched with sadness, touched with doom. Or was that doom just his own sense of the impossibility, after all, of being saved by her?

As he had not yet found a tenant there was no need for him to move, but now that he had made his plans he wanted to get out, to run quickly onward all alone towards the future. The flat was already beginning to feel weird and quiet, like a revisited place, afloat in time and streaked with hallucinations. Betty was there, poor dead Betty in a place she had never known and where all his thoughts about her had been secret. He had opened a drawer and found another photograph. He had always hidden these relics from Dorina. Poor Bet. Smiling, young, dim, far off and dead. Sometimes at night he thought about her mortal remains. Once he tried to find her grave, but there were only stretches of mown grass. He had never raised a memorial. While he lived Betty's story was not yet over, and when he died it could not be told.

He must put off seeing Dorina until he had found a job. He would send Ludwig with a present. The funny thing was that he and Dorina understood each other perfectly in spite of all the people who crowded in between them. That was a secret which the others would never know. Some pure ray, perhaps even simply of pity, from that girl came uncontaminated to his heart. She alone truly divined his inward collapse, and yet she knew not what she knew. He had always been surrounded with women who wanted to run him. Dorina had never wanted that. Her compassion was part of her own helplessness. He thought, from her and from her alone I can accept pity. The thought made him feel humble and good. That was what women were for, to make a man feel good in spite of everything, but why had it never really worked for him? Dorina should have been the perfect rescuer. Yet somehow big Mitzi's mushy affection relaxed his nerves more than Dorina's pure love.

The front-door bell's violent ringing pierced his reverie so rudely that he could not at first think what had happened to him, it was like being shot. He felt instant terror. The police? The final accusation? Who could be calling on him at this hour and ringing his bell with such dreadful urgency?

Austin stood by the door.

"Who is it?"

Someone spoke outside.

Austin opened the door. A man stood there. The man was Garth.

"Come in, Garth," said Austin. He held the door open and his tall son came in.

Austin went back into the sitting-room. Garth followed, dropping a brief case and a mackintosh and the evening paper with weary deliberation onto the floor. He gave his father a faint smudgy smile and then started to stare around him. He looked very tired and brown and in need of a shave. His clothes were greasy and tight-fitting like some sort of ancient uniform. How tall he is, thought Austin, he has lost all the soft looks of boyhood. How tall, how thin, how stern, how dark his hair, how hard his face, he is like an Indian.

Austin said, "My God!" and fell into a chair. "I didn't expect you till July."

"Didn't you get my wire? Things look different here. You've moved things."

"Yes. I didn't expect you till July."

"I decided to chuck it all up. Where's Dorina?"

"She's visiting Mavis."

"Do you mind if I use the telephone?"

Garth lifted the telephone and dialled. "Is that the Air Terminal? Could I have inquiries, please? My name is Gibson Grey. I rang a little while ago about a suitcase. Yes, a dark blue suitcase, off the plane from New York. Yes, I see. Yes, I filled in that form. You'll let me know if it turns up. Thank you. Good night."

"What is it?" said Austin.

"I've lost my suitcase. I put it onto a bus at London Airport, at the back, you know, and then couldn't get on myself. I had to come on the next bus twenty minutes later, and then at the Air Terminal, you know, where that thing with the luggage goes round and round—"

"Round and round?" said Austin.

"Yes, you know, it's a circular thing and the cases go round until someone picks them up. Well, when I got there my case wasn't on the thing. Someone must have seen me miss the bus and pinched it. Or else it just stayed going round and round until it was obvious its owner wasn't there and someone took it away."

"I'm so sorry," said Austin. "Perhaps it'll turn up. Was there anything valuable in it?"

"Only a manuscript."

"A philosophical manuscript?"

"No. A novel. Unfortunately it's the only copy. But it's of no importance. How are you, Father, are you all right?"

I used to be Dad, thought Austin. But of course I couldn't be now. How different Garth looked, a strange tall man in need of a shave, a visitor, an intruder, a judge. "I'm fine," said Austin. He added, "I'm so glad you've come home."

"Home," said Garth. "Yes, I suppose this is it. How are things, how's everybody, how is Ludwig, is he still staying with that Ricardo person?"

"Yes. Oh, Ludwig's engaged."

"Who to?"

"Grace Tisbourne."

"I'm sorry about that," said Garth. "Sorry, I can't talk. I'm just crazed up by that aeroplane. If you don't mind I'll just make myself some scrambled eggs and turn in."

"I'm afraid there isn't any food in the house—at least, there was a loaf only I threw it away."

"Is there any milk?"

"No, sorry, you see—"

"Well, I'll just have a hot bath and turn in."

"The hot water's turned off," said Austin desperately. "I'm sorry. You see, I'm just leaving on holiday."

"Where are you going?"

"To the seaside."

"You're going to the seaside at midnight?"

"Yes, why not?"

"Well, can I stay here while you're away?"

"Of course."

"Good-bye then. Forgive me, Father, I really cannot talk. I'll carry your cases down."

"Wait a moment," said Austin. "I'm not going on holiday. Dorina's left me. I've lost my job. I'm going to let the flat. I'm going to take a room at Mitzi Ricardo's. It's all temporary of course. I'm terribly sorry. I mean Dorina hasn't really left me. It's all a mess. But it'll be all right, you see. I'm so sorry—"

"Don't," said Garth, *"Don't."*

There was silence. Austin panted.

64

"Must you go, Father? It's so late."

"Yes."

"We'll talk later then."

"Yes," said Austin, near to tears.

"Oh by the way," said Garth, "there was a letter for you downstairs. I put it in my pocket."

Garth handed over a type-written envelope. Austin looked at the stamp and started to tremble. He hastily tore it open. It read as follows.

My dear Austin,

Please forgive me for not having written to you for such a long time. You have been nevertheless much in my thoughts, and this particularly of late, since I have decided, for a number of reasons of which I shall tell you at leisure, to retire early from my employment. As you know, I had intended to settle in the East. But I have found the ideas of home and of family more magnetic with the advancing years than I should have supposed possible. In short, I have decided to come back and to make my home in London. In the meantime we have both grown older and I hope wiser. I will say no more. But believe me when I tell you how warmly and eagerly I look forward to our reunion after these many years apart. God bless you. In the cordial expectation of seeing you later this month, I remain, ever your affectionate brother,

MATTHEW

"I haven't an idea what to do, it's worrying me out of my mind," said Mrs. Carberry to Mavis Argyll. Mrs. Carberry was talking about her retarded son, Ronald. Ronald was ten. Mrs. Carberry had four other children. Mr. Carberry drank. "Of course I pray about it all the time, I pray when I'm working and all. But it doesn't seem to make it any easier to see what to do. Walter wants me to put him into that home, you know, the institution place, the child irritates Walter so, and sometimes I'm near agreeing just for peace' sake, Walter was on at me again last night, he says it isn't fair to the other little ones to have a sort of loony in the house, not that Ronald's like that really, but he's disgusting, you know, and the others can't help being nasty and that makes him worse, and he's a real little hobgoblin sometimes, and with the eldest in trouble it's enough to do, but I can't let him go away, I just can't, I sometimes think it would break my heart, when I see his little simple face, it's not his fault he's so wearying. If he goes into that place he'll have no one to love him and he could die of that, and I'd be thinking of him every night, poor little boy, wetting his pillow with tears and wanting his mummy."

The painters had just gone. Mrs. Carberry, who helped out, was loading the washing-up machine. Her eldest son was in trouble with the police. Her husband was a tyrannical brute. Mavis thought, this woman has real troubles, not like my nervous evanescent woes. Yet Mavis's woes were real to Mavis and though she was sorry for Mrs. Carberry she could not quite conceive as three-dimensional that awful world where children whined and a man shouted.

"If only he could come here, Miss Argyll," said Mrs. Carberry, "just for a time. He'd be no trouble, the poor little mite. The welfare people would pay and he'd go to his special school like he does now and I'd see to him."

"It wouldn't work," said Mavis. Mrs. Carberry had suggested this before. Mavis hardened her heart. Mrs. Carberry was offering her this waif. If once Ronald came to Valmorana he would never leave.

Mrs. Carberry did not argue. She looked tired, vague, old, older than Mavis although she was probably fifteen years younger. Mavis was putting on weight, but she had kept her looks in an almost uncanny way. Mavis was fifty, but could look twenty-five. Dorina eternally looked eighteen.

Valmorana was Mavis's mother's old family home, a white, Italianate Victorian house in a quiet tree-hazy corner of Kensington. In her days of Catholic piety Mavis had wanted to give it to the nuns of the Sacred Heart. She was to have been a nun herself and Valmorana was to have been her dowry. But a valuable London property cannot with an impulsive gesture be pressed into somebody's hand. The nuns were canny, worried about the cost of maintenance, worried about possible litigation with the local authority, worried about Mavis's cousins, who had written them a nasty letter. While negotiations were still going forward Mavis changed her mind about everything. She decided not to become a nun, she decided there was no God, she decided to have as many love affairs as possible, and did. Later still, appalling misery brought her back to the Sacred Heart door, godless but desperate. Her childhood Catholicism, distilled by utter loss of faith and now sweetened by disillusion with the world, awaited her in those musty dusky rooms where long black skirts rustled and distant doors closed quietly. Then again she would have given them the house. But the Sacred Heart nuns were shrewd and thrifty. Of course they wanted Valmorana. But they wanted it on their terms. They also wanted Mavis. After some months it somehow turned out

67

that the house had become a girls' hostel of which she was the warden. The money came from the nuns, the local authority, and rich Catholic friends. Mavis took the responsibility and the risks.

She did not regain her faith and she sometimes hated the religion of her childhood with a spitting passion. But she led perforce, and with every wry reservation, a sort of dedicated life. The enterprise was a modest one, she never accommodated more than two or three girls at a time, and though always busy she was never overworked. Her clients, muddled, illiterate, often delinquent, always pious, interested her but usually did not touch her deeply. She was efficient, and smiled covertly when the good nuns spoke of "grace." She enjoyed her efficiency and enjoyed, like a voluptuary, her regained innocence. During the wild years she had woken every morning to some guilty problem. Above any pain except that of guilt one can hope to climb by seeing what is above, by seeing that there is something above. Guilt and remorse had trapped her during those years. Now she woke to clarity, to an emptiness full of the urgent needs of others. She had achieved, by accident and in a second-rate way, what she had once desired as a high spiritual prize, a life that was like water, a sort of colourless see-through blow-through existence, full of tasks and without ties.

Well, there was one tie of course and that was Dorina. Valmorana was Mavis's by entail under the will of her mother, who had died long ago. Mavis's father had married a second time, again a Catholic woman, and again one who died young. In fact Dorina's mother perished in childbirth and Mavis had to act the little mother. Dorina was a good deal younger and had been still at school during the wild years. She had been a funny little girl, prim and secretive and taciturnly self-sufficient. After their father's death she had had somehow, only Mavis could never fully attend to it at the time, a rather miserable adolescence at several uninspiring schools, handed around in the holidays. There had been strange incidents. "I am afraid your sister attracts poltergeists," one headmistress had complained severely to Mavis, who had her own ghosts to contend

68

with. In fact Dorina's presence at Valmorana provoked incomprehensible electrical storms. Pictures fell. Windows cracked. A noise like a grand piano falling down the stairs occurred once without visible cause. However, when Dorina was eighteen these phenomena ceased.

Dorina left school and came to live permanently at Valmorana in the early days of the hostel. Though intelligent, she had never managed to pass any exams. She was often vaguely ill and was regularly suspected of tubercular tendencies. She helped a little in the house, she took a typing course, she worked part time in a library. On the whole she did nothing much, managing to create in the midst of hurlyburly a quietness of her own. She was the spirit of the garden, the spirit of the stairway, always somehow passing by with flowers in her hand. The tough inmates laughed at her, but treated her as a mascot.

Often she exasperated Mavis, often she touched her. Mavis knew that her sister was not happy. Sometimes, looking at those secretive eyes, she wondered if all Dorina's ghosts had not somehow been simply drawn inside her. There were strange things still. What went on inside? Did Dorina regard Mavis's girls as interlopers and false children? Was Mavis mother even now? Mavis had never made a proper home for her. Was it even possible that Dorina felt resentment about money because she herself had been left penniless? Of course the sisters loved each other and Dorina's art could sometimes make things seem idyllic. The nuns, who on the whole kept out of the way, made little sorties to try to get hold of her, but she vaguely eluded them. She seemed even more calmly godless than Mavis. She never worshipped or seemed to feel either the need of it or the guilt of abandoning it. Her spiritual world was other.

All sorts of plans were made for her but she soon rendered them all hazy and inconclusive. Dorina's attention to it could make any plan seem incoherent. It was in any case obvious that marriage was her lot and Mavis devoted time and thought to a selection of suitors. Dorina was passive. Mavis invited young men. The idea of Dorina married caused her various kinds of pain. She sometimes invited Austin too, and he sometimes came, not of course as a suitor, that idea never entered her head, he was much too old and generally hopeless, but because he was Matthew's brother and she was sorry for him. Dorina was sorry for him too. Being sorry for Austin was a sort of occupation for both of them. Austin, who had a general talent for inspiring pity, had officially "gone to pieces" after Betty's death. Unfortunately this was just the sort of thing likely to interest a young girl.

Of course Dorina had, because of Matthew, another source of interest in Austin. Matthew had been one of Mavis's earliest admirers and something had happened between them. Mavis had chosen the nunnery. Matthew had left the country. What exactly had happened was now utterly shadowy even in Mavis's own mind. It had been a muddle. Matthew had vanished forever and communication had ceased. Mavis never spoke of it or even thought of it except when she occasionally realized with irritation how fascinating it had all been to Dorina. Of course it was never discussed. And now here was the nemesis.

Later on it seemed inevitable that Austin and Dorina should want each other. Mavis accepted the situation with a smile but she could not like Austin and this sort of false relation with Matthew was distasteful to her although the marriage occasioned no communication between them. There was something for which she could not forgive Matthew and of which she did not wish to be reminded: perhaps his ineffectual suit, perhaps the fruitlessness of her own choice. Sometimes she thought that her own failure to marry Matthew was actually the cause of Austin's marrying Dorina. It was not just that Austin was an object of interest because of the Matthew legend. Austin's relations with his brother were obscure and intense. Might not this repetition be a highly determined event in some fraternal drama? If so, so much the worse for Dorina. Mavis was not surprised when there were difficulties, though she could not quite see what they were. They never *quarrelled*, it seemed. Mavis was pleased when things broke down.

70

She would not ever have been wholly pleased if Dorina had married happily. What could she have been to a ful- filled Dorina except an ageing maiden aunt? She had never seen herself in that light in relation to her younger sister. As it was she could now be useful to Dorina with a full heart. These unmagnanimous frailties in herself Mavis saw with a cool eye. And in general she welcomed the possi- bility of perhaps getting rid of Austin altogether.

Not that it was at all clear that this was what was envisaged. Dorina used to come and stay fairly often, relapsing when she came into her old dependence on Mavis. She kept her little room still unchanged at the top of the house. Once she came and said to her sister, "I think I'm not going back to Austin, at present at any rate. We are better apart for a while. We both have to sort things out. We need a little holiday from each other." She added, "He's glad I'm here." Mavis could understand that. Austin was an intensely jealous and possessive man. He probably felt that his young wife was, at Valmorana, almost literally cloistered. Further, Mavis did not ask and Dorina did not tell.

Mavis was at this time distracted by an outburst of problems about the future of her enterprise. The house was still her property. The convent suddenly wished to transfer the whole thing to the local authority. The rich Catholic families objected. The local authority offered to buy the house at a figure Mavis would not consider. Meanwhile the roof needed repairing, the whole house needed rewiring, everything wanted painting. The local authority now offered a grant in return for a short lease. The convent agreed to carry on the old regime pending negotiations. A Catholic businessman said he would pay for repairs. These were now almost finished. The place was empty, the old smell was gone, the welfare people were offering new furniture. Valmorana looked like an ordinary house again and brought to Mavis, suddenly on stairs and landings, memories of her father.

Her own future of course was equally at stake. If she leased the house to the local authority she would not stay

71

on as warden. This was tactfully plain to everybody. A number of good people had approached her offering other posts, some of them very interesting. The last few years had been ruled by necessity. But had they been perhaps a little dreary? The idea was disconcerting. Mavis found herself curiously restored to ordinary life and ordinary choices. There was no reason why she should be ruled by her false reputation for holiness. She had not after all given up the world and a surprising number of things were still possible. Mavis felt that she had emerged again into the light, not really such a different person in the end.

Mavis was now thinking, no, I will not give way about Ronald Carberry. The little boy had a touching face. But he was unmanageable, unworkable, would never be fully a human being. Mavis knew that if she was not careful she would have Ronald Carberry forever. She did not want that sort of responsibility, she did not want to re-enter the hot muddled personal unhappiness of the ordinary human lot. That at least her imitation dedicated life had enabled her to shun.

Mavis had left the big kitchen and repaired to her drawing-room. To keep herself sane she had reserved, in a separate part of the house, her own rooms, full of furniture and pretty things from the old days. She watched now out of the front window as Mrs. Carberry walked away slowly down the road carrying her old shopping bag and looking down at the pavement as she walked. Mrs. Carberry believed in God and Jesus Christ and the Virgin Mary in much the same way that she believed in Walter and Ronald and Mavis. The sun was shining, making a flowering cherry tree at the corner into a winged gallery of rosy light. The petals were falling slowly to the pavement through the still air like autumn leaves. Mrs. Carberry walked into the slow rain of petals with her head down, hump-backed with anxiety. Mavis felt relief when she turned the corner. She moved to the side window which looked down on the garden and watched Dorina, who was standing barefoot in the middle of the lawn.

Dorina when alone, and Mavis had often thus watched

her unseen, had the vague pottering ways of an animal, expressive not of boredom so much as of an absolute absorption in the moment-to-moment processes of life. Dorina was trying to pick up a twig with her toes. She tried to grip the twig by flexing her toes about it as if they were fingers. This failed, so she then manoeuvred it between the big toe and the second toe, lifted her foot a little and surveyed it. Then she tried to toss it away, failed, and had to lean down to extract it. She remained bent over and picked a daisy. She straightened up and examined the daisy and then pressed it rhythmically against her lips several times. Then she turned on her heel and, still holding the daisy, began to comb out her hair with her hands. She had light brown hair, not very copious but rather long, which made a little rill down between her shoulder blades. She wore it loose usually or in a plait. Beyond her was a yellow privet hedge, red tulips nearly over, a prunus tree, the high white wall. She looked like a young girl in a picture who had eternally nothing to do except wait for her lover. It was hard to believe that she was over thirty. Mavis watched her with annoyance, curiosity, pity, love and a kind of fear. If only she had married an ordinary public school boy with a job in the City, instead of a weirdie like Austin with a funny hand. She was enough of a weirdie herself.

"Dorina!"

"Darling!"

"Come up. I want to talk to you."

Dorina was in the room. She was wearing a creamy and purple sprigged dress almost to her ankles. She had a long thin pale face and large grey eyes. A Victorian water colourist could have conveyed that frail yet bony look. She was taller than Mavis. Mavis was getting plump. Her hair was fuzzier and shorter than Dorina's and always untidy, fading now into a peppery sandy colour which would one day quietly become grey. Her eyes were less big, her nose less aquiline. Mavis wore a flowery dress too with a frilled hem. Both sisters still dressed to please their father, who had been a lawyer with a sparetime passion for painting.

He had adored his pretty daughters. He could not have done with a boy. Dorina had done quite a lot of painting too when he was still alive. Neither of them had much talent.

"Oh dear, I meant to help with the washing up."

"Mrs. Carberry was here. It's done."

"Did she bring Ronald?"

"No. I'm discouraging visits. She wants to park him here for good."

"Well, why not?"

"Think, child!"

"He's awfully touching."

"He's awfully touching. But he's somebody's life-long problem and not ours."

"I hoped Louis would come this morning." Louis was Dorina's name for Ludwig.

"Clara Tisbourne rang up," said Mavis.

"Oh. Did she say anything?"

"Yes. Her mother died last night."

"I am—so sorry—" Dorina looked frightened. Any news of a death affected her in a personal way. "I hope she didn't suffer—Mrs. Ledgard."

"No. It was expected after all."

"One never expects a death, it isn't possible."

"Maybe. And another thing. Gracie's engaged."

"Who to? Sebastian?"

"No. Ludwig."

"Gracie engaged to Louis. Oh." Dorina turned away towards the window. She said, "Gracie's lucky. Well, so's Louis. She's nice. But how odd."

"Yes, I suppose it is odd," said Mavis. Her own feeling had been a kind of little dismay on Dorina's behalf. Ludwig was such a thoroughly decent boy and he had comforted Dorina in some way, perhaps by being someone whom she and Austin had discovered and liked jointly. He was a part of their public world. Dorina and Austin had so little social public world in common. Now, it occurred to Mavis, he was gone. Gracie would not tolerate his rather peculiar friendship with Dorina and all those almost daily go-between ministrations. Perhaps it might be a blessing though if it made Dorina make up her mind about Austin. Clara Tisbourne had also told Mavis that Austin had lost his job.

"Did Clara say anything else?"

"No." Let Austin tell her in his own time.

"Charlotte will have the Villa."

"Clara says she thinks it's left to both of them."

"I want Charlotte to have it," said Dorina. "Poor Mrs. Ledgard. Oh dear."

"When are you going to see Austin?" said Mavis. "You can't decide anything till you see him again. You're just getting sort of comatose and dreamy staying on here and deciding nothing."

"I'll write to him," said Dorina.

"You're always writing to him. Don't write to him, see him. All those letters going to and fro and Ludwig arriving with flowers—that's no use—"

"Don't, Mavis. Do you ever feel that life is empty and awful?"

"Yes. But it's better to have it empty and awful than full and awful like Mrs. Carberry. Oh *Dorina*—"

Dorina was in tears.

"I'm going to make the lunch," said Mavis.

She went out not exactly banging the door but closing it briskly. She felt horribly haunted by Dorina's troubles, almost made unclean. Only spirit could break these spells. Perhaps she had better ask Mrs. Carberry to pray for them all.

"We're on an island," said Austin. "You and me, Mitzi, we're on an island. Where's Ludwig?"

"He's taken Gracie to the cinema."

"Good. Was I saying? We're on an island. Man needs a woman, tenderness, nothing like it, always one at the right time. Have s'more whisky. I'm thingummybob and you're what's-her-name, years and years on this island and all the time there's a wee wifie waiting—"

"Austin, you're drunk."

"Oh I'll get there in the end, Mitzi, it's lovely there, you know, at least it will be after they're all dead and the old dog will recognize me and wag his tail—"

"I'd like to have a dog. I've always wanted a dog. Only you couldn't keep one in London really."

"And the wee wifie's waiting and turning her spinning wheel like a bloody sibyl and the years are passing and all the time I'm down on the beach crying my eyes out because the great big nymphie won't let me go home."

"Austin darling, you've only been here two days and—"

"I won't ask you to sit on my knee, Mitzi, the chair might bust. Don't you grieve though, one day you'll meet a man who's bigger than you are. You know I'm glad I've lost my job, it makes me feel free. Begone dull care. Oh I've had such awful news, you don't know what awful news I've had."

"About Dorina?"

"No, not about Dorina, no such luck, I mean luck for *you,* dear. Dorina's safe, she's all right, she's safe in her cage and they're feeding her with seed cake through the

76

bars. She'll wait for me, she's got to, bless her innocent little palpitating heart."

"What's this news you've had, Austin?"

"No news. One has always known the worst. In the womb one knows one's doom, one lies in the tomb, shut with the executioner into a little room. Only one forgets it mercifully, it slips one's mind. We all know the day of our death only we forget it. Shall I tell you a story?"

"About Dorina?"

"Always on about her, aren't you. No, not about Dorina, she's sacred, she's above us, she's separate from all this, she's an angel, she's on her island and we're on ours. I'll never talk to you about her, never, if I ever talk to you about her may my tongue wither. Pass the bot, there's a good girl. Was I saying? God, I so much wanted a daughter. What was I saying?"

"Austin, you're drunk, you'd better go to bed."

"But not with you, my pettikins. Even big girls can't have everything they want. Keep your dressing gown buttoned, duckie, I don't want to see your nightie. Shall I sit on your knee?"

"Austin—"

"I'm not as drunk as you think. I'm just telling dull care to begone. Shall I tell you a story?"

"The bottle's empty."

"Shall I tell you a *story?*"

"All right, but—"

"Once upon a time there were two brothers. Now this story isn't about me and Matthew. I know you think it is but it isn't. There were these two brothers and they lived on the top of a high mountain, and down at the bottom of the mountain there was a deep blue lake and at the bottom of the lake there lived a lady—"

"How did she breathe?"

"Shut up. And this lady was the most beautiful and desirable thing in the whole world and one day the younger brother said to the elder brother, Brother, let us go down and get this lady, let us appropriate this lady, and the elder brother said, One lady between two is no good, I resign my part in the lady, go you and get the lady for

77

yourself. So the younger brother climbed down the mountain, which was very steep, did I mention that, it was very steep, and he got the lady—"

"How?"

"Never mind. Then when he was climbing up the mountain with the lady the elder brother looked down and saw and he couldn't bear it and he took a great boulder and rolled it down the hill and killed the younger brother—"

"Killed him?"

"Yes. Squashed him out as flat as a kipper."

"And what happened to the lady? Was she killed too or did she marry the elder brother?"

"That was the funny part. It turned out there wasn't really a lady at all. It was all made of plastic, like plastic flowers. And the younger brother was bringing it back to show it to the elder brother just for a laugh."

"So the elder brother killed him for nothing."

"It's not so simple. You keep saying things but it's never as simple as you think. Mitzi, what's that?"

"What?"

"That noise. Mitzi, there's somebody out on the landing —Quickly, go and look, quickly—"

Matthew, who had been listening at the door for some minutes, turned and scuttled away down the stairs. If he could immediately have undone the street door he would have darted out and run away into the night, but as he was still fumbling with the catch Mitzi appeared on the landing and switched the light on.

Matthew looked up. He saw a tall portly woman, with short pale bobbed hair and a large pink face, dressed in an old dressing gown. In the dim light and the shapeless robe she looked rotund and heavy, armless and legless and big-breasted like an archaic stone goddess. Mitzi looked down. She saw a stout bald elderly man with bulging bloodshot eyes and a frightened expression, holding a brief case. He looked like a tax inspector. They had never met each other before.

"What is it?" said Mitzi.

"I am extremely sorry," said Matthew. "I just came in

through the door and was about to call up the stairs. The bell appears to be out of order. I fear in any case that I may have entered the wrong house. I am looking for a Mr. Gibson Grey, a Mr. Austin Gibson Grey."

"The bell hasn't worked since the blitz," said Mitzi. "Could you wait? I'll see if Mr. Gibson Grey is in." She had decided that this individual was about to serve a writ on Austin for nonpayment of a debt.

There was no sign of Austin. He had gone through into the adjoining kitchen. She found him there leaning over the sink and panting. He had been dashing water onto his face and his hair was wet and dripping.

"There's a—"

"I know. It's my brother."

"Your brother?"

"I'll go down and see him in a minute."

"What are you doing?"

"Just breathing."

"Do you think he heard?"

"Yes."

"Does it matter?"

"Yes. Could you give me some of that brandy? The whisky's all gone."

Mitzi took it from the cupboard and poured him some. He drank it in single draught and started coughing.

"Where is he?"

"In the hall."

"Go and look, would you? He may be just outside."

Mitzi came back. "He's sitting on the stairs at the bottom. Shall I—"

Austin strode past her and out of the room. As he came onto the landing he took his glasses off and put them in his pocket. Matthew rose and they met at the bottom of the stairs. Austin extended his left hand.

"Matthew! How delightful!"

"Austin— Austin—" Matthew took the hand in both of his.

"Forgive me," said Austin, "I have to go out this very minute to make an urgent telephone call. You must excuse

79

me. I would have loved a talk but it must wait. Please excuse this rush."

"May I come with you?"

"It's just at the corner. Perhaps I can get in touch with you. Where are you staying?"

"Brown's Hotel."

"Good. Well, here we are and I must make my call. I'm afraid it'll be rather a long one. So nice to see you. We must get in touch. Please don't wait."

Austin got inside the telephone box. It was very brightly lighted inside. Outside was dark. Matthew had vanished. The bright lights were hurting Austin's eyes. He lifted the receiver and started dialling nines. Then a violent airy impulse took him about the waist and swung him far away. He pursued himself through space. He was lying on a tilting board which turned out to be the door of the telephone box. Just before it was going to tilt him into a pit he lurched forward until his face was pressed upon a black pane of glass. Through the glass he saw two shimmering orbs, like the face of an owl. Matthew was peering in at him from outside. He tried to turn his back but he seemed to have six rubbery legs which were gradually being folded up. He was a space craft landing on the moon. No, he was on that swing again, flying back the other way. His vision was darkening into a night sky of pullulating dots. One knee struck a concrete wall and there was pain somewhere. One foot seemed to be trying to run away down a rat hole. Something funny was spinning round and round in front of his face. It looked like a telephone receiver swinging round and round and round upon its flex. He must be on the floor. But then where were his legs?

"Are you all right?" said Matthew.

The telephone receiver was saying something too.

A woman's voice said, "Do you want the police?"

"Yes," said Austin, "I want to report a murder."

Nerves, thought Matthew, pure nerves. Typical. I couldn't leave it till tomorrow, could I. After that talk with Garth I imagined Austin thinking, he came straight to Garth, he talked me over with Garth, that he hadn't time to come and see me, oh no, I'm second best, he spends the evening with Garth and decides to see me later, everyone takes precedence over me, he wouldn't come hot-foot from the airport just to see me, would he. That's what I thought of him thinking. I can do Austin better than Austin does himself. So I come rushing round here in a nervous frenzy and commit that crime on the stairs. Did he know I was listening? And now this tele-phone box crime. Why couldn't I go quietly back to my hotel? Am I afraid of him, or what?

A little farther on Matthew passed the home-coming Ludwig in the darkness, but of course they did not know each other.

A little farther on still a police car went by with its siren screaming.

My dear Ludwig,

Your last letter has filled your mother and myself with consternation. When you spoke of this matter earlier we did not, I am afraid, realize how serious you were. This step which, led by understandable feelings, you propose to take seems to us not only injudicious but wrong. We are fortunate enough to live in a democratic state and should surely obey or at least confront its laws however temporarily repugnant, as Socrates did with the laws of Athens. The accident of your birth in England seems a quite insufficient reason for this grave step, which must be seen by the English authorities themselves as a mere device or subterfuge. The United States government has a long arm. Are you certain that you cannot be extradited as a deserter? Your letter was vague on this point. We are very alarmed indeed about your position and feel uncomfortable about your motivation. You know how with gratitude your mother and I regard our deliverance in this land of freedom. Naturally we share your horror of this terrible war, though we cannot agree with you that it is wrong to wage it. Some wars are less evil than what they combat, in the present case totalitarian government, which we have experienced and you have not. Naturally too we do not want to see you in uniform. You are our only child. Perhaps you do not realize how ardently we have prayed that this cup might pass from us, and that you would not in fact be drafted, as this seemed at some time likely. Of this I say no more. Duty has nothing to do with what we however passionately desire. We feel in this

82

eventuality that you cannot adopt what seems so odd and makeshift a solution without in the long run thinking ill of yourself, even apart from the danger of your being extradited. We understand about your work and about the pleasantness and ease of life in England, but you are not an English person. You have the precious privilege of an American passport which must not be lightly given away, and there are claims which America has upon you because of us, because of your education, because of the true ideals for which, however imperfectly, this country stands. You are young and young people are greedy. But you have many years ahead, God willing, and England and a time of work there can be enjoyed later. If you do not now somehow make yourself straight with the American power you will be unable to return here for many years or perhaps ever without severe penalties, such as imprisonment, and you know what terrible places are these prisons, where you could even be killed by the other prisoners. You must know that if you do not meet this matter properly now, in some way, and meet it right here at home, you are choosing exile from what you are fortunate enough to call your homeland. You would be certain to wish to return later, we feel sure, and to come whatever the cost, this we fear. Your suggestion that we should, at our age, remove our home yet again seems to us merely thoughtless. We do not want to return to Europe where we have no happy memory. We have so far managed to keep your decision from the neighbours, who about your return constantly inquire, but we have discussed the matter with Mr. Livingstone. Having regard to the date of drafting, he advises that you profess to have been travelling in continental Europe and not to have received the papers. This untruth, though as such repugnant, seems the best method to put yourself right with the law. When you have come back here we can consider best what to do with regard to your attempting to get perhaps exemption. The tribunals are more sympathetic now and there are a lot of different possible courses, but these must be arranged for over here. Above all you must come back soon, or any further delay is now very dangerous and we so terribly fear your being extradited, which would be ruin of your life. Will you please send a cable to say that you are coming. You are causing us very great anxiety and pain. Your mother sends her love and hopes you will soon be with us once more.

Your affectionate father,
J. P. H. LEFERRIER

Dearest Karen,

Will you be my bridesmaid? This is my way of letting you know that I am engaged, affianced, a *promessa sposa!* No, not to— But to that American boy I told you of, Ludwig Leferrier, the young ancient historian! So I am to be a don's wife after all! (Do you remember "tinker tailor" in the dorm and Ann crying because she always got "thief"?) I didn't expect it, when I first met him I thought him awfully censorious, and then suddenly I started seeing him as Sir Lancelot. I feel rather frightened and old but fearfully happy. He's handsome in a grave sort of way but sort of furry too, he's awfully clever and serious, not a bit like— Do you remember saying let's never get married unless we feel fantastically lucky to get him? I feel like that about Ludwig. May you, darling, be equally blessed. I have always regarded you as my sister since that first morning at boarding school when you told me I didn't *really* have to turn my mattress every day! I gather you are still down at the Mill House. Let me know when you'll be in town and we'll talk clothes and love! Lots and lots of the latter from your childhood pal,

G.

Sebastian,

What did I tell you? Please see the enclosed cutting from *The Times*. You know what your tactical mistake was of course? Interested as I was, I even gave you, on *that* evening, a hint of advice. I was *then* almost resigned. I know I have been a complete idiot where you are concerned. I gratuitously confessed my love (which men despise) and I let you have me when I was sure you loved another (which is genuinely contemptible) and you can do what you like with me and you know it. However, since this morning there is a new world in which it still remains, oddly enough, for you and me to make each other's acquaintance. We did rather start at the end, didn't we? I think now something rather formal would be in order. The parents are still much involved in their childish pursuits, Pa with his pigs and Mama with organizing her terrible boutique, but I can give them the slip on Monday. Let us then lunch at an expensive restaurant of your choosing, yes? I shall probably be staying with Ann Colindale, not at the parental mansion. She is in love, by the way, but not, wise girl, with you. Don't tell Gracie I'll be in town.

Your slave,
KAREN

Are you really very sad about Gracie?? My darling.

Dearest Sis,

I have told the parents that I cannot, because of an examination (a fiction this), attend the funeral games. I hope you enjoy them. Poor old Grandma. Everyone will be rejoicing, won't they, especially Aunt Char. What news of the carve-up? Aunt Char will be able to act out her fantasy of cocking a snook at the family. Us I am afraid she has never liked since the days when she babysat us while the Ps were out on the tiles. Now maybe she'll light out for Monte Carlo. I would if I were her.

About the egregious Leferrier. (What does "egregious" mean exactly? I must look it up.) He is decent and clever and too good for you and I respect his decision not to return to that ghastly place. Perhaps now at last you'll stop flirting. I have had to speak to you about this before. Flirtatiousness cuts you off from people. Some women (e.g. our mother) are eternally cut off from the world by a flirtatious temperament, only they never realize it. Yes, he's decent and I'm glad. Or am I? Am I not a little jealous? Will not our old alliance suffer? Ralph Odmore says that Sebastian (ought I to tell you this?) is dashed.

Ralph still doesn't know how I feel about him. We have dignified conversations about European history. God. I confess I'm relieved you aren't wedding Sebastian. Fore-suffering all, like the Grecian sage, I know that whatever the fate of my passion for Ralph all will in a year or two be dust and ashes. So young and so untender, love's victim though I be. I pant for Ralph, yet panting know that all is vanity. A family connection would prove an embarrassment.

Talking of embarrassment I have had another of *those* letters from Mum, partly tosh about Grandma (faugh!) and also about the Gibson Grey biz about which she is agog, and into which pie she proposes to plunge up to the elbow with the highest of motives. (People like our ma should be forbidden to write letters.) God, how I think one should leave other people's things alone and not crawl all over them. I see our dear Ps as two giant snails with waggling inquisitive eyes leaving long slimy trails behind. Do not let us be like them. Fear it, sweet Gracie, fear it, my dear sister. Aunt Char is at least a decent sardonic letter-alone.

I now have an appointment with Ralph in the cricket pavilion of which nothing will come. Look after yourself, my child. What you and Ludwig have so far *done* about it I forbear to ask, though I should certainly like to know.

Ever your loving sibling,
Patroclus Tiresias Tisbourne

My dear Dorina,

Thank you very much for your little note about poor Mama. Expected though it was, we are all very grieved and will miss her sorely. I will not dwell on this further. She was a wonderful person, and as you may imagine our hearts are full. And Gracie's engagement, in a happier way, has made us feel the fateful passage of time.

May I take this little chance to say something? We were very sorry indeed to hear about Austin's misfortune about his job, of which I gather you have now learnt. George, who sends his best regards by the way, is scouting around for a suitable post and has told Austin this, which has relieved Austin's mind very much indeed, so don't you worry either. Job-hunting can be so depressing. Meanwhile, may I suggest that you yourself should come and stay with us for a while? There are times when it may be better to be away from one's own family, on neutral ground as it were, and in a new scene! Even lucky I feel this now and then! Regard it as a holiday, as a treat. Also I am sure it could help you to talk a bit to an outside well-wisher. You understand. And we could invite Austin or not as you pleased. You know how very sincerely we hope for both your happinesses. To see you here would, I need hardly say, gladden our hearts after our recent troubles. Do say I may fix with Mavis for you to come.

Ever, with love,

CLARA

P.S. We have just heard that Matthew has come home! What a surprise! Austin tells us he came straight to Austin from the airport in the most touching way. Austin seems delighted about his return and one cannot but think this a happy augury!

Dearest Gracie,

All my congratulations! I have just seen it in *The Times*. May you be happy and glorious! Nor will I withhold the tribute of saying that the news caused me pain, I will not specify how much! I will always feel something special about you, even when we are both ninety. Why it didn't come off with us I think we both very well understood, though it would be hard to say and now will be never said. I liked your intended a great deal. I understand you will in all likelihood be decorating the Oxford scene? When a decent interval has elapsed I will invite you both to lunch. That will occasion another pang. Dare I hope in your bosom too a little? I say no more. All greatest happiness to you, dear Gracie, and love from,

Yours, a good loser,

SEBASTIAN

Dear Louis,

I have heard of your engagement and write to congratulate you so much upon it. Gracie is a lovely girl, and we are all so glad that you will stay in England. I expect you will now be very busy as engaged people are. But I hope you will still find time to come and see me. I have expected you on several days but you did not come, though I understood from Austin that you would come. Your visits are precious because I know you are on Austin's side and with many other people I am not sure what side they are on. This connects with what we spoke of when you were last here. I am sorry to be so sunk in my own concerns. I know I am not important except to myself and I suppose to Austin and Mavis but I am at a loss. I am sorry this letter which was meant to be very short is getting incoherent. I just meant to say that I value you because of Austin and because you are a good person and have been a good friend to me. Please continue to visit me now and then if you can find time. I am rather depressed. With my very best wishes to you and Gracie,

Ever,
DORINA

Dear Leferrier,

I believe I may be the first to bring you the glad news, since the Master's letter won't get into the post till tomorrow, that you have (of course) been elected to the fellowship in ancient history. We immensely look forward to you and are in a fever lest you may have changed your mind about us! I personally tremendously enjoyed our arguments. The school of Lit. Hum. is, as you know, trinitarian in form, its pillars being in this case yours truly, as the Greek and Latin language hand, MacMurraghue, whom you didn't meet, as the philosopher, and now yourself as the ancient history merchant. MacMurraghue is incomprehensible and distinguished. Our joint pupils will be lucky men. Our common room, though not quite a small Athenian state, is a gay enough place. May I say how glad I and MacMurraghue (and also the Master, who I fear designs you to be Dean!) are that you are a single man. There are too few merry bachelor dogs left among us young Turks. I did enjoy getting drunk with you on that second evening and I shall take pleasure in returning to the charge about your heresy concerning the *De Rerum Natura* and the Delphic Oracle! And I hope you have forgiven me for describing your interest in Aristophanes as limited to his value as a source of information about the price of sausages! In anticipation, in short, of *larx,* this being I fear not the sort of solemn letter you may have expected to receive from a prospective colleague and an Oxford dignitary,

I nevertheless sign myself,
Yours sincerely,
ANDREW HILTON
Fellow and tutor

My dear Austin,

I am sorry that I visited you so precipitately and so late on the evening of my arrival. My heart was full of you and I had to come to you directly, it could not have waited till the morning. Please forgive my rather abrupt appearance and departure. I have called twice since but got no reply, though I think Miss Ricardo was in on the second occasion. Your telephone appears to be out of order. May I suggest that we have lunch soon, somewhere quiet, perhaps my club? I think I should tell you this much of my plans. I am looking for a house and propose to settle here for good. I do not intend to hunt for old acquaintances and I shall not be calling at Valmorana. I have diplomatic cronies in London if I crave for company, which I do not expect to do. But I very much want to see you. I found (this condenses a long story which I will tell you at more leisure) that it was impossible to settle elsewhere with any peace of mind while our old difficulties remained as an unresolved cloud upon the horizon. I do not presume to imagine that I can help you. But you can certainly help me. And if I speak in this context of fraternal affection these are not, as far as I am concerned, empty words.

As ever,
your devoted brother,
MATTHEW

Dear Ludwig,

I'm sorry we've kept missing each other. I hope you got the note which I left on the door of the flat. I shall be back there on Friday. I've been in the East End job-hunting. I want to find something straightforward to do for other people. I can't express to you how sick I got of philosophy, much more so than when we last talked. I said then it was rubbish. I think now it is muck. More of this when we meet. I haven't said, and I say now, how good it is that you are marrying Gracie Tisbourne. Good for her, since she is getting a first-class chap, and good for you since you are getting what you want. I wish you happiness, and the things which are more important than happiness. You know what they are. About my father: I cannot think very highly of Miss Ricardo as a companion for him, but I am glad that he is where you are. My intuitions about him and you at Cambridge, Mass., were just ones. Do stay by him. At present I can do nothing for him, except keep clear of him and also of Dorina and Uncle Matthew. In families people are often automatically gifted with an ability to cause awful pain by moves which are innocent in themselves. I don't know how much you have studied, and if so understood, our curious scene. Anyway, *stick to Dorina* whatever happens as well as to Father. She is probably best at Valmorana for the moment and so long as you go there Father will feel easier about her. Excuse all this family rot. When we meet let us talk about quite other things.

Yours,
GARTH

My little bird,

How is it with you? I think about you constantly. I will send Ludwig over with some flowers. When you have the flowers, will you please send one back to me the way you used to? Your husband is still a sentimental old silly where you are concerned. I miss you horribly day and night. You know I told you in that note about having chucked up my job. Well, I think I will stay on a little longer in the

Ricardo lodging house so as to get some money by letting the flat while I look for a better job. Mitzi is a blousy old whore but kindly and lets me have the room cheap. I believe she is having some sort of romance with her photographer. As I expect you have heard Matthew has turned up again. He came round late one evening, rather hang-dog. I'm afraid I was somewhat brisk with him and indicated in the politest possible way that he should keep clear of my affairs. I rely on you to support me in this. (Please, Dorina. Important.) I haven't seen him since but he has written me a hypocritical letter, wherein he says incidentally that he would rather hobnob with "diplomatic cronies" than be seen dead with "old acquaintances"! (That might interest Mavis.) I fear he has become quite incurably grand and will not be met with in our little world any more.

About us, it may be better at the moment to continue things as they are. I feel you are *resting* at Valmorana and you are safe there. If the Tisbournes suggest your going to their place, for God's sake don't go, they are prying peepers and first-class trouble-makers. George very kindly announced he would find me a job! I told him to go to hell. Rest well, dear child, and become better in your heart and your soul. Quietness will make you feel whole again and will dispel those anxieties which made us both so naughty. Then you will come back to your tiresome old husband who loves you—who loves his dearest little bird so much. Let me know, as always, how your days go, what you do. I so much want to know that, to be able to picture you.

Ever, ever, ever,
AUSTIN

Dearest Patrick,

Grandma's funeral was a riot, I wish you'd been there. The graveyard bit was gloomy of course and I found myself shedding tears. Poor old thing, she never had much fun. Aunt Charlotte cried and Mama patted her face (her own face not Aunt Char's) with a *black* hankie. Papa wept a bit, would you believe it, I was quite shaken. He is very *sensible*. (The French word.) He never got on with Grandma of course, but he took it all in a literary sense. He was talking about mortality and so on in the car, the brevity of life and all that. That was in the car *going*. In the car coming back he was enormously cheerful, as indeed we all were. Aunt Char looked twenty years younger. Mama was chattering about the Spode dinner service and the Georgian silver. Then everyone came back to our house and there was a sort of *party*. *Sir Charles* had come. (I cannot get used to his elevation.) (We were spared Hester, Sebastian, and your beloved.) And a lot of rather chic people I didn't know, and some of the linen people from Ulster, only they sheered off when they saw the *drink!* You see, everyone stood around for a while trying to be solemn, and then we heard a burst of gay laughter from the kitchen where Papa and Sir Charles had opened a bottle of champagne. Then we all converged on the kitchen and there were drinks all round, and people were sitting on the kitchen table and draped round the hall and stairs with glasses in their hands and corks were popping, it was quite a wake. Ludwig was there of course and he obviously rather disapproved, but he had a drink to please me and then cheered up. Yes, of course he is too good for me, and I thank heaven fasting. He will be a good *husband*—dread word—you see how old I have become that I can even utter it. He is clever and wise and sweet, and if he is solemn his other half will provide the laughs. I am glad, chicken, that you are jealous! But fear not for our alliance, that is eternal, and a brother is forever. Oh dear, Ludwig wants me to write to his parents and I don't know how. I suspect they are *difficult* (religious!), so unlike our dear parents whom you were so idly knocking. *Ours* have, so far as I know, never prevented either of us from doing anything that we wanted ever, which is not bad for aged Ps. As for your *curiosity* about what Lud and I are *doing,* you must *reck your own rede* and be contained! Best of luck with Ralph Odmore, whom I always think of (sorry, lover boy) as a grubby urchin. But of course he's huge now. I suspect he's cleverer than Sebastian. Only I can't help hoping your being hooked on your own sex is just a phase, and you aren't going to be like Oliver. I think the other sex is always more fun. Write soon. Much love, little one. Your matronly sister,

G.

Yes, about the aged Ps not getting imbrued in the Gibson Grey mess. As I think Ma told you telephone-wise, Matthew is back. There's another man I want in my net! I'm told he's got fat, though.

Dearest Clara,

I was glad and sad to hear of Gracie's engagement. Our age-old plan for our young had something too-good-to-be-true about it, hadn't it? I think, probably from some time ago, they had both deeply decided otherwise, and I daresay they are being sensible and it serves middle-aged dreamers right! As Charles is always telling me, one shouldn't dream too much about other people's destinies, even if they are one's children. I hope Gracie will be very very happy and I look forward to meeting the boy.

I am told Matthew Gibson Grey is in England. Is this true? Do you know his address? Charles is very keen to get hold of him about some government thing, to serve on a commission or something. I thought he was going to join a religious order in the East? I suppose that was just a legend. Matthew is the sort of person who generates legends. Poor Austin can't be too pleased. Even if the old story about Betty isn't true, Austin can hardly want Big Brother as a spectator of his current catastrophes. But perhaps Matthew is only passing by? Will we see you at the Mill House this weekend? Mollie says she has invited Penny Sayce again but *not* Oliver and Henrietta! (Apparently Geoffrey cannot stand Oliver.) We count on you for the weekend following, of course. Charles sends love. He *did* enjoy himself at the funeral!

Au revoir and love,

HESTER

I gather Garth Gibson Grey is home too and has become a dropout. I'm so terrified Ralph will be one. Thank heavens he and Patrick are pals now. Patrick will be such a steadying influence.

My dear Charlotte,

I should have written to you much sooner to say how sorry I was to hear of your mother's death. These are not empty words, and it is not just that in every death we mourn our own. I saw little of her lately, but I recall with gratitude her vigour and directness in the days when she used to help me financially with my girls. Her charity was always judicious. I only wish I could have recruited her as a fellow worker. She came of a good breed, and it is only sad that so much energy and character had to be confined to the narrow field of family life. What a general she would have made!

On another topic. I am so worried about Dorina. Clara has invited her. She won't go. (You know why.) I think indeed she cannot go to Clara's, but she does desperately need to see somebody other than me. In a way I am the last person who can help her at present. She is fond of you and respects you. Will you not come and see us, especially now that you are more free? Ring up soon about this. Only don't tell D. I asked you to come!

I hope it's in place to add that I am so glad that you will now be in easier financial circumstances! One does like to see the big money going, for once, to those who deserve it and are one's friends! Forgive this faintly cynical note, which issues, as you know, from affection! Come soon. With love,

MAVIS

P.S. Is it true that Matthew has come home? Could you let me know if you hear anything about him?

My dear Father,

I grieve deeply at the pain which I am causing to you and to my mother, and I beg you to forgive me and to try to understand. This is not anything hasty and surely you know me well enough to realize that "the pleasantness and ease" of England is not something which could tempt me away from my duty if I thought that it lay elsewhere. I cannot be an active partner in an iniquitous proceeding. That this war is an unjust war and a crime I have many times argued to you and I will not rehearse the arguments. We see this differently. All right. But granted that I believe what I do believe, I cannot be morally justified in donning the American uniform. I should regard myself with abhorrence, as a murderer, if I were to let conventional attitudes or public opinion or even my love for you lead me to be a slaughterer of the innocent. If ever I saw my duty plain before my face it is here, and I cannot do otherwise than refuse this summons into a place of wickedness.

As for obtaining exemption, I do not see that, since I am not a pacifist, I could do so on any ground allowable by the tribunals. This is a matter on which I have reflected for years and about which I feel clear. Meanwhile do not fear that I shall be extradited. The British government is very unwilling to extradite any American "objectors," and my having been born here makes extradition unthinkable in my case. I feel there is moreover nothing improper in my now presuming upon the "accident" of my "English" birth, for it seems, in all the circumstances of my having come to study in London, together with the crisis which has overtaken me here, to be no accident after all but a disposal of destiny for which I should be humbly grateful.

It is indeed arguable that I ought to come home and be martyred, tear up my draft card, refuse to join up, as many others have so admirably done, and then let them do their worst. That would be to act the Socratic part. Socrates did not allow the laws of Athens to force him into wrongdoing. He kept on speaking the truth and was prepared to take the consequences. I have thought long and carefully about this and have decided that this particular martyrdom is not enjoined upon me. I do not dread, indeed I would welcome, a term in prison, but if I were to drink of this cup I should lose my passport, my access to Europe, and possibly any further chance of pursuing my studies. I would find myself forced to become a full-time protester. And this, I am certain, is not my task in life.

You, who have so often bid me ponder the parable of the talents, should understand this. Plato said that justice was doing one's own job. I must pursue my chosen studies and develop my mind and make it fruitful or else perish in my soul. I could not live the life of protest. I am not in any sense a group man. I should become rancorous and ultimately vapid. I am a contemplative and could never be a man of action. I know myself, and the *duties* which being myself imposes. Please please understand that this is not an idle or frivolous decision, but engages all the deepest things that I am. I make it as before God.

I have a piece of news which I hope will give you pleasure and seem to you like a hopeful sign of some later time when we shall have survived these woes. I have become engaged to be married to an English girl. Her name is Grace Tisbourne. I enclose, as you will have seen, a photograph of her. (It isn't a very good one. She is much more beautiful than that.) Her family are very good, her father is a high civil servant, her brother is at a private school (what they call a public school over here) and she is a wonderful and sweet girl. She would like very much to write to you and will probably do so in a little while. Do rejoice with me if you can in this. And see that now I *must* envisage a time when we shall all be united in peace and happiness in Europe. Please see it this way. I love you and I honour you and if I could obey you I would. But I must first obey my conscience, as you yourselves have always taught me to do. Please understand that my decision is firmly taken. And please write soon and forgivingly to

Your loving son,
LUDWIG

My darling husband,

Thank you for your sweet letter. No Louis and no flowers however. Never mind. I miss you terribly too. In a little while we'll meet, but not yet. You are very understanding, who else would understand so well? There is a sort of nothing here, a nothing in me— I'm sure everyone else thinks that something definite is up, whereas— Oh I am a troublesome girl to you and you must forgive me! I just have to be alone for just a bit longer, just breathing, existing. You like to know what I do. I do little things. Today I worked in the garden. I clipped the privet hedge and mowed the lawn. And I painted a cupboard and stuck some pictures from magazines onto the door of it. It is very pretty. You shall see it. I will do one for us. I am rather worried about your letting the flat, though I suppose it is necessary, is it? It seems silly to say it, but it sort of cuts off our retreat for the moment, I mean it is home after all. I know I left it but it is there. You will think I am being very stupid, but I feel suddenly homeless. Please let this time be short, and don't let anyone get into the flat that you can't easily get out again, will you. Had you not better take legal advice about it? And do be careful who it is, the tenant I mean, there's so much of *our* things in the flat, there's letters and things and all your old stuff in that trunk and private things. Don't destroy anything please, but lock it all up somehow won't you. I do hope you will soon get a better job, I'm sure you were right to throw up the other one, and go back to the flat again. I liked to think of you there in *our* place. I hope you are comfortable where you are. I think Mitzi Ricardo is a nice person. Give her my best wishes. And give my love to Garth. Don't worry about Matthew. He won't come here. So we are in our seclusion and all is well. And of course I won't go to the Tisbournes. I am not too troubled with the strange things, and I am reading a lot. I will send you a book at the weekend. I would like us to be reading the same book. Forgive me and don't stop loving me, as indeed ever and ever I love you.

Your nothing-wife,
DORINA

My dear Dorina,

Thank you for your letter and your kind wishes. I am sorry not to have seen you, but I am afraid I am terribly busy at present. I have to be a lot in Oxford where I am to take up that college appointment that I told you of.

So I am afraid I shall have to resign my task as messenger!
I hope all will be well with you, and I trust we shall meet
again later on. With best affectionate wishes,

LOUIS

"May I see a bigger one?" said Gracie.

The jeweller went to fetch another tray.

Ludwig kicked Gracie's ankle.

"A diamond ring is just about the soundest investment you can make these days," said the jeweller. "Diamonds are still a girl's best friend, ha ha."

"How much is this one?" said Gracie.

"That is six hundred pounds."

Ludwig kicked Gracie again.

"That is a really marvellous ring, madam, a remarkable individual." He called the diamonds individuals. They all looked the same to Ludwig.

"I don't like the setting," said Gracie. "What about this one?"

"Superb! Eight hundred pounds."

Is this some sort of joke? thought Ludwig. He had suggested that they should find a little Victorian ring in Notting Hill. Gracie had led him to Bond Street. Ludwig was not used to this kind of shop. Nor, clearly, was Gracie.

Ludwig was living in a daze. Ever since he had become engaged the world had looked completely different. A strange white light shone upon things, like a theatre or television light, so that everything was too bright and a little blanched. This light was not quite itself happiness, though Ludwig had no doubt that he was happy. He had even less doubt that he was deeply in love and that Gracie was too. They were still shy with each other, or they were shy in a new way. They did not always know what to talk about. There was the uneasiness and anxiety of real romance, so unlike what is dreamed of. There were curious silences, when they would look at each other and then laugh and clasp hands and kiss. They had not yet been to bed. This tormented Ludwig, not only with physical desire, but also because he felt himself a failure for not being able to take charge. He had still not even managed to discover whether or not Gracie was a virgin. And there had never quite been a context in which he could tell her about his own, as they now seemed, rather dreary and forced adventures. The possibility of something was discussed, if at all, obliquely. Ludwig would say, "Why don't we come back to my place this evening, after we've had dinner?" And Gracie would say, "I'd rather not. It's so crowded, and I feel Mitzi's against me, and Austin makes me feel funny." Then Ludwig would say, "When are your parents going away for the weekend?" and Gracie would say, "They've put it off again." A hotel seemed so vulgar, and would she come? If only he could have afforded a car. There remained the Park. Could he tear Gracie's tights off behind a bush? Sometimes he felt desperate enough to. But without a lead from her he could hardly suggest it. Would an English suitor have let this absurd situation continue? What would Sebastian have done?

Nights were thus unsatisfactory, and during days Gracie seemed to assume that they would be almost all the time together. This much human company was a novelty for Ludwig, and there were occasional moments when he reflected with dismay how absolutely he had lost his solitude. He and Gracie scoured London like tourists, always following her suggestions and her plans. They went down the river to Greenwich, they visited the Tower, they explored the churches of the City, they went to Hampton Court and Kenwood and Chiswick House, they kissed each other in the National Gallery and the Courtauld Institute and the Victoria and Albert Museum, they were at theatres or concerts almost every evening and sat in innumerable pubs between Ludgate Hill and the Gloucester Road. Gracie scarcely drank alcohol but adored pubs, which were new to her. Ludwig, who had not a very good head, found he was drinking too much. Then there were the restaurants.

Gracie, always ravenous and always slim, would eat well twice a day. She liked the Savoy, Pruniers, Wheelers. She admired the Mirabelle. She cared for the Caprice. Ludwig found he was spending a great deal of money. The remains of his American grant were fading away. And his Oxford salary would not begin until September.

Of course it was all delightful. Gracie enjoyed the sometimes pointless details of life more than anyone he had ever known. She could make a treat out of anything. When they met it would always be at some obscure surprising place, which nobody but Gracie would have thought of as being a place at all. Then there would be a little walk, they would feed the ducks in the park, or the fish at the Dorchester, or look at some tiny monument, or visit a shop which sold the best nougat in London, or go to the Wallace Collection to hear the clocks strike twelve and then go on to a pub with a funny name, passing by a flower shop where Ludwig would buy flowers to be later ceremonially thrown into the Thames from a particular bridge. Gracie seemed to have become, since their engagement, more beautiful and stylish than ever, and he felt intense possessive pride as he paraded his delicious fiancée in theatre foyers or through the streets of the West End. They were often thus privately in public but, evidently at Gracie's wish, did little visiting. They were invited jointly to a number of gatherings, but somehow or other Gracie usually found a reason why they could not go. Ludwig sometimes uneasily wondered whether this was because she wanted to avoid Sebastian.

Their talk was constantly of trivialities but Ludwig had never found trivialities so almost spiritually absorbing. They chatted about food and people and their London travels. Ludwig noticed that Gracie enjoyed each experience but without in any way wanting to connect one with another. Sometimes she asked him questions about history, but these were not so much requests for information as occasions for him to charm her with his omniscience. "Why you know everything!" she would cry with shining eyes, after he had stated some of the better-known facts about Pericles or Cromwell or Lloyd George. She made no effort

101

to remember anything that he told her. Sometimes she asked more metaphysical questions such as "Do fleas suffer in a flea circus?" or "Why do we call high notes high notes?" He always attempted an answer. About Oxford, which had been a taboo subject until the great news came, they now talked lightly, talked houses, old or new, town or country. On its deeper mystery Ludwig brooded alone, tipsy with the joy of it.

Yet elsewhere there were quite other and terrible things. He tried at intervals to talk to Gracie about these things but it seemed so portentous and artificial to trouble her happiness with this talk. "It's past," said Gracie once. "See it all as past and done. You've made the decision. Let it glide away now. Let it go." In a way this was wise advice. And Ludwig decided that Gracie's reluctance to discuss his great issues was due not to any indifference but to fear. She feared still that he might depart, she feared his fears and his agitation about matters which she could not fully understand. He had asked her to write to his parents, but she kept putting it off. This perhaps was understandable. It would not be an easy letter to write.

The great issues themselves pained him all the time. His parents' opposition hurt him because of old habits of concord and obedience. He had never been explicitly at odds with them before, although quietly their lives and opinions had diverged. Their arguments could not move him, but the sheer fact of their opposition stirred and wounded his conscience in obscure and frightening ways. He could see, and even be touched by seeing, that they cared what the neighbours thought, they feared the laws, they feared the police, they did not want to be "out of line," they did not want their fragile achievement of Americanness to be damaged, they feared that the long arm of American power would somehow seize him, disgrace him, destroy him. That they saw the war differently was probably their most rational area of disagreement, and that was difficult enough. They loved one America, and he, if he loved at all, loved a different one. But he could readily have endured his pain at their distress if only he had felt absolutely sure of himself.

102

He had no doubts about his judgement of the war. When he looked outward all was plain and clear. But when he looked inward . . . Did his parents really believe that he was moved by worldly motives, that he could prefer English cosiness to his duty, or that he was simply a coward? Could he believe it himself? Of course he liked England, of course he wanted Oxford, of course he was a coward, anyone would be, no one wanted to fight that war. The trouble was that on this side of the Atlantic there was no test to which he could put himself to make sure that he was acting on principle. Here there was nothing hard at all. The hard things were all over there. Ought he not to go back and suffer? How necessary was suffering? How necessary was it to *him?* How was Christ to be imitated? Ought he not to go through the centre of this drama rather than round the edge? Was it fair to those who could not escape, thus beautifully to do so? As he had said to his parents, he could face prison, he could even have loved it, but he could not face the haunting possibility of having his wings clipped forever. No passport, no Europe, no scholarly world, no using of his real talents. That was the hell that he feared. And in acknowledging, as he must, these motives, was he not, in taking what was in effect the easy way, but an inch away from dishonour? Very occasionally he even conceived that he ought simply to go back and don the uniform as most of the others did. Why did he think he was so special?

And now he had Gracie, a responsibility forever and a link with the easy world which he so much loved and feared. The English milieu into which she brought him was relaxed and liberal and hazy. Here no one seemed to conceive that he could have any problems about going back. No one seemed to want to talk about it or to be interested or to understand. Or perhaps they felt a certain delicacy. It was hard to tell with these people. Meanwhile the big talk with Garth to which he had been so much, even for months, looking forward had not yet taken place. He had only seen his friend once briefly before Garth's disappearance to the East End, and not at all since his return. Was Garth avoiding him because of Gracie? It was but too possible that Garth despised him for this match, and felt already that they were hopelessly divided. It was also possible that Garth's affection for him was wounded because Ludwig was no longer solitary. Whatever the reason, Garth remained elusive. To hell with him, Ludwig sometimes thought, if he's got so damned touchy. If we can meet, good, if not I'm certainly not going to chase after him. He greatly needed that talk, however.

Now here was Gracie asking to see yet another tray of rings.

As the shopman moved away Ludwig said to her in a low voice, "Look, honey, this stuff isn't our class. I can't afford you a ring like any of these. That one costs more than I've got in the bank. Let's get out of here, come on. Tell the man we'll think about it."

Gracie flashed him a dazzling smile and began to turn over some even grander rings.

"Gracie!" said Ludwig. There was a hint of the authority of the husband. He had already ceased to call her "Gracie" except at very solemn moments.

"Sssh!" said Gracie, "you're distracting me."

"Honey, have a heart—"

"It's an investment."

"But, sweetie pie, in order to invest money you have to have the money to start with."

"Shut up, Ludwig, you're not paying for this ring," said Gracie. She said to the shopman, "I think I'll have this one. Will you take a cheque? I have my passport and a banker's card. Or you can ring my bank."

The shopman was happy to trust madam. Gracie wrote out a large cheque.

"Don't wrap it up, I'll wear it. Ludwig, could you put it on my finger now? No, on this finger. That's right." She darted the stone to and fro to catch the light.

"I congratulate you on a wonderful purchase," said the shopman, "and may I wish you happiness. A diamond is forever."

Ludwig staggered out into the dusty sunshine of Bond Street. He grasped the skirt of Gracie's cool crinkly stripy dress in a hot hand. "Poppet, are you mad? You haven't got that much money."

"Yes, I have," said Gracie coolly, "now. Don't mess my dress, Ludwig." She hailed a taxi. "The Savoy, please."

"What do you mean 'now'?"

"Grandmama left everything to me."

"To you—everything?"

"Yes. The house, the stocks and shares, the great big bank balance, the lot. Ludwig, I am rich. You are marrying an heiress."

"God!" said Ludwig. He fell back in his seat. "But, poppet, can that be right? I mean *all* to you?"

"All."

"And nothing to your mother or Aunt Charlotte?"

"Not a bean."

"But shouldn't you give it to them? I mean, it's not right—particularly Aunt Charlotte—"

"We must respect the wishes of the dead. My, have you ever seen such a large diamond really close to?"

Suddenly everything was frightening.

A young man on the doorstep was delivering flowers.

But flowers were for Alison, they must be. Only this week Alison was dead.

Charlotte could read the name of the flower shop on the paper, but there did not seem to be any note attached. The flowers were pink gladioli. She motioned them away.

"Are they for Mrs. Ledgard?"

"No, they—"

"There must be some mistake. Are you sure this is the right address?"

"Yes, I—"

"All right, thank you," said Charlotte. She snatched the flowers and shut the door quickly.

She carried them into the drawing-room, which smelt soothingly of lemony furniture polish. She examined the bouquet carefully. There was no note. They must be for Alison, from somebody who didn't know. Ought she to take them to the churchyard, or would that be stupid? It didn't matter. Then suddenly she thought, they are from Matthew, for me. There had been no word from Matthew since his return, no word indeed for years. And now these flowers. She closed her eyes.

When she opened them she saw through the window that the young man who had delivered the flowers was still standing outside. He seemed undecided. Then he saw Charlotte looking out at him. The next moment the front-door bell rang again.

Charlotte thought, it's the wrong address, he's realized it's the wrong address. The Matthew idea was too good to be true, obviously absurd. She picked up the flowers and opened the door and handed them back to the young man. "I told you so."

"What?"

"That this is the wrong address." How cruel, thought Charlotte. It was years and years since anyone had given her any flowers.

"I am very sorry," said the young man, "I must apologize. You obviously don't know who I am. My name is Garth Gibson Grey."

But that's impossible, thought Charlotte. Garth Gibson Grey is a boy, a schoolboy.

"We haven't met for some time, Miss Ledgard."

"I see," said Charlotte. She saw a shabby tall thin dark-haired man, rather sallow, with a hard bird face. He looked like a thief. Only now she could also see the gawky boy who had, in years which she had somehow mislaid, become this man. "I'm sorry I didn't recognize you. But who are the flowers from? You see, my mother is dead."

106

"The flowers are from me."

"But my mother is dead."

"For you."

"For me? But why?"

"Why not? I just thought I'd call on you. I just thought I'd bring you some flowers."

"It's a long time since anyone gave me any flowers," said Charlotte.

"That's why I thought—I mean—"

"You thought it might have been a long time?"

"No, I—"

"A wreath perhaps. That would be more suitable. Yes. I thought at first they were from someone else. Well, thank you." Charlotte took the flowers, which Garth was proferring again. They felt dead and sinister.

"I won't detain you," said Garth, as Charlotte showed no signs of asking him in. "I just wanted to bring the flowers and to say that if ever there was anything I could do for you I'd be so pleased if you would let me know."

"What on earth could you ever do for me," said Charlotte, "and why should you assume that I want anything done? I really cannot think why you're here."

"Oh well—you know—there's always something one person can do for another, even if it's only posting their letters."

"I can post my own letters, thank you," said Charlotte.

"Well—forgive me—" said Garth.

"What for?"

"For having been a fool. I meant well."

"I am afraid I don't understand this conversation," said Charlotte. "No doubt I am getting old and out of touch with young people. Perhaps I don't understand the language of flowers any more. Are you what is called a flower child?"

"Oh no, nothing like that. I just—I'm so sorry—"

"Not at all, not at all," said Charlotte. "Thank you so much for the flowers."

They stared at each other, seeking words. Then Charlotte made a sort of flapping movement with her hand and shut the door. She let the gladioli drop on the floor and stood by the door listening to Garth's receding steps. The tears which were her constant companions now came again into her eyes.

Leaving the flowers where they lay, she went slowly downstairs to the kitchen. If only there had not been that moment of thinking about Matthew. She had been so unkind to the young man, pretending not to understand him. To be thoughtlessly pitied by the young is, after all, one of the least of the trials of age and should be endured with grace. She saw in herself the loneliness of the old and the artificiality of trying to help them. And yet, and yet, she was not old. How quaint of the boy to come round, when he hardly knew her. Had he heard about the will? Everyone must know by now. How agonizingly she felt it as a disgrace.

Upon the draining board lay the two halves of one of the Spode plates which she had broken last night. Just a little while ago it would have seemed worthwhile to mend it. For years she had cosseted these things which now suddenly all belonged to Gracie.

It was not that she had particularly thought of them as her own. She had looked after them as she had looked after Alison because here was home, here was duty. Now there was neither home nor duty any more. She owned her toothbrush but not the mug in which it stood, she owned her dress, but not, although she had worn it for years, the onyx necklace about her neck. Everything was entirely as usual, and yet utterly alienated, as if what one had taken to be someone's house had turned out to be an antique shop. Just for a moment perhaps all these things were proclaiming a secret truth, that they were tough, old, cold, and practically immortal. They had existed, they would exist, until they were burnt or smashed to pieces. They were unconnected and heartless. Ownership was an illusion.

Hardship reveals eternal truths, but only for a moment, since human beings soon recover and forget. Charlotte had not yet recovered and still saw with the awful eye of vision. Of course it was a matter of pride to continue polishing and dusting. But there was no spirit left for mending plates. And this was not really because all those dear old plates now belonged to Gracie, but because it was suddenly clear that life was extremely short. Life was short, ownership was an illusion, nothing really mattered very much. All the same, I ought to have been nicer to that boy, she thought. My life is near its end, she thought. She dropped the two halves of the plate into the refuse bin.

The house was quiet and weird. Clocks ticking in it seemed to be saying something new. Charlotte listened. It was odd how absolutely gone Alison was. The house had already forgotten her. The room had been cleaned, the medicines thrown away, all the untidiness and litter of illness and death had been swept up. Did all human things disappear so quickly and so completely, leaving onyx necklaces and tall-boys in cold possession of the centuries? And as the familiar place had slipped forward into another time, so Charlotte herself had changed. Home and duty and pity had prevented more than a rather cursory sense of herself. She had felt sorry for herself, but, as she now realized, in a vague and undifferentiated way. For the intense anxious sense of herself with which she was now suddenly invested she was quite untrained. She had never been a specialist in self-awareness and Alison's presence, though it had occasioned brooding, had also prevented it from being too detailed. There had always been, after all, Alison to be sorry for. Her mother's illness, her mother's pitiful fear of death, had kept mortality at bay. Alison had always been there, in between Charlotte and death. Now that defence was removed. Charlotte stared at death and it seemed very close to her, it had quietly came closer, it spoke to her in the ticking of the clocks, Charlotte's own death, her very own.

Of course it had all been natural and inevitable, the way it had worked out. Of course Charlotte had had to look after Alison, it had to be Charlotte, since Clara was married with two children, and to him that hath shall be given and from him that hath not shall be taken away even that which he hath. That bit of the Bible's true anyway, thought Charlotte. The grace and hope of religion had

109

withdrawn from her long ago. All that was left was fatalism and a special taste in the bitterness of truth. Her life had passed her by, not really lived, not really hers. Only her death was hers, now silently drawn so close.

Everyone would be very kind and, within the limits of their own self-interest, considerate. Gracie would press her to stay on, would offer money, Clara and George would probably move in, Charlotte would become, in the nicest possible way, their housekeeper. Soon Charlotte would be looking after Gracie's children as she had, it seemed like yesterday, looked after Gracie. A single woman was a great blessing in a family. Usefulness was not at an end. There would be points and purposes in life, never quite her own points and purposes, but was not blood thicker than water after all. The strength of the family bond made other things in her life seem arbitrary by comparison. Usefulness was her destiny. Gracie's children, Patrick's children, were her fate in the years to come. She had no private destiny and nothing extraordinary could ever happen to her now.

The only trouble is, thought Charlotte, that I hate all these people. Through so many years she had detested Alison's sickliness, Clara's worldliness, Gracie's pertness, Patrick's cleverness, and George's unspeakable assumption that Charlotte was eternally in love with him. Had she ever loved George? Perhaps. But now George was just something hanging in the corner of a spider's web. Clara had eaten and digested him long ago, and only the memory of a legend lingered on to taint George's invariable kindness, Clara's too attentive sweetness. Yet it remained that these people were all she had, they were her daily bread, as Matthew, who had once mattered so much, could never be.

Charlotte went slowly to the door. The cold stale smell of loneliness came to her from the dark stairway and her face felt naked and cold with solitude. Would anybody ever look into her face again and really see it? She came up into the hall and saw a bunch of flowers lying beside the front door. She especially disliked gladioli. She plodded

110

downstairs again and began to arrange them in one of Gracie's cut-glass vases.

⚜⚜⚜

Dorina shrieked. The water closed over her head.

She woke up. That dream again. Had she really shrieked or had it been just a dream cry? Was it night-time?

She saw that it was day. A hot sun was burning a line down the centre of the drawn curtains. She was lying in her petticoat on the bed in her little attic bedroom. It was afternoon. Mavis was away and she was alone in the house and had sought refuge in sleep from a fearful consciousness. But such awakenings were terrible, when nightmares could escape into daylight rooms and the emptiness of the house invited hauntings.

She sat up and pulled her dress on and continued to sit on the edge of her bed. She remembered Louis's letter and now he would not come any more. The insincere letter had hurt her. Of course he could not realize how important it was to her to see him. It was not just the link with Austin, though that was important, the little gifts that came. It was that Louis was a part of the ordinary world, through him she could still glimpse ordinary things, ordinary streets, ordinary conversations, laughter. Laughter had somehow gone out of her life. When had it gone? As for the streets which surrounded Valmorana, where she went to shop for Mavis, they were full of portents. Strange looks, strange numbers, dead birds.

Valmorana seemed to have few memories, it had become, when Mavis transformed it, a different place. Only in the drawing-room the shade of their father lingered a

111

little, and in the garden beside the privet hedge, gentle, intense, stooping. Twice widowed, he had been in love with his two daughters, two lovely replicas of two lovely wives. Death had been an angel to him that was terrible and yet gentle. He had been happy when he was older with the two girls and with his painting. But that quiet spirit could not help Dorina now.

She never told Mavis how much she feared the weird unfortunates who usually filled the house and how the cries of those unwanted babies sickened her. Grotesque faces peered at her and mocked her timidity. Yet the uninhabited house was perhaps worse. She could not picture the outside of the house from within, it was as if it had no outside, but spawned inwardly, breeding new darkness and full of the obscure frightening smell of menstrual blood. Thus she dreamed about it often, dreamed of a huge sprawling place in the centre of which were rooms, or a room, which she had never seen before. She could never quite get into this room, which was large and dark with no external windows, reddish usually, full of red furniture or lit by a dim red light, and she would glimpse it with amazement and horror through a doorway, or more often from a gallery or peephole where she looked down into it from above, empty and dusty and full of big old-fashioned furniture. Sometimes too she would see something in it which she knew to be a ghost, the figure of a woman projecting from the waist upwards high up in the wall opposite to her, like the prow of a ship, and moving slightly as if tortured. Once or twice in waking hours in Valmorana she had for a second seen or imagined a similar figure.

Of her private horrors she did not now speak to anyone, not even to Mavis. The quality of them would have been hard to tell. Memory and dream sometimes became confused and things of the mind crowded close behind a screen. There were figures like statues upon the roof and in the garden and dogs with strange heads. She had talked a little to Austin in the early days, but her experiences terrified him so dreadfully that his terror frightened her out of further confidences. To terrify others, that was worst of all. Later he said he had not believed her, and she smiled.

What had then frightened her most was her sense of other horrors in him, quite different and worse perhaps, which she was stirring. How fatally and truly they had found each other, so suited and so kin. If only one of them could have been ordinary. And yet how much she had been led, to begin with, by a sense that, for him, she could be. She had seen herself saving Austin, doing something as comprehensible and commonplace as that. She wanted to cook for him, and for a while she did. She wanted to sit by his fireside and sew.

Sometimes she could not keep fear out of her eyes. Austin imagined that she was afraid of him, and in an unforgettable time of revelation, sitting alone, she had realized that she was afraid of him. It had all started in tenderness and pity. How had this fear got in? Was she perhaps just afraid for him, afraid of his nightmares? No, she feared him and he knew it, and this was yet another barrier for love to surmount. For there was love, not just compassion in her, not just possessiveness in him. He was not just the greedy boy who grasps the pretty bird and breaks its wing. Of Betty they never talked. Dorina had never even seen a picture of her, though oddly enough as a child she might have met her, only she never did.

It was only very lately, only perhaps when she had received Louis's horrible letter, that she had fully realized how much her love for Austin cut her off from other people, as if she were being gradually cornered by a relentlessness of which he was the almost unconscious agent. He seemed to feel almost any contact between herself and others as a betrayal. If she were to see the Tisbournes, or even Charlotte, he would scent a plot. Matthew of course was out of the question. And Garth was taboo. She would have liked to see Garth, to see him all grown up and different, but the embarrassment and anxiety which had always attended her relations with him would doubtless have become even worse. And Austin would think they had discussed him. Now even Louis was gone. It was as if something were closing in for the kill.

Dorina knew that many of her thoughts about her situation were ridiculous. But she knew also that she was not mad. When the pictures had fallen off the wall other people were more frightened than she was. These things were, perhaps, chemical. What she most feared was spiritual, some end point where even love died tortured. She feared the final inhumanity of man to man which she saw on the television set in the kitchen. Now the girls were away, she watched the television often, fascinated by these amazing images. She could never get used to it. She knew that there were such cruel things in the world, even in her own little world. Mavis had once suggested that she should see a doctor, once suggested that she should see a priest, but Dorina knew that this was pointless, quite apart from the hurtfulness of it to Austin.

Her only way back to the world was through her husband. Only here could magic be changed into spirit in the end. And now she had run away from him. Or was that what had happened? Was it simply fear of him that kept her here? He had never been really cruel to her, though he had stormed at her often, he had wept at her, he had accused her of destroying him. He had wanted protection, but she was danger. Once she thought that he was drugging her, but that was only imagination. She had felt her whole consciousness battered by him, as if because he so desperately wanted from her what she could not give there was a little less of her left every day. She had had to escape to breathe, to be. And yet in escaping she had made yet another obstacle between them of a quite new kind. For Austin was relieved at her departure. Of course he wanted her back, he wanted some new and better dream of his marriage, but meanwhile he too breathed. He surrounded her with anxious possessive jealous tenderness, but in obedience to what he professed to think were her wishes he did not come to see her. He wandered about outside her prison like a fierce protective wolf. She heard him baying in the night.

Thus they remained utterly obsessed with themselves and each other, and some natural healing process of which Dorina felt she ought to know the secret could not take place. If only there were somewhere else towards which she could look. Mavis talked sometimes, her eyes far

114

away, a little embarrassed, preaching to her, about simple duties simply understood, about obvious needs and obvious claims. But nothing here was simple and obvious, and almost any move was fearful. She might have prayed to God to dissolve the obsession and to show her simplicity if only she had believed in Him. His absence at least remained significant to her, but it was an utter absence of help, an absence of recourse. Worship would have been a relief, like tears. *C'est impossible de trop plier les genoux, impossible, impossible.* Who had said that to her once? The voice of some teacher, otherwise forgotten, came to her from convent days, from earliest childhood. Should she not kneel, and would it aid her, even if there were no God? Sometimes she did kneel in her room at night, but rose quickly, knowing that she knelt to demons.

❦❦❦

"She says she's been attacked by an owl," said Ludwig.

Mitzi was sitting in her little kitchen, pouring some whisky into a glass with a shaking hand.

"She's drunk," said Austin. He had just come in out of the rain, looking tired and bedraggled, his mouth drooping.

"I'm not drunk," said Mitzi, "and I *was* attacked by an owl. I sat all the evening in that pub and you didn't come."

"I only said I might come," said Austin.

"If I hadn't been wearing my head scarf it would have clawed my eyes out."

"I must ring Gracie," said Ludwig.

"Go to bed, Mitzi," said Austin. "I'm sorry I didn't turn up."

"Where were you? God, my head hurts. I was so frightened."

"I got so bloody depressed I went for a long walk, I can't remember where."

"I don't believe you. You've been to visit your little wifie."

"Oh shut up," said Austin. "I haven't. And don't talk about Dorina like that. I'm soaked. I'm going to bed."

"To wifie, to wifie. You'll hug a pillow and pretend it's her."

"Good night!"

Austin departed through the sitting-room and slammed the door.

"Are you all right, Mitzi?" said Ludwig. "I must go and ring—"

"No, I'm not all right. I've been alone all day and then waiting for that drip. I don't know why I bother with him, he's just a scrounger. Here, let me look at myself, it feels funny, it's hurting."

Mitzi was still wearing her glossy black mackintosh and a damp pink scarf round her head. She got up unsteadily and peered into the little mirror propped on the dresser. Then she pulled the scarf off. There was a long sticky red gash down the side of her face, from the temple to the jaw.

When Mitzi saw the wound she began to wail. She wailed rhythmically like a dog and tears spouted from her eyes. "Oh Christ, look at that."

"Dear me, you have hurt yourself," said Ludwig. "However did you do it?"

"I told you, I was attacked by an owl!"

Whatever happened, he thought, she must have been pretty drunk not to notice it till now.

"Ooh, ooh, ooh," wailed Mitzi. In a moment it would be hysterics.

"Sit down," said Ludwig. "Sit down, Mitzi. Here, have your whisky, please don't cry."

Mitzi laid her forehead on the table and wept, trying to grasp her whisky at the same time.

"What's the matter?"

Ludwig jumped.

Garth was standing in the doorway, his face wet with rain, his hair blackly streaked about his head.

"She says she's been attacked by an owl. Look."

"Better wash it," said Garth. "Move the chair here beside the sink, come on. Where's the disinfectant? Yes, bring that bottle and a clean cloth— Well, find one, look in those drawers. Put the towel round her shoulders. I suppose the water's hot, good. Take that glass away from her. Now stop that noise, please, *stop that noise!*"

Mitzi stopped her wailing. She sat helplessly, looking up at Garth while he bathed the wound, her mouth wetly open and tears coursing down her face. She looked like an enormous baby.

"The water's very hot," said Garth, "but that'll do it good. Now a clean towel, please, a *clean* towel. Fine. Now you'd better go to bed. Leave it uncovered. It'll be stiff tomorrow. If it looks at all septic go to a doctor. Now off to bed."

"We'll have to help her," said Ludwig. "She's rather drunk."

Mitzi was whimpering again, very softly, almost droning, gazing away across the room and patting the scar rhythmically with her fingers.

"*Go to bed,*" said Garth. "We'll help you. Where's her bedroom?"

"Next landing."

Mitzi, holding her glass, was propelled through the sitting-room, towering over her helpers like the image of a goddess being wheeled slowly along. The stairs were difficult, as Mitzi insisted on clutching the glass with the hand which was also holding the banisters. A trail of whisky followed them up.

"Just tumble her on the bed," said Garth. He extracted himself from under Mitzi's huge arm, switched the bed-room light on, and then went away down the stairs and closed the sitting-room door after him.

Tumbling her on the bed was not so easy. Ludwig, suddenly left with all her weight heeling over upon him, nearly lost his balance. Then somehow they both fell onto the bed together. Mitzi's elbow descended onto his chest like a pickaxe. Ludwig gasped. The next moment he found himself gripped in a fierce gorilla-like embrace.

It took Ludwig a moment to realize that the big girl was actually embracing him, another moment to discover that struggling was useless. Mitzi was immensely strong. Ludwig tried to raise his knee up between them, but Mitzi's giant arms, like two sinuous tree trunks, had drawn their bodies close together. He felt her panting whisky-laden breath upon his face and then a huge tongue appeared to be licking him.

Ludwig relaxed and said in a small firm voice, "Mitzi, let me go, *please.*"

There was a crying sound, as if somewhere a little girl was weeping. Then the terrible grip relaxed. Ludwig, bruised and breathless, fell off the bed. He found he was kneeling beside it. For a minute he had been in black darkness. Now he was surprised to find that the light was on and that he could see Mitzi's large pale freckled tear-stained face very close to his own, all crumpled up with weeping and curiously spotted with blood from the long gash, which was bleeding a little. Big hands touched his shoulders gently. "I'm sorry, Ludwig. I must be drunk. I'm so unhappy. And that owl frightened me so."

Ludwig kissed her on the brow. Then somehow he had dug one arm in underneath her neck. He felt the warm vertebrae. He kissed her on her hot wet alcoholic mouth. He got up, dignified. "Good night, Mitzi."

"Good night, darling Ludwig."

He went out and turned out the light. Unless drink sent her to sleep at once he would almost certainly meet her in her dressing gown later on. God. He had nearly reached the sitting room door when it occurred to him that he was sexually excited.

Garth had left Ludwig to put Mitzi to bed, not out of any embarrassment which related to her, but because he was afraid his father might emerge and he did not want to be seen with one of Mitzi's arms hung around his neck like a bolster. Thus he would not appear to advantage.

118

And as he had not seen Austin for some time he felt that their next meeting should be initiated with some due solemnity. He had come tonight to see Ludwig.

However when the door closed behind him he forgot Ludwig and Mitzi instantly and was back again in a little street on the west side of New York. It was in the early hours of the morning and he was alone. It was very stupid to be alone in a small New York street in the early morning hours. He had been to a party and had felt such horror of his fellow guests that he had refused all offers of lifts and had set off by himself and found the way back longer than he had realized. He had met a few solitary walkers and eyed them and been eyed by them. A police car kerb-crawled him and then drove away leaving the scene empty. A little later he saw something happening on the other side of the street. Three people were standing there in a group. Then suddenly they were all in wild motion. Two of them were attacking one. It was all taking place underneath a street lamp, brilliantly lighted, perfectly clear, theatrical. The two attackers looked like Puerto Ricans, the attacked was a Negro. A knife clattered to the ground. Garth saw another knife entering the Negro's clothing at his side, heard him scream. The Negro, who was not a powerful man, was flailing with his arms and screaming. "Help me, help me!" he cried to Garth, and out of the mêlée he seemed to lean towards him like a child starting from its mother's arms. One of the men had gripped the Negro's arms from behind and was drawing them back. Number two had picked up the fallen knife and was pulling the Negro's shirt at the neck as if he wanted to take his tie off. "Help me, help me!" Garth, who had stopped, watched. While number one held on behind, number two had bared the man's throat and, slowly and deliberately searching with his left hand for the place, drove the knife in at the base of the neck, just above the collar bone, where it would go straight into the subclavian artery. Garth saw the knife blade flash and heard one more scream, the last one, before he turned and walked on. He did not run, he just walked at a fast steady pace, not

119

looking behind him, and took the next turning and the next and the next. After that he walked till dawn.

Ludwig came in, looking rather red. "Gee, she's large. I wonder how she did get that wound."

"Is my father in?" said Garth.

"Yes, but he's gone to bed."

"Good. Can we stay here?"

"I guess so. This is Mitzi's sitting-room really, but we all use it."

"Your room's upstairs?"

"Yes, next door to your dad."

"Then we're better here."

"Look," said Ludwig, "do you mind if I just telephone to Gracie. I was going to telephone to ask if I could come round, but now——"

"Good heavens," said Garth, jumping up, "don't dream of changing your plans for me, especially not at this hour. I'll be off."

"Stop, *please,* Garth. I see Gracie all the time, and I've hardly seen you. I'm not staying the night over there, nothing of that sort, it'd just be coffee. Garth, please stay, I *must* talk to you, please. Gracie won't mind."

"All right."

Garth sat, and heard through the open door Ludwig talking to Gracie on the telephone. "Yes, honey, I just got back from the meeting, it went on longer than—— No, I guess I won't if you don't mind—— That's right, I might get some work done—— Good night, honey pie, sleep well, sweetie puss, yes, darling, and you—there—dear—um—yes—good night, little chicken." Kisses. Click.

Garth noted that Ludwig was already prepared to mislead his fiancée.

Ludwig was red again, perhaps because he realized that Garth had overheard the conversation. "Whisky?"

"A little. Has my father got a job yet?"

"I don't think so. Not unless he has today."

"How's Dorina?"

"I haven't seen her. Why don't you go?"

"I can't," said Garth. He must not go near Dorina. He

120

wondered how much Ludwig understood of all that. "When are you getting married?"

"September. It's a big do, I'm afraid."

September. Ridiculous.

"Say," said Ludwig, "when I'm married we'll still be friends, won't we?"

"Yes." But it was unlikely. Marriage made people worldly. Even now Ludwig seemed to have less edge to him. Garth stared at Ludwig's greyish furry head, close cropped again now, his earnest long-lipped face and often-blinking puzzled doggy-brown eyes. Why had this chap once seemed so important?

"Have you seen your Uncle Matthew yet?" said Ludwig.

"No. I don't suppose I shall. I'm not going to be at the Buckingham Palace garden party. Why?"

"He sounds an interesting guy. I'd like to meet him."

"He is an interesting guy," said Garth. He had already decided to keep clear of Uncle Matthew. Uncle Matthew knew too much. And look what he had become. "But he's a false prophet."

"A false prophet?"

"He's an entangler. He'll entangle you if he can. He's a fat charmer, charming his way to paradise. He's the sort of person who makes everyone tell him their life story and then forgets it."

"You seem to feel strongly about him," said Ludwig.

"I don't." Garth was about to tell Ludwig that if Ludwig fell in with Matthew he would have to fall out with Austin, but he decided not to. He could not set up as his father's keeper, it was a false role. And some things must be left to Ludwig's intelligence. "I haven't seen him for years, actually."

"Gracie seems to be very keen on him," said Ludwig. Garth said nothing.

"Say, did that bag of yours ever turn up?" said Ludwig.

"No."

"Austin said there was a novel in it."

"Yes, but it's not important. I would have torn it up anyway. It was a false sort of thing—personal muck—you know. I'm not a novelist."

121

"What was it about?"

"Well—it was about a chap who saw somebody stabbed in the street and felt it meant something absolutely important to him, and kept trying to explain this to everybody, to his parents and his girl and his teacher and so on, and nobody understands and then they think he's mad and imagined it all and in the end he commits suicide."

"It sounds jolly good," said Ludwig.

"Don't be silly, Ludwig," said Garth. "You must have developed softening of the brain since you came to England."

"Don't bite me. I can't conceive of anything you wrote not being somehow good."

"I'm not a writer, that's the point, not an artist. You may know a truth but if it's at all complicated you have to be an artist not to utter it as a lie. Almost everything uttered is lies."

"What about philosophy?"

"That's the worst lie of all, because it's so gentle."

"Gentle? Why did you give up philosophy?"

"Because I saw a man stabbed in the street."

"So the novel was about you?"

"Yes, in a trivial way. The hero was me, I suppose all first-novel heroes are the author. But it didn't e⁻ress the point, not *the* point."

"Who was the guy who was stabbed, I mean the real one?"

"I don't know. A Negro. He was done in by a couple of thugs. He may have been a thug himself. It was late at night, no one around. He shouted for help. I watched. Then I walked on."

"I guess I'd have walked on too. But you feel guilt?"

"No, I don't," said Garth. "Part of the point is that I don't feel guilt."

"I would," said Ludwig. "I feel guilt about everything. But if you don't feel guilt why is it so all-important?"

"Oh don't—" murmured Garth, "don't—"

"You know, I've so much wanted to talk to you about my situation."

"You mean your engagement?"

"No. My not going back home to fight."

"Oh that. What about it?"

"You're the only person I can tell this to really. My parents feel ashamed of me. They think I'm ungrateful, they think I'm scared, they hate my breaking the law. They don't want me to stay here, they think I'll be extradited. And of course they don't really want me to fight either. They're all mixed up. I'd like you to read their letters."

"Are they leading you to change your mind?"

"No, of course not. But I feel sometimes that I'm in a dishonest position. To go back and resist is okay. To stay away and resist—well, it's not resisting, it's having the best of all worlds and leaving the suffering to them."

"Bosh," said Garth. "You'll suffer, you'll see to that. As for being lucky, why shouldn't you be? On the other hand, if you feel so unhappy about it why don't you go back?"

Ludwig looked miserable. "I don't see why I should," he said. "I'm no politician. I'm a scholar."

"Stay here then. What do you want me to say?"

"Garth, you don't understand. The war's wrong. We agree on that? Now—"

"Not all that again," said Garth. "Of course the war's wrong, in an abstract sort of way. But even if you were to go and fight it, that wouldn't matter. Do that, if you so much want to please your parents."

"You haven't got it! I feel it's dishonourable to do what's right in an easy way, and yet—you see I keep thinking and thinking about that war and all the suffering, the bombs, every day, at this very moment, and the kids and the women—"

"I daresay you do think about it. Thinking about the misery of the world is a favourite contemporary occupation. And if you can't think the television set will think for you. I keep thinking about that chap being knifed and about those students I saw having their heads battered. I daresay those chaps are sitting it out in some brain-damaged twilight at this very moment. But so what? The

123

mind is a mechanical sort of cinema show with a rather small number of reels."

"I feel it's dishonourable not to go back and be martyred and yet to go back would be totally irrational. And by staying I do what's objectively right, in that I refuse to fight in that war."

"So you have to choose between unreason and dishonour. All right. The only thing that's certain is that you will choose."

"You're not being very helpful," said Ludwig.

"You want total reassurance. I can't give it."

"I don't. You didn't talk like this at Harvard."

"At Harvard I couldn't see. Now I can. At least I can see more. The point is, it doesn't really matter very much what you do. What you do will be decided by causal factors in your nature which in a way are deep, and in a way are utterly superficial. Deep because they're mechanical and old. Superficial because their significance is, in relation to the real you, trivial. In a way nothing matters very much, though in a way everything matters absolutely. It needn't matter what you do, though it can matter a good deal how you do it. Meanwhile virtue is just a necessary illusion."

"It matters whether I act rightly or not," said Ludwig doggedly.

"Not really, and not in the way you mean. You and I are conditioned anyway to do what's normally thought of as right. Any of the acts you are capable of contemplating will be 'right.' So why worry about that?"

"What should I worry about then, according to you? Politics?"

"Good Lord no. Or yes, maybe, if it's one's job. It isn't yours or mine. Strictly politics ought to be done at the ground level where your whole being is testimony and there isn't anything abstract any more and nothing in it for you, especially anything interesting or personal. And at that level distinctions break down and it isn't really politics. One should do simple separated things. Don't imagine you *are* that big complicated psychological buzz that travels around with you. Step outside it. Above all don't feel guilt or worry about doing right. That's all flummery. Guilt is the invention of a personal God, now happily defunct. There is no Alpha and no Omega, and nothing could be more important than that. Remember I once quoted to you that thing of Kierkegaard's about metaphysics, that in order to sew you must knot the thread? Well, that's wrong. You don't have to knot the thread, you can't knot it, you mustn't knot it. You just keep pulling it through."

"I'm not with you," said Ludwig. "What are you going to do with yourself? What does all this amount to in practice?"

"I'm not sure yet. I used to think I had a special destiny. But I've made a discovery. Everybody has one. So I don't feel so bloody anxious now about mine. Thank God I lost the novel. It could have been a temptation."

"I thought on your curious view there wouldn't be temptations any more," said Ludwig.

"Oh there are temptations, there are trials, there are even goals."

"Mention one."

"To give up the world. To have nothing, not even hopes. To make life holy. You remember in the Iliad when Achilles' immortal horses weep over the death of Patroclus and Zeus deplores the sight of deathless beings involved in the pointless horrors of mortality?"

"Is that 'holy'?"

"Yes. Gods can't really grieve. Men can't understand. But animals which are godlike can shed pure tears. I would like to shed pure tears. Zeus sheds none."

"Are you on drugs?"

"Don't be ridiculous, Ludwig."

"This stuff is beyond me. Have some more whisky?"

"No, thanks. And another thing—"

"I'm not sure I can stand any more."

"I went to see Charlotte today."

"Aunt Charlotte? Yes."

"I annoyed her, hurt her. Never mind. One can't get everything right. Could you tell Gracie something?"

"Gracie? Yes."

"From me. Tell her she must at once and very humbly beg Charlotte to stay on in that house. I mean obviously Gracie isn't going to turn her out. But Charlotte's so bloody miserable, if everyone isn't careful she'll just take off, and then she'll be very much harder to help. Gracie must beg her to stay, and say she'll make a flat specially for her or something. It's not easy, I mean to get the right tone and all that. But it's urgent, it's a matter of days and hours. Tell Gracie that if she's got any love for Charlotte, Charlotte needs that love in action and in evidence right now. Okay?"

"Okay," said Ludwig, rather expressionlessly.

"You think I'm an interfering bastard?"

"No. I think what you say is, to use one of my old-fashioned words, right. Say, how did you know Gracie had inherited the house?"

"I read it in your letter, the one to your father that's lying on the desk. I read it when I came in, just before I heard you and what's-her-name talking in the kitchen."

"So reading other people's correspondence is not incompatible with holiness?" said Ludwig.

"No, I don't think so. I must be off. I say, could you give me a pound to help me through tomorrow. Give, if you don't mind, I never take loans. Thanks a lot. Good night. And don't forget. No Alpha, no Omega. So it doesn't matter."

What a load of balls, thought Ludwig after his friend had departed, is he nuts or what. All the same, he's a remarkable guy. He's got thinner and crazier since Harvard.

Ludwig looked at his letter to his father, which was still lying on the desk.

My dear Father,
    I write to tell you first of all that my fiancée Grace has inherited a great deal of money, since she is the sole heir of her lately deceased grandmother. . . .

Had he thought that the news would console his parents? Yes. And why not. All the same.

He tore up the letter.

126

"One should do simple separated things. Don't imagine you *are* that big complicated psychological buzz that travels around with you. Step outside it. Above all don't feel guilt or worry about doing right. That's all flummery. Guilt is the invention of a personal God, now happily defunct."

Austin Gibson Grey, standing outside the door, heard his son's precise slightly staccato voice holding forth and ground his teeth with rage. Should he, he wondered, bound suddenly into the room, hissing and grimacing like a Japanese warrior? No. He went slowly back up the stairs. He was hurt that Garth, whom he had hardly seen, should come to visit Ludwig and so evidently avoid him. And he was ready to scream with incoherent irritation at Garth's moralistic eloquence. Whatever it was all about, it certainly wasn't about that. And it wasn't *like* that either. Life was misery and muddle, it *was* misery and muddle.

He stopped outside Mitzi's door. He could hear her crying quietly inside, grieving for her lost health and strength, grieving for her youth, grieving about heaven knew what, him perhaps. The weeping was sing-song, a soft long wail in a descending octave, a few sniffing breaths, a whimper, then the wail again, very soft, mechanical. Should he go in and comfort her? She was drunk and would be wet and sentimental. He said sharply outside the door "Stop that!" There was silence. He went on into his own room.

He took off his jacket and shirt and trousers and put on his pyjamas over his vest and pants. He removed his

127

glasses and lay down on the bed. At once the demon asthma was present. A stifling pad was pressed over his face, a steel cord tightened about his chest. He sat up again, leaning forward and breathing regularly. It was all so familiar and it would never leave him as long as he lived. He stared at his right hand and tried to flex it. With his left he reached for his tablets. They gave him nightmares, but they drove away the demon for a time. He shook up his pillow. Dust came out of it. He coughed and fumbled for a cigarette.

His room had got into an extraordinary mess. Every room he lived in did. Unwashed clothes were everywhere, smelling. Old cigarette packets and coins and string and squeezed-out tubes and razor blades and yellowing sheets of evening papers lay about. Why did his life somehow generate this excrement? He had applied for jobs. He had written cunning letters offering himself as one whose dedicated wish was to be an assistant librarian, a clerical officer, a part-time teacher, a secretary in a publishing house (they said one must type, but did not specify how fast), a personnel manager, a club organizer. What he thought of as rubble jobs. But no one wanted him. The Labour Exchange said they could get him a job as a nurse.

Meanwhile he had not managed to let the flat. Perhaps Garth put off prospective tenants. It suited the holy boy to live rent free. Two possibles failed to get in at all, since Garth was away. Another man only wanted it for the week of the Motor Show. There were debts and very little in the bank. He had borrowed a few pounds from Mitzi. Garth was shamelessly penniless. While Gracie Tisbourne had, they said, inherited hundreds of thousands. Why were things thus? Would it be possible for him to grit his teeth and become a nurse? No. Names were important. If he took a rubble job he could always laughingly call himself an executive. But a nurse was a nurse.

He cared what Dorina thought, he cared what Matthew thought, he cared what Garth thought, he even cared what the bloody Tisbournes thought. Why should he be always the slave of his audience? Well, he was. What was so relaxing about Mitzi was that he did not care a fuck what

Mitzi thought. Or Ludwig. There was peace there. But the others were his torment. How the Tisbournes would dance and sing if he became a nurse. "Darling, Austin's got a job, guess what!" And Dorina. How could he bear to be such a failure in her eyes? He had felt so proud on his wedding day. How had his marriage then become so vulnerable and exposed? He must be able once again to mystify and impress Dorina. She would lend herself to the mystification as she had always done.

He must get a job. He must get the flat back. He hadn't even let it yet. He must make Dorina stop being whatever she was being. Afraid of him? How he feared that fear, how he feared her horrible ghost-haunted thoughts, she was for him a fatal and destructive girl. Yet how precious she was and how much he loved her. He would kill anyone who came near her. How much longer could he keep her immobilized and spellbound at Valmorana? Of course she understood, she knew his jealousy, perhaps she feared it. She would keep still, as still as a frightened mouse, as still as prey. But supposing somebody were to kidnap her? The vile Tisbournes had asked her to stay with them. Supposing Mavis were to interfere or Garth or—

He could hear Mitzi stirring, hear the sound of her door opening. He switched off the light. There was a soft knock and Mitzi said, "Austin, are you awake?" He lay back silently. The door opened an inch or two. "Austin." He closed his eyes. He had read in a book that the eyeball reflects light. She must not see his terrible open eyes. The door creaked as it opened wider. He lay tense and stiff, feeling that he would scream if he were touched. The door closed again quietly and the feet shuffled away. He was on Calypso's isle. But was Ithaca still real? He turned sideways pulling a blanket up. Suppose Ludwig were to write him a testimonial? What happened if the money simply ran out? Was it conceivable that he could ask Matthew to lend him money? No. Would Ludwig lend him some of Gracie's hundreds of thousands?

He was beginning to see those clear coloured images, the gentle precursors of sleep. Now he saw again the blue lake in the quarry to which he had climbed down on that hot summer's day. Matthew would not come. Matthew was a timid boy. Scrambling down was easy, but to climb up was impossible, the loose stones came away, running past him in long rattling sluices. Matthew was laughing. Weakness, impotence, rage made him limp, the sun blazed in starry tears in his dazzled eyes, he could not get up. Now Matthew was throwing stones down at him and laughing. Weeping with rage he climbed and climbed. Something struck him and he fell and an avalanche of rattling stones cascaded him down to the very edge of the blue water. He had hurt his hand.

Sleep took him and he began to dream a dream which he had had many times before. Betty was not dead after all. She had been kidnapped and taken away and kept in a big house by somebody who gave her drugs. She was alive still but drugged. He saw with horror her dazed vacant face. Yet he did not want her to awaken. That must never be.

"Honey bun," said Ludwig to Gracie, "Austin has asked me to lend him money."

"Oh," said Gracie. "Did you?"

"I lent him five pounds."

"That was quite enough," said Gracie. "I hope you won't lend him any more. After all, you aren't going to be paid until September."

Ludwig pondered on this. "Sure," he said. "But I just mentioned it in case *you* might feel like lending him some."

"I don't," said Gracie.

That was that.

The fact that he was quite accidentally going to marry a rich girl had made more difference to Ludwig's consciousness than he would have believed possible beforehand. The prospect gave deep and warm satisfaction. He had become more extravagant. A life-long habit of anxiety about money was distinctly weakened. And when Austin had asked him for a loan he had felt pity for Austin and also a kind of contempt, which was new. He noticed the contempt with dismay. Had he then so quickly deserted to the side of the rich? With even more dismay, after parting with the five pounds, he reckoned out that before September he would have to ask Gracie for money. So far she had been delicate enough not to offer him any.

Being paraded around as a fiancé was something he had not yet got used to. He had not got a finance's temperament. "Have you met my fiancé, Ludwig Leferrier?" Ridiculous word. And what about "husband"? "Have you met my husband?" "May I present my wife, Grace?" "Did you know, Leferrier's got a rich wife?" What would Andrew Hilton think? Gracie's husband. Husband. The word became senseless to him. One day he looked up its derivation and was appalled. Gracie and Clara were busy planning the wedding. They asked if Ludwig's parents would be coming. He did not know. He decided that if his parents seemed to want to come he would ask Gracie to pay their fare. It was all rather awkward and curious. And meanwhile he and Gracie were still careering around London like tourists. And they had still not been to bed.

Ludwig thought a lot about Garth and tried to see him again, but Garth had once more disappeared. Of course Ludwig had been a dull companion because he had wanted only one thing from Garth on that evening, the ratification of his own decision. When one has momentously decided one does not want to be told that "it doesn't matter." Of course Ludwig had acted rightly. But he should have argued more intelligently with Garth. Garth's theories had seemed mad, but now they recalled to him things which he had thought for himself in the quiet room at school. Of course he did not agree with Garth. But he did need

131

what only arguing with Garth could give him, a clearer theoretical grasp of his own action. It was all hazy in crucial places. And he did need, just for once, to be praised by someone he respected. If only his parents' attitude did not force him to think about other people's opinions so much. Those awful touching letters stirred his imagination and robbed his decision of its cool certainty. When he slept he doubted himself in dreams. One terrible night a huge half-naked woman in a helmet and starred and striped panties, looking rather like Mitzi Ricardo, brandished a spear at him and shouted "Defend me!" The dream Ludwig fled crazed with terror.

"There's a fly in the milk," said Gracie, "could you rescue him?"

Ludwig removed the struggling fly on a teaspoon.

"All right, Ludwig, leave him now, he'll dry his wings. God helps flies who help themselves."

They had been at a sculpture exhibition in Holland Park and were now in a Kensington High Street tea shop. Gracie had eaten two chocolate éclairs and was now eating a meringue.

"Do you mind if I smoke now, moppet?"

"All right, barbarian. Why is the smoke at one end of a cigarette grey and at the other end blue?"

"I think it's a matter of—"

"You know, you really must meet Matthew."

"I've just been thinking that," said Ludwig.

"Why?"

"Oh, I don't know—" I'd care what *he* said, thought Ludwig. He had heard Matthew much talked about. Opinions about him seemed to differ.

"You'll probably meet him at my parents' awful cocktail party."

"Must we go?"

"It's *for* us! Yes, I have plans for Matthew. Matthew is our fate."

"How do you mean, sweetie? I'm *your* fate!"

"Yes, darling, I just mean we'll take him up. He's awfully amusing."

"Okay, poppet." Ludwig was aware that married people

132

usually used pet names. His father called his mother "Mudge," his mother called his father "Topper," he had never discovered why. He had not yet determined Gracie's secret pet name.

"He's much cleverer than Austin, or Garth."

"By the way, angel, I've a message for you from Garth."

"From *Garth?*"

"Yes. He says he thinks you should tell Aunt Charlotte very soon how much you want her to stay on at the Villa. You see, he called on Aunt Charlotte and he formed the view—"

"Really, Ludwig," said Gracie. She put down her fork. *"Really!* Do we have to be told what to do by Garth Gibson Grey?"

"No. I agreed with him too, of course. And I'm sure you don't need to be told anything. It's just that he thinks Aunt Char might take off soon if— You see, he formed the view—"

"I'm not interested in what view he formed. He's conceited and interfering, he's as bad as my parents. I don't want to know his beastly thoughts. There's something cold and dead about him, there's a dead mark on him— Ugh!"

"Well, Gracie, sorry dear, I—"

"And as for begging Aunt Char to stay on at the Villa, I shall do no such thing. I shan't ask her to go, but I shall leave it to her to move out without being asked."

"Gracie!"

"Really, Ludwig, you must learn to *think* about these things. Honestly. If I ask Aunt Char to stay now it would be very unkind to ask her to go later. And how do I know what I want to do with the Villa? I may want to sell it."

"Yes, I see—"

"Or we may want to live there ourselves. We shall need a town house. And there's all our children."

"All our—yes—"

"It would be terribly short-sighted and silly to make Aunt Charlotte feel it belonged to her, as she must feel if she were to stay on now. Of course I'm not a monster, I'll do something for Aunt Char later on. But I want to under-

133

stand my own situation first of all. There's nothing one regrets so much as one's thoughtless acts of generosity. They're usually just conceit anyway, one wants to see oneself acting nobly. Garth would have an idea like that, he'd so much enjoy begging Aunt Char to regard the house as hers."

"He's rather sure of himself, I know—"

"He's not, he's afraid of life, he's a timid man like his father, only vainer. That sort of priggish vanity makes nothing but trouble. You do see what I mean?"

"Yes, sure—"

"And I think it's extremely impertinent of him to offer us advice."

"Yes, I guess so." Ludwig was stunned by her grasp of the matter. And after a moment's reflection he saw that she might very well be right. Would he and Gracie ever live in the Villa? And their— Oh God.

"I wish we had a place of our own right now," he said. "Maybe I could find other digs where you wouldn't mind coming. You know, Gracie, I'm a man after all and, well, we are engaged, aren't we, and—"

"It's an exceptionally hot summer."

"Honey, don't tease."

" 'Time on my hands and you in my arms.' "

"Gracie, stop it. Do you want me to insist, do you want me to get tough and bully you?" Was she capable of making him wait until the wedding day? Oh Christ.

"No, Ludwig. Darling. My parents are going away next weekend, they're going to stay in the country with the Odmores."

"Oh that's great! That's—"

"Ludwig—"

"Dovikins—"

"You wouldn't ever talk to Garth—about that—would you?"

"Sweetie puss, of course not, cross my heart."

"I'd rather you didn't talk to him too much, he's a wrecker, a hater."

"Okay, honey bun."

A few minutes later they were holding hands on top of

a bus. Ludwig remembered he had meant to tell Gracie that after all he felt that he ought to go and see Dorina. But as he hadn't argued about Charlotte or even about Garth it would sound rather artificial to raise Dorina now. Let them all go. It was only three days to the weekend. Whoopee!

⚛⚛⚛⚛

"It must be wonderful to have so many wonderful memories," said Clara. "You've achieved so much, it must be marvellous to look back on it all."

"I hope you're going to write your memoirs for us," said George.

"And to have visited so many famous places, to have been *everywhere,* I do envy you, you must have the most super photograph album."

"I'm afraid I never took any photographs," said Matthew.

"Charles is very disappointed you won't come on the commission," said George. "But I don't blame you. Those things are so boring. I expect you feel you've earned a rest."

"How will you employ your time?" said Clara. "Will you buy a house and fill it with that wonderful collection of china we've heard so much about?"

"I don't know," said Matthew.

"Whatever you're planning, we must *help*," said Clara. "More gin?"

"No, thanks, I must go. Let me know when you get some news of Charlotte."

"We're not really worried about Charlotte," said

135

George. "It's typical of her, really, to clear off into the blue with an enigmatic farewell note. She just does it to annoy. She's probably staying at a hotel round the corner."

"I wouldn't have expected her to be so unkind," said Clara.

"Naturally she's sensitive," said George.

"Yes, but a little magnanimity—"

"On Gracie's part?"

"No, on Char's—"

"I suppose pressing her to stay on at the Villa just did no good," said Matthew.

"Well—er—" said George, exchanging a glance with his wife, "I don't know that she was pressed. And after that crazy will, Charlotte would probably have cleared out anyway. She has a little annuity, she's not destitute."

"You know, I've been thinking," said Clara to her husband. "Mama asking for Treece like that at the very end—Treece is our family lawyer, you know—perhaps she wanted to change the will back again. I'm sure she did. Poor Mama."

"Poor us," said George. "Treece was so embarrassed, wasn't he, when he had to tell us we'd been disinherited."

"Yes, I know. Bad Mama!"

"Ingratitude is the last privilege of the dying."

"But its all going to Gracie is quite nominal, isn't it?" said Matthew. "She'll distribute it, surely?"

The husband and wife again exchanged glances. "I'm not sure that you know our Gracie," said Clara. "We often feel *we* don't. Of course Gracie *would* scoop the pool without lifting a finger. Things have always been like that for her. The gods love her."

"I really must go," said Matthew.

"Gracie will be so sorry to miss you, she's so full of you these days, she's making Ludwig quite jealous!"

"I look forward to meeting Ludwig," said Matthew.

"He's sweet. You'll meet him at our party. You will come, won't you?"

"Shall we call you a taxi?" said George.

"No, it's such a lovely day, I think I'll walk back across the park."

136

The park was in meadowy summer glory, with long plumes of uncut grass making a luscious light yellowy green between the splashed shadows. The air was thick with soft polleny smells which made breathing a luxury. Trees hazed the Albert Memorial and smudged the rosy front of Kensington Palace and long golden vistas showed multicoloured strollers with their dogs. Nearer to the water pink-footed geese and white-faced coots paraded in the groves of rhus and bamboo. A jay called in the bushes and signalled with its blue wing.

Matthew wondered in what modest hotel room, made hot and hideous by the sunshine, Charlotte was sitting tensely beside her suitcase, so determined to hurt and to be hurt. He wondered about Austin. He wondered about himself.

Talking to Taigu in Kyoto it had all seemed to become clear. Taigu was sad, but he had helped Matthew to his decision all the same. In matters of the spirit the difference between false and true can be as narrow as a needle, but only for the very great does it disappear altogether. Matthew had so long dreamed of the *place* which awaited him at that tiny monastery, a seat kept there for him, not quite so glorious as the empty thrones which Giotto imagined in paradise, but just as certainly reserved. Almost like an economist he had reckoned it out, how his future would pay for his present. He had advanced the day of his retirement with the impatience of a man awaiting his beloved. The anticipated savour of that time was as honey to him. Then he would be at peace and his life would begin.

But, as in almost every human life, something had gone wrong somewhere and the *malin génie* had got in and twisted something, ever so slightly, with huge huge results. Shifting his bulk about restlessly, Matthew had sat upon the floor of Taigu's little paper-screened room, while Taigu sat motionless cross-legged, and they talked the thing to a conclusion. Outside the snow fell, then sun yellowed the shoulders of the mountains against a pale blue sky. A single branch of evergreen curled agonizingly against the wall behind Taigu's shaven head. Matthew's feet were

137

laden with cold, his legs aching with hours of sitting on the floor. Wind rattled the screens. A bell rang. Taigu sighed. It was no good. A human being has only one life. And Matthew had had his.

Yet what had that life amounted to, he wondered. How could a successful career vanish and seem to leave so little behind? There were his youthful hopes and vanities, his happy sense of himself as exceptional, and here was this—heap. While others had employed these twenty, thirty years in art, in marriage, in raising a family, he seemed to have done nothing that had achieved any permanent form at all. There were no jewelled external things: works of art, acts. There were not even any people who had really stood the test: loves, but no love. Of course he had made a great deal of money. Could something as vulgar as that matter? "He had great possessions," he quoted gloomily once to Taigu, who picked up the reference and laughed. Taigu often laughed at inappropriate moments. Matthew could not see the joke.

Not that he had been bored ever. But it appeared that a life could be interesting, amusing, full of the urgencies of state, and ultimately trivial. He had seen important things, he had seen terrible things. He had seen poverty and war, violence, oppression, cruelty, injustice and hunger. He had seen decisive moments in men's lives. He had witnessed a scene in the Red Square when demonstrators were arrested, and when an ordinary citizen, an accidental passerby, had suddenly gone across to join them and had been arrested too. Matthew knew some of the men involved. They were still in labour camps. Some were in "hospitals." Their lives were ruined. Oh he had seen these things, but always as an outsider, as a tourist with diplomatic immunity from the misery of the world, returning to evening drinks in a carpeted embassy hung with minor masterpieces by Gainsborough and Lawrence. He had never truly lived in places where duties were terrible and their consequences life-destroying and long.

Thus he had been cheated by the *malin génie*. A life which had seemed an interval, and which now was seen to have been filled with trash, had made him what he was, a person profitlessly spoiled. To have settled down now in Kyoto, to have lived in that strange world with the idea of which he had so long ago fallen in love, would be a falsity. He could only have played at the contemplative life, only enacted it, producing something which might be very like the real thing but could not be the real thing. Could not be, because a human being has only one lifetime and cannot but be fashioned by it. There are no intervals and one is what one has thought and done. For Matthew, it was too late. He had made his beloved wait too long. This was the bitter truth which Taigu made him at last clearly see as he twisted and turned his fat bulk restlessly upon the tatami.

Of course there were various second bests, but Matthew was in no mood for second bests. He could rent a little flat in Kyoto, and live there quietly, hanging around the monasteries, talking Buddhism with the masters, writing a book about it all. He could take up an art or craft, painting perhaps, or pottery. Wisdom was to be had so. Or something humbler. "You might work in the garden here," Taigu said to him, immobile with calm eyes. But if one were never to have the pearl of great price? No.

Then there was Austin. Matthew sometimes felt that Austin would be amazed if he knew how much, on the other side of the world, he had been thought about. In a way it was a consolation to Matthew to know that his preoccupation with Austin was not, though it might have been, the only barrier to his vocation. Could one have taken such an unresolved personal anguish into that great silence? To have had his life, at this stage, wrecked simply by Austin would have been—ridiculous. But now, since what he had so greatly desired was not to be, there were older and in some ways more natural duties which asked to be heard. Matthew knew that if he had always carried Austin within him as a poisonous and unassimilable alien body, the Matthew which Austin carried must be that much greater and more venomous.

In a way, Matthew thought, it all rests on nothing, it's all in Austin's imagination. In reality he had done nothing to Austin. Or had he? Even at the quarry, Austin said that Matthew had thrown stones, but this was not true. Or had he perhaps shuffled his feet a little to make the stones run down the gulley? He remembered seeing those stones cascading down and feeling pleased, before he heard Austin cry out. He had certainly, at the beginning, laughed. Could a man receive a life sentence for laughing? Yes. The rest had seemed like that, based on nothing, or practically nothing, or perhaps everything. Would he ever be able to talk about it with his brother, gently and with good will?

Running straight to Austin on that first night, with that almost uncannily grotesque outcome, had been a silly nervous thing to do. The sense of inevitable blunder, inevitable resentment, was unnervingly familiar. Someone who was always contriving things like that deserved to be hated. Since then, politely, Austin had evaded him, never at home, never free, courteously, on picture postcards, refusing, for excellently plausible reasons, all Matthew's invitations. I shall have to change my tactics, Matthew thought. The thing had already begun to seem like a quest. It was ironic that the great task of his retirement seemed to be simply to cure his younger brother of a crippling hatred. Yet if it could be done was this not a great thing? For him, yes, thought Matthew. But for me, emptiness. Thus duty often is, he told himself, for the doer, emptiness.

The thought of Mavis Argyll sometimes flitted through Matthew's mind. It flitted now, against the summery trees, the shade of a young girl. How he had changed, how she must have changed, since those days. He had not seen or communicated with her for twenty years. He supposed that, in the roulette of London social life, he would probably meet her somewhere or other eventually. Various people, some of whom did not know of his old connection with her, had spoken to him of her and of Valmorana. Matthew felt no emotion in his memories, in fact he scarcely formulated any memories. His life had long ago blotted out Mavis and all his purer romantic love had become centred on something very different from a woman. He felt a certain curiosity sometimes now about the past. What exactly had happened, who had given up whom and why? Had Mavis felt resentment at not being more ardently pressed, at being perhaps too readily surrendered? She was a Catholic and he was a Quaker. She had had a religious vocation and he had respected it. Had they really loved each other so much, and if they had could they ever have parted? He remembered that he had been unhappy but he could not recall the unhappiness. If he met Mavis would they be embarrassed? Only for a moment surely. He would not write to her. It was indeed essential that he should leave her alone since he must not, whatever else he did, go anywhere near Dorina. His friendship with Betty had had such stupid wretched consequences.

Meanwhile how would he live? A sense almost of ennui came to him out of the trees which seemed now to be drooping and darkening before his eyes. London seemed a city not even wicked, but devoid of spirit, dusty, broken. God had died there since Matthew was young and Jesus Christ, who might have been waiting for him in England, was gone too, faded utterly, his old Friend and Master, gone. How abhorrent to him now was the image of the Crucified One, the personal local Godhead of Christianity. In Singapore once a girl who knew that he collected porcelain had given him a nineteenth-century Chinese vase on which a Rubens crucifixion was represented. Matthew viewed this curiosity with fascinated horror. The intrusion of that theme was a vulgar outrage. And here in England, where it might have been forgiven, have been the bearer to him of something ancient and holy, he found it offensive too and shuddered away from its message of anxiety, suffering, personality and guilt. He thought, the West studies suffering, the East studies death. How utterly different these things are, as indeed the Greeks had always known, that deeply secretly Oriental people. Greece, not Israel, had been his first real mentor.

He had intended to make contact with the London Buddhists, but London itself had already made this project futile. He knew that these people would merely annoy him. He was spiritually disinherited, spoilt, left absolutely on his own. Sometimes it even seemed to him that Taigu, in those last talks, had condemned him to death. And

141

he wondered, as he walked down a vista of tired trees heavy with their leaves, whether just this particular emptiness were not the nearest he would ever come to enlightenment.

"Matthew! I say, Matthew, wait for me!"

It was Gracie Tisbourne, running, long-legged, brown-legged, as graceful and sinewy as a Spartan maiden. She ran up to Matthew and touched him lightly on the shoulder as if she were playing tig. She was wearing a short green-flowery dress and her silvery-golden hair had blown in a wispy network of glowing threads over her small eager face.

Matthew smiled at her, feeling intense irritation. He wanted to be alone with his thoughts. He did not want to walk across the park with Gracie, he felt frenzy at the idea of half an hour's compulsory conversation with this coy and spritely wench. Her curiosity, her archness, her air of flirtatious affection, her appalling youth, grated upon his mood. He thought, I cannot and will not talk with this girl all the way across the park.

"I'm sorry, Gracie," said Matthew. "I'd love to talk to you, but I'm just nerving myself to do my daily stint of jogging."

"Of *what?*"

"Jogging. You know. It's an American invention. It's a kind of rather leisurely running designed for elderly people with heart conditions. I have to do half an hour a day. Doctor's orders. So off I go and please forgive me, see you another time."

Matthew started to run, first quite fast and then more and more slowly. He ran away at random through the trees, puffing along, crossing paths at random, scuffing through grass, glimpsing distant water, running away from Gracie, running away from himself, running away from the spoilt emptiness and the death of his gods.

He reached the Serpentine beside the Peter Pan statue and sat down gasping and exhausted with an agonizing stitch in his side. This had been one of the sacred places of his childhood, but no child Matthew awaited him here and the statue, defying the universe upon its bronze

142

pyramid of animals and dragon-fly-winged fairies, looked merely grotesque and quaint. Childhood was so far away and no whiff of freshness from there came to him mingled with the cool smell of the water. The pavilions and fountains at the end of the lake minded him of China, not of childhood. Gaily painted ducks sailed under tangles of green willows but for him the scene was grey and his heart beat within him like a resonant gong in an empty hall.

Gracie, running as fleetly and effortlessly as a young antelope, flew lightly towards him and plumped down on the seat beside him, smelling of flowers, not even out of breath.

"You haven't done half an hour yet. May I run with you?"

"No, I'm not going to do any more."

"I love this place, don't you. Aren't the little rabbits sweet, and the mice. See how they're all shiny from being stroked by the children. Oh Matthew, I do so want to talk to you. I haven't seen you properly at all yet. You know, you could be such a help to me. You were so nice to me when I was a little girl, I've never forgotten, and you're so wise and I do so trust you and admire you, you don't mind my saying so, do you? It's so wonderful if somebody young can be friends with somebody old, don't you think, we have so much to learn from you, I don't feel a gap at all, I feel you know me very well, maybe better than anyone, you can see right into me and right through me, you could help me to find myself. You aren't cross with me, are you? We must talk together, mustn't we, for ages and ages and ages. I do feel you could tell me the truth about myself, even if it meant being quite severe. Will you come to tea with me soon? When will you come to tea?"

Oh dear, thought Matthew, oh dear. Not now, he could not bear them now, the hot eager simple emotions of a young girl. How paradoxical that the young are so elementary and formless at a time when they feel their lives to be of a maximum significance. How could one tell them the cruel truth that one is just not interested? He shifted

143

away from her, from her long glowing rosy-brown legs and the fresh appley smell of her dress.

"Just now I'm going to be away for a bit, but later on perhaps—"

"Oh and another thing, Matthew, I want you to have the Villa."

"The Villa?"

"Yes, to live in. You can't go on living in a horrid hotel. The Villa's empty, you know, and I somehow *see* you there. You needn't pay any rent. You've got to have somewhere to put your vases and things, and house-hunting in London is such hell now. You could have it for the whole summer or the whole year or longer if you wanted. You see, Ludwig and I will be living in Oxford."

"No, no," said Matthew.

"Just while you're looking round for somewhere permanent then. Oh do live in the Villa, it would give me such joy! You could move in tomorrow."

Matthew saw himself in the Villa, in quietness, closing the front door.

A large golden retriever was lifting its leg against one of Peter Pan's fairies. "Poor old Tinkerbell," said Gracie with a giggle. "Do you believe in fairies, Matthew?"

"Yes." There were no more gods, but all the minor magic remained, beautiful, terrible, cruel, and small.

Matthew saw the fey wild-haired face of Mavis Argyll, she floated again before him, enchantress, temptress, and as her translucent robe drifted across the scene the ducks quacked and the dogs barked and the lake water glittered amethystive beneath its flowing willows and the willows tossed their pale locks wantonly and an aeroplane bound for London airport buzzed murmurously above them like a great honey bee. Matthew opened the door of the Villa and Mavis Argyll came in.

"I'll think about it," he said.

"Ludwig."

"Yes, chickadee?"

"Have a milk chocolate kitten."

"No thank you, angel."

"Ludwig."

"Yes, honeybunch?"

"You're not going to be very pleased with something I'm just going to tell you."

"Oh Lord, you're not going to—"

"No, nothing awful. It's just that Mama and Papa are not going to go to the Odmores this weekend after all."

"Oh God! Oh no!"

"It is a nuisance of them, isn't it?"

"I'm not going to stand for this," said Ludwig.

"How do you mean? There's nothing— Oh Ludwig, *no*— We've got to go down, the cocktail party is just starting, they'll expect us, they'll look for us, and Matthew's coming specially to meet you."

"Bugger Matthew."

"Ludwig, what are you doing? You know the door doesn't lock and—"

"I'm going to jam it with this chair."

"Oh do be careful, you'll break it. Oh Ludwig, please, mind the tea tray and—Oh dear, why did I tell you—"

"Come on, Gracie," said Ludwig. "Get undressed." He slipped out of his jacket and began to take off his tie.

"Not—no, no—not suddenly like this, please—"

"Yes. Suddenly like this." Ludwig undid his belt and

145

dropped his trousers off. The little attic room was hot and stuffy and thick with evening sunshine.

"Ludwig, I couldn't bear it if Mama and Papa came, they're certain to come to fetch us, and—"

"Take your dress off, Gracie."

"And I haven't anything—"

"I have. Come on."

Ludwig took off his shoes and socks and pants and his shirt last of all. He stood before her naked, sweaty, hairy, erect. Gracie stood there in her silky cream-coloured party dress, her hands at her bosom. Ludwig pulled the little narrow bed out from under its white shelf and ripped the counterpane off it.

"Ludwig," said Gracie, "I've never done this before. I've never seen—before—"

"I've done it, but it never meant anything till now," said Ludwig. "Forgive me." He was trembling. He felt ugly before her, gross, smelling of sweat and sex. She had never seemed more delicately inaccessibly desirable. He had never made love to a virgin. What would it be like? How could she not detest him? He saw her revulsion and her fear, and for a moment he thought of getting dressed again. But if he did so there would be this new barrier between them, everything would be even more difficult. And by now desire was too fierce, he was faiting with it.

"Gracie, please, darling— Help me too— Undress. It has to be."

Gracie unbuttoned her dress. Her things fell into a pile on the floor. Her eyes were vague with fright. She was shuddering, her teeth were chattering, and when he touched her breasts and then drew her body up against his, she felt rigid and cold though he could feel her heart striking against him. She leaned stiffly upon him, cool and dry and quivering against his hot greasy sweaty passionate flesh. "Oh Christ," he said. "Quickly. Quickly." She climbed awkwardly onto the bed and lay passive as he knelt and eased himself upon her. Tears came out from under her closed eyelids.

146

"Where are those two children?"

"Chattermagging upstairs as usual."

"Who do you think will arrive first?"

"Pinkie, you do agree about having Char?"

"Of course, we can't let her drift off."

"Austin has been borrowing money off Ludwig."

"I wonder if we should offer him a loan."

"A small one."

"He wouldn't accept it actually."

"You relieve my mind!"

"Will Austin come?"

"He'll come for Gracie, he always loves her Natasha act."

"I suppose you didn't invite Mavis and Dorina?"

"I sort of did, but they won't come."

"Here's somebody. It's Hester."

"Hester darling, you're first!"

"How awful, I always am!"

"No Charles, no Sebastian?"

"Charles is coming from the office, and Sebastian's cramming, he's so sorry."

"Have you heard Gracie's latest? She's let the Villa to Matthew for the summer."

"Why, Penny, hello. Clara, here's Penny."

"Clara has just been telling me Gracie has let the Villa to Matthew."

"I think that's sinister."

"Oh hello, Charles, Mollie, Geoffrey!"

"Have you heard Gracie's latest?"

147

"Pinkie, do tell the butler he needn't announce people."

"Where is Gracie?"

"She's upstairs with— Oh Mr. Enstone, how good—"

"Is Matthew coming?"

"We hope— Oh Oliver, good. Your mama has just arrived."

"I hear Karen has chucked art school."

"Dr. Seldon, how kind—"

"Is Karen coming?"

"She's in the country, she's becoming a pig maid."

"A what?"

"What a mob. Oh hello Ann—"

"Geoffrey has taken up pigs."

"Ann dear, how lovely you look—"

"Gracie has let the Villa to Matthew."

"Pinkie, who is that young man by the door?"

"You mean the one in turquoise?"

"May I introduce myself. My name is Andrew Hilton."

"Oh Mr. Hilton, how good— Mr. Hilton, Mr. Enstone. Pinkie, Mr. Enstone needs a drink—"

"Where's Gracie? I thought it was all in aid of—"

"I hear Gracie's marrying a German."

"Sssh, he isn't German, he's American."

"Is that him over there?"

"I suppose that is a boy, it's so hard to tell these days."

"Why, Richard, how super to see you."

"Mollie Arbuthnot is opening a boutique in Chelsea."

"Penny, you know Richard Pargeter, don't you."

"What do you do, Mr. Hilton?"

"I teach Latin and Greek. What do you do, Mr. Enstone?"

"I'm afraid I'm a clergyman."

"Isn't Ann Colindale looking stunning."

"Is Matthew here?"

"I don't think so, Oliver."

"Pinkie, where *are* Gracie and Ludwig?"

"I hear Austin's son is back."

"He's on drugs."

"They all are."

"Penny Sayce looks ancient."

148

"You'd look ancient if your husband had just died of cancer."

"Poor Penny— I say, Ann, whoopee, long time no see."

"What with Martin dead and Oliver queer and Henrietta most peculiar—"

"Hello, Richard, let's have lunch."

"Hello, Ann. Excuse me I must just—"

"Oh hello Richard— I'm afraid Karen isn't here."

"Where *is* Gracie?"

"Oh Char darling, you've come, how marvellous, Penny, here's Charlotte— Pinkie, give Charlotte a drink, one of her specials, Char, do sit down, I know you're not a stander-upper."

"Oliver Sayce lets his ten-year-old sister drive his sports car on the M-One."

"Mollie Arbuthnot's boutique will sell only white things."

"There's Richard Pargeter, you know he's divorced again."

"Pinkie, do go and call Gracie and Ludwig, they're being so naughty."

"Oliver Sayce is making a fortune in the antique book trade."

"I'm dying to see Gracie's German."

"Is Sebastian here?"

"Don't be silly."

"Sebastian is studying chartered accountancy."

"Isn't that Charlotte Ledgard?"

"I thought she'd run away to sea."

"She only ran as far as Bailey's Hotel."

"Why, Matthew, how marvellous! Look, everybody, here's Matthew! Matthew, you remember Penny— Geoffrey, do come and—Matthew, how lovely—"

"I think I see some familiar faces."

"Rather the worse for wear."

"Clara, I—oh hello, Matthew!"

"Matthew, how super!"

"I thought there was going to be a pregnant silence."

"Matthew is rather like a visiting general."

"Everyone has recovered."

149

"Clara, I think Gracie and Ludwig have gone out. I called, but there's not a sound from upstairs."

"Karen Arbuthnot has become a pig maiden."

"Matthew has got fat and old."

"We all have."

"Is that really Sir Matthew Gibson Grey?"

"Clara, we want Gracie!"

"I thought Matthew had become a monk."

"Perhaps he has, it's so hard to tell these days."

"Penny Sayce believes in salvation by bridge."

"Pinkie, are you sure that Gracie and Ludwig—"

"Afraid my Latin's a bit rusty. Did some New Testament Greek of course."

"Richard, let's have lunch."

"Charles and Geoffrey are discussing the crisis."

"May I get you another drink, sir?"

"Thank you, dear boy."

"Henrietta Sayce has won the under-twelve bridge championship."

"Is Dorina here?"

"Don't be silly."

"Dr. Seldon is discussing liver fluke with Geoffrey."

"I don't think people should invite doctors, they're such a memento mori."

"Do you think that butler's just hired for the occasion?"

"Of course he is! Richard thought the butler was real!"

"Matthew and Oliver are discussing Oscar Wilde."

"Why, Austin, isn't that lovely, Austin's come— Pinkie, here's Austin, how super—"

"Is that Austin Gibson Grey?"

"He looks like a poet."

"Where *is* Gracie?"

"Is that Gracie's intended?"

"No, darling, that's Ann."

"No head for languages, I'm afraid."

"Richard Pargeter is going to buy a yacht."

"Is the young man in turquoise Ludwig?"

"Austin, I'm still job-hunting for you—"

"George, for God's sake don't waste your time."

"I did want to say if ever you're short we could—"

"Thank you, George, I would actually like a loan, how much could you let me have?"

"Well, er I'd have to—Clara's signalling, excuse me—yes, Austin, we'll definitely arrange—excuse me—"

"Matthew looks like a businessman."

"My dear, he is a businessman."

"Char darling, you're puss in the corner as usual."

"You know I hate parties."

"Who are you pushing, Richard P.?"

"Sorry, I just wanted to get at Matthew."

"Penny dear, Hester has just been telling me about Mollie's boutique, it will sell nothing but white things."

"Geoffrey's pigs have all got liver fluke."

"I say, Clara, Austin accepts our offered loan with enthusiasm."

"Never mind, Pinkie, I must be getting drunk."

"Clara, what a super party."

"Clara, where *is* Gracie?"

"Pinkie, do go and look for them—"

"Oh hello, Austin."

"Hello, Matthew."

"Your job must be very interesting too, Mr. Enstone."

"How about a drink sometime soon, Austin?"

"Sorry, Matthew, I'm just leaving town."

"Is Ludwig the man with the lace ruffles?"

"No, that's Oliver Sayce."

"Hester, we were so sorry Sebastian couldn't make it to the Mill House."

"Look, Matthew and Austin are talking!"

"No, they aren't. Austin's talking to Charlotte."

"About time somebody did."

"Wish I'd made it to Oxford."

"Austin is drunk."

"So am I."

"So is Mollie Arbuthnot."

"Where *are* Gracie and Ludwig?"

"Karen Arbuthnot has got liver fluke."

"Austin is sloshed."

"He's gone off to the loo."

"Where is the loo?"

"Char, I do want to talk to you—"

"Mr. Enstone and the young man in turquoise are boring each other into agony and have had empty glasses for ten minutes."

"Oh Char, you do make me blush, I'm a rotten hostess."

"Yes, wonderful place, Oxford."

"Mr. Enstone, I must introduce you to Lady Odmore, she's so interested in the liturgy. Mr. Hilton, do meet Oliver Sayce, he's in the antique book trade."

"Oh hello!"

"Hello!"

"I feel quite faint with relief."

"I've been wondering who you were all the evening."

"Char, listen darling, you're going to come and live here with us, we've decided it all, there's plenty of room and we just couldn't bear it if you were anywhere else, you can sleep in George's study and have Gracie's room when she moves, we'll bring the car at the weekend and collect all your stuff from the Villa, and then we shall be so snug here when we're all together, so let's say it's fixed and—"

"It's very kind of you, Clara—"

"Not at all, my dear, you know how anxious we are—"

"It's very kind of you, Clara, but I have just made another arrangement."

"You can't stay in that hotel—"

"I'm going to live in Austin's flat, we've just fixed it, he's letting me have it for a low rent. I feel I need a place of my own."

"Char—you're going to live in Austin's flat?"

"Not *with* Austin, dear."

"Gracie and Ludwig are the limit."

"Matthew is leaving."

"Austin is locked in the loo."

"Everybody, Matthew is leaving."

"Oliver and the turquoise man have gone to the pub."

"Matthew has left."

"Hester, you and Sebastian must—"

"Thank you, dear Mollie—"

"We must leave too—"

"Clara, thank you so much—"

"Geoffrey is carting Mollie."

"Love to Karen."

"Love to Sebastian."

"Love to Henrietta."

"Love to Ralph."

"Good-bye— Why here they are!"

"Gracie and Ludwig, just when everybody's leaving!"

"Gracie and Ludwig, how wonderful they're looking!"

"Just like a god and a goddess!"

"Wait, everybody, Gracie and Ludwig—"

"Gracie and Ludwig!"

"Hooray!"

My dear George,
   It was so kind of you to press a loan upon me, but I think that I can manage perfectly well without your help.
                                        Yours,
                                           AUSTIN

My dear Karen,
   Thank you for a super luncheon, for which it was sweet of you to pay, and excuse this short note as I have exams.
                                        Love,
                                           SEBASTIAN

My dear Louis,
   Do come and see me, all well of course and nothing else to say,

                                        Love
                                        DORINA

My dear Austin,
   I am now living at the Villa, at home every morning and very anxious to talk to you. Will you ring?
                                  Your affectionate brother,
                                           MATTHEW

LIVINGSTONE SUGGESTS PLEAD TOTAL CONSCIENTIOUS OBJECTION LETTER FOLLOWING LEFERRIER

Dearest Patrick,
    No time write as busy Ludwig all time forgive,
                                    eternal love,
                                        GRACIE

Dearest Hester,
    So glad you will come to the Mill House, we are dying
to see you and Charles and Sebastian down here, I will
telephone about time, Karen sends love,
                                    With love,
                                        MOLLIE

Dear Ludwig,
    Were you at that party? I loved it, especially the later
stages. Come and house-hunt.
                                    Yours,
                                        ANDREW

My dear Sebastian,
    Your unspeakable communication received, meet me
six Tuesday Kings Arms Sloane Square. Will telephone.
                                Your wounded bird,
                                        K.
And please come Mill House parentwise?

My dear Mr. and Mrs. Leferrier,
    Just to say briefly at once how very glad we all are
about the engagement of our dear daughter to your son,
I am sure they will be very happy. My husband and I so
much hope you will come and stay with us for the wedding
and I will write soon with details of times. With our
warmest wishes,
                                Yours sincerely,
                                CLARA TISBOURNE

Dear Ludwig,
    I have moved to Stepney, but let us meet soon. I feel,

for reasons which are not obscure and perhaps not important, depressed.

> Yours,
> GARTH

My darling husband,
I hope you have found a job, I have no spirit to write, but I am well, and I hope to see you, not now, but soon, and this with the ever-love of your ever-wife,

> DORINA

Dearest Gracie,
Thanks for your rotten letter, I am very miserable, but I know you don't care,

> Your bitter brother,
> TISBOURNE

My dear Father,
Thank you for your cable, that won't do I'm afraid, but I will await your letter.

> Your affectionate son,
> LUDWIG

P.S. I have just discovered that my fiancée is very rich. I didn't know this before. I have obtained the Oxford appointment.

Dearest Dorina,
Just to say that we so very much hope that you will come and stay with us *soon,* which we feel sure will benefit *everybody*.

> With much love,
> CLARA

Dear Mr. Secombe-Hughes,
I do hope you will let me have some money soon as I am beginning to be in financial difficulties, excuse this letter, I am too embarrassed to say this when I am at work, and please excuse me,

> Yours faithfully,
> M. RICARDO

P.S. I now have six IOUs.

Dearest girl,
     I haven't written for two days, I know, I am wretched too, I have no job, I will write properly soon. Oh God I love you.

A.

Do not go away anywhere with anybody even briefly.

My dear Charlotte,
     Thank you for telephoning, yes, could you come and see us tomorrow if possible, Dorina urgently needs rational company and I urgently need advice.

Love,
MAVIS

P.S. Have you seen Matthew?

Dear Ralph,
     All right I was a fool to tell you, but you were worse than a fool to react as you did, and we cannot leave things here. I am in agony. Sorry.

PATRICK

My dear Mavis,
     I would like to see you if you would like to see me. Would you? And if so will you telephone me?

Best regards,
MATTHEW

Austin Gibson Grey lay half-dressed upon his unmade bed and watched his long thin window change from a summer blue through purple to a lurid London night red. Having got drunk at the Tisbournes' party, he had made a complete nonsense of all his arrangements. He had let the flat to Charlotte for three pounds a week, party because he was sorry for her but largely to spite George and Clara and also out of vanity. The trouble was that five minutes earlier he had accepted George's offer of a loan. Could he use George's money to subsidize Charlotte to spite George? No. So he had to write to George to refuse the loan after all. And meanwhile he was broke. He had only gone to the party for the drinks and the sandwiches, having had no lunch, and to see Gracie of course, and then there were no sandwiches, only rotten cheese biscuits, and no Gracie.

Charlotte's money would hardly cover the rates. He owed a month's rent and a quarter's electricity. He owed for clothes and for some books which he had already sold. He had sold his watch and his stamp collection. He had already borrowed as much as he could hope to get from Ludwig and Mitzi. No job that he would dream of taking had been offered. He would not be triumphed over. He was at the end of his tether. In fact he had been there for some time. Of course he could cancel Charlotte. But all he had left now was his pride.

It's all so petty, he thought, but it's destroying me. He had to eat, and Mitzi's suppers were getting smaller and smaller. Anyway there were days when he hated Mitzi.

If only there were somewhere he could get away to, somewhere to which he could take Dorina, making mock of them all, somewhere in the south beside the sea, where the wind was warm and Dorina could walk barefoot in the waves and pick up shells to give him, and he would be clean and free and cherished. At present he felt too demoralized even to take a bath and his body smelt. Anyway Mitzi had turned the hot water off to save money.

He had still not been to see Dorina, and with everything in this muddle he could not go, and now that Charlotte had insinuated herself into the flat there was nowhere to bring Dorina even if he did get a job. He hated Charlotte. And he had read a letter from Dorina to Ludwig which he had found in Ludwig's room. It was quite a simple letter, but it was so affectionate and pleading. He hated Ludwig. He sat up jerking his pillows about. The pillows were old and greasy and wafer-thin and emitted dust. There was no clean linen any more. The warm purple powdery dirty London air drifted through the window and sifted down into his lungs, making him gasp. He had mislaid his tablets. Wolfing cheese biscuits at the Tisbournes, he had bitten his tongue again, it still hurt.

Someone knocked on the door and Austin hastily covered himself. The room was dark and a tall figure stood in the faint illumination from the landing. "May I turn the light on?" said Garth.

The light went on as Austin was fumbling for his shirt. His underwear was filthy.

"Sorry, I didn't realize you'd have gone to bed."

"I haven't gone to bed," said Austin, "I was just—resting." His shirt seemed to be inside out.

"Can I help you, Father?"

"No." Austin got his shirt and trousers on and pulled up over his rumpled bed an Indian counterpane so worn and frail that if he had let it out of the window it would have floated away like thistledown.

Austin sat on the bed. Garth sat on the floor with his back to the wall. He had a bulky bundle with him and looked, as the young can, poor and shabby and elegant at the same time.

"Well, how are you, Garth?"

"Very well, Father."

"Has Charlotte moved in?"

"Yes."

"Have you moved out?"

"Yes. I've got all my things here."

"You mean in that bundle? Need you look quite so like Dick Whittington? Did that suitcase ever turn up?"

"No."

Austin kicked a pile of underwear away under the bed with his heels. He felt hungry and nervy. The sight of Garth's ostentatiously calm face filled him with irritation and pain. "Well, Garth, tell me about your life."

"Several things, Father. First of all could you lend me the key of that blue trunk, you know, at the flat, in the kitchen cupboard?"

"Is it locked? I don't keep keys. I don't even know what's in it."

"It's full of pictures and things—I mean photos—remembrances of my mother—all her stuff."

"Oh—" He must have locked the trunk against Dorina. Why did it seem so aggressive of Garth to speak of Betty as his mother, indeed to speak of her at all?

"You'll have to break it open," said Austin.

"You don't mind if I take one or two of those things, that big photo with—"

"Oh take the lot, take the lot."

"Have you got a job yet, Father?"

"No. Have you?"

"I'm still looking for the right one. At present I'm just washing up."

"Washing up?"

"Yes. In a Soho restaurant."

"I think I'm a bit old for washing up," said Austin, "but it may come to that. You said there were several things. That's one, or maybe two. What's the next? Need you sit on the floor? There is a chair."

Garth continued to sit on the floor. "Would you mind if I went to see Dorina?"

"Yes," said Austin. "Wait a moment." He felt a jolt of terror. "What for?"

"I feel I could help," said Garth, speaking slowly. "I thought at first I couldn't. But now I feel I can. I've been talking about her to Ludwig."

"Oh, have you?"

"I feel everything should be opened out a bit more, there should be more fresh air and talk. Dorina needs to talk to people. I don't mean doctors or anything like that. She needs news of other people's troubles. She needs ordinariness."

"And you imagine *you* can provide that!"

"Well, *would* you mind?"

"Yes, I would," said Austin. "You don't understand anything about Dorina and me and I forbid you to meddle." He tried hard to keep his voice steady, but embryos of anger were swelling in his chest and constricting his lungs. Dorina and Garth would walk hand in hand in the garden and talk about him. They would look into each other's eyes. This was an old nightmare. Huge balls of anger grew inside his chest.

Garth was sitting very still with his hands on his knees, his serious face puckered up with care and cunning. The light was bright in the room and the night was hot and red outside and moths flew in and out like paper fragments.

"All right," said Garth. "I'm probably a fool. I just hate to see you so sort of tied up and so full of resentment against everybody and so anxious. One's got to overcome resentment. That's one of the most important of all things. Just see that it's possible. If you can once see that it's possible you can see that it's easy, and if you can see that it's easy you can do it. You should just try to forgive us all."

"Go away, will you, Garth, please," said Austin quietly. He feared that awful seizure, that black outburst of anger that ripped out of him when it came like a physical eruption, as nauseating and inevitable as vomiting. Blackness poured out. Betty, walking in the garden, hand in hand with Garth.

"I know I'm making you angry," said Garth. "It's not

161

easy to talk to you like this. Anger is frightening. And you are my father. I just felt I had to sort of testify. Please think about it and forgive me. I won't ask if you'd mind if I went to see Uncle Matthew, I know you would. But I must say one thing. I think *you* ought to go and see Uncle Matthew. There's no need to make any drama about it. Just go and see him. Ask him to lend you some money."

"Garth, get out, would you," said Austin. "There's a good boy."

"You could break this circle if you wanted to—"

"Get out."

"And the sky wouldn't fall if Uncle Matthew met Dorina in an ordinary way—"

"You don't know what you're talking about," Austin uttered in a low screeching voice. "You're mad. Don't you know that Matthew and your mother, don't you *know*—?"

Garth shifted a little, rocking his head slowly to and fro. "I suspected," he said, "that you thought—that you imagined—something of the sort—"

"And then you suggest to me—"

"But I don't believe it."

"You don't—?"

"No. Nor do I for a second believe that you really believe it. Sorry, Father."

Austin swayed, clutching himself, giving out a low raucous cry. He seized the tumbler which stood on his bedside table and threw it at the wall. It failed to break and rolled back to his feet. He seized it again and rising up hurled it at the side of the window frame. The tumbler shattered and one of the window panes cracked. Garth was gone. Austin was lying on his bed, biting the thin greasy pillow and uttering big quiet tearless sobs. Papery moths flitted above him. Some flew against the blazing electric light bulb and fell down onto his twitching back. Later he went to sleep and dreamt of Betty falling into a well. The water closed over her head.

Dorina had read an African folk tale about a woman who was turned into a doll. The doll was somebody's wife and was kept in somebody else's pocket and brought out every now and then to be looked at as two men walked along a road. One of the two men was her husband, but was it he who had transformed her into a doll or the other man and whose pocket was she kept in and how did it all end? She could not remember.

Charlotte was very neat this evening. She had a smart summer suit on, off-white with cinnamon stripes. She was slim and tall and her sleekly waved hair was purplish grey. She sat primly with knees and feet together. Already that morning she had cleaned Austin's flat from end to end. Then she had had a bath with expensive bath salts.

Mavis was untidy. Her blue nylon overall was spotted with grease. Her hair moved cloudily, her eyes were dreamy and young. The house was still empty and echoing, its future uncertain, time on a brink. She had told Mrs. Carberry she might occasionally bring Ronald with her to work. But she was not to think that Ronald could be foisted, that no.

Mavis and Charlotte and Dorina were sitting in the drawing-room drinking elderberry wine. Mavis and Charlotte sat together. Dorina sat a little apart at the open window, looking out at the garden, at the spiky pink roses and the starry daisies on the lawn and the privet hedge pale as yellow marjoram bleaching in the sun. The garden was so much like the inside of her head. It was hard to realize that other people could see it too.

Mrs. Carberry was crying in the kitchen. Her eldest son had been arrested for stealing. Her second son was on probation for drugs. Her husband had hit her. There was a handbag that she wanted, crinkly blue leather with brass rings, but it was too expensive. Perhaps it would be reduced in the sale.

"Did you see Matthew at that party?" said Mavis.

"Yes," said Charlotte, "but he didn't see me."

"Is he much changed?"

"Yes."

"He wrote to me."

"Did he?"

"He said he wanted to see me if I wanted to see him."

"And do you?"

"One is curious."

So Matthew had written to Mavis. Charlotte wondered, can I rebuild my life even now and be an independent person walking on the face of the earth, set free from people's pity? Can I build walls against the seas of sadness and resentment and jealousy or must I be their victim after all?

"So you think that's why Austin was so anxious to let you the flat?"

"Yes."

"What do you think, Dorina?"

"I don't know."

"Will you came and stay with me, Dorina?"

"Dear Charlotte—"

"Don't press her, let her think about it."

"You think Austin felt she might come and stay with you in his flat as a sort of halfway house?"

"Yes."

A grass snake got in with the goldfish once. Dorina's father tried to lift it out with a stick. It would have eaten the fish. Accidentally he killed it. Dorina ran away weeping. There were such terrible things in the world.

Mavis felt a great void where her faith had been. This feeling was new, she had not missed it before. Yet it was not that she suddenly felt it was valuable. She had sacrificed her life for something of no value. Yet the sacrifice itself was of value. Could that be so?

Mrs. Carberry had seen such awful scenes on telly before her husband came home and switched over to the World Cup. She saw some men out in the East shooting a prisoner. He was all tied up and they held his head down and shot him with a pistol. Sometimes the television men would say, hold it, don't kill him till our cameras are ready.

"I do think Dorina should come and stay with me."

"So do I."

"She could do me a lot of good. You could do me a lot of good, Dorina. Why not think about that? Stop thinking of yourself. Think of me."

"Dearest Charlotte—"

It was hard to picture the outside of the house from the inside. It was as if the inside proliferated, breeding all sorts of new dark uninhabited rooms. Sometimes it smelt of blood. But the garden was separate and clear, another kind of dream place, lit by a cool grey sun by day and night. There were statues there. One's mind, wasn't that just chemistry too?

"I think I'll go out into the garden."

Once she had thought that Austin was drugging her. But of course that was just a fantasy.

"Yes, do, it's so sunny."

"If you ever want anywhere to run to, Dorina, run to me."

"Dearest Char—" Upon the white treads of the stair the flies are dying, sprayed by Mrs. Carberry. Are they in agony? What is it like for a fly to die? Dorina feels she ought to kill them quickly by stepping on them but she cannot.

"Do you think she ought to see somebody?"

"You mean a doctor?"

"Or a priest."

"I don't know."

"Austin's the trouble, not her."

Mavis felt a void where her faith had been, an empty space left underneath her heart, only she had not noticed

165

it for years. She had made a great sacrifice for nothing, she had made a mistake.

"So you will see Matthew."

"I suppose so."

"Isn't it funny his living at the Villa. Who would have thought it this time last year. It's funny, yes, funny."

"I wonder if he still owns that cottage."

"You mean in Sussex where Austin and Betty were staying when Betty was drowned?"

"Yes."

"He sold it to a cousin of Geoffrey Arbuthnot."

"Ludwig hasn't been to see us."

"He is sick with love, happy boy."

"Happy since he is loved."

"Happy anyway. It is better to be sick with love than just sick."

"Are you all right, Char?"

"Yes. And take that look off your face. I'm not one of your cases."

"Don't be a fool, Char."

"I can hear somebody crying."

"It's Mrs. Carberry. Her husband beats her."

"Men. They really are worse than us, aren't they?"

"Yes."

Dorina walked across the grass. She held her plait of hair in her hand and hauled on it a little. She was barefoot. It was impossible not to step on the daisies. If only she were feathery-light and could float along with the soles of her feet just touching the little humpy centres of the daisies. They would tickle a bit, and her feet would be stained yellow with pollen.

"Dorina."

Someone had spoken her name very close by. Was it Austin? Alarm made her heart rise and race.

"Dorina. Here."

A voice was speaking to her from the other side of the privet hedge. Dorina looked quickly round, then she sped through the gap in the hedge.

On the other side was a smaller lawn, hidden from the

house, an old brick wall where the garden ended, a stripy clematis, a white broom in flower.

On the lawn, stark, like a man on a stage, in a picture, someone was standing. He was tall, dark, lanky, sallow, shabby, familiar.

"Garth!"

Dorina put her hand to neck and sank down on the grass. Garth knelt down beside her grinning.

"Hello, Dorina, I wasn't sure you'd recognize me."

"Garth—how—oh you have changed—you've grown up."

"Well, of course I've changed, it's ages since we met. I just came in over the wall. I wanted to look at you."

"To look at me?"

"Yes. I was beginning to be unsure whether you really existed or not."

"I'm sometimes unsure myself."

"I say, what are you going to do about it all?"

"About Austin?" She looked past his dark head at the big stripy mauve faces of the clematis flowers. Suddenly talking to him like this was odd but somehow not difficult. "You tell me what to do."

"I'll tell you one thing. You must stop being so afraid of him."

Dorina considered several answers and then just said, "How?"

"I don't know. Your fear sets him off. It excites him. Like a tiger smelling blood. Stop being so quiet. Stop doing everything in slow motion. You must feel like a prisoner. Break out. Go somewhere. See people. Above all, see him, and if he's tiresome, shout at him."

Dorina just shook her head. "If I leave here anything I do will hurt him and, as he thinks, expose him to ridicule."

"Well then hurt him, expose him to ridicule, wake him bloody up."

"Garth, how can you—"

Garth rose to his feet and Dorina rose too. They stood intently facing each other with hands hanging. In the heat of the evening Garth's face was marked with trails of sweat.

"Oh well, I'm glad I've looked at you, that might help somehow."

"Garth, don't go for a moment. Better not tell him you've been here."

"Oh hang him!"

"Please. And Garth— Have you seen Matthew?"

"No, but I will. I shall have to. What is more my father will have to."

"Why 'have to'?"

"Because he's fascinated by him, because he needs him, because in the end he probably loves him."

"If I really thought," said Dorina, "that Austin loved Matthew—"

"What?"

"It would all go away, the nightmare would go away, it could—"

"Who knows? Maybe. But there are strange loves in the world. Good-bye. I say, Dorina, may I kiss you?"

Dorina stood quiet, arms pendant, while Garth put his hands gently on her shoulders and carefully and deliberately kissed her first on the cheek and then without haste upon the lips. Then he glided away, waved a hand, hauled himself up onto the wall, waved again, and was gone. The bright vision of him remained for a moment only silhouetted against blue sky.

Dorina looked quickly round. The garden, which had been for a while so real, had become itself again, empty and still under a grey sun, a thought-place. She touched her face, which was moist with his salty sweat as if with tears.

Austin had been crying last night. Mitzi had heard him sobbing and had opened the door. His room was obscure. She said, "Austin, darling." He made a sort of animal retching noise. Then he turned on the light by the bed and made an awful face at her. It was a dreadful squashed-up face of violence and loathing. It haunted her sleepless bed, huge and hostile, like the owl which had rushed at her out of the dark. Or had she imagined that owl? Then he turned the light out again. Mitzi fled.

Now it was the next morning and she was sitting in front of her typewriter in the office. Her ankle ached and the scar upon her face itched and pulled the skin in towards it, so that she felt grotesque. She kept scratching, drawing blood, dabbing with her handkerchief, looking at herself in the mirror. She loved Austin. Of course she had always loved him, but now it had blazed up. Great gusts of fiery emotion blew upon Mitzi as if she had opened the door of a furnace. She had not known how much difference it would make to have him with her in the house tucked up safe and snug every night. It gave her a feeling she had not had since she had been a little child with her mother. I love him and I'll keep him, she thought. He came to me. He said we were on an island. I love him and I'm not complicated like the others. I don't drive him mad and make demands. He can be bad to me and it makes no difference, he knows that. His dreadful face floated before her glorified, the mask of a lion, terrible and noble.

"Miss Mitzi, may I ask you something?" said Mr.

Secombe-Hughes behind her. He often called her that, perhaps facetiously.

Mitzi, who had been absently scratching her breasts, quickly buttoned up her blouse. "Yes, Mr. Secombe-Hughes?"

"May I take a photograph of you?"

"Well—"

"As a little gift, a token."

He was smiling his most bardic smile and had combed his grey hair, which stuck wetly and greasily to his head, curling up a little at the ends.

"Yes."

"Come."

Mr. Secombe-Hughes held out his hand and Mitzi, rather surprised, took it. Their relationship seemed suddenly to have altered now that she was to be photographed. Mr. Secombe-Hughes led her, or rather pulled her, out of her office and into the studio. At the far end, a relic of a bygone day, there was a backcloth representing the terrace of some great house and beyond it a lake and some mountains. A white painted cast-iron seat stood in front of it.

Mitzi sat down. "I've got this car."

"I have received a good offer for the business. I am thinking of going back to Wales. Back to my village."

Well, I hope to God you'll pay me first, thought Mitzi. "I've got this car."

"Don't worry. I will arrange you. May I?" Mr. Secombe-Hughes's hands were gently moulding her, soothing her. He had turned her head to hide the scar, caressed her hair, drawn his fingers across her cheek, pressed persuasively upon her collar bone. He had lifted her arm so that it trailed negligently over the back of the seat. Now his hand had somehow got into the crook of her knee. "And may I dress you in this? It belonged to my mother." He was holding a huge white shawl embroidered with white flying birds. He had drawn it round her neck and was tucking it down across her breasts. Mitzi relaxed, laughing.

"There are seals there," said Mr. Secombe-Hughes, who had withdrawn now. He was using the oldest camera, which he still said was the best one, and he had covered his head with a black cloth and his voice was muffled. "There are seals there and big crabs and wet rocks as pink as the dawn and little secret inlets where the sea is like cream and there is light yellow seaweed like light tossed hair. And the cormorant flits like a ghost low over the waves. And there is solitude and the wild pained cry of the seagull."

"Where?" said Mitzi.

"In Wales. At my village."

I feel so relaxed, thought Mitzi. Mr. Secombe-Hughes ought to have been a masseur. The great white silky shawl caressed her, smelling of an old old perfume, a sweet powder from a powder puff of long ago. Mitzi's ankle had ceased to ache. With dazed wild joy she realized that it had become better. She bounded up the rocks, away from the sea, towards the castle, where Austin was waiting for her on the terrace, where she had chained him to the castle wall with a silver chain, and between every link of the chain there was a pearl, and when the sun was low in the sky they sat and kissed each other upon the terrace and listened to the wild pained cry of the seagull and watched the cormorant flit like a ghost over the waves until the great moon arose and the moonlit sea was like cream in the little inlets.

The great square eye gazes at her and Mr. Secombe-Hughes's muffled voice rises and falls and fades like the sound of the waves.

"Miss Mitzi, I love you, will you marry me?" Mr. Secombe-Hughes is kneeling beside her and the white shawl is disordered.

"I must have fallen asleep for a moment."

"Will you marry me?"

"The sea, I dreamed of the sea. A castle on an island."

"We would have a little office in Aberystwyth."

"Oh please, no, Mr. Secombe-Hughes, I cannot love you."

Mitzi struggled away and rose to her feet. He remained kneeling.

"Miss Mitzi, please now, you must have known of my

love, you seemed to accept it, only in my difficulties, one is a gentleman, I could see you understood. I have written a poem about you in Welsh in five hundred lines. We could have an office in Aberystwyth and a cabin by the sea, you dreamed of the sea."

"Please, Mr. Secombe-Hughes, I never accepted your love, I do not want to marry you, please get up."

He got up. "Miss Mitzi, let me at least love you. It is something if a man can at least love a woman. There is so little in my life. It would give me something to dream of, something to write about. A man must have something to dream of. I could send letters to you and poems and little flowers from the rocks. I understand. How could I hope? But just let me—go on loving you—and perhaps—sometimes—you might come to Wales to see me—and I would dream of you and think about you in the night-time."

"I don't want you to think about me in the night-time," said Mitzi. "Your love makes me feel unclean, I don't want it. I want the money you owe me, all of it, and then not to see or hear of you again. Don't touch me, please, I'm in love with somebody else."

There was silence. Mr. Secombe-Hughes picked up the shawl from where it had fallen to the ground. Mitzi rushed to the office for her coat and bag. "I'm sorry," she said, as she ran out of the door. She felt unclean. She needed Austin.

Later on she started to cry and wondered what Mr. Secombe-Hughes had done after she had gone away. She felt very sorry for him. But he sickened her all the same.

The privet hedge glimmered in what seemed to be star-light. Do stars really give light? Stars which no longer exist still shine upon us, they say. Only in London there are no stars and the night sky is a fiery purple. Austin's hand quested over dry earth between stems. His glasses had fallen off as he leapt from the wall. Then he saw them lying upon the lawn like wicked lost eyes reflecting a little light.

Something touched his cheek. It was a spider's web which he had just broken. He felt or saw the spider running darkly upon his coat and shuddered it away. The grass was dewy and he slithered his feet over it snakelike. A tall pale thing stood near, a statue which he had forgotten.

He had been out all day wandering, getting through the hours. People gave him strange looks. He visited museums but could see nothing. He sat in the National Gallery reading the evening papers. Sometimes in the afternoon he slept in the park. He had dreamed again that Betty was still alive, a drugged captive in a castle. His clothes were covered in dry grass and his nose itched. He usually returned home late to avoid Mitzi, who was becoming amorous.

There was a light in the drawing-room, a gap in the curtains. Would he see Dorina? Would she see him and scream? Would she faint, keeling over from her chair onto the floor? He had seen her faint so once. How he loved and feared her frightened face. Her tender vulnerable person filled him with sweet anguish, as if he should have found a little wounded animal, and then not know how to cherish it.

Such feelings in their married life together had made up a trembling and precarious happiness. He had always loved her with tears in his eyes. She had played at helplessness to please him. They had played together and this had seemed to bring back his innocence. But her laughter had always sounded of mortality and her uplifted hand had always seemed involuntarily to point at terrible veiled things.

Austin reached out his left hand and gripped the window sill, resting one cautious silent foot upon the gravel. He saw Dorina seated in the midst of gold like a Madonna in glory. He fell against the wall of the house. Only it was not Dorina, it was Mavis, sitting opposite to him at a table and writing a letter. She looked a tired sad angel. She looked up dreamily and murmured something, a name.

Austin retreated. He desired to call out, to break the spell, but he feared the irrevocable. With everybody against him was it indeed conceivable that he might lose Dorina? He was in an unlucky inauspicious time when any move would be a wrong one. Was it simply that his wife had left him and was afraid to say so? No, she would not murder him by going elsewhere and being with others, she would never betray him.

Any violence there had been before had seemed like play. But now he could not raise his voice even to say, "Come back, that is enough." Some mechanism geared his lightest movement so that if he touched her he would break a bone. He must let her wander and return of her own accord, even if fear drove her screaming to him. In the end her own ghosts would send her back. He must wait, he could afford to, she was tethered to him by an unbreakable cord. She was, however far she might roam, forever his prisoner.

Austin went back, slithering over his trail in the dew. He trampled upon flowers, touching the warm crumbling surface of the brick wall. A thick plait of wistaria made a step for him and cracked under his weight as he pulled himself up. A moment later he was walking along the street, dusting himself down, his heart loaded with misery.

"Oh Mr. Gibson Grey, please."

Two figures were standing on the edge of the pavement near a street lamp.

"Mr. Gibson Grey. You are Mr. Gibson Grey, aren't you?"

"Yes."

"I thought you were one of our gentlemen."

Austin recognized the charwoman, Mrs. Carberry. A boy of about ten was holding her by the hand.

"Good evening," said Austin.

"I thought it was you," said Mrs. Carberry, "though the lights aren't very good, are they, and I haven't any glasses on. I don't think the lights are as bright as they used to be at night, since the new government. I wonder if you would be so kind as to help me?"

"Yes, certainly," said Austin.

"It's Ronald here. This is Ronald, my boy, my third boy that is, and there's two girls younger and much less trouble. Ronald, this is Mr. Gibson Grey. You see, Ronald doesn't want to cross the road. He's not like other children, he's difficult, though God know it's not his fault. Come on, now. See." Mrs. Carberry was tugging Ronald, who was hanging back. Austin caught a glimpse of the boy's face, curiously plump and pale, creased up with fear and will.

"There aren't many motor-cars at this time, well, there's one," said Mrs. Carberry. "I don't think it's the cars he minds, I wouldn't want to get him half over and have him dragging his feet like, he's that strong you know, there's just something about this road that gets at him in his mind, he's so fanciful you see. I wonder if you'd just be so kind as to take his other hand and we'll walk him over, I believe he feels better when there are two, when his father used to hold his hand he was always better with a smile on his little face, like he never smiles now, poor pet, perhaps a man would help, he won't do a thing for me these days. Now take the nice gentleman's hand, Ronald, and we'll all three go across as safe as safe. Would you mind, sir?"

"Of course not." Austin moved round and took the boy's other hand. The hand hung limply and when Austin had taken it it felt weak and small. He had to grip it firmly as there was no answering pressure. It was like holding a dead mouse. Could sickness of the mind deaden the body so?

"You'll have to pull a bit, sir." Austin pulled. Ronald walked. Ronald turned a face like a pudding plate up towards Austin and they walked across the road all three.

"Oh thank you, sir, you are so kind, thank God you came along, I could have been there half an hour, and I didn't want him half-way across dragging his feet with the cars coming."

"Shall I see you home?" said Austin. "Will you be all right?"

"Oh yes, it's only that road, and he likes the tube train, poor mite. You see, I get him out of the house when I can, his father shouts so, I used to take him to his auntie weekends, only she's took against him. We're quite all right now and I do thank you so much, sir."

"Good night."

Austin returned to himself. For several whole minutes he had been thinking about something else. Now the old buzzing cloud swept blindingly about him once again. Matthew had said that he would not go to Valmorana, but Matthew could break his word. What was it that Mavis had said when she had looked up so dreamily from her letter? She had said "Matthew." The universe said "Matthew."

Austin walked blindly on. Could he still be rescued by Dorina's love and was the miracle still possible and did Ithaca still exist? When the spirit deadens it takes place so slowly, but there are moments when a man can see himself becoming more callous because he has to survive. A false alarm on the night bell once answered, it cannot be put right again ever. What did Mrs. Carberry think about him, he suddenly wondered. Had she seen him climbing over the wall? But then it did not really matter to him or to anybody else what Mrs. Carberry thought. If God existed He too would be indifferent to the thoughts of Mrs. Carberry.

176

"Hong Kong must be a very interesting city. Yes, thank you, spinach, no potatoes."

"Yes, fascinating."

"Why did you decide not to stay in the East?"

"Oh well, I didn't really fit in there. I thought I'd better come home. Home is better, after all."

"Yes, of course."

"One is more at home."

"Yes."

Perhaps it's frivolous of me, thought Mavis, but I can't bear his having got so fat, and he's become pompous and sort of Oriental and old. He could be my uncle.

"I'm afraid I've put on some weight since we last met," said Matthew.

"Oh no."

"You look just the same."

"I've faded."

"Fading suits you."

"Like a piece of old chintz."

"Yes, there's no doubt that I've put on weight."

She is defeated, he thought, tired out by years of a rather dull life. We are both weary, we have not the energy for real communication, we are cautious and afraid of hurts and entanglements. We are saddening and disappointing each other.

"Did you ever try dieting?"

"No, I've rather taken to the fleshpots in my old age."

He has become so rotund, she thought, even his head has become fat. And his eyes are a sort of viscous fishy

177

blue but so bloodshot that they look almost purple. He probably drinks too much.

"So you're thinking of selling Valmorana?"

"Yes." She supposed she was. The nuns were bankrupt and moving house and the local authority wanted impossible things. And she had been putting everything off until she met Matthew. What a desolation she had now prepared for herself. Why had she been so sure that he would be a source of new life? Had he expected this of her? She read disillusion in his eyes.

"It's quite a good moment for selling house property."

"Is it? Good." They say he made a fortune in Hong Kong, I can believe it. "I'll get a flat. Much more convenient."

"Much more convenient."

I'm boring her, he thought. They were having lunch at the Café Royal. Matthew had no servants at the Villa yet. He had thought that food and drink would help. Now they had both eaten and drunk too much in desperation.

The texture of the face matters so, she thought. That flabby ageing surface invited no touch. She had imagined a great magnetic force drawing them together, she had imagined tears of joy. She had recalled him so clearly, smooth-cheeked, clear-eyed, plump and blond. But that image was already fading.

"Will you have cheese or pudding?"

"Cheese, please."

"I'll have the chocolate mousse. Yes, and cream."

No wonder he is so fat, she thought. Why does he stare so as the waiter pours the cream? His eyes are suddenly glistening with interest.

"And I think I'll have some cheese too. Waiter, cheese. And I trust Dorina is well?"

It was odd how tamely these names now came into their conversation. We should be faint with emotion, thought Mavis, but this is a kind of game. It is as if we are dealing with everything, making it safe and ordinary, and then setting it aside. Austin had already been perfunctorily dealt with. The whole past was being sadly folded up and put away. Was it for this that they had met?

Perhaps it was. Suddenly it occurred to her, I am no longer attractive; and then that was what it all meant.

"Dorina's very well. When Austin gets a job I expect they'll get together again."

"I expect so."

It was a mistake to meet like this, he thought. Eating and drinking are so gross. She has got fragments of biscuit all down the front of her dress. We ought to have met at nine o'clock in the morning on a bridge. After all, and though we hoped otherwise, something is utterly lost to us. How could it not be so? We surrendered each other bloodlessly without a fight. Our love was puny, not powerful enough to live on and be changed into anything which could nourish us now. We deserve this fiasco.

"And Tokyo must be a very interesting city too."

"Yes, fascinating."

There is nothing either in the world or out of it which is good without qualification, except a good will.

Bosh, thought Garth, eating baked beans on toast in a Lyons tea shop in the Tottenham Court Road.

Nothing was good without qualification. Will was just ropes and pulleys. Moral conceit was an aspect of mental health. Usefulness mattered, but only in the obvious sense. And not mattering, that mattered too.

He had kissed Dorina. That was important, but only in a momentary separated sort of way. It had no consequences nor even any implications. Had it been an innocent kiss? Yes. But was it her innocence or his which made it so?

179

Should he go and see Uncle Matthew? If he did it would be artificial and dramatic, the sort of thing he had intended henceforth to eschew. It would also be something important but of a different kind. It would have consequences. Did he after all want somebody's approval? Matthew's? Or somebody's love? Matthew's?

He had kissed Dorina. Did his father's marriage still exist and could it be salvaged? Was it any business of his?

In the restaurant in Soho where he washed up every night an out-of-work actor caller Trevor was making advances to him. Everyone employed there talked about sex the whole time. Garth hated sex. In America he had made experiments and felt ashamed and disgusted. Better to live alone. Why had he never discussed these things with Ludwig?

He was worried about his future and his state of mind. After the excitement of coming home he had felt a failure of energy. He had considered work which he might do and had discussed it with very busy people. The contingent details of choice disturbed him. Everything that was offered him was too particular, too hole and corner and accidental, not significant enough, though at the same time he realized with dazzling clarity that all decent things which human beings do are hole and corner. That was indeed, as he had told himself earlier, the point. But when it came to it he found he could not profit from his own wisdom and because his power had momentarily weakened he felt ordinary things like loneliness.

Meanwhile life was inconvenient, impecunious and tiring. He dashed about most of the day doing voluntary work and discussing jobs. At night he washed up and listened to filth. He had desired the freedom of having nothing to lose, no possessions, no ambitions, no hopes, but this did not feel like it. Into his mind and even into his plans were crowding other matters with which he had not reckoned and which he had proposed to do without. Concern for his father for instance. He had envisaged a cool duty but not this muddying anxiety. People occupied his thoughts and made him feel interest, even curiosity, even the possibility of resentment.

And there were odd compulsions such as this compulsive feeling he now had about going to see Uncle Matthew, as if this had to be done before anything else could happen. What did he want from Matthew? The idea of virtue is a fake-up, he thought, it's like God. When one understands that one can begin to live. Did he imagine he could explain it all to Matthew? Nothing could be more dangerous.

Matthew held in his hand something which was for him one of the most beautiful things in the world. It was a shallow Sung bowl with a design of peonies cut under the glaze. Its colour was a sort of milky ivory, what an angel might conceive of if asked to conceive of white. Its texture was something indescribable, a combination of softness, hardness, smoothness, depth and light.

He placed the bowl on the table next to a Ting cup in the shape of a chrysanthemum. The cup was paler, another unearthly shade, the colour of water, not as we ever see it but as God sees it.

His collection had arrived in several packing cases. He had unpacked some of the things. A history of his life, in a way. Old friends.

He and Mavis had parted almost resentfully. So much for that. I am not what I seemed to her, he thought, and doubtless she is not what she seemed to me, but it is our lot to be irrevocably condemned to seemings and to deserve them too. We were both, when it came to it, determined to be disappointed. We were mean with each other. What in a way saddened him most of all was the sense of having repelled her physically. This brought on a mood of regret for his youth which seemed, after many of his recent emotions, almost pure.

Mavis had been an objective, and now that she had somehow swept fruitlessly past him he felt the problem of what he was to do with himself even more keenly. He had come home because there was nothing else to do, he had come home because of Austin. But Austin was proving another blank. Meanwhile Matthew frequented his club and chatted politics with Charles Odmore and Geoffrey Arbuthnot.

He now felt his worldliness as a kind of galloping sickness. His unoccupied mind craved diversions, detective stories, television, gossip, drink. Once or twice he thought of telephoning Taigu. But Taigu hated the telephone and such a conversation would be merely upsetting, unkind, undignified, bad form. What could they say to each other by long-distance telephone call? Matthew did not want to lose face with Taigu by exhibiting bad form. Such miserable dignities were left to him. Perhaps he would end up writing his memoirs after all.

Austin preoccupied him, with a hopeless brooding anxiety which now concerned the past more than the future. He dreamed about Austin almost every night. He re-enacted the scene in the quarry. He dreamed about Betty. He dreamed about Dorina. He did not dream about Mavis. He avoided the Tisbournes. They seemed to make him quite automatically play a part which he found distasteful, that of the successful public man. They gave him cues, they egged him on to ever more playacting, they applauded. He would have quite liked to see Charlotte, and even felt he ought to, but kept putting it off. He would have quite liked to meet Ludwig Leferrier, but was afraid that if he tried to he would end up having tea *tête à tête* with Gracie. He would have quite liked to see Garth, but that was out of the question. He needed occupation, but not of the kind Charles Odmore kept proposing. He tinkered with the house. Now there was his collection to arrange. He had acquired a charwoman and a motor-car and an Irishman to cut the grass. He feared for himself.

Someone was ringing the front-door bell. Matthew was

in shirt sleeves. He could not find his jacket. After a moment or two he went to the door as he was. Austin was standing on the doorstep.

Matthew's immediate thought, in the midst of his emotion and his surprise, was how young and good-looking his brother still was, with the sun shining on his fair hair.

"Come in, Austin," said Matthew, as coolly as he could.

Behind Austin, also glowing in the morning sunshine, stood Matthew's new motor-car.

Austin followed him past the packing cases into the drawing-room, where on the table and on the mantelpiece vases and bowls stood about still wispy with straw.

"The famous collection," said Austin.

Matthew thought, he is a bit drunk. Dutch courage. "Yes. I haven't really got space for it here. I may lend some of it to a museum."

"You mean until you move into an even larger house?"

"Well, I—I really need some showcases—but they never look quite right in a house—it's a problem—I've never had it all together before——"

"What did you do with it when you were out there?"

"Oh it was stored in various places. I went on buying new stuff."

"A sort of compulsion I suppose, like drinking."

"I suppose so."

"I can't see it. Not one of my vices. But it seems pretty stupid to own it if you put it in a museum, doesn't it?"

Austin reached out and seized a *famille rose* vase and held it up frowning in front of his face. Instinctively Matthew stepped forward and took it from him.

They stared at each other. Then Austin laughed.

"Sorry," said Matthew. "Have a drink."

"I could always use a drink. Whisky, thanks. Neat, thanks. You won't? Yes, you even look like our father now that you're old. I think if that gentleman hadn't been so damned abstemious I might have been—well, what might I have been— Do you mind if I sit down?"

"I'm no abstainer," said Matthew, "only it's a little early. I'm glad to see you, Austin."

"Are you?"

"Yes. You know I am."

"I can't think why. Oh yes I can. So as you can thank God you aren't me."

"No, not only for that reason."

Austin laughed again. "That's nice. Not only for that reason. You're a caution. Well, you wanted to see me and here I am." Austin had sunk into a chair, his legs cocked over the arm. Matthew prowled, touching the china.

"So you decided to come and have a look at me after all."

"No. You're no oil painting, as my friend Mitzi would say. Do you know about my friend Mitzi? Oh yes, you've met her, haven't you. The twenty-stone Minerva with the heart of gold. She's not my mistress, by the way."

"I didn't suppose she was."

"Hang what you supposed. I came because—let me see, why did I come—because you asked me to and now that our father is in Abraham's bosom you are the head of the family, if there is a family."

Matthew felt cool now. He was glad that Austin had had a drink or two. A little craziness would help here. He was determined not to let this meeting fail in the way his meeting with Mavis had failed.

"Then let me enact the head of the family," said Matthew, "by asking you whether you've got a job yet."

"No, I haven't, and since we're on the subject I'm broke. Could you lend me some money?"

That's what he came for, Matthew thought. Of course. He felt exasperated and disappointed but still determined to keep Austin with him until—until what? What did he want, what seriousness could they possibly achieve? How, he now realized, his whole scene had changed since he reached England. Something had dwindled, some pure fire. Give Austin the money and let him go. Human beings are better off without pure fires. But it's what I need, thought Matthew, not what he needs, that makes this so important for me.

"Yes, of course," said Matthew. "I'll just find my cheque book." He began to ferret about in the desk.

"You despise me, don't you," said Austin behind him.

"No," said Matthew, still searching. He found the cheque book. He could keep Austin now until he wrote the cheque. He turned round and sat down. "Austin, can't we stop being enemies at last?"

"No."

"Can't we forgive each other—or rather can't you forgive me?"

"No."

"Please try," said Matthew. "As you said just now, I'm old—"

"That hurt, did it?"

"Please. I'm old and you're not young. And we're not just two acquaintances, we're part of each other. While this bitterness exists there's a part of each of us that is poisoned. Can't you feel the poison in yourself?"

"Yes," said Austin. "But there's only one way to cure that. And it isn't by forgiving you, as you rather mawkishly put it. What does that church language mean anyway? There isn't such a thing as forgiveness. It's a theological myth. You should know that, since you're such a religious expert."

Austin had abandoned his nonchalant posture, leaning forward now in the chair and staring at his brother. Matthew leaned forward too. It was as if they were playing chess. Outside, under the walnut tree, the Irishman was pushing the mower over the lawn.

"Never mind the word," said Matthew, "there are movements of the spirit which break down resentment, which let love and pity in—"

"I don't want your pity."

"I was thinking of yours."

"My pity for you? Don't make me light, Sir Matthew."

"I know you see me as a success," said Matthew, "but I'm not a success. Everyone has wounds which they hide and failures and humiliations which torment them. I want and I need to be at peace with you. How this thing grew up between us God knows—at any rate God if He existed would be the only one who could know, it's so damn complicated and so deep and so beyond the conscious

185

will of either of us. But never mind how it grew. We don't need to know that in order to make it cease. To make it cease is perhaps something oddly simple. There's that much good in the world, at any rate."

"I don't know that there is that much good in the world," said Austin. "And why do you imagine that I want you to be at peace with me? Why should your peace be an aim of mine? If you were at peace that would be your final triumph. That at least you shan't have while my will can prevent it."

"Your will can prevent it forever," said Matthew, "so you needn't feel any anxiety on that score. But why *choose* strife and unhappiness? Because this does make you unhappy, doesn't it?"

Austin after a moment's pause said softly, "Yes." Then he leaned back in his chair, still staring. He added, "But why should I want happiness more than anything else? You don't."

"I'm not sure about that," said Matthew. He wondered about it for a moment. Ease of spirit, absence of anxiety, absence of *fear*. These were the ingredients of happiness.

"Oh get on with it," said Austin. "Write the bloody cheque and let me go. I swallowed my pride and came here partly because I'm financially desperate and can't live on air and my girl friends any longer, and partly because I've realized I don't care a damn. I'm at the bottom, I don't care, I'm free, it just doesn't bloody matter any more. Can I have some more whisky?"

"Yes. Austin, listen. I have never purposely or willingly hurt you in my life."

"That's a lie. Please write the cheque before we start, ha ha, becoming emotional."

Matthew searched for his pen. He said, "Would a hundred pounds do you for the moment?" He had intended to offer a larger sum but he thought, let him come again.

"You're cunning," said Austin. "Keep little brother on a lead. Interview him every month. That's your idea, isn't it? You want to make me into your remittance man. And then you say you have no ill will towards me."

186

"I want to see you again."

"Oh come on, come on, give me the money, and make it two hundred while you're about it. I want to pay poor bloody Mitzi what I owe her, I've been borrowing from that poor cunt, excuse my French, that's what I've come to, Sir Matthew."

"I'll give you two hundred," said Matthew. "Austin, I beg you, just try to conceive that we might be friends. Why should we be the slaves of this sort of black magic? I'm harmless to you."

Austin got up and helped himself from the decanter. "I hear you've been seeing Mavis."

"I had lunch with Mavis. Don't worry. It wasn't a success. No need to get excited."

"I'm not excited. Just keep clear of Dorina, that's all. Leave *us* alone at least. I think I'd kill Dorina rather than let her have anything to do with you."

Matthew said, imitating Austin's quiet voice, "Well, that won't be necessary. In any case there isn't any harm I could possibly do to your marriage even if I tried."

"Not this one," said Austin. "I'll see to that."

"What do you mean, 'not this one'?"

"Don't pretend, because we haven't discussed it, that you don't know, and that you don't know I know!"

"Be careful, Austin."

"Be careful, be careful, nothing hasty, love and reconciling, anything but the truth, write the bloody cheque, will you."

"What are you talking about?"

"You know Betty committed suicide because of you."

Matthew sat at the desk and wrote the cheque. Pay Austin Gibson Grey the sum of two hundred pounds signed Matthew Gibson Grey. He said, "Austin, please keep some contact with reality. Betty's death was an accident."

"So we all said. But it wasn't, you know. Betty drowned herself."

"Austin," said Matthew, "keep a grip on yourself. And curb your spite before it drives you completely crazy. Betty didn't commit suicide. She couldn't have."

"How do you know? As you said yourself, everyone has wounds which they hide."

"I saw—" Matthew checked himself. "Betty wasn't a suicide, she wouldn't and couldn't have done it. And if she had, it certainly wouldn't and couldn't have been because of me."

"Why are you so sure?"

The door bell rang. "Excuse me," said Matthew. He handed the cheque to Austin and went out to the front door. The person on the doorstep this time was Garth.

Garth said, getting under way with what sounded like a prepared speech, "Uncle Matthew, you know who I am, I hope, and I trust you'll forgive me for taking this step of calling on you without ceremony. I thought of writing and I thought of telephoning, but—"

"Your father's here," said Matthew.

"Oh," said Garth, pressing his lips together. Then he said, "In that case perhaps—"

"Bring him in, bring him in," said Austin from behind.

"Come in," said Matthew.

Garth followed him into the drawing-room. As they came in Austin, who was holding the cheque, folded it in two and began tearing it up into little pieces. He screwed the pieces into a ball and laid the ball tenderly in one of the Chinese bowls.

"Hello, Father."

"Hello, Son. Touching meeting." Austin sat down. "I suppose you two have been chatting about the Absolute."

"I haven't seen Garth for years," said Matthew. "I hardly recognized him. Have a drink, Garth."

"No, thanks." Garth was looking round the room. "You've got a lot of things."

"Possessions, yes."

"Why do you call them that?"

"Well—they are—possessions."

Matthew looked at Austin, who met his eye with a look almost of complicity. Austin looked quite calm. How could he be so calm after all that emotion, after all those lies? Austin was relaxed, the put-upon spectator. He would sit out his son's visit. He would not tactfully make way

188

for Garth, leaving Garth behind to discuss Austin with Matthew. Meanwhile Garth was testing the atmosphere, wondering what to do. God, he's like his mother, thought Matthew, watching the thin frowning nervous face. Betty had been a bony untidy charmer with straggling black hair, but red-cheeked, with some gaiety. Betty was drowned in a deep lock on the river, her hair floated upon the water, it was an accident.

"Well?" said Austin. He smiled at Matthew. His consciousness at that moment was almost affectionate.

"Another time," said Matthew to Garth.

"Sorry," said Garth. "Sorry to butt in on your—your—Sorry."

Outside in the garden the Irishman was sitting underneath the walnut tree drinking orangeade out of a bottle.

Matthew felt as if some insect were clinging to him which he wanted to brush off against a hard surface. He would not let Austin drive Garth away like this. He would not let Austin win.

"I'm afraid I've got to go," said Matthew, looking at his watch, "at once. I've got an appointment." This was an invention.

Austin rose and they all three walked rather slowly to the front door, which Matthew opened. The boy is angry with me, he thought, and he felt pain. He very much wanted to speak to Garth, to touch him, but it was impossible. It is not my fault, but the boy is angry. They stood on the pavement. Austin was still smiling a spiteful defensive hurt smile.

Matthew said at random, "This is my new car."

For a second all three were blessed with an interest in something alien. The car was admired.

"One of those big jobs, eh, very nice."

"Excellent colour, that dark red."

"Automatic transmission. Do you miss the gears?"

"Very good for traffic."

"Splendid London car."

"Once you've had automatic transmission you can't be without it."

189

"Can I give either of you a lift?" said Matthew, wondering where he was going.

"Well, yes, thanks," said Austin.

"Where are you going?"

"Victoria."

"That's on the way. Garth?"

"I'll come for the ride. You can drop me at a tube station."

"Would you like to drive, Garth?" said Matthew as they moved to the car. He wanted to make some gesture to please the boy.

Garth hesitated. He touched the car. He obviously wanted very much to drive it. He said, "No, thanks."

Austin was peering in at the dashboard.

"Would you like to drive?" said Matthew to Austin.

"Yes, I would," said Austin, "if you don't want to."

"I don't mind. I'm not used to driving on the left yet, actually."

"Must feel odd."

"Don't know my London."

"Where are you going, Matthew?"

"The British Museum. I'll take over from you at Victoria."

"If you're going to the B.M. I'll come too," said Garth. Austin laughed.

They got into the car, Austin at the wheel, Matthew beside him and Garth in the back.

"Better get out of here by the back way, Austin, avoid the main road, right then left. No, left. Never mind, take the next turning. How are you getting on, Garth?"

"Fine."

"Glad to be back in England?"

"Yes."

"Found a job yet?"

"No."

"Austin, please don't drive so fast, Austin, *please*—"

Austin applied the brakes violently and the big car jerked, shrieked, bumped over something. Somebody screamed. Matthew, before his head struck the windscreen, had a vision of a little girl of about six in a pink dress running into the roadway after a ball. The car moved on quietly, stopped against the curb, half slewed across the road. Matthew held his head. He looked back. The little girl was lying on the tarmac. Austin was holding the wheel and staring straight ahead as if he were in a trance.

Garth got out and Matthew followed. He saw, very bright and clear, the dusty hot street, the child lying still with the sun shining on a bare arm, the texture of the pink dress, a trickle of blood increasing, a woman in an overall kneeling in the road. The woman was gasping, trying to scream with each gasp, trying, until someone stopped her, to lift up the child's head.

Garth said, "We must telephone, get an ambulance and police."

A number of people had collected and two other cars had stopped. It was a poorish street, a long wall with gates in it, several small terrace houses and a bomb site with a caravan. Garth said, "There's a telephone box—" Someone said, "I've already—" The sun shone on trickling blood and a pink dress and things from which Matthew averted his eyes. There was no doubt that the child was dead. Someone had picked up the ball and was holding it helplessly in his hand. The woman was swaying and choking, wailing raucously, her mouth wide open and dripping. A man who had come out from the caravan sat down on the pavement with his back against the wall.

Austin was standing behind Matthew. Garth was talking to a man at the telephone box. There was the sound of a siren in the distance. Matthew held his head with both hands. Something was blazing just above his eyes. He said to people standing nearby, "The child ran in front of the car."

"Yes, it wasn't your fault."

"Did you see it?"

"Yes, it wasn't their fault."

"The child ran out."

"The car was travelling too fast."

"Matthew," said Austin over Matthew's shoulder, "will you say that you were driving?"

"What?" said Matthew.

"Will you say that you were driving? You're sober. It wasn't our fault. No one can say that it was our fault. You're sober. Do you understand?"

Garth came back. "They've telephoned for everybody."

"Matthew, will you say that you were driving? Do you understand me?"

Someone had taken charge of the woman and led her back to the pavement. The child lay alone, no one near her now. The blood had made a sticky pool in the gutter. The woman sat on the curb, sobbing now. Two women, passersby, were crying too.

"My little girl, oh my little girl— It wasn't their fault. She ran out. It wasn't their fault. It was my fault, my fault—"

"Be quiet, Mary," said the man who was sitting against the wall.

Someone said, "Are you the child's parents?"

"Yes."

"My little girl, my darling, oh my darling—"

"I can't stand this," said someone.

"It wasn't their fault."

"The car was travelling too fast."

"But the child ran out."

"It could happen to anyone."

"Matthew," said Austin. "I'm not sober and you are. Will you please please say that you were driving? No one saw. It wasn't our fault, was it, it really wasn't our fault. Will you say that you were driving?"

"No, I'm sorry," said Matthew, "I can't." He went and sat down on the pavement with his back against the wall, near to the child's father. His head was on fire. Perhaps his skull was broken. If only that awful sobbing would stop.

Ambulance men were stooping over the poor remains in the road. The man who was holding the ball had put it down in the gutter where the blood had reached it. Austin, pale-faced and shuddering, was talking to the police. Matthew fainted.

Dearest Hester,

Have you heard the absolutely awful news? Austin Gibson Grey, driving Matthew's car, ran over a child and killed it. A little girl, about six, Matthew said. Isn't it *ghastly?* Apparently the child ran straight under the car, it wasn't Austin's fault. But how terrible, imagine it, I suppose it could happen to any of us. I just don't think I could live with myself after a thing like that, could you? Imagine facing the child's parents. An only child too apparently. I am so sorry for Austin—and one can't help feeling it *would* happen to him. Matthew got a nasty crack on the head hitting the windscreen and has been under the doctor. Oh dear, I can't think of anything but poor Austin, I must write to him, and I'm sure he'd be glad if you wrote too.

On brighter topics, we've fixed the wedding for August 18 after all, as Ludwig will be busy in Oxford from September, and I do hope you and Charles won't be abroad then. They've been offered a college house, which will solve the accommodation problem for the moment, but I do rather see them in the country. There are such lovely Cotswold houses near Oxford. Remember the lovely one Richard Pargeter bought after his second marriage and then they were divorced before the central heating had been installed? Is it true by the way that he's taking out Karen Arbuthnot? I should think he's old enough to be her father! Anyway, I rather fancy Gracie as the Lady of the Manor. It's nice to have a rich child!! Let me know when you'll be in town, I've found a new Italian restaurant, scruffy but delicious. Are you coming to the opening of Mollie's boutique?!

With love,
CLARA

P.S. When will Sebastian know about his exam? Do write to Austin. Isn't it *awful?*

Dear Patrick,

I send this by the hand of Williamson minor to say that no I will not see you this evening. After our talk at the pavilion, which I should have thought made the situation abundantly clear, it seems to me pointless to continue arguing. I know you want to because even argument with the beloved object is something gained. But for the beloved object himself it is just a bore. I am sorry that my reaction seemed to you to be, to use your own words, "mindlessly conventional." It is not, actually, convention but psychosomatic instinct which is in question. I enjoyed your company before your curious declaration because you seemed to me to possess an interesting mind. Now that you have, by your own volition, drawn my attention to your hair, eyes, nose, breath, complexion, patchy signs of incipient whisker, in short, and I use the word in a general sense, to your sex, I cannot feel the same unmixed interest which I felt when I conversed freely with what I could take to be an unembodied intelligence. Moreover, I now have no inclination to continue colloquies into which you have obviously entered, recently at any rate if not at first, with ulterior motives. Be man enough to see the point and get over this absurdity. And meanwhile keep out of the way and for Christ's sake keep your mouth shut and don't make spaniel's eyes at me in chapel. I presume you do not want to figure in my life merely as a pest. Excuse this rather peremptory manner, but I am older than you and know a good deal more of the world. In case it might help the healing process I may as well tell you that I am in love with a girl. And let us both shut up about this matter as from now. Sorry.

RALPH

My dear Ludwig,

Your mother and I have talked the matter over again with Mr. Livingstone and he thinks that your wisest course is to plead total conscientious objection. With our religious background, and with Mr. Livingstone's backing, which he promises to give, there is every chance that this would be allowed. What your legal situation would then be in relation to the draft I am not sure, and whether you would be required to do some other form of national service might depend on the view of your case taken by the tribunal. I am making further inquiries about this aspect of the matter, and also about what legal assistance we shall require to contract for. I am afraid it may be an expensive business, and possibly a lengthy one, and should be set in train *at once*. I suggest that you write to the military authorities, whose address I trust you have retained, *today,* and inform them that you have only just received the documents, that you propose to return to the United States forthwith, and that you are a total conscientious objector. (Do not use the word "pacifist" which has some unfortunate connotations.) Emphasize that your objections are "religious in origin." Mr. Livingstone thought that this would be a judicious phrase. If by any chance you have not retained the address of the military authorities, send me a cable and I will ascertain its details. It is important to get these right. Any suggestion of slovenliness on your part at this stage could give the wrong impression and damage your chances. Act please on this advice *today,* as delay could be most hazardous.

About what you term your engagement, your mother and I have mixed feelings. We want above all things your happiness, and we are sure that Miss Tisbourne is a charming girl. You are possibly a little young to consider marriage. Moreover your immediate future is, to say the least, uncertain. We are glad to know that you did not learn of the young lady's fortune before you courted her, though we are in any case aware that you are above any mercenary motive. We trust that she and her family knew of your initial ignorance of her circumstances. (When you say that "her family are very good," do you mean that they are "high society"?) As I say, we are concerned above all for your happiness and we beg you in this matter to make no definite plans for the present. The young lady looks very young, scarcely more than a schoolgirl, and this is not, as I am sure you will on reflection agree, the moment for you to take on the responsibility of a young wife. Also, and quite in general, your mother and I feel dismay at the prospect of your marrying an English girl. This is not a matter of racial prejudice, but of geography. You speak, it seems to us rather lightly, of our all being united "in Europe." Is this the wish of Miss Tisbourne and her family that you express here? As we have told you, your mother and I have no wish to uproot ourselves at our age and no inclination to return to part of the world which has for us only the unhappiest of associations. Please consider carefully what you feel to be your duty in this respect. You will in any case have to return to this country for some time to sort out your position in relation to the authorities. My advice is that you should explain the whole matter frankly to Miss Tisbourne, if you have not done so already, and explain that you cannot in the circumstances make any definite matrimonial plans. In the farther future, when you have made yourself right with the authorities, Miss Tisbourne and her family might be pleased to come over here and present themselves to us, and this would also be the occasion of a proof of the longevity of your mutual affections. Meanwhile please do not enter into any definite arrangement. You must also of course inform the Oxford College that you cannot at present take up your appointment with them. It is flattering that you should have obtained his honour. You might in the circumstances suggest to them a visit of a year's duration perhaps in several years' time. We are surprised in fact that the college should appoint you, having regard to your anomalous position in relation to the United States government. Possibly they are ignorant of it? It is, I need hardly tell you, your duty to inform them of it fully, and when you have done so there is little doubt but that they will advise you to return to your own country at once.

I am sorry to write in this vein and to consel so urgently

a severance from a life which I am sure is pleasant to you, but this is a matter of great seriousness. I cannot feel confident that you are entirely well informed about extradition, which is a nightmare to us. If you do not put yourself right now, the consequences to you will be lifelong. A delayed or irregular return will mean imprisonment under the harshest conditions from which you might emerge mentally and physically damaged and with loss of civic rights. The alternative is permanent exile. Consider what, with your whole life before you, you would be choosing. My son, do you really want to become an outlaw and an exile from the country which has given to us refuge, freedom, an end of wandering and fear, and to you the full status and being of an American? You have gained without effort or desert a privilege which millions, including your parents, have had to achieve by years of painful striving, and for which millions of oppressed people have yearned in vain. Ludwig, you are an American. Do not lightly throw this precious title away, but realize rather that it involves responsibilities and ties of a deep and lasting nature.

I say nothing here of your scruples and reasonings about the war. I trust profoundly that the compromise which we have suggested will be acceptable to you. Above all, you must act immediately. Your mother sends her fondest love and joins me in begging you to do as we suggest.

Your affectionate father,
J. P. H. Leferrier

My darling husband,

I have heard the terrible news of the accident. Mavis told me this afternoon. Do not be angry, I ran straight round to Miss Ricardo's house immediately, but you were not there and Miss Ricardo said she didn't know when you would be in. I would have left a note then, only I had no paper and I was so distressed. She said she would tell you I called. Do not be angry with me for going round, I felt I had to see you at once, I am so terribly upset, I have been crying ever since. Do not blame yourself, my darling, do not blame yourself at all. Mavis said the child ran straight in front of the car and no one, not the best driver in the world, could have avoided what happened. Oh do not be too grieved and unhappy and do not blame yourself for this awful thing. It was brought about by chance and not by you. I want to see you so much but will now wait for you to write to me. Oh let us meet soon, let us be together soon. This separation has been my fault and I weep for it and ask your forgiveness. Let us somehow be together again soon and keep all the world out as we used to do. Forgive me for going round to the house, it was all such a shock and I felt I had to see you. Write soon to your loving child, your wife,

D.

Dear Mrs. Monkley,

I write on behalf of my brother and myself to send our profoundest and most heartfelt sympathy to you and your husband on this irreparable loss. My brother, as the police agreed, very much thanks to your own generous and prompt evidence, was not to blame for the accident. However we cannot but feel a responsibility and a grief which will remain with us always at having been the instruments of this dreadful occurrence. We need your forgiveness for having unwittingly so altered your lives. I cannot find the words to express our sorrow at this thing, and our sense of having engendered, however innocently, a life-long responsibility. Our lives can never be the same now, any more than yours can. I hope you will forgive and accept, from both of us, this clumsy expression of our grief. It was kind of you to let me know the time of the funeral. I will certainly attend. My brother, whose work precludes his attendance, sends his profound condolences. I will, as I said on the telephone, hope to call on you and your husband a day or two after the funeral. If there is any help which my brother and I can give you in your bereavement we would esteem it a privilege to give it. Please excuse this clumsy letter. We are more wretched than words can express at what has happened. I will be at the funeral.

Yours sincerely,
MATTHEW GIBSON GREY

My dearest little girl,

Thank you so much for your sweet letter, which cheered me up a lot. Please *don't* come to Mitzi Ricardo's place. I'd rather you didn't come there. It's not a very nice place. I only wish I had a place that was worthy of you, Dorina. A palace with a great garden and I'd set you in the midst with fountains playing all round you. I will see you *soon*. I will write again when all this ghastly biz is over. I don't want you mixed up in it. It's such a mess, and I've got hundreds of things to do like going to the bloody funeral and seeing the parents and so on. The father is being rather awful about it all. Oh God I wish it hadn't happened. It was all because Matthew would insist on my driving and made us go round that back way. I am still in a state of shock and I am thinking of seeing a doctor. But don't let my darling girl worry about me. I am *all right* and I will survive and recover, I have had worse blows than this. Don't go away anywhere, will you, and don't come to Mitzi Ricardo's place again. We'll meet soon, I'll write, and yes we'll be together again before long and keep them all out. Look after yourself and keep yourself safe and secure for your loving husband,

AUSTIN

P.S. How did Mavis know about the accident? Did Matthew tell her?

Dearest Gracie,

So Austin has run over a little girl. Good for him. He has certainly maximized happiness in the Tisbourne family. Ma was incoherent with delight about it when she telephoned and I could just imagine her face, pulled into that false sadness with glee looking through. And don't tell me you don't feel exactly the same. I would be moderately bucked myself if I hadn't got other troubles. As it is, I wake up in the morning and feel at once that at least *something* nice has happened.

I have told my love. Ralph rejected me, not nastily but with a much more awful high-mindedness. And now he refuses to see me and has written me a disgusting missive.

199

I am sorry I wrote you a horrid letter by the way. Misery has made me benevolent, I can't at the moment see the point of being unpleasant to anybody, I am even nice to my housemaster. A matter on which you can help me: Ralph alleges he is in love with a girl. Who is she? Could you try to find out? You might ask Karen Arbuthnot, who knows everything.

I don't know what to do about Ralph, I am more in love than ever and feel utterly sick with it. I sweat and my hands tremble and I can't eat. Do you feel like this about your Ludwig? (Have you—by the way??) What restrains me from instant suicide is a tiny hope. Ralph's grand disgusting letter felt at first like a kick in the guts. But later on I thought that a longish letter, indeed a letter at all, was a sign of interest. What do you think? I may be deceiving myself. But there's just enough left of the sense of a game to be played to keep me out of the mad-house. I am not sure what I shall do. I am tempted to write twenty pages in reply. But possibly the wisest thing might be to answer laconically saying okay, and then wait for him to make a move! But will he? Supposing he just doesn't? Oh God. Anything rather than the end.

Your demented brother,

PATRICE DE LA TOUR DE TISBOURNE

P.S. Send me some cash, would you? God, to think how I buttered up that old lady, artlessly sending her gems from my stamp collection, all in vain!

Sebastian,

Thanks for seeing me again and congrats on passing your exam. If you imagine that your casual politeness will eventually quench my flame you have miscalculated. In fact you would be sorry if I stopped loving you. How much does your heart really ache for Gracie? I felt that your remarks last time were designed to annoy me (good sign) rather than to express your irreparably wounded feelings. You made a hearty luncheon, my darling. (And you let me pay again. You really are *super!*) I think, by the way, that Gracie and Ludwig have taken the plunge. This is just inference from Gracie's appearance. She doesn't confide in me any more. What a fool you were not to pull her into bed. She was dying to be forced.

I'm coming up again on Friday for the opening of Mama's ghastly boutique, and I'll be chez Ann Colindale as usual. Ann is lovesick too, we sigh by numbers. I am going to take a secretarial job in town. I am sick of living in a vicious circle of pig grub and pig shit down here. I haven't broken it to Pa yet, I'll ring you Wednes. Dins Fri? Much love, dear sweet beautiful Sebastian, from your, very much in love with you but putting a brave face on it,

KAREN

P.S. Did you hear that Austin Gibson Grey ran over a child? I am so sorry for that man. I think he is in love with Gracie, incidentally. What a planet.

Dear Mr. and Mrs. Leferrier,

You will know about me from Ludwig and how we are to be married. I am so happy and I love him very much and I am so much looking forward to meeting you both. I hope you will come to the wedding. He has shown me your pictures, the coloured ones with the maple trees and the black-and-white ones of the house with the veranda and your little dog, I am very sorry that he died lately. It is not very easy to write to people when you don't know them but I felt I so much wanted to say a word to you. I love your son so much, he is a marvellous man and I am sure we shall be very happy. I am certain that I shall do all that I can to be a good wife to him and to make him happy throughout his life as you would wish him to be. We are to have a College house in North Oxford. I am not sure if that is in the country or not, we are going to see it shortly, it is most exciting. I wish you could be here to come with us. But I hope you will be over soon, I so very much want to meet you. I enclose another photograph of myself, a rather better one, and photos of my parents and my brother, and a new photo of Ludwig which I persuaded him to have taken specially. It was quite difficult to persuade him, he is so modest! My parents both send their very warmest wishes and look forward to having you here as their guests. My mother will be writing to you again. Thank you for having such a wonderful son. I love him very much! See you soon I hope.

With my very best wishes,

Yours,

GRACE

My dear Austin,

I have written to the parents and I will attend the funeral. I have made your excuses for not attending, since you say you don't want to. My own ailments are better. I hope you are not filled with grief and I hope you are not blaming yourself. As far as I can see the accident was genuinely not your fault. You were not used to the car and I ought not to have let you drive it. It is fortunate indeed that the police did not test you for alcohol, as I fear that evidence would have gone against you. You have Mrs. Monkley's immediate self-accusations to thank for that escape, I think. I will go to see them after the funeral to see if there is any help I can give. It is indeed a terrible affair. But as I say, do not blame yourself. It was my suggestion that you should drive.

Concerning your extraordinary remarks about Betty perhaps it is better to say nothing. Except this: I know, and you must know, that what you said was so cannot have been so. If I knew you less well I would be more disturbed. Enough. I am glad that you came to see me. It is a great relief to feel that communication between us has been resumed. When this shadow has lifted a little I trust and believe that you will come again. And I hope that you will reconsider your decision about financial help. I can render it easily. I care about you very much.

Ever your loving brother,

MATTHEW

My dear Matthew,

How awful about the child. I am desperately sorry. I told Dorina at once of course and she rushed round to that place where Austin is staying. I am rather relieved that she didn't find him. She has written to him. I feel if they were to meet just now they would upset each other so much it might do some new kind of permanent damage. This seems almost like superstition. But I never knew two people so framed to do each other harm within the very context of their love. That they do greatly love each other is part of the paradox. Or is this all idiotic? I often tell myself I *ought not* to protect Dorina. Perhaps there is an old possessive instinct involved here. There is no doubt that she is afraid of Austin and her fear touches me and makes me afraid too.

I am sorry to talk about her when it is your terrible experience and Austin's which should be the main concern. Yes, one will be haunted always by this, it cannot be otherwise. Thank you very much for telephoning me about it. May I come with you to see the parents? It may seem presumptuous to say so, but in a way I am used to this sort of thing. (Though every case is special, of *course*.) May I come? I very much want, after that stupid luncheon, to see you again and talk properly. Matthew, thank you for telephoning, it was the right thing to do. Do not grieve too much. Ever, with love,

MAVIS

My dear Father,

Your letter has caused me much distress. I fear we are moving farther apart and it is becoming difficult even to argue. I cannot plead total conscientious objection since I do not, in my conscience, totally object to war. I think some wars are justified. I just happen to think that this one is not. I cannot, at a crucial moment in my life, and even to encompass a purpose which in itself is right (i.e. my not fighting) solemnly allege something which is not true. Nor do I conceive that you would wish me to do so. In fact the purpose is not separable (I think) as a worthy end if the means to it are false. My total attitude of rejection of this policy of the United States government is what must here be considered. And I am only (in my own eyes and I am sure in yours) likely to be thought just if I am honest all the way through. I think that to wage this sort of unbridled aggressive war upon a backward country in defense of some nebulous idea of containing communism

203

(which cannot in any case be contained by these methods) and in defiance of international agreements and the territorial integrity of the country concerned is a wicked action. To make millions of innocent people suffer terribly over years and years in this sort of way is wickedness. If ever one can see and identify and have the duty to denounce wickedness in a government it is here, and the fact that it is one's own government only makes the duty more urgent and indeed precious. I know I have said all this to you before, but please see this *passionate* sense of our government's wrongdoing behind my decision about my own life. For these reasons, and *not* because I totally object to warfare, I have decided not to fight this war, and I have decided, which is in many respects a harder decision, to give effect to my rejection of United States policy by staying in England. (There is no question of extradition. I have gone into this matter with the college lawyer.) That England is "pleasant" to me is, in relation to my choice, accidental. I am at an age where I have to choose my task in life. And I believe that my task is to be a scholar and not a politician. To return to the States in order to become a rather reluctant and inefficient "protester" would be a pointless sacrifice of my talents and of my true duty which I cannot feel called upon to make. And that, believe me, is the only alternative to the course which I have chosen. Please reflect on this and see what is good in this course, even if you disagree with some of my reasoning and some of my values. Also please see the decision as now firmly taken and finished. There is no going back. I take up my Oxford appointment in September. The college knows all about my position, I have explained it in detail to the Master and the governing body, they understand and they *approve*.

I am getting married on August 18. This too is a step upon which I have reflected deeply and about which I have no doubts. Gracie is young and she has not had an "academic" education, but she is very intelligent and shrewd. She is not a flibbertigibbet or a "deb." No, her parents are not "high society." I just meant, I think, that they are middle class people with a decent income and a nice home. I am not sure quite what I meant. You will like her and them very much. I hope by now you will have had her letter. Please please understand and forgive and consent to these new things in my life. I am twenty-two and I must make my decisions for myself, however painful it is to be at odds with you and with my mother. I hope, and indeed know, that you have always found me in the past an affectionate and dutiful son, and such you will find me in all essentials always. Please consent to my proceedings and give me your blessing. I very much hope that you will come to the wedding. Gracie (or as I suppose I must get used to saying, Gracie and I) will most gladly pay your fare. With deepest respect and love to you both,

Your son,
LUDWIG

My dear Matthew,

I learnt of the accident and of your indisposition with the greatest sympathy. Please convey my sympathy to Austin too. It must be dreadful to be, however innocently, the instrument of bringing such awful unhappiness into the lives of others. It gives one a terrible sense of mortality and makes one feel how we are all, in respect of the inevitability of sorrow and death, "members one of another."

I saw you, and was sorry not to talk to you, at Clara's party. I expect you know (well, now I come to think of it there is no reason why you should) that I am renting Austin's flat for the moment. I would be very glad to see you there (or indeed anywhere) at any time. You will know of recent sad changes in my life. I feel that I am growing old, I feel lonely and in need of the support of old friends, in which (in my case) rather small battalion I certainly count you.

With affectionate regards and best wishes,

CHARLOTTE

Dear Mr. Secombe-Hughes,

I am sorry not to have been to the office for the last few days, you will understand why this is. Also, a friend of mine had an awful accident and I have had to help. I feel

205

bad about last time, and I must have seemed unsympathetic and ungrateful, especially about the poem. I would like to read it if you translate it into English ever. And I was touched about your mother's shawl. The fact is I have been worried about personal things and you did take me by surprise and that made me want to run away because I didn't know how I ought to talk to you about it. I very much hope you will see your way to paying me what you owe me if the business is sold. I enclose the IOUs and you will see there is quite a bit owing. My friend who had the accident still needs me for some days but after that I will come to the studio. I hope very much that you will settle up with me as requested in the time between, sending some of the money anyway. I hope you will excuse me for writing so openly to you, and understand about the other time. Respectfully, with good wishes,

Yours truly,
M. RICARDO

Dear Ralph, Okay, have it your way.

Good-bye.
PATRICK

Dear Mr. Gibson Grey,

You got off easy. Driving under the influence and not used to the car. I saw you were under the influence at once, and if that policeman hadn't been a clot he'd have had you for it, and if my wife had kept her trap shut. We could have had a lot of damages out of you and you could have been in a lot of trouble. You took our little girl away from us. You were only thinking of your own skin, weren't you, when you were talking to the police, I could see that your knees were knocking together and when you saw you'd got off scot bloody free you looked that pleased, I wanted to wipe the look off your kisser. Well, maybe you've noticed that a letter from *Sir Matthew* has been lifted from your table. By me. I went round to your place and your big girl friend obligingly showed me into your room and there was the letter lying open, which I took the liberty of pocketing! How's that for evidence? You could face a stretch, you know, and your brother would have to give evidence against you, he'd have to, if the police had that letter, so he'd be for it too, he said nothing like that when they asked him questions, he'd be up for perjury. Think of yourself doing bird and your grand brother with the title in the next cell! Well, I don't want to put you in quod or make trouble, all I need is money, and I'm reasonable too. See? I'll call on you about it. That letter's in the bank, so it's no good running round here. My wife knows nothing about this, and if you know what's good for you you'll leave her out of it. She's got enough trouble, after your drunken driving. You got off easy, and if you've got any sense you'll see it stays that way. I'll call about terms. You're lucky I'm reasonable, someone else might have been vindictive.

Yours truly,
NORMAN MONKLEY

The waste land where the caravan stood was covered with thin grasses which had grown quite tall and been dried by the sun into a wispy patchy yellow. Their blanched dryness expressed desolation to Mavis as she sat on one of the divans and looked out of the window. She expected to see scattered bones. The humpy shadow of the caravan fell across the pallid parched expanse. Traffic rumbled and the air was hazy with dust and the terrible ennui of a hot London afternoon.

Mrs. Monkley had set out tea, with her best matching cups and enamelled souvenir spoons. The caravan was tiny and depressingly neat. There were two divans and a fitted table and a television set and a little sideboard with a lace cloth and a budgerigar in a very small cage. Mr. and Mrs. Monkley seemed small too, as if they had been made with the fittings. Perhaps they were simply used to moving their bodies in this space. Matthew, sitting on the opposite divan, seemed huge and had already knocked over a brass ornament and a sugar bowl without seeming to notice. Mavis shrank into herself, feeling wizened by a stale misery which had little to do with Mr. and Mrs. Monkley's bereavement.

Matthew had just handed to Mrs. Monkley an envelope which Mavis assumed contained money. Mrs. Monkley handed it quickly to her husband, who put it away with a reverent air as if it were a holy relic. What sum of money did the envelope contain and how had Matthew decided on the figure? Matthew had adopted a soft and fluent way of speaking which was quite unlike his usual utterance.

He seemed to her like an elderly snake charmer whom she had seen once on a visit to the pyramids. He and Mrs. Monkley did most of the talking. They understood each other, responding in a sort of quiet litany. Matthew was charming Mrs. Monkley. He had taken charge of the scene. After all Mavis was unnecessary, worse than useless. Mavis looked out of the window at the blanched grass and knew that she was soon going to start to cry and would not be able to stop. She would cry for herself and for her wasted life, and for all wasted and desolate lives. The child's death in itself seemed to have little meaning. It was a tiny kernel in the midst of all this misery, tiny and almost pretty like the ridiculous enamelled spoons.

Mrs. Monkley kept blaming herself, even blaming the child. Sometimes it sounded as if she were asking Matthew's pardon. And Matthew spoke as if it was he who had occasioned the whole thing. Austin was not mentioned, not out of delicacy but as if he had been forgotten. Mavis kept seeing the running child in her mind's eye. Mrs. Monkley had been showing the family photograph album. Mavis had dreamed about a child being run over, only the child in her dream had been Dorina. At the funeral Mavis had walked beside Matthew, silently, with the quiet possessiveness of a blood relation. But they had not spoken to each other, only smiled at parting, their smiles flowering sadly. Austin had not been present. Nor, of course, had Dorina.

"It was a beautiful funeral," Mrs. Monkley was saying, "a beautiful service. Her coffin looked so tiny, didn't it, I wouldn't have believed she was in it if I hadn't seen her with my own eyes lying there before, you know. The men wanted me to go outside but I wouldn't. Going away and leaving here there in the cemetery was so strange, as if it were wrong to leave her all alone at last, that was what somehow made me feel most of all that she'd gone, when we all went away together and left her there alone. And there'll be days and months and years that will pass by now and she'll be there in the one place always. And at night I'll think of her, when it rains and the wind blows, and think how she's there all alone at last."

Mrs. Monkley was possessed, as all truly bereaved people are posessed, by the soul of the departed. She could speak of nothing else and could ease her pain in no other way. She and Matthew had been talking for an hour. She had shown him the photographs, the school reports, the toys. Mrs. Monkley spoke in a tearful voice, but had control of herself. Mavis felt like screaming, seeing the scene with a strange precision, and yet it was full of gaps, of whitenesses. Perhaps I am going to faint, thought Mavis, it is so hot and airless here. She saw Mrs. Monkley's blue eyes staring with the effort of remaining tearless. She saw Mr. Monkley's brown moustache and the many soft rubbery wrinkles on his brow. She saw Matthew's round brown eyes and the frown of concentration and solicitude which he wore all the time, his face puckered with the anxiety of letting Mrs. Monkley talk and of interrupting her at exactly the right moment with exactly the right words.

"It was sad too to see the flowers lying there," said Mrs. Monkley, "she wouldn't have liked that, to see the flowers lying there dying, not in water like, it would have been distasteful. Yet I couldn't really take them away, could I. When we'd buy flowers sometimes she'd want to hurry home to give them a drink. Perhaps it was some kind of prophecy like, she always knew about death somehow and would ask about it, so unlike a child. She'd ask about Arthur, that's our budgie, when he'd die and how old budgies lived to, and I'd never tell her and then Norman told her one day and she cried because she thought poor Arthur would die before she did, and now she's in her grave and Arthur's alive still. She loved that bird, she used to dream we'd gone away and forgotten and left him to die, and then she'd be crying again, how that child could cry, she'd cry just for the pity of things, she was that tender. She never let us kill an insect but she'd catch it in a jam jar and let it free outside. She was always on about death, she asked and asked about it when her grandma died, we didn't let her see the body of course. I said it was just falling asleep and waking up with God. But I can't find it in my heart now to believe she is with God.

I can't think she's anywhere, any more, that's what's so funny. It leaves such a gap in your heart. And the worst is I keep forgetting she's gone, every morning when I wake up I have to remember it all over again, and all through our lives she'll be somehow not there, and we'll think now she might be leaving school, now she might be getting married, now she might be having little children of her own. And she won't be there at all. I suppose life is a matter of getting used to more and more awful things, but I can't think I'll ever get used to this. Every morning when I wake up I think she's still alive. I can't think she's with God. She doesn't exist any more anywhere. That's what's so funny, isn't it."

"All human lives are short," said Matthew. "We all look forward into a mystery and we die soon. She had a happy life and never suffered even at the end. Remember her happiness."

He is putting words together, thought Mavis. What she says is true, what he says is false. It is not his fault. A real experience of death isolates one absolutely. The bereaved cannot communicate with the unbereaved. Only one is not bereaved for long.

She recalled her own mother's death, the long tangles of golden hair, the pillow wet with tears. Her mother had cried herself to sleep. Mavis, a child, had felt engulfed in a blackness which it seemed could never end. Yet soon she had felt trivial worries, trivial joys. We are soon faithless to the dead. About her father's death she had been stoical for Dorina's sake.

"I can't quite believe it somehow," said Mrs. Monkley, "it's all so recent as if we could still put the clock back and make it not to be. It hasn't had time to become real yet like real things in the past. There's the little dress I was making for her, there's the picture she painted at school and brought home to show us. I wish I could believe in a life beyond the grave. It would comfort me to feel that she was with her father and that he'd meet her there when she felt all strange and new and take her by the hand and lead her to Our Lord like I thought it might

211

be once when we died and met our dear ones beyond the grave."

"Her—father?" said Matthew, glancing at Mr. Monkley.

"Oh yes, she's not his child," said Mrs. Monkley. "Her poor father died and Mr. Monkley is my second husband."

"I am her father in the spirit, you know," said Mr. Monkley, and patted his eyes.

"Quite," said Matthew.

"I think we must go," said Mavis. "It's been very good of you to see us and give us tea. And I hope you'll think of us as friends, and if we can ever help in any way—"

"We appreciate that," said Mr. Monkley, "and we'll do just that, won't we, Mother?"

"But I'm not a mother any more," said Mrs. Monkley.

"You may have another child," said Mavis.

"I've had my womb removed," said Mrs. Monkley, "it got diseased, you see."

"We must go," said Mavis.

Matthew got off the divan, toppling a plate of cakes onto the floor. Mrs. Monkley had felt it necessary to set out a massive high tea, which had remained almost entirely untouched. Mavis had destroyed two sandwiches, mainly with her fingers. She and Mr. Monkley now picked up the cakes. Matthew and Mrs. Monkley seemed not to have noticed. Mr. Monkley's moustache somehow edged them to the door and escorted them out. A hot dry wind was blowing outside. Three steep steps led them down into the dusty prickly dry grass which poked Mavis's ankles and tickled her knees. A long "oooh" came from within the caravan. Mrs. Monkley had started to cry, at last.

"Good-bye."

"Good-bye."

"You'll be good friends to us, I know," said Mr. Monkley, "to me and to Mother, we appreciate it, we appreciate your visit and your kind recognition of our loss."

Mavis and Matthew walked across the bumpy ground to the road, hurrying discreetly so as to get out of sight. A taxi appeared and without a word Matthew hustled Mavis into it. He gave the address of the Villa. They sank back into the soft gloom of the interior.

Mavis felt that her face had suddenly become all hot and wet, dissolved into tears. With a kind of frantic haste she and Matthew began to embrace each other, lips seeking lips in a frenzy of sudden need. She struggled to adjust herself against his bulk, dropping her handbag, a shoe coming off, as he clumsily clutched her and kissed her again and again. And now as her tears flowed she felt, mingled with the liveness of her body, a pure sensation which she had not in many many years experienced, the sensation of intense fierce undiluted happiness.

Norman Monkley and Austin were sitting in Austin's bedroom. It was ten o'clock in the morning. Norman sat on the bed. Austin sat on the chair. There was not much space. They conversed in low voices.

"I've told you I haven't any money," said Austin. "What's the use of going on at me in this way? I'm very sorry for what happened. But it wasn't my fault, your wife said so. And I wasn't drunk."

"You was, you know," said Norman. "Got any cigs here? Well, mind if I roll my own? Have one, they're not bad."

"No, thanks. And anyway as the police didn't test me then the thing is closed. You don't understand the law. That letter of my brother's which you stole isn't evidence of anything except that you're a bloody thief. I deny that I was drunk and no one could prove the contrary, the whole thing's closed, finished, over."

"My little girl is closed and finished and over," said Norman, "but not this business, it's only just beginning.

There's no great hurry. But money I'll have, and regular, otherwise trouble."

"Mr. Monkley—"

"Call me Norman. We'll be seeing a lot of each other."

"Get out," said Austin softly. He gripped the edge of the flimsy counterpane, feeling cold fear. Behind the figure of Norman rolling his cigarette there opened a terrible landscape, a premonition of living death. He was not sure whether or not that letter could be used as evidence against him and there was no one he could ask. Matthew had done for him again.

"I'll go when I'm ready, don't take on. As I said, I'm a reasonable chap. I've had a terrible loss and I want some compensation for it. That's fair, isn't it. Fair's fair. You can't give me and my wife our little girl back but you can give us money. Money's not much but it's something. And buying things always consoles a woman. Look at it in a human way. And don't be so frightened, you look sick with fright, you'll be vomiting in the basin in a minute. No need to be so frightened of poor old Norman. Norman's a nice chap really."

"I'm not frightened," said Austin. "I'm angry."

"Yes, yes, your teeth are chattering with anger. Don't let's argue. Suppose you just give me twenty pounds now on account and then when we've both thought it over we'll fix a nice round sum to be paid every month, in memory of my little girl, think of it that way. I don't want to be nasty. I won't ask more than you can easily give, I'm not a fool. I know you're not a big man. We could be friends, you know. You ought to want that after what you've done. Now what about twenty pounds?"

"I haven't got twenty pounds!" said Austin.

"You can get it," said Norman. "A chap like me couldn't, but a chap like you always can. You could borrow it from your brother, he's a Sir and he's stinking rich, I know that much."

"You're dreaming," said Austin. "You have no power over me. That letter you stole proves nothing. Now please go away. Please."

"If you want to try it out in court of course, then it's

214

up to you," said Norman. "But if you think about it a bit you'll decide not to. Your brother would tell the truth, in court. I know a bit about him, he's religious. I've been studying your family since we sort of ran into each other. If it comes to it, he won't protect you. He won't disown his letter. He'll tell the truth. And then you'll be for the high jump. You could get a cool ten years for manslaughter. And the tough lads inside don't like child-killers either."

"That's not true, I couldn't be sent to prison!" said Austin. Could he be? Would Matthew testify against him?

"Or may be I might drop round and talk it over with him."

"With who?"

"With your brother."

"You leave my brother alone! You wouldn't get any change out of him, anyway."

"Wouldn't I? Not to help little Austin?"

"Stop, you don't understand—"

"I do though," said Norman. "And what I don't understand now I will soon. You've got a fellow traveller. You and your brother interest me. I'll work it all out. I'm a bit of a psychologist really. I've written a psychological novel. I'll bring it round next time I come, you might like to read it. And your brother might help me find a publisher. He's a book-writer himself, isn't he?"

"I will not read your novel," said Austin. "I will not see you again. Get out."

"If you'd rather I dealt direct with your brother—"

"I said get out."

"Don't start screaming. I'm not going without some money. I'm in no hurry. I can wait while you go and get it." Norman turned lazily about and stretched himself out on the bed.

Austin stared at Norman's rather dirty suède shoes. Then he closed his eyes. He said to himself, don't scream, think. Get rid of this swine somehow and then— "Listen," said Austin, "you said you were a reasonable man. If I give you five pounds now, will you go away? I'll raise some more in the next few days. I'm broke and I can't

215

produce money just like that. Please accept a fiver and go and I promise I'll raise some more."

"All right," said Norman, after a judicious silence. "You see how decent I am really. I'll accept a fiver now and some more in a few days. I meant it about being friends, something like this is a real bond. You will read my novel, though, won't you?"

"Yes," said Austin.

"And discuss it with me?"

"Yes," said Austin.

"Good. Now where's the fiver?"

"Wait a minute," said Austin. He went out of his bedroom and stood upon the dark landing. Run out of the house, and run and run and run? He walked slowly down the stairs. The stairs smelt of dust and despair and mice and old old cooking.

He went into Mitzi's sitting-room. Mitzi was there, dressed in a tattered pink negligee, a little too small for her. She pulled it together with a coy movement. "You might knock!"

"Mitzi darling," said Austin. "Will you lend me five pounds?"

"I can't, dear," said Mitzi, "I really can't. I've got to stop lending. I haven't a sou until old Secombe-Hughes coughs up. Very sorry and all that. Please don't be cross."

Austin left the room. He caught a last glimpse of Mitzi's large breasts bulging out above her brassiere, wisply veiled by the negligee. Outside on the chest on the landing lay Mitzi's handbag. Austin opened it. It contained a five-pound note, a one-pound note, and some silver. Austin took the five-pound note and closed the bag again. He mounted the stairs.

"Here you are," he said to Norman, who was still reposing. "Now go."

"I thought you'd cut and run," said Norman. "Thanks. Now I've been thinking—"

Austin took Norman by the shoulders and pulled him gently to his feet. Still holding him he stared into his face. Norman had greasy brown hair and a longish brown moustache and a dimpled chin. He had large sentimental

216

brown eyes. Austin patted Norman's cheek. "Run along, Norman, there's a good boy."

"We are friends, aren't we?" said Norman.

"Yes, sure."

"I'll come again Tuesday evening, I'll bring my novel, okay?"

"Okay. Run along now."

As Norman's steps receded and the front door banged Austin came slowly down the stairs. The door of Mitzi's setting-room was open.

"Austin. Did you take a fiver out of my bag?"

"Yes."

Mitzi was sitting now on her sofa, legs wide apart. She was not looking at him. Two huge tears like drops of mercury emerged slow and glistening from her eyes. Austin came over to her. He drew her knees together with his hand. Then very carefully he sat down on them and rolled her over sideways on the settee and nestled his head against the large bosom. Mitzi sobbed, then sighed.

❦❦❦❦

"I like flies more than spiders," said Gracie. She drew her fingers through a spider's web in the corner of the empty room. "You can see flies washing their hands. It makes them so much more like us."

"Poppy dear, I want you to come and have supper at my place," said Ludwig.

"Why?"

"Just because it *is* my place. A man must have a base of his own. I want to be the boss, I mean the host, just this once. I want to cook you an omelette. Why won't you come?"

"You know why, Ludwig."

"You needn't see Austin."

"That big girl frightens me."

"Poppy, you're being silly." Gracie had somehow in the last few weeks become Poppy. She had been Poppet and Moppet, then Poppy. She would be Poppy now forever. It was nice that she had a special private name at last, though it was not a name that he liked except here. He was still "Ludwig." That was part of Gracie's curious little formality with him. He was scarcely ever even "darling" these days. But they were yet closer than before. She would be his Poppy, he had a Poppy, until the end of time.

Meanwhile the day of their marriage shimmered in front of him like a triumphal archway. They would pass through it into privacy and silence. The anxious happy pain of their present relationship would be no more. They would be unimaginably different and quieter with each other. They would not be together all the time. Married people were not. Now each day was still a delightful invention. When Gracie's parents were away they made love. This often happened now, though whether by arrangement Ludwig did not ask. He and Gracie were still shy lovers. They had no words for things that happened or might happen. Ludwig was drunk with this guiltless bliss. Their very shyness graced their proceedings with a sort of innocent radiance which made him realize how much before he had always felt ashamed of love-making. So he lived now with Gracie in that strange lurid anxious light of passion and innocence and felt as pure and as frightened as if he had been chosen to be sacrificed to a deity in whom he most profoundly believed.

In fact as time went on there were intervals. Ludwig had been engaged just long enough to feel the return of a sense of self-preservation which the uncertainty of a precarious love can temporarily banish even from selfish people. He stopped taking Gracie to the British Museum. It was impossible to explain to her who the Assyrians were nor did she really want to know. Exhausted with happi-

218

ness, he needed the cool touch of the impersonal. Visiting the place by himself he felt in the oblivion of personality with which the great things quietly overwhelmed him a sense of relief. Nor did he feel guilt at this. He had to *be* the person whom she admired, and this must involve these breaks in his consciousness of her which were after all no treason. To have a goddess living in one's heart was not always to be busy at devotions.

Ludwig had still not yet met Matthew. This was not entirely an accident. There had been possible occasions, but Ludwig had lightly shunned them, although Gracie kept repeating how much she wanted them to meet. "I do so want to see you two dear things together," she said to Ludwig, who was quietly annoyed. That Gracie "adored" Matthew was a sort of bird cry of what Ludwig now reluctantly thought of as her "set." One day he realized that the cry was set going largely by Gracie. It was a part of Gracie's image of herself that she "adored" Matthew. Of course, this was harmless but it somehow depressed Ludwig and made him conscious of something which he usually ignored, his own vanity. Like many scholars and artists Ludwig was able to combine profound modesty in his work with a considerable degree of self-satisfaction.

Matthew was much talked about in the "set," not always with respect. "Matthew the Hoax of Hong Kong" he was called by Sebastian, whom Ludwig had lately met at one or two rather screamy parties. And Karen, whom Ludwig had not yet encountered, appearently referred to him as Matthias Menuhin, which was supposed to be a joke, meaning that he was a great fiddler. Ludwig had early on made up his own mind, on little evidence, about Matthew. It was in this context that he was made aware of his own good opinion of himself. Sebastian was interesting and clever. So was Oliver, so were many other people whom he encountered in the environs of the Tisbourne household. But they caused him little anxiety because he did not feel about any of them that they were in his class. With Matthew, this might prove to be a different matter. And that Matthew was nearly three times his age was something which his instincts found curiously irrelevant. If Matthew were not a carefully cultivated ally he might prove to be a poisonous and formidable foe. Ludwig put off discovering which it was to be.

His parents had not yet replied to his last letter. It was no use telephoning. He and his father could not communicate by telephone. The impulse to go to them, to embrace them, to explain, returned to him constantly and freshly, succeeded by the remembrance that now he could not go, he could never go, to them. Gradually he began to feel more resigned to the possibility that they would not bless his wedding day. His task were to get married, to get settled, to work, and only after that would he be able to win over his parents. If only they would forgive and accept him he would be completely fulfilled and happy. Of this he felt sure, although there was always something else in the picture, a little speck of unaccounted-for pain floating before the eyes and never quite brought into focus.

He could not really discuss it with Gracie. Part of the difficulty was that Gracie had no concept of America. She regarded it as a far-off barbarous country which was no concern of hers or, any more, of his. Could one be indifferent to something so large? Apparently. Gracie professed optimism about his parents, though he knew that she was secretly anxious and looked out every day for their reply to her letter. But her anxiety was personal and simple. She saw his parents, as she saw Oxford and the Parthenon Frieze and the Ancient World, as extensions of Ludwig, and that was as far, across the waves of the Atlantic, as she could discern. So Ludwig's thoughts about honour were private thoughts, and he sought wisdom from an Athena who was not Gracie, and certainly not the problematic idea of his native land. Who after all was America? A freedom fighter, a slut, a demon, a Daughter of the Revolution? What now was he to her or she to him; and what was this speck of anguish which floated constantly before him? He would fix his eyes instead upon the grey-eyed one, the pure one. This henceforth must be the religion of his solitude.

Of Garth Ludwig had seen little. Garth had now got

some sort of job which Mavis Argyll had arranged for him at a semireligious "mission" in the East End. He was regarded by Gracie and her friends as a "drop-out" in a sense which implied "a failure." There was among these young people no tendency to idolize a pointless rejection of society. Ludwig, who had at first thought them worldly, now increasingly saw their point. He felt in any case less impressed by Garth. Garth was so evidently not "going anywhere," whereas Ludwig was, even Sebastian was. This sense of Garth's pointlessness was increased for Ludwig by Garth's own gloom. Doubtless he was depressed in a simple way by his surroundings and the dullness of his work. But someone like Garth had no right to be depressed. At Harvard he had spoken with glittering eyes of the freedom which comes to the truly destitute. There was no air of triumph now. Moreover it seemed to Ludwig that Garth only called on him in order to deliver a sermon, to tell him that he ought to look after Austin, or that Gracie ought to look after Charlotte. Garth had questioned Ludwig quite adroitly once about his own problems but Ludwig had answered evasively and Garth had gone away abruptly with a wave of the hand. There is a great force in him, thought Ludwig, a great fire, but all the same he will waste himself.

As Garth faded, Oxford became more real, not a dream place of the future but a real city with libraries and shops and pubs. Gracie and Ludwig were in fact at this very moment in Oxford, standing in an empty upstairs room of a house in Rawlinson Road, in a flat which the college were going to let them have for a small rent. They were to have the big upstairs half of a red brick Victorian house. Downstairs lived a friendly elderly lady, a Miss Thorrington, who had been a pioneer of women's education and who had talked to Ludwig about Socrates. Outside the window, through which Gracie and Ludwig were now gazing, lay a small neat garden with a square of lawn and red walls to match the house and two cherry trees which Miss Thorrington said were a glory in the spring-time. Beyond were more trees, other gardens, other houses. It's all so particular and cosy and small, thought Ludwig, with

a weird alarm. Must he then begin his married life surrounded by cherry trees, mossy brick paths, windows of
a certain size and shape? These definitions seemed too tiny
for the world in which he had dreamed he would live with
Gracie. But the little particularity and accident of it all
was, it seemed, just what Gracie liked best, and her delight delighted him. Gracie loved everything—the coloured
tiles in the sitting-room, the stained-glass window on the
stairs, the rockery in the front garden, the way the gate
fastened, Miss Thorrington's cat.

Last night, under the wing of Andrew Hilton, they had
actually dined in college at the High Table. Gracie had
said beforehand that she was terrified and would be able
to say nothing. She sat next to the Master and chattered
without stopping throughout the meal. She and the Master
never seemed to stop laughing. She got on well too, in
a joky English way, with Andrew Hilton and with several
of the other fellows including the philosopher MacMurraghue. At a later stage of the evening, while Ludwig and
Andrew were arguing about triremes, Ludwig heard Gracie
and MacMurraghue passionately discussing how to get
wine stains out of tablecloths. When at last Ludwig saw
Gracie to her hotel she said to him, "I think I shall like
Oxford just as much as you will." He rejoiced. He then
returned chastely to college and drank another bottle of
wine with Andrew. They decided to give a joint class on
Aristophanes in the Michaelmas term, a prospect which
filled Ludwig with heady enthusiasm. Andrew then wrote
some very funny improper Latin verses. Ludwig could not
remember going to bed and woke up with a hangover.

Now as he looked down on the gardeny suburban scene
through the dusty window pane he thought *Oxford, Oxford*. Here his mind would live and grow in quietness and
in truth. And for a moment he felt almost faint with a
sort of physical pleasure which had nothing to do with his
pretty fiancée.

"Supposing, to save your life," said Gracie, "you had
to hold onto a trapeze with your teeth, do you think you
could do it?"

222

"No," said Ludwig. "Whatever put that into your head, Poppy?"

"I was discussing it with MacMurraghue at dinner. In fact one's back teeth are awfully strong, and if—"

"Darling Poppy! Look, darling, you will come to my place, won't you, just to say hello to poor Austin?"

"You said I needn't."

"I keep thinking about that child who was killed. I feel so sorry for Austin. If you just smiled at him it would help. So little for you, so much for him."

"Do you rate my smiles so cheaply?"

"Darling, you know I—"

"Ludwig, we'll never have rows, will we, like other married couples do, never, never?"

"Never."

"Austin's unlucky. I fear unlucky people. It's contagious."

"We ought to share our happiness, Poppy."

"No, I'm afraid. That's a very dangerous idea, Ludwig. Our happiness is not a great sum which we've got and can give. It's just a dream. We haven't achieved it. We don't deserve it yet. I have nothing for anybody else. I just want to seize you and hold you. The generous years may come later. If there is any later."

The dusty floorboards converged on a window framing cherry-leaved vistas of brick houses. The neat trapped garden was sweet and desolate with ordinariness. Such indeed, if one was lucky, was life. They would lie in bed and see the cherry trees in flower. She was right to fear the gods.

"We'll be happy here," said Ludwig. They moved into the next room.

"And *this,*" said Gracie, "shall be the nursery. Miss Thorrington will baby sit. I've already asked her."

There was a strange hazy look in her eyes. Oh God, thought Ludwig, perhaps she's pregnant already!

Dorina sat surrounded by her judges. She fought back tears. Garth was smiling at her with a smile which she could not understand. There was no complicity in his smile however. It was meant simply to help her. It was not meant to remind her that he had kissed her. Although they were both conscious of that too.

Clara was ending a rather long speech. "So as I see it, my dear, you can do no harm and only good if you come and stay with us. George entirely agrees and joins me in inviting you. Austin can come and see you there. We'll look after you. We'll sort of chaperone you. You can go out with Austin and then come back and stay with us, you can do whatever you like and feel protected. You'll be like our daughter and Austin can come and court you! Don't you agree, Mavis? Mavis and I have talked it over, we've all talked it over."

"It's the first I've heard of it," said Charlotte.

"I did try to telephone you," said Clara.

"The telephone's cut off."

"George will pay Austin's telephone bill," said Clara. "We needn't even tell Austin."

"Does Austin know?" said Dorina, "I mean about this idea of my coming to you?"

"Not yet," said Clara. "We thought we should tell you first and tell him when you'd agreed."

"He won't like it," said Dorina.

"Really, Dorina," said Clara, "you mustn't be so slavishly sensitive about what Austin will like or not like. That's always been part of the trouble. Please forgive me for speaking so frankly. Besides," she said, aside to Mavis, "I don't think he'll mind *now*."

They behave as if I was not here, thought Dorina. How can they speak like that. She understood perfectly what Clara meant. She looked at Garth to see if he understood. He smiled his mysterious helpful smile.

Mavis, with lips a little parted, was gazing vaguely across the room. Her eyes were big and dazed. Last night she had lain for hours in Matthew's arms. He had wanted to make love to her but she had not let him. They had talked softly for hours about themselves. Next time she would not refuse his love, she would give herself utterly. Tonight, perhaps. Dorina knew, of course. Mavis had returned late. Dorina had been waiting up alone. Dorina said, "You smell of tobacco. You smell of man." They had not talked of it further.

Charlotte was thinking of an aching tooth and of three pieces of paper which she had in her pocket. She touched the tooth with her tongue, the papers with her fingers. She had not meant to pry into Austin's things. She had found a key on the dresser which fitted an old trunk and had opened the trunk looking for sheets. It was full of a jumble of old letters and photos. She saw a photograph of Matthew, young, plump, graceful, with copious fair hair, hands in pockets, laughing beside a river. After that she had started to delve further and had found something which had led her very much to speculate. Charlotte too was in the secret of Mavis's vague look. Not that Mavis had told her. Charlotte had seen Mavis and Matthew together, laughing in a certain sort of way, and Charlotte had become stiff. She felt this stiffness in her now, the stiffness of age and envy and barren hate.

Clara thought, I am putting on a silly sort of manner, I always do when Char is there, she sort of makes me. Why can't I sound more sincere? After all I am sincere. "Most sincerely, dearest Dorina," she said, "we do just want to help you. A change would do you good. We'll invite Austin. We'll give a little party for you. Anything."

Dorina shuddered.

"A sort of engagement party," said Charlotte, and laughed.

"Don't be silly, Char. I mean Dorina can have her friends over at our place—"

"I have no friends," said Dorina.

"Come, come," said Garth. Everyone stared at him, expecting him to say more, but he said no more.

"I haven't any friends either," said Charlotte. "I think Dorina should come and stay with me. Wouldn't you like to, Dorina?"

"Yes," said Dorina, "but—"

"It wouldn't be suitable, Char," said Clara. "We're much more ordinary than you, if you see what I mean. Dorina needs the ordinary."

"I agree that you are more ordinary than I am. But do you mean that Dorina and I might drive each other even dottier than we already are?"

"Don't be silly. I just mean we've got more of a real base than you have. After all a happily married couple—all right, we know we're very bourgeois—but we can give a sense of security—we can organize things—if she needs to see anybody or—"

"You mean if she needs to see a psychiatrist?" said Charlotte.

"No, no, I just thought—nothing in particular—Dr. Seldon for example, he's so understanding—in a way it'll be easier for her than here with Mavis."

"Does Mavis agree?" said Charlotte.

"Yes," said Mavis, looking at Charlotte for the first time. Their eyes met with a shock. Could Mavis read Charlotte's thoughts, Charlotte wondered. "I think a change from here will do Dorina good."

It will do her good, thought Mavis, I am not just pursuing my own ends. I never thought of it in this way before, but perhaps Clara is right. Dorina and I have always kept up the fiction that all is well. Maybe Dorina should see a psychiatrist. But she would be ashamed to see one under this room.

Dorina thought, they want to tidy me away. As things are at the moment I stand between Mavis and Matthew.

Matthew cannot come to this house with me in it. I contaminate it, I contaminate Mavis. Matthew must not come near me because of Austin. My case has got to be tidied up and closed. They want to arrange for Austin to come and collect me. But I can't go to the Tisbournes, I can't. Oh let me not weep now.

"Thank you, Mrs. Carberry," said Mavis.

Mrs. Carberry put down a tray of tea and biscuits. Mrs. Carberry was thinking about Ronald. Ronald had been crying all the earlier part of the morning at home. Mr. Carberry, who was out of work again and living on National Assistance, had shouted, "Take that bloody brat out of this house before I murder it." Mrs. Carberry had brought Ronald to Valmorana although she knew that Miss Argyll did not really like this. Ronald was now crying in the kitchen downstairs. Mrs. Carberry was listening hard to see if Ronald's crying was audible in the drawing-room. She thought it was not, but then she was becoming increasingly deaf. The doctor could do nothing about that any more than he could about her arthritic leg.

"What do you think, Garth?" said Clara.

"What does it matter what Garth thinks?" said Charlotte severely, but with a friendly look at Garth all the same.

"I am only here by accident," said Garth. He had come to consult Mavis about the future of his job. Something was wrong, he wanted his life to have some sort of significance which it lacked. "What I'm doing is all bits and pieces," he complained to Mavis, who seemed surprised that he thought this mattered. "Our work is like that," she said. "Perhaps the best thing in the world is just visiting old people. What do you expect?" He did not know what he expected. He felt that he could not think *properly* about anything, and perhaps the solution was not to think at all. Yet was that *his* solution? He was going that afternoon to see Mrs. Monkley, who had had some sort of collapse and was in hospital. He was looking forward to this because there was drama in it. He had thought a lot about the little girl and he felt very sorry for the parents and for Austin but he could not conceal from himself the fact that he found it all a bit exciting. It was life-giving, even pleasurable. Because of Austin, these things were significant, just as what was happening at this moment was significant. It was helping dreary people with whom he was not dramatically connected that made his life seem grey. He had not anticipated this at all. Of course he must change himself, but how? He admired Mavis's slightly cynical professionalism the more because he felt it was not natural to her. As Clara and Mavis and Charlotte were still looking at him he said at random, "I think Austin and Dorina should go away together for a holiday in Italy. Uncle Matthew will pay."

"A sort of honeymoon?" said Charlotte sarcastically.

"Are you serious?" said Clara.

Mavis just shook her head.

Dorina dissolved quietly into tears.

"Now look what you've done!" said Clara.

"I'm sorry," said Garth. He wished he could talk to Dorina alone. Now whenever he came to Valmorana she ran away to her room. He felt sure he could help Dorina, but it was the old dramatic feeling again.

Mavis thought, why is all this happening, I did not intend it. I was talking to Garth and then Charlotte arrived to see Dorina and then Clara arrived as if she expected to take Dorina away in her car. And Clara seemed to know about me and Matthew, well I suppose everybody does by now. Does Dorina imagine I organized this scene? Does she think I'm trying to get some public sanction for throwing her out? She thought, I shall discuss it all with Matthew tonight, he is so wise. Thank God. Tonight. Yes, yes, yes.

Mavis said, "Darling, you shan't do anything you don't want to do, that's clear at least."

Dorina wailed, "But I don't know what I want to do!"

Garth said, "Well, I'm off. I can't help. I just think nothing makes sense here until Dorina and my father get onto ordinary speaking terms again. Sorry, and good-bye. Cheer up, Dorina." He left the room. He ran into Mrs. Carberry on the landing. She had been sitting on the stairs. He thought she was eavesdropping. But in fact she was just taking a short holiday from Ronald's tears. Just to be quietly somewhere by herself was a relief to Mrs. Carberry now. It was one of her few positive pleasures, just to sit like an animal and breathe. She was too deaf anyway to hear what was going on in the drawing-room.

Garth went on down to his bicycle. It was simple and satisfying to get around London on a bicycle. Garth liked to see himself as a cyclist. He put on his bicycle clips, seeing himself. He wished he could talk to someone who was intelligent and educated enough to be impersonal, and not a woman, of course. A pity Ludwig was locked away inside his ghastly "engagement" and its horrible social world. Garth felt too that Ludwig was somehow disappointed in him, and that grieved him. He was somehow disappointed in himself. As he cycled away he thought again of Mrs. Monkley and cheered up.

Mavis led Dorina weeping up the stairs as if she were a little girl who had disgraced herself in the drawing-room. They went into Dorina's bedroom. Dorina spent more and more time in this room now. Dorina lay down on the bed and stopped weeping almost at once. Mavis sat down beside her and sighed deeply. A happiness concerned with Matthew floated Mavis upward like a rising tide.

"I'm sorry," said Dorina. "I know I must go away from here. It isn't just— Clara is very kind. But if I go to her she'll be busy about me all the time, and I— Oh how I wish everybody could forget me. I'm such a *thing* for you all— It's a form of wickedness. I mean it is in me."

"Don't be so foolish, my darling."

"It's an illness then. I don't want to see Dr. Seldon."

"You shan't see any doctor if you don't want to."

"I know I must see Austin soon. Garth is right. But any particular moment for seeing Austin seems the wrong one, if you see what I mean. It's all become such a drama. And everyone's watching and they're so interested. I wish I could go away somewhere where no one knew me."

"Don't grieve so, my pet. It'll all come right somehow. I'll ask— Look, take two aspirins and rest for a while. Then you'll feel better."

"I'm always resting. I do nothing else."

"Well, stay here now. I'll come back soon. Perhaps we might go out for lunch."

"I don't want to. Sorry, Mavis. Don't let Clara take me away. I'll go away soon somewhere, I promise, I know you want— But not with Clara. I'll see Austin soon. But I won't go to Clara's, please—"

"Dear dear child, I love you," said Mavis. "You shan't go anywhere. You shall stay here with me. Time will help us somehow, it must."

"There's nothing left but time, is there," said Dorina. "That's the only thing that's inevitable here. Yes, yes, I'll rest. I may sleep. Go, please, dearest Mavis."

"Shall I pull the curtains a little?"

"Yes, please."

The door closed softly and Dorina's tears began to flow again. What had happened to her mind? She knew in some sort of abstract way that she must see Austin, talk to him, try to make things ordinary and workable again. But in the part of her mind that dealt with real day-to-day things this simple act seemed impossible, and it was almost a luxury to give herself over to fears of all kinds. If only she could become unknown, become nothing. So many people thinking about her, this paralysed her.

She lay on her back in the shadowy room. There was a dark patch upon the wall and a strange truncated shape leaning out of it. With her will she could send it away, and yet with her will it crept, making the room horrible. Why was she thus destined to carry her fears outside her? She lay looking with fixed fascinated lightly weeping eyes upon the room of fear.

When Mavis came down to the drawing-room Clara and Charlotte were just leaving. They seemed to have been having some sort of argument which they wanted to continue elsewhere. Mavis was relieved.

"It was premature, that's all," said Clara. "Give her a day or two to get used to the idea. You do understand, don't you, Mavis? I've thought a lot about it and I'm quite certain she should come to us. It'll sort of break the deadlock, if you see what I mean. Don't you agree?"

230

"Yes, I do understand," said Mavis. "You're very kind. Give it a few days. Are you going too, Char? Come back soon. Good-bye, dear. Good-bye."

Mavis forgot them before the purr of Clara's departing car had made itself heard. She sat down in the drawing-room in the most comfortable chair. She let the sweet thought form itself in the silence. Mostly it was with her simply as a cloud which gilded all that she looked upon. Now she spelled it out in letters of gold. She was in love and she was loved. The angel of miracles had come to her, to her. Each day luxuriously she put off the full realization of her felicity. She teased herself with thinking that it could not be, blessed with the knowledge that it was. Out of this, she thought, good will come to everyone. Out of this, in the end, we shall all be saved. She lay there limply with closed eyes and almost slept for sheer joy.

In the car Charlotte was saying to Clara, "I think I shall have to have all my teeth out, my gums are rotting. Does my breath smell awful?"

"Not at all," said Clara, averting her head.

Charlotte touched the pieces of paper in her pocket. A handbag was a thing she never carried. She did not possess one. She had seen and understood Mavis's dazed look. She knew what happiness looked like. She had never experienced it herself but she could recognize it in others. The sight sickened her.

She felt constrained with Clara. For nearly a week now Clara had taken to sending her picture postcards every day, carefully chosen, with some sort of tender witticism inscribed thereon. Clara had done this once before when Charlotte had been in hospital for the removal of a cyst. Did Clara think that Charlotte was ill again? The stream of affectionate postcards irritated Charlotte and somehow alarmed her. She felt she was being touched by a slimy hand. One thing she would not stand for was being treated as sick by Clara.

"Thank you for the postcards."

"Not at all."

231

"But why send me postcards all the time? I'm not a schoolchild with the measles."

"I thought—I just felt I—"

"I suppose you'd like to feel I put them in a row along the mantel-piece?"

"I just wanted to—"

"Oh never mind. Do you really want Dorina to stay with you, or is it just some sort of ploy or pose?"

Clara, driving, was silent for a moment. "Why are you getting at me so?" she said. "Of course I really want her to come, and I really think it would do her good. Almost any change would. Don't you think so?"

"Maybe," said Charlotte. "I haven't any theory really. How about Gracie? I can't see her nursing Dorina, can you?"

"Gracie is full of her own life. I'll nurse Dorina."

"How kind and good you are!"

"Char—please—"

Clara suddenly steered the car in to the side of the road, stopped it, and burst into tears. It was a quiet road in Kensington, pretty with pastel-painted stucco and wistaria. Charlotte was surprised, upset. She turned and stared at her sister.

Clara took off her smart hat and tossed it into the back of the car. She rumpled her cascade of well-waved, well-dyed, chestnut brown hair. Tears blurred the carefully applied make-up. She looked uglier and younger. Charlotte was appalled.

"Sorry, Char."

"I should be saying sorry," said Charlotte. "What's all this in aid of?"

"Oh nothing to do with you, sorry, I mean it's not your fault. It's just everything. I suppose I'm growing old. I know everyone sees me in a certain sort of way, as a sort of busy interfering person, you know, and I act it too, I act it, but it's not me at all. Oh I can't explain."

"I think I understand," said Charlotte. "Sorry, old thing."

"Even George doesn't really see— Well, George is a man, he has so many interests and he's getting so important

232

now, he has all sorts of things to think about which aren't personal things, and I have only personal things, and when they sort of fail or become different one feels so let down. And I do try to help people and I do sometimes really do it, and it's not just a ploy or a pose."

"Sorry, Clara. What do you mean by personal things failing or becoming different?"

"Oh well, the children. I don't know. I feel I've lost Gracie. And Patrick was just rude, rude, all the time when I went down to school. He said he had his own troubles. He said, 'Oh fuck off, Ma.' He actually used those words to me. And I can't get on with Ludwig really, I think he despises me. No, well, he just thinks I'm a nonentity. I suppose I am a nonentity. I'm just George's wife and Gracie's mother and so on, I'm nothing in myself and I can't even help people properly, everybody just laughs at me, I know they do. Oh I do wish Gracie was marrying Sebastian. Sebastian understands me and Ludwig never never will. I could have loved Sebastian like a son. But Ludwig will never even notice me. I'm already beginning to look forward to my grandchildren. That's how desperate I am, that's what it's come to. And I'm not fifty yet. I feel I've got nothing in my life at all."

Charlotte looked at the row of pretty little houses with their wrought iron porches and their climbing roses and their well-clipped creepers, all very trim and very expensive. She thought, I am an absolute swine, but there it is. It's years since I really thought about Clara. And now there's nothing I can do for her, I can't even think what to say to her. I am so absorbingly sorry for myself I can't even enact being sorry for Clara. Anyway she'll hate me later on because she broke down like this.

"Sorry, Clara," she said again. "I think we're both still suffering from shock from Mother's death. That changed so many things. We'll settle down again. Life isn't an ideal business at the best. We are all disappointed. One just has to jog along, give cheerfulness a chance to break in. One should count one's blessings. There are a few."

Clara pushed back her hair and started the car again. She said, "I never thought to hear this sort of dreary worldly wisdom from you, Char. You were always the intense one. However, I expect you're right. Where shall I drop you, at the flat?"

"No, I'm not going to the flat. Drop me at High Street Ken Station. Cheer up, Clara. Things aren't too bad. The children are just going through a phase."

"Life is a phase," said Clara. "Here's High Street Ken if you really want it."

"You're bloody lucky to have any children," said Charlotte.

"I know. Good-bye, Char. Forget all that stuff. Good-bye."

As soon as Clara's white Volkswagen had turned the corner Charlotte hailed a taxi and went on to the flat. She climbed the stairs, came in, listened carefully, as she always did, prowled, and then went into the little sitting-room. She always feared that somebody, Austin, Mitzi, Garth, would have come in in her absence. I don't belong here, she thought, I must move. But with her tiny income, where to? She could not rent even a single room in this part of London for what she was paying Austin. She would have to move out to—where? Already the solitary evenings were terrible. She saw herself in the mirror, blazingly blue-eyed and full of strength, her pale grey hair tied in a negligent yet elegant bun, her plain dress sufficiently smart. She looked like the head of a women's college, an eminent doctor, a scholar, all the things she might have been and ought to have been and was not. She looked brave. She also looked unmistakably like a single woman.

She sat down and drew out of her pocket the three items which she had been carrying with her. She laid them on the table. The first was a snapshot which had been torn into several pieces and then mended (not by her) rather crookedly with sellotape. It was a snapshot taken many years ago and showed Matthew and Betty outside Matthew's cottage in Sussex. Betty looked sportive, juvenile, very dated. She was wearing shorts and a satin blouse and high-heeled shoes and a great deal of lipstick, and her hair was bobbed and stiffly waved. She was turning towards Matthew and laughing. Matthew was staring

234

self-consciously at the camera with his distinguished scholar-of-Trinity look, which was also curiously dated.

The next item which Charlotte laid on the table was a letter which had also been torn to pieces and also mended (not by her) with sellotape. It was in Betty's rather schoolgirlish hand and it read as follows.

> Dearest Matthew, yes, we'll meet then Piccadilly station as you suggest. I am sure Austin doesn't suspect. Thank you for everything!
>
> Much love,
> BET

Charlotte stared at this thoughtfully for some time. The letter and the snapshot she had found together in an old leather wallet. The third item, which she now began to consider, she had discovered separately among a lot of Betty's old school magazines at the bottom of the trunk. It was a certificate issued by a sports committee of the Fulham Swimming Baths to attest that Miss Elizabeth Granger had obtained a first-class diploma in General Swimming, comprising breast stroke, crawl, butterfly, and life saving.

Charlotte pushed her chair back. One of her lower front teeth was loose and she rocked it painfully with her tongue. It had been general knowledge that Betty Gibson Grey could not swim. Yet why was it general knowledge? Because Austin had always said so. And when had Austin always said so? After her death.

In retrospect it seemed an odd marriage. Betty was not considered to be a good match by those who care about good matches. She was a typist in a firm that did business with Austin's firm. Clara had said she was "without distinction but jolly." Betty had certainly been, in the mode of a bygone age, jolly. She danced and sang and played the guitar badly. Her guitar in fact still existed, at the back of the cupboard where Charlotte found the trunk. Presumably on Dorina's advent the relics of Betty had been just bundled into the darkest place. Charlotte could not imagine Dorina sorting these things out and asking

Austin if they should be kept. Dorina walked innocent and blind over the remnants of her predecessor.

Poor Betty. Destined for a happy ordinariness, what demon had set Austin in her way? And how was it that Austin was so attractive to women? Every woman thinks of herself as a healer. Did they somehow sense the leprosy within and feel confident that they could take the world-resentment out of those fine eyes? Dorina had thought it.

Poor Betty. How had a good swimmer managed to drown herself accidentally in a calm river on a summer afternoon? She fell into a lock. Armidale Deep Lock, the name came back to Charlotte. Austin found her there already drowned. Well, she could have hit her head on the side of the lock, only no one had suggested that.

Austin was a curious man. He inspired love. He inspired fear. Dorina feared him. Everyone had got used to regarding Dorina as a crazy little thing. But perhaps Dorina was not being just irrational and neurotic. Perhaps there was some quite other pattern behind it all.

Charlotte took the things from the table and put them back where she had found them in the trunk. It was lunch-time, whatever that meant now. She leaned into the darkness at the back and drew out Betty's guitar. She touched a string and it twanged with a surprised painful loudness in the quiet flat. Charlotte sat down nursing the guitar. She forgot Austin and began to think about Matthew. Tears came to her as she sat alone and rocked her decaying tooth with her tongue and strummed tunelessly upon the strings of the guitar.

During luncheon at Pitt's Lodge Clara was exceptionally gay.

George said, "You're in high spirits, darling. Have you bought a new hat, or what?"

"No, Pinkie, it was just this morning at Valmorana. It's awful to laugh, I know, but it really was such a hoot."

"Well, what did happen, you tell me."

"We were all so solemn and what everbody said was quite idiotic, it didn't make sense. Dorina said, 'I have no friends,' and Char said, 'I have no friends either.' "

"It sounds like an Oxford group session."

"And Mavis said, 'You shall do whatever you want,' and Dorina said, 'I don't know what I want,' and Garth said Austin and Dorina ought to go to Italy at Matthew's expense!"

"Oh was Garth there? Has he got a finger in the Dorina pie?"

"And then Dorina started howling and had to be led away. And Char was being sorry for herself as usual."

"We must invite Char."

"We might invite her with Penny."

"You know Char hates bridge. Where are the love birds, by the way?"

"Oh dear. They're out looking at a car. Oliver Sayce is trying to sell them his ghastly sports car."

"I can't see Ludwig at the wheel of a sports car."

"Let's hope reason will prevail. I so don't want Gracie to learn. After what happened to Austin one wonders whether one wants to drive at all."

237

"Did you remember to go to Mollie's boutique?"

"Yes. I bought a horrible white tea cosy with white embroidery on it."

"Put it away for a Christmas present."

"And that reminds me. Richard Pargeter rang up. He wants us to go with him in his new yacht to the Mediterranean."

"He'll drown us."

"He wants us to chaperone him and Karen Arbuthnot."

"Did he say so?"

"No, but that's it. I must say I'm surprised at Karen. I always thought she was keen on Sebastian."

"And Richard is no chicken."

"Richard has been around forever. Mollie is putting a brave face on it, according to Hester. She says Karen can't resist boats."

"I can though. Must we go?"

"It would be rather fun, Pinkie. The Greek islands in September."

"Could we take Patrick?"

"Patrick disapproves of Richard."

"Our son is austere. By the way, I suppose you didn't persuade Dorina to come and stay?"

"No, Pinkie, but I will. I want Dorina and I'm going to get her."

"Dearest Clara, you think of everybody but yourself."

❈❈❈❈

Garth sat beside the bed in the middle of the big sunny ward. There was a murmur of sympathetic embarrassed visiting-hour conversation, the awful doom-ridden tension between the healthy and the sick. The place was blanched and lineny with an apocalyptic impersonal light, and people shaded their eyes and lowered their voices. Death lived there and was only casually absent. Garth was holding Mrs. Monkley's hand. He had taken hold of it, squeezed it, and now, as it still clutched his, could not relinquish it.

"I don't know what's the matter with me," Mrs. Monkley was saying. "I feel all collapsed inside, as if my innards had gone, the doctors don't say, I feel as if I was dying and I wish I could die." All the time she spoke huge tears slowly flowed and her eyes, though directed to Garth, did not focus upon him.

"You will recover," he said.

"No, I won't. I know other people recover, but I won't. My little girl was everything to me, she was my joy, everything I did I did for her. It's not the same for Norman, being her stepfather, he doesn't feel it like I do. It's awful to say it now, but he never really loved the child properly, she was a nuisance to him, a child is a nuisance if you don't love it, a child in that little caravan, of course there were difficulties and bad times. Nature means something, you know, and it wasn't Nature for him like it was for me. We were on the housing list years, but when her father died, my first husband that was, we went down to the bottom again. I loved him, I can't believe it now they've both been taken, it's too cruel, he was such a wonderful man, an educated man, he was a schoolmaster, he knew everything. Rupert was his name and he named the little one."

"What was her name?" asked Garth. It was odd that he had never heard it.

"Rosalind. Like in Shakespeare, I forget which play. He said she'd be a tall girl. But she was just a little bundle when he died, he died of his stomach, and now they're both gone— She was such a wonderful clever child, just like her father, bright as a button at school— Oh I can't believe it when I wake up every morning."

"Don't give way," said Garth. "We all have to die.

It's a short walk through a sad place for the best of us."
He could find no words to engage with hers, no eloquence
to answer hers. He said, just in order to ask a question
which she could easily answer, "What does your present
husband do?"

"Oh he's in the motor trade, on and off that is. He's
been in prison. That's why I married him really. When he
told me he'd been in prison. I was that sorry for him."

"You've been good to him."

"Not really. We always quarrelled. And I couldn't help
comparing him with Rupert and I'd say so too. It was a
lot for a man to bear. And the caravan was too small and
the money came in dribs and drabs and he'd hold out on
me and we quarrelled about Rosalind. She was such a
good dear little thing she could never bear to hear our
voices raised after she'd been put to bed, though she was
that tired as Norman would never turn off the telly, we
used to quarrel about that too, and she'd come wriggling
out of her little cubby hole in her nightie and holding up
her little hands and sometimes we'd stop, even Norman
would, for very shame at the child. Oh I could bear it all
when she was there. I'd think about her away into the
future when she'd be a tall girl at the university maybe,
and it was like a line of happiness going right away into
the future. And now I'll never see her again, never hold
her in my arms again, oh how can it be, just because she
ran out of the door at just that moment, just that particular moment, if only I'd called to her, spoken to her just
once again—"

The white apocalyptic light was splintering in Garth's
eyes, there were tears somewhere, his tears, strangers. He
thought, this is what it is really like to look at death. He
thought of the dark New York street and the cry of "Help
me" and the heavy body slowly let down into the gutter
and the figure of himself walking on, walking on. That
had been the text written in small letters. This now, the
blankly sunny hospital ward, Mrs. Monkley's clutching
hand, her endless crying, her lips wet with tears, this was
the text written in larger letters and held up before him.

240

This was the rhetoric of the casually absent god. But could he read it, and was it even meant for him to read?

There were connections, but could they work in his life? Because a child could step into the road and die there was a certain way in which it was necessary to live. The connections were there, a secret logic in the world as relentlessly necessary as a mathematical system. Perhaps for God it was a mathematical system, the magnetism of whose necessity touching the here and now was felt as emotion, was felt as passion. He had recognized, at times, that touch and trembled at its awful certainty, being sure that he could not now be otherwise contented. It was an eternal doom. These deaths were merely signs, accidental signs even. They were not starting points or end points. What lay before him was the system itself. What burnt him was a necessity which was the same throughout. But could this searing darkness be for him other than an experience? Was this his fallen state? Was this every man's fallen state? Experience was impure and inextricably mingled with delusion. Even words tormented to the utmost retained that haziness and warmth without which perhaps poor humans cannot live. Yet what was action without these, could one go on in the dark after meaning had died? Absolute contradiction seemed at the heart of things and yet the system was there, the secret logic of the world, its only logic, its only sense.

❈❈❈❈❈

Mavis lay back relaxed in a big armchair at the Villa. It was late evening. Matthew, with a glass of brandy in his hand, sat in an upright chair leaning towards her.

Only one lamp was alight. They were not touching each other. There was no need. That would come. Passion and happiness joined their bodies.

Speech was loosened and had become perfect. They talked intermittently, often at random. Everything needful had been said. Now everything in the world could be said and there was a huge calm expansion of time.

Matthew had unbuttoned his waistcoat. He felt comfortable and justified inside his body at last. Mavis's faint touch upon his wrist, now withdrawn, made him feel light and pure as if a golden line had defined him altogether and lifted him slightly out of the grosser world: while yet, luxuriously incarnate, his desire waited, confident and curbed.

He saw in Mavis the counterpart of his own feelings, as she lay back, her shoes kicked off, her dress undone at the neck, her hands caressing her throat and breasts, her fuzzy halo of greying hair spread out behind her head, as it turned heavily to and fro.

"So you see," Mavis was saying, "I just don't know what to do for the best about Dorina. I fear making some terrible mistake. There's some very delicate thread which only she can unravel. One can't cut the knot. Sometimes I've felt that she just wanted me to force her to do something. But even if she did really want it I doubt if it would be wise. What could a psychoanalyst make of that child? There are some things which are very obvious and it could take a lot of time and a lot of pain to go over them. But psychoanalysis is such a blunt instrument. Dorina knows, she *knows*."

"Knows what?" said Matthew.

"The obvious things. Sometimes I think it's like a puzzle and she can see and yet not quite see. I watch her sort of knit her brows over it. She'll have to find Austin again, they'll have to come together very quietly at some moment when *she's* ready. It may be quite soon."

"You are stating the problem, not its solution."

"Stating it in a certain way excludes certain solutions."

"Quite. Do you think," said Matthew, "that there is only one thing the matter with Dorina, or are there many

242

things, all quite unconnected with each other? When someone's in trouble like that one is often tempted to simplify, to think there's one answer, one exit."

"I don't know," said Mavis. "I believe there's one thing. I believe it will all come right together. But then I do so much want to—as it were—release her—I mean as one might release a bird. Especially, and this doesn't make my thinking any clearer, now. My darling."

"Yes. Yes. Do you think that she can—if that is the word—save—Austin?"

"Yes. I believe it."

"You don't think it, you believe it?"

"Yes. I suppose it's like religious faith here. One has certain beliefs *for* other people, half trying to help them with the beliefs."

"I know. Austin needs a job. I've been trying. George has been trying. It's not so easy. His age and lack of—And some sort of idea about him that's got around."

"I know."

"It could all get pretty incurable."

"Yes. But I don't think any one thing should wait on another. I want Dorina to see him soon, to want to see him. If he has any good angel—"

"Yes, and he knows it," said Matthew. He added, "There's no point, you know, in my seeing her."

"Yes. That's impossible."

They looked at each other.

"If only, if only—"

"What, Mavis?"

"If only they could both be somewhere absolutely else and happy."

Matthew held her serious gaze. "That's not good enough."

"I know that too. But there are moments when one gets tired out with loving and finding it's all vague in the end, not a great river moving a delicate mechanism, but just—spray."

Matthew smiled at her. "I think your river and your mechanism *here*—"

"Yes, yes—"

243

"But I wish too— You at least can speak of love. What can I do for Austin? You know I came back for Austin?"

"I know you did,. and it makes me specially happy it makes everything far better—*here*—"

"Bless you."

"Isn't love the name of what made you come back for Austin?"

"How far can a name penetrate into darkness?"

"Let it fly there—like a flaming arrow—"

"You are full of metaphors tonight."

"I am full of—oh—poetry—love—"

"Mavis, I—"

"I know."

"Come."

⬥⬥⬥

"You will read my novel, won't you?" said Norman. "I mean it, I want to know what you think. It's a psychological thriller really, make a marvellous film. It's about this chap who never has a chance in life, he's a clever chap, as smart as paint, but he has bad luck, has an accident when he's five, well, it's not an accident really, his father throws him out a window and he damages his jaw and has an impediment in his speech ever after so that he can sort of talk but people always misunderstand him and think he's saying something else, some of these bits are a scream, but sad at the same time and sort of symbolic, and then he meets this girl, well, I won't tell you the whole story otherwise there won't be any suspense, and it ends with his getting a gun and going into a supermarket and shooting down everybody within sight and—"

"Excellent fellow," said Austin.

"Well, here it is, I've got several copies. I keep it in this steel box folder thing with a spring, it's rather heavy. We can discuss it next time."

"What makes you think there'll be a next time?"

"Stop kidding. I want to get your brother in on the act."

"My brother would crush you like an insect."

"I don't see why he should. He's sorry. He's a damn sight sorrier than you are. Now get this straight. I'm not blackmailing you."

"You are. You're breaking the law. And I've got your letter to prove it."

"Well, as to the law, you're the one who's for the high jump. My letter was just an emotional outburst."

"If you approach my brother he'll go straight to the police."

"No, he won't. He'll make terms. For your sake and because he's sorry. I only want a little. Christ, can't you understand. I've had this awful loss and—"

"Wait till I get a job," said Austin. "I'll give you a little now and then, just because I'm—sorry—I am sorry, you know. But I can't now—I haven't *got* anything."

"I asked for twenty pounds and you got twenty pounds. I bet you've got plenty stashed away."

"Oh God—"

Austin had gone round to the flat when Charlotte was out looking for something that he could sell. There was nothing of value except a little diamond ring and matching brooch belonging to Dorina. He sold these for twenty-two pounds and suspected that he had been cheated. The shop man could see that he was desperate.

He had tried to compose and leave behind a letter telling Charlotte that she must pay more rent, but he could not find the words. He would write the letter later on tonight.

Austin and Norman were sitting in Austin's room in the twilight in the same positions, Norman on the bed and Austin on the chair. Austin hated having Norman in the room, but he did not want to be seen with him in the street. Norman was loathsome, shameful. This nightmare

245

couldn't go on, it couldn't. But to be in that mess with Matthew publicly—

"I only want ten quid next week," said Norman. "I know you've got it, you're just holding out on me."

"I haven't got it!"

"You can borrow it from your bank."

"I can't! I've had an overdraft for months—"

"How you get it is your affair. Only ten quid. You can get ten quid, chum. Well, thanks for this and I'll be moving on. I'll be back this time next week. Then we'll fix something regular. I'll be resonable and decent you know. And I won't go to your brother if you don't want, provided you pay up. Shake hands to show there's no hard feelings? I say, what have you done to your hand?"

"My father threw me out of the window when I was five."

"You're kidding. Well, *auf wiedersehen.*"

The shadowy Norman took himself off. Austin sat groaning softly with his hands over his face. The future had become impossible, unlivable. Had he got Norman now for life? He must just refuse to pay, he could not live with an arrangement like that, being bled by Norman, it would drive him into insanity. Supposing he went to Matthew and told him everything and simply asked for his help? Matthew would know what to do, Matthew could not be cornered and defeated. When he had told Norman that Matthew would crush him like an insect he had spoken out of some very old feeling which he had had about his brother, an ancient feeling without a name. But no, he could not go to Matthew and let Matthew triumph over him. That would break the springs of survival forever.

"I say, Austin, why are you sitting all in the dark?" Mitzi switched the light on.

"Don't do that, don't *do* that, damn you."

"Sorry." Mitzi switched the light off again. "Austin, who was that funny-looking man who came up? You sounded like conspirators whispering up here."

"He was offering me a job."

"Oh good. What in?"

"The blood transfusion service."

"Oh, is that——?"

"Fuck off, Mitzi, will you."

"Austin, don't be cross. Would you like some coffee?"

"I'd like some whisky."

"There isn't any whisky."

"Then go to hell and leave me alone."

Mitzi went away and Austin forgot her. How he had hated selling Dorina's little ring. He had kissed it. Why was he not wearing it round his neck like a charm? If only her prayers would avail, if only something would avail against the devils in his life.

"I went there but he was gone," said Mitzi, "gone."

It was the next evening after the visit of Austin's mysterious friend. That morning through misty sizzling rain, Mitzi had gone to the studio. She had had no answer to her letter or to several telephone calls. She had put on her glossy mackintosh and made her way there through the mist. The streets were lined with black bobbing jostling umbrellas, like an ill-omened ecclesiastical procession. It was a horrible morning, warm and wet and grey and full of doom.

Mitzi wanted not only her money, she wanted to see Mr. Secombe-Hughes again. He had grown a little in his silence. Now she saw that it was stupid of her to be so unpleasant to him, it was unnecessary, a mere reflex. She was not so rich. And the world was a sad enough place without her little nastiness to Mr. Secombe-Hughes, who was guilty of nothing worse than writing a five-hundred-line poem about her in Welsh.

She felt tense and expectant as she neared the studio, nervously pleased to think that for once she could easily gladden someone. When she got there the door was locked. Dripping on the step she fumbled for her key. Then as she set her foot inside the sound of her footstep told her that the place was empty. Stripped. She walked through her own little office into the big room beyond. It gaped with emptiness, even the linoleum had been removed. There was a litter of newspapers and a smell of cats and a black trickle of water coming in under the garden door. Only the old familiar castle scene still hung upon the wall, hazy and desolate in the rainy light, as if it were raining in there too upon the wet glittering terrace and the pitted iron-grey waters of the lake. Mr. Secombe-Hughes had decamped.

Taking my typewriter with him, she suddenly realized. That was gone too. And her wages. And the poem in five hundred lines in Welsh. Was there no message left for her, a letter propped on a window sill, a little notice, an address? No. She kicked about in the heap of newspapers and found a faded yellowy tassel from an old silken shawl. Mr. Secombe-Hughes had had, after all, a soul. Tears came into her eyes. Her typewriter was gone. Her bank account was empty. Mr. Secombe-Hughes was fled. He was, she thought, a gent. She shed tears in the dim empty room as the warm wind pattered across the skylight and the water streamed steadily down the glass and the lines of rain descended into the brown lake. Mr. Secombe-Hughes was gone.

"He was gone," said Mitzi, "gone forever, taking my typewriter with him." She had nothing now, not even the IOUs which she had sent him through the post as a reminder. She reached out for the bottle.

Will she never go, thought Ludwig. Gracie will be here soon and nothing is properly ready and she will talk talk talk and I don't want her in my room when Gracie comes and oh God I think she's going to cry. "You can trace him," said Ludwig. "People don't vanish. He'll turn up."

"Gone forever," said Mitzi. She had put the silken

248

tassel into her handbag, where it had disintegrated into a tangle of yellow string.

Mitzi was wearing a grubby blue overall which was too tight for her. With her short fair hair tucked behind her ears she looked like an inflated schoolgirl. She unsteadily poured out some more whisky, making a wet ring with her glass upon the crisp new tablecloth which Ludwig had bought for the occasion at Barkers. She pushed aside the knives and forks which he had carefully set out and placed her elbows on the table. Her mouth drooped.

Ludwig had at last persuaded Gracie to come to supper in his room. It was an important event. He had reluctantly given in to her in the matter of Oliver Sayce's sports car, a waspish MG, of which they were shortly to become the owners. Gracie seemed to have no intention of learning to drive. Ludwig knew nothing about the interior of cars. The MG was not in its first youth. Oliver Sayce, who had followed his father into the antiquarian book trade, was a formidably efficient Etonian in jeans who was constantly tinkering with the car, which was called Kierkegaard. Constant tinkering, Ludwig suspected, would be needed to keep Kierkegaard on the road. Oliver Sayce's eyes had expressed deep wild relief when the sale had been provisionally agreed upon. "He goes like a bomb," said Oliver. Ludwig did not care for bombs. "We'll give him a gallop on the M-One on Tuesday," said Oliver. Ludwig could not help hoping that Kierkegaard, without actually crashing, would somehow disgrace himself. Meanwhile, in return for Ludwig's resignation in the matter of the car, Gracie had agreed to come to supper in his room on condition that she did not have to meet any of the other inmates of the house.

To preclude such encounters Ludwig had decided to cook everything on his own gas ring. There was to be consommé with a little sherry in it, omelette with cold potato salad, apple strudel, and cheese. He had suddenly felt so happy as he was laying the table. He was thinking about the house in Oxford and how it would be. Then Mitzi had arrived, carrying her glass and bottle.

"I just don't know what I'm going to do," said Mitzi.

249

"He was a gent, you know. You never met him, did you. He was a dear. He wrote such marvellous poetry in Welsh. He was a kind man. He was gentle, gentle all the way through. A gentle man. A gentleman. Is that what it means? Not many men are really gentle. I do wish you'd known him."

"He isn't dead, for God's sake!" said Ludwig with exasperation. "There's no need to talk about him in that lugubrious way. And now, Mitzi, if you don't mind—"

"I cared for him," said Mitzi. "He cared for me. But it was not to be. It was not to be."

"Oh there you all are," said Austin. He came in and sat down at the table opposite Mitzi.

"You look a wreck," said Mitzi. "Where have you been all day?"

"Out."

"Where out?"

"Coming, going."

"Going where?"

"To see a lady."

"What lady?"

"A lady who lies fast asleep in a room in Tregunter Road. She has been asleep for sixty years. She was eighteen when she fell into a trance. And there she lies still in all her girlish beauty. When a man kisses her she will wake up but in the twinkling of an eye her beauty will fade and she will rise up in her bed a wrinkled old hag of seventy-eight, but as she's good for a hundred thousand pounds it could be worth somebody's while."

"Did you kiss her?" said Ludwig, judiciously stirring eggs.

"No. I gazed upon her loveliness and tiptoed quietly away."

"You're drunk," said Mitzi. "You don't know anybody in Tregunter Road."

"Can I have some of that stuff?" said Austin. He took one of Ludwig's wine glasses and slopped some whisky into it.

Norman had telephoned. Norman was coming again tomorrow.

"I see you're entertaining Mitzi," said Austin. "I'm jealous. Can I come too?"

"I'm not entertaining Mitzi," said Ludwig. "I'm entertaining Gracie. I've persuaded her to come here at last."

"Persuaded her?" said Mitzi. "I suppose present company isn't grand enough for the young lady?"

"Oh Gracie's coming, is she," said Austin. "Good."

"It isn't that," said Ludwig.

"I don't see what else it can be," said Mitzi.

"Can we join you?" said Austin. "You needn't feed us. We can just sit by and drink."

"I'd rather you didn't, if you don't mind," said Ludwig. "I'd prefer to see Gracie alone, please understand."

"So we *aren't* grand enough," said Mitzi. "I suppose we should feel honoured that Miss Gracie comes slumming here at all. Miss Dorina has never even set foot in the place."

"You keep off Dorina," said Austin. "You understand nothing about her and you never will."

"Oh of course no one understands *her*," said Mitzi, "she's so deep. It's just that these mystery ladies get rather boring for us ordinary mortals."

"You're jealous," said Austin. "Just shut up about Dorina."

"I am *not* jealous," said Mitzi. "Why should I be jealous of a poor sick girl who isn't even in her right mind?"

"How dare you speak of my wife like that!" said Austin, rising to his feet. "She's worth a hundred of you, a thousand. Don't you dare utter her name! She is my wife and I honour her and I love her."

Ludwig said, "Please would you mind going and fighting somewhere else?"

Mitzi rose. She towered across the table. "Your wife! Your wife! You're very quick with that cosy little title, but you don't go to see her, you don't ask *her* for help, she isn't supporting you. You came rushing to me to be rescued and then you insult me in my own house—"

"Please," said Ludwig. "Gracie will be here in a minute and—"

"You wanted me to come here. You were wagging your tail like mad when I said I'd come. It wasn't my idea."

"It was your idea! You had it all worked out. You just prey on people. You're just a mean cadger. You have all the instincts of a common sponge. Even when you sent Ludwig along to me you had to say 'Here's a rich American, you can fleece him for anything you like.' He said that about you!"

"I said no such thing."

"You did, you did. You're a liar as well as a parasite. You prey on women. You've driven your poor little Dorina round the bend. You probably wore your first wife into her grave. You'd get your claws into Gracie if you could. You watch out, Ludwig, he'll get hold of Gracie too if he can—"

"*Please,* Mitzi, *please,* Austin—"

"Get out of this room," said Austin. He began to move round the table.

"This is my room. You can get out of it. And you can get out of this house too! You've ruined another day of my life. You've ruined one too bloody many. Oh God how I wish I'd never met you!"

"You don't know what awful trouble I'm in," said Austin thickly. "You don't know what an awful strain I'm under. You wouldn't be so beastly to me if you knew."

"Little man, little man!"

"You're drunk, Mitzi."

"*Please,* you two—"

"So are you. 'I had a little husband no bigger than my thumb, I put him in a pint pot and there I let him drum'!"

"Shut up, you bitch. Do you want to make me hate you?"

"Don't you dare touch me, Austin Gibson Grey. I may be lame but I could beat you with one hand."

"Please don't fight in my room! Oh look out, look out!"

Mitzi had given Austin a violent push. He staggered. The bottle of claret tilted over, the saucepan of beaten eggs fell off its perch on the fender. Austin lost his footing and crashed down in the fireplace.

"Damn you!" he shouted. "You've broken my glasses. Oh God I've hurt my arm so. Damn you, damn you!"

Ludwig began to pull Austin up. Mitzi sat down and burst into clamorous tears. "It's all because I love you, you fool, you dolt. I'm the only person who really cares. God knows why I do. You're a rat, you're just a blond rat. You'll be sorry one day. I'm the only person who really sees you and really loves you. And you make my life a misery—"

"I've got the bloody wine all over my suit and you've broken my only pair of glasses, you bloody bitch! Oh hello, Gracie!"

"Gracie!" cried Ludwig. He stepped out of the eggy mess in the fireplace.

"The Duchess has arrived," said Mitzi. She began to dry her eyes on the tablecloth.

Austin said, "Gracie, I'm very sorry. I'm afraid you aren't seeing us quite at our best."

"We're drunk every day, but not always brawling," said Mitzi. "Take a seat. This is Liberty Hall. Have a drink."

"Oh Poppy, I'm so sorry—" said Ludwig.

"No, thank you," said Gracie.

Gracie had done her scanty pale hair up into a tiny knot of a bun. She was wearing a longish green silk dress and carrying her mackintosh and a bunch of irises. She looked old-fashioned and appalled.

Austin was brushing down his suit. A long red stain ran from jacket to trousers. He picked up the twisted frame of his glasses from among the egg. He gave a maniac laugh.

Ludwig ran round the table. "Poppy, darling—"

"She's Poppy now, is she," said Mitzi. "Or is it Popsie?"

"Mitzi, will you please get out," said Ludwig. "And you too, Austin. I'm sorry, but—"

"I know you do pay the rent, but this *is* my house," said Mitzi. She rose, tall and huge-bosomed in the tight overall.

"Mitzi, get out, there's a dear—"

"No one bothers to be polite to me, oh no, I'm just poor old Mitzi, poor old bag. This man scrounges off me.

253

And as for you, Ludwig Leferrier, I seem to remember you were glad enough to hug me and kiss me only the other week, and now it's 'Get out.' All right, I'm going. And I'll take my little man with me. Come on, Austin. We'll go and sit in the kitchen."

As they went away down the stairs Ludwig and Gracie stared at each other.

"Poppy—"

"Wait, Ludwig."

A door closed below.

"Pack your things, Ludwig."

"What do you mean?"

"Pack your things. You're not spending another night in this house."

Ten minutes later Ludwig and Gracie were getting into a taxi. It was still raining. Gracie said "Kings Road."

They got in and fell back into a darkness which smelt of rainy clients.

"Poppy—"

"Ludwig, did you really kiss that woman?"

"Yes. But, my darling, please understand. She was drunk. Garth and I had to put her to bed. I was pushing her onto her bed and she just put her arms round my neck. I felt sorry for her, I kissed her sort of out of pity, and anyway she'd got hold of me round the neck, it wasn't— Honestly, she fills me with repulsion—I just pitied her, it wasn't any—"

"You aren't very chivalrous, are you?" said Gracie.

"Oh God," said Ludwig.

There was a moment's silence. Then Gracie began to put her arms round him. "It's all right. But don't do it again."

"Oh Poppy, you are good to me! Poppy, where are we going now?"

"We're going to see Matthew."

"Matthew?"

"Yes. We're going to the Villa. You're going to stay there with Matthew. I've just decided. I want you two dear men to be together."

"Oh God!" said Ludwig again.

"Do take your coats off," said Matthew.

"I'm sorry we're a bit wet," said Ludwig.

"Not at all, not at all. Mavis, could you turn the electric fire on. Please sit down. Have a drink."

"A little water for me, please," said Gracie, "and a biscuit if you have such a thing."

"Oh dear, haven't you dined? Mavis and I dined rather early."

"Oh yes, we've dined, haven't we, Ludwig," said Gracie, kicking Ludwig.

"Yes, yes, thank you, sir."

"I think there are some biscuits in this—"

"And so it is all right, Matthew, isn't it," said Gracie, "for Ludwig to stay here?"

"Of course it is, Gracie, it's your house. It's very kind of you to let me stay here."

"Ludwig can have the white room, you know, the one with the cats."

"Yes, indeed, I'll be very glad to have Ludwig here."

"I feel we're imposing on you," said Ludwig. "I mean— Yes, a little whisky, thank you—"

"Not at all, not at all."

"I think I must be going," said Mavis. She and Matthew exchanged glances.

"All right," said Matthew. "I'll just see you to the door. Excuse me, will you."

Outside in the hall, with the drawing-room door safely shut, he drew Mavis up against him and murmured *Damn!*

In the drawing-room, Ludwig was saying in a low voice, "We're being an awful nuisance, I can see that. Matthew doesn't want me in the house. He's never met me before. He must be cursing. And there was no need to say we'd dined. I'm ravenous, I had no lunch—"

"Have a biscuit then!"

Matthew came back.

"It gives me so much pleasure to see you two dear men together."

Matthew and Ludwig smirked.

"More whisky?"

"No, thank you, sir."

"Another biscuit, darling Ludwig?"

"Thank you, dearest Gracie."

"Well, I shall leave you now," said Gracie. "It's such a weight off my mind. That house was just not a suitable place for Ludwig. Now, good night. No, I must go and you must get acquainted, you must have a real talk, man to man. It makes me so happy to see you together, it gives me such a happy secure feeling. Good night, good night."

Matthew and Ludwig returned to the drawing-room.

"Shall I show you your room?" said Matthew.

"Look," said Ludwig. "I really feel I'm intruding—Gracie means well, but—"

"Not at all. Here, have some more whisky, I'm having some."

They sat down and looked at each other.

Ludwig saw a fat bald slightly cunning-looking elderly man with a large expanse of expensive tweed waistcoat.

Matthew saw a slim cropped-silver-fair-haired American with a Germanic face and an awkward manner.

"Austin won't like this," said Ludwig.

"We really must stop minding too much what Austin will like or dislike," said Matthew, "don't you think?"

"Well, maybe—"

"So you are marrying Gracie."

"Yes."

"And you are not going to fight."

"No."

"And you are not going back."

"No."

"Are your parents upset?"

"Yes."

"Not easy, not easy," said Matthew. "I'm sorry. No, not an easy choice. Tell me about it."

Ludwig looked into the round cunning brown eyes. He was being charmed. He had been warned of this.

A packet of cornflakes somersaulted to disgorge its crisp innards over Rodney's boots. Golden sick he thought as he laughed crazily golden shit golden entrails fit for a bloody King, himself the King. Now something was snaking slowly into Rodney's field, it was a trail of glittering red blood, the blood began to soak the cornflakes in the silence that went on. Outside the glass silent policemen flitted by, Rodney saw them flit. He raised up his revolver and they disappeared. I am King of the world he thought and he laughed again. I can fuck the world, worldfucker goldfucker me. He stooped and raised a handful of the sodden cornflakes gloatingly to his mouth.

Austin groaned and pushed Norman's novel back into the heavy box file. The steel clip leapt to and pinched his fingers. He had got a makeshift pair of glasses but they made his eyes ache. Norman himself would be here in a minute. Austin had three pounds to give him. He had acquired the three pounds by selling two of Ludwig's books at Foyles. He had purloined the books just before the removal men came to take them over to the Villa. Everything went Matthew's way in the end.

"Well, what did you think of it?" said Norman, flashing his white teeth under his healthy bush of dark moustache. He was lounging on the bed. The morning sun was thick and dusty.

"Very good," said Austin. "Very effective imagery."

"I'm glad you mention the imagery. You see it is a serious book. I thought of calling it *Death in the Supermarket*—"

257

"Excellent title."

"But I decided not to because that just sounds like a detective story—"

"Yes, of course."

"While this is sort of a metaphysical novel, really."

"Very metaphysical."

"You didn't think the characterization was weak?"

"Not at all."

"The humour's a bit sick, isn't it?"

"Very effective humour."

"Didn't you like that bit where he's trying to explain that the girl's arm is caught in the escalator and they think he's a Pakistani?"

"Very funny. I mean very touching."

"You see, he got all covered in dirt falling down that lift shaft and they think he's a Pakistani!"

"Very amusing."

"And then there's that bit—"

"Look," said Austin, "I have actually read your bloody novel, well some of it. I'll help you to try to get it published. I'll help you like that in any way I can. I'm sorry for what happened—"

"How do you mean?"

"I mean about your little girl, what's her name—"

"Oh yes, Rosalind."

"I am sorry and I haven't forgotten about it—"

"I should hope not. It only happened three weeks ago. I say what *have* you done to your hand?"

"I caught it in an escalator."

"Are you being funny?"

"Look, as I say, I'll help you about the book. And here's three pounds which I got in a bloody rotten way. And that's the lot, Mr. Monkley."

"Please call me Norman."

"That's the lot, Norman. I can see you're not a monster. You're an artist, a man of sensibility. You're a talented chap. You're not a blackmailer."

"Oh yes I am," said Norman.

"So you admit it?"

"I admit nothing."

"Well, as I say, that's the lot, you can't get blood from a stone, if I make a fortune I'll give you some. Now let's drop all this unpleasantness and have a drink, shall we?"

Austin brought out some of Mitzi's whisky. There wasn't much left.

"Wait a minute," said Norman. "You and I just don't understand each other. It comes of me being so nice. I'm going to get money and regular money out of either you or your brother. I don't mind which. I'm quite easy about it. You say you can't manage. That's okay by me. I'll go to him."

"I told you, he'd have you arrested, he's not like me."

"No, no, he'll look after little brother whom he loves. He can afford to, he spent his life fleecing Chinamen. All I want is a reasonable recompense, a small pension like. It's not blackmail. It's more like sort of sentiment. He'll understand."

"He'll murder you."

"Not he," said Norman calmly. "He's a gent. And I'm a man of sensibility. We shall understand each other." Norman reached out and poured the remains of the whisky bottle into his tumbler.

"Here, leave some for me, I haven't had any yet!" said Austin.

"'I haven't had any yet!'" Norman mimicked. "The trouble with you is, you've never grown up. You're not mature. You're still little brother running along behind and crying 'Carry me!'"

"Give me some of that whisky," said Austin. He stood up holding out his empty glass. He was trembling.

"Sorry, adults only," said Norman. "This is man's stuff. I'm going to do business with big brother. We'll make arrangements about you. I'll tell him you sent me."

"Give me some of that whisky, give it to me, I want it!"

"'Give it to me, I want it!' Poor little boy. Ooh look out, there goes your glass, why it's a real tantrum. My God, I think he's going to cry! I'll tell big bro about that too."

"That's—my—drink—" said Austin. Some ancient panic had indeed brought the tears into his eyes. Familiar impotent anger flooded his throat. He made a lunge for the whisky glass which Norman was waving tantalizingly before him.

"Naughty temper, naughty!"

Norman twisted away from the clutching hand and deftly tapped Austin on the chest, jolting him back onto his chair. Norman was intoning, "I'll tell—big brother—on you—" Austin rose again, pawing, flailing, grabbing. Norman was laughing. Norman's foot shot out and Austin yelped with pain. He swiped blindly at the dancing glass, which flew and shattered against the door. "Calm down, bugger you— Look out, do you want me to hit you properly?" Norman's fist met Austin's shoulder, but Austin was already on top of him.

"You—swine—"

"Get off me—"

Austin's left hand gripped the metal box file containing the novel. He swung it wildly, one knee on the bed, as Norman began to topple off onto the floor. The corner of the file drove into the back of Norman's head with a violent crack.

Five minutes had passed. Norman was still lying absolutely quiet on the floor. The back of his head was bleeding a little.

Panting with emotion and fear Austin had waited for him to move, to rise. Then had shaken him, pulled him, then desisted. Norman lay there on his side, surrounded by broken glass, his face pale, his eyes closed. He looked a different person. Austin could hardly recognize that remote altered face, which was not like that of a sleeper.

Austin sat on the bed and panted. He reached down and fumbled with Norman's wrist. There seemed to be no pulse. The hand fell back onto the floor with a thump. He tried to feel for a pulse in Norman's neck, but the soft quiet warmth of the flesh filled him with fright and horror. He felt that he was going to be sick. He stepped carefully to the basin and leaned over it shuddering and making noises in his throat. Then he returned to the bed. The awful sound of that blow, and now the absolute silence, the silence of responsibility and doom. Norman was as still and as remote as a wax effigy dressed in a suit of clothes. The clothes looked weird on him, like clothes on an image. It had all happened so quickly, how could what had happened so quickly be so irrevocable and full of consequences?

Austin could feel in his own body the force of the blow. Already he was reluctant to touch what lay at his feet. Norman lay heavy and without motion like a huge long thing inhabiting the room, not like a presence but like a portent, a piece of incomprehensible stuff put there as a threat or as an ugly joke. What on earth was he to do with Norman? Norman was so heavy, Norman had no business here. How could he get rid of him?

Austin got up again and ran some cold water into the basin. He splashed some down onto Norman's face. He stirred him with his foot. The thing lolled. Not a move, not a breath. If only it were somewhere else and not here in his room. Austin's mind ran about ratlike seeking an issue. Suppose he were to call a taxi and— No, that was no good. He must ring up a hospital, get an ambulance. But suppose Norman were really dead, as dead as he looked? Austin would be— The police would come and— It would be the end of Austin—

He opened the door and listened. The house seemed to be empty. Mitzi had gone out earlier that morning to be interviewed for a job. What could he do? How could he hide what had happened, tidy Norman away and make this awful thing not to be? He had an absurd impulse to thrust Norman in under the bed. Put Norman in a cupboard. It had already begun to seem like the name of a thing. A dead Norman in the room, big, weighty, long. In a sudden frenzy he kicked the silent form, shook it, slapped its face. It sickened and appalled him. Was he vainly insulting what was indeed already a corpse? The thing rolled back into stillness, it was invincible. Austin stared at it and moaned aloud. Then he ran down the stairs to the telephone. He dialled the number of the Villa.

261

"Could you get a mirror?"

It was fifteen minutes later. Matthew had driven round at once.

Austin went to Mitzi's bedroom. There was a large hand mirror on the dressing table. He hurried back again and gave it to Matthew.

Matthew awkwardly laid the surface of the mirror against Norman's face.

"It's too big, I can't get it—"

"Shall I move—"

"No, that'll do."

Matthew drew the mirror away. There was no haze on it.

"Matches."

"What?"

"Matches. I want to—"

Austin handed a box. Matthew struck a match and approached the flame to Norman's strangely pale cheek, to his nose.

"Look out, you'll set fire to him, what the—"

There was no recoil, no movement.

"He's like a bloody waxwork," said Austin.

"I think he may be dead," said Matthew.

"Then what are we going to do?" said Austin. "I'm not going to admit to having hit him."

"You got him just on that spot— Let's sit down for a minute."

Matthew was panting, as Austin had been a while· ago. Austin was cold.

They sat down at opposite ends of the bed, looking down. Austin withdrew his foot from the touch of Norman's trouser leg.

Matthew was deliberately controlling his breathing. Austin's teeth were chattering slightly. He made them stop.

"Of course we must get help at once," said Matthew. "But let's give ourselves two minutes."

"Can't we get him away from here in your car?"

"No, of course not. Think."

"We could pretend we'd found him in the road—"

262

"No!"

"Well, what's the two minutes for?" said Austin.

"To get your story clear. You hit him in self-defense. Well, you did, didn't you? Why were you fighting, anyhow?"

"I'm not going to admit to having hit him, I tell you," said Austin. "It was an accident, the whole thing was an accident."

"You'll have to tell them—"

"No," said Austin. "You're not going to make me do that again. Not again. You'll drive me mad. Can't you see? I'd tell them you did it, I'd say anything. I'm not going to be caught by the police, they'd accuse me of murder, it would end me, it would kill me—"

"All right," said Matthew. He seemed calmer. He was pursing his lips now like a scholar considering a conjecture.

"Suppose we say—"

"Shut up. Let me think."

Austin rocked himself and moaned softly. Norman's socks, Norman's shoes, Norman's feet, so appallingly, irrevocably there.

"Are you sure the house is empty?"

"Yes."

"Now how could he have got such a wound accidentally?" pursued Matthew. "Not by falling in this room, I think, there's nothing he could have hit his head on with that degree of force. He must have fallen down the stairs. I think that's the only possibility. Did he drink any of that whisky?"

"I can't remember," said Austin, "I can't remember."

"Well, he smells of whisky now all right. He fell down the stairs. What could he have hit his head on?"

"The edge of the trunk on the landing below," said Austin. "It's got brass corners."

"He fell down this flight of stairs and hit his head on the edge of the trunk. While I'm talking you can be picking up the pieces of glass."

"Where shall I put them?" said Austin.

"In the wastepaper basket for the moment. And rub over that bit of linoleum with the newspaper. Was he arriving or departing? Departing. He had been talking to us both and we had had a drink. We had the impression that he was a little tight when he arrived. Why had he come? In order to bring his novel, no, in order to pick up his novel, which you had already read. Which you had already read. I have not read it but you asked me to be present to discuss possible publishers. We suggested —no, we said we'd let him know— That's right, now could you take the novel out of the box file and put it on the window sill. Wash the edge of the file, put it under the tap, yes, now give it to me. The novel was brought here in a large envelope since destroyed, yes. We all talked on the landing. Norman was still holding his glass, got to explain why he's covered in whisky, yes. Talking to us he stepped back and missed his footing. That'll have to do. Now help me to move him down these stairs. You'll have to do most of the work. Get hold of his jacket."

"I can't—only with one hand—" said Austin faintly.

"Pull, pull, I'll do the best I can. Don't pull his shoe off, hold his ankle."

"I think I'm going to be sick."

"Do what I tell you. Pull."

Norman moved. He slid along the linoleum as far as the top of the stairs. Austin noticed with a dazed horror that Matthew was actually holding one of Norman's hands.

"Do you think we—roll him down—"

"Don't be a fool," said Matthew. "Now you go first with his feet. I'll hold his shoulders. We'll sit him from stair to stair. Kneel down to it, kneel. Better hold onto his— No, lift his feet. Wait, wait till I put this paper behind his head. Gently, I want to keep his head up, gently—"

"You think he isn't dead?"

"I don't want any blood on my clothes, or on the stairs."

"Oh Christ, is he bleeding much?"

"No. Now take a rest here."

They rested with Norman sitting up between them, leaning back against Matthew's knee. Matthew had his arm round Norman's shoulder. One of Norman's shoes

264

was coming off. Austin pressed it back on again and felt the firm warmth of the foot. This couldn't be happening. How long did it take a body to get cold?

"Now again. Come on. That's right."

Norman's bottom bumped smoothly from stair to stair. His head kept falling forward with a jerk.

"Christ, his bloody head will fall off," said Austin.

They reached the landing. Austin took his hands away.

"We've moved him a little from where he was originally lying. It would be this corner of the trunk, wouldn't it? Might be a smear of blood on it. So." Austin averted his eyes. He sat down heavily on the stairs. "Now in a minute or two I am going to ring for an ambulance. Meanwhile we must work. I want you to do these things. Take a dustpan and brush and see that's no glass upstairs. Bring it all down and put it in the bin, no time to dispose of it otherwise. Wash the floor and dry it. Were both the tumblers broken?"

"Yes."

"Well, take up another two and moisten them with whisky—"

"There isn't any, he had it all."

"Then put a little water in the bottle and—"

"I can't," said Austin, "I can't, I can't, my mind's gone blank."

"All right, just sit still."

"Suppose he wakes up and accuses me? Oh God, he is dead, isn't he? Oh God, what am I to do—"

"Keep quiet."

Austin continued to sit on the stairs. He looked through the open door to Mitzi's sitting-room into a sunny dusty haze. Matthew was grunting, moving up and down, his legs brushing against Austin's shoulder.

"Where are the brushes kept?"

"There."

"I'm putting the file in here."

"Yes."

"Where can I burn things?"

"Kitchen boiler."

"Where do you keep glasses?"

"There."

Some thing flashed over Austin's head and shattered to pieces on the landing. "What was that?"

"His glass."

"Why break another one?"

"Only one glass broke. Couldn't sort out one from two."

"I don't understand," said Austin, "oh I don't understand—"

"Get out of the way, would you," said Matthew.

"You've broken one of Mitzi's best cut-glass tumblers," said Austin. He walked towards the sunlight. He tripped over something. It was Norman's arm.

"You remember what happened," Matthew's voice followed him out of the darkness. "You asked me to meet Norman, we discussed the novel, we decided nothing, we said we'd let him know, he was talking on the landing, he stepped back—"

"Yes."

"We had the impression he was a little drunk when he arrived."

"Yes."

"I'll do the talking."

"Yes."

"Austin—"

"Yes."

"If the police suspect anything at all this story won't stand up."

"You are Sir Matthew," said Austin. "They'll believe you." He went over to the cupboard where Mitzi kept the drink.

Matthew was on the telephone. "There has been a serious accident—"

There was a little gin. Austin drank it from the bottle. He sat down and a hazy dead feeling came over him. He had no worries, he had no responsibilities, he was being looked after. He laid his head back in the chair and went straight off to sleep.

266

My dear Oliver,

Please forgive us, but after careful thought we feel that Kierkegaard is not for us. Such a distinguished vehicle deserves a connoisseur, and we are rather dull people, we have decided probably mere "family car" owners. We terribly enjoyed the "spin" and we thought Kierkegaard did very well. Blowing a gasket is something which might happen to anybody. (I am not sure what a gasket is, but I understand this to be the case.) And it was just bad luck about that policeman. We got home all right, and were glad to hear that you did too. No, you certainly cannot pay for the hire of the automobile. We enjoyed the day very much in spite of the tiny mishaps. We look forward to seeing you on Thursday at the Odmores' party. With all our thanks to you and best wishes from us both,

Yours,
Ludwig

P.S. I am so glad to hear that your little sister is to be our second bridesmaid! I do look forward to meeting her.

Dear Patrick,

Don't you think that you are behaving rather childishly? There is no need to shun me like a leper just because I don't belong to the brotherhood. The way you are avoiding me is becoming, I feel, conspicuous. I hope you didn't think my letter to you was offensive or priggish or pi. It wasn't intended to be. I just felt it kinder to make things clear. Also, and in general, I think it is foolish of you to embark upon a path which seems to guarantee a lifetime of misery. Meanwhile, I confess that I miss our discussions on history and philosophy. Perhaps after this salutary interval of clarification we might, if you still feel inclined to, resume them?

Yours,
RALPH

My dear Karen,

I don't seem to have heard from you for some time. Don't think I'm complaining, I just notice a gap in my post. Also, my spies tell me that you are going off with Richard Pargeter on his yacht. Is that wise? I should have thought Richard was a dead end for any girl. However, I am, as you know, old-fashioned. Isn't it about time you bought me another meal? Will you be at the party? I met your mother in Sloane Street and promised to visit the boutique. Perhaps you would support me. I may ring up. Excuse the above frankness of your old friend and well-wisher,

SEBASTIAN

Dearest bro,

I've been in such a tizzy, going to Oxford and that, please forgive neglect. The flat at Oxford is sweet, so cosy and ordinary, it make me happy in a special new way. I think loving Ludwig is improving me morally. Is this possible? By the way, there's been another jolly disaster, or has Ma already told you. The father of that little girl that Austin killed fell down the stairs at Austin's place after getting drunk discussing a novel he'd written with Austin and Matthew and managed to break his skull and is still in a coma. There's potted history for you.

What news of the Ralph biz? By the way, I have got the answer to your question about Ralph's heart condition. It appears that Ralph loves Ann Colindale, who loves Richard Pargeter, who (currently, he never does anything for long) loves Karen, who (although she denies it) loves Sebastian, who love me, who loves Ludwig who loves me. So that's *that* situation tied up.

Other news in brief. Ludwig has moved to the Villa and I am over there all the time now so I see a lot of Matthew. He asked after you. Sebastian says Ralph has permish to come up to the Odmores' party. I suppose you can't make it? The parents are well. They are still trying to get their hooks onto poor old Dorina. They also plan to cruise to the Greek islands with R. Pargeter. You are not included since you are understood to disapprove of him. I enclose a cheque.

Your loving sister,
G.

P.S. I have decided to have a second birdesmaid, little Henrietta Sayce. She and Karen will look so pretty together, with the same dresses, one big and one little.

Dear Mrs. Monkley,

May I on behalf of my brother and myself express our profound sympathy with you in respect of your husband's recent accident. As I am sure you appreciate, everything possible has been done for him. My brother and I did what we could at the time, and the doctors in charge of the case are as competent as can be. I have arranged for him to have a private room and extra nursing care. I gather he is still unconscious and it is as yet too early to know what will happen and whether serious brain damage has been sustained. We must all, in our various ways, hope for the best. We were glad to hear of your release from hospital, and Miss Argyll (who also sends her condolences) and myself will hope to wait upon you in the near future. With deepest sympathy and sincere good wishes,

Yours sincerely,
MATTHEW GIBSON GREY

My darling Mavis,

Thank you for your careful letter (which I have destroyed) about the matter I spoke to you of. I think we had both better now, in a sense, try to *forget* this. What has happened has happened and what has been done, rightly or amiss, has been done and will have whatever consequences it will have. Let us meanwhile bury it in decent silence.

With Valmorana and the Villa both impossible we are like the babes in the wood, are we not, my dear. I suggest National Gallery tomorrow, British Museum on Tuesday, and Wallace Collection on Wednesday! It is not satisfactory, but at least it is temporary. August will dispose of Gracie, who now treats this house as her own, which indeed it is. And meanwhile: can you not persuade Dorina to go to the Tisbournes, who are so anxious to have her? Clara says Richard Pargeter would be very willing to take Dorina along on this yacht cruise which they seem to be contemplating. Quite apart from our interests, I think this change would do Dorina a world of good.

Mavis, you have asked me to live in the present and I am (especially in view of what I spoke of at the beginning of this letter) prepared to do so for the moment. But one day I shall again think of the future, and think of it as inseparable from you. A habit of unhappiness may be hard to break. But we are not too old to break it. Nor is it too late to think extravagant and beautiful thoughts. I love you. Let us be ambitious for ourselves. I kiss your hands. Tomorrow.

MATTHEW

My darling husband,

I was so terribly sorry to hear of the accident to poor Mr. Monkley. How unfortunate, and how unhappy it must have made you that it should have happened in your house and just when you were so kindly trying to help him. I am so sorry.

Mavis wants me to go to the Tisbournes. They are going to go on some sort of cruise, I am not quite sure when, and want me to come too. Mavis is very kind and doesn't press it but I know she wants me to go. I do not want to go. The idea of the "cruise" fills me with horror and the Tisbournes being so sympathetic to me the whole time reduces me to whimpering. Sorry I cannot express this, I am very unhappy. I know it is all my stupidity and my fault. Austin, can we not find a solution for ourselves, this endless dependence on other people is so bad, oh I know, I know, that it is my weakness that has made us so. From where can strength come? How I wish we could go away together, you and I, though I know we have no money and I am so unable to deal with the world. Oh what can we do? Dear husband, I think of you so much, especially in the night-time, and pray to you in my thoughts, for you are all that I have. There is no God, but I pray to you and lodge there in the thought of you all the good that I know or dream of.

Austin, will you come to see me here? I, we, have put this off for reasons which we both understand. You have hoped for better fortune, a new job, getting the flat back and so on, and I have hoped—for a calmer mind. But maybe we are wrong to wait, and cannot without somehow coming together attain any of these goals. I have thought a lot about this. I do not want to displease you. If you would like to see me please come. Telephone first. But if you would rather wait a little longer I am happy to wait too. I am happy always in your will. Apart or together, I am a place of safety for you. You know that. Ever your patient and loving wife,

DORINA

My dearest son,

Your father has suggested that I should write to you so that you can be sure that he and I are of one mind in this matter. I am not very good at this sort of letter and I did not earlier write because the discussion was between yourself and your father, you understand. Dear Ludwig, I cannot express to you how much we miss you. To say that I think of my dear son every day says little. I think of him every minute and remember what times in our day and night are his bed-times and his getting-up-times, and every night and indeed always in my thoughts I pray for him that he may be protected and guided to do the right.

So it is. Ludwig, we have had such a nice letter from Miss Tisbourne. Please thank her from us both. I think we cannot write to her, it is too hard to write. She seems good-hearted though rather a young child, it seemed to us. We still hope and trust that you will put off this marriage, which seems to us, with your general position in so much doubt, to be not well thought of. A marriage is forever, as I am sure you feel this as we do, and it may be that this very young lady, though so charming, is not the strong and spiritual stay which you, which any man, has need of upon that long road. Please consider this carefully, Ludwig. And do not think that we are just prejudiced and unable to understand the "tone" of a society which might seem to us, as perhaps it does to you, a little "grand" or even worldly.

About the other matter I do beg you to come home and sort it out. How can you go on to your work at Oxford with this hanging over your head? At least come home and face it and do so before making any more plans to get married. Mr. Livingstone tells us that you can now plead objections to war on general moral grounds which need not be actually religious. You speak of being "honest all the way through." Dear son, it does not seem to us that you are being honest all the way through if you seek all the advantages and shirk all the unhappy consequences of the position which you have taken up. If you wish to bear witness this cannot be done by running away but only by "facing the music." Your father and I have talked this over again and again and again, among ourselves and with Mr. Livingstone. You know that we do not wish you to be in trouble. But neither do we wish you to seem and perhaps to be a coward. And if you do not come back now you will be in very much greater trouble later on. Even leaving aside the concern which I know you have for our feelings, surely you cannot sincerely believe, at your young age, that you will never want to set foot in the United States in your life again. We so much fear that you will suddenly decide to come later when it will all have such terrible consequences. And who knows what will happen in Europe? Oh Ludwig, come back. Now and only now can all be put right. Mr. Livingstone is sure that it can all somehow be arranged for the best and we can see about it when we can talk to you properly ourselves and see your dear face. Please reply soon and say that you will come. Time is very pressing in your situation. And please, surely this is simple and reasonable, at least postpone your wedding. That cannot be difficult. Write soon, my dearest son, and relieve the anxious loving mind of your devoted mother,

R.F.

We were surprised to hear that the college authorities approved. Can they really have understood the situation?

My dear Ludwig,

Thank you for the excellent stuff on Aristophanes, it's just right. How modest you are! With you doing the history and me doing the poetry we shall be able to put Big A. on the Oxford map as he hasn't been for ages. We *shall* have fun next year and I can't tell you how much I look forward to it. I hope you will be down at the weekend as suggested? There is a big auction sale of self-styled antiques and you and Gracie might pick up one or two things for the flat. By the way, I think your lovely fiancée has made a conquest (I mean other than of the undersigned—and of the Master)! Going down to the room of the brutish MacMurraghue to borrow a trifle of sherry I saw on the table his form for next term's lectures decorated as follows: "Gracie is and *ought only to be* the slave of the passions." Make what you can of that! But fear not, McM., though a philosopher, is a gentleman. Oh what fun we shall have! See you at Sat. I hope.

Yrs,
ANDREW

My dear Charlotte,

I am sorry not to have replied sooner to your charming letter, and very sorry not to have seen you. Wherever were you hiding at that party? Let us indeed meet. Only it cannot be for a little while as I shall probably be out of London. I have to go to Cambridge to see a man at the Fitzwilliam about the possibility of putting my collection of Chinese porcelain on permanent exhibition there. And I have other calls to make. It is remarkable how busy one can be when one is allegedly "retired"! However we must definitely meet before long and talk about old times. When I am back in London and the timetable looks a little less horribly full I shall give myself the treat of a quiet luncheon with you. So I will get in touch with you later if I may. Meanwhile my very best wishes to you and au revoir.

Yours,
MATTHEW

My dear Ludwig,

I'm sorry I haven't seen you. I've been, in what seems a rather ineffectual way, very busy. This Mission, which used to be a Christian Mission to Seamen, is now (and no doubt more valuably) scarcely more nor less than an old-clothes shop. You would be surprised how many people, especially children, are ill clad in our Welfare State. However I'm not writing about this. I shall be moving soon anyway to a housing thing at Notting Hill. Do persuade Gracie or someone to go to see Charlotte. I gather she's still all alone in my father's flat. Women like Charlotte are crazier than you think. It's no good my going. She'd think I was pitying her. (Rightly.) Also: she should be got out of the flat soon so that my father can have somewhere to take Dorina. These little mechanical details are often important. Here, money helps. Matthew and Gracie both have that. Can't they for Christ's bloody sake use it intelligently? Or why can't Charlotte go on this cruise everyone seems to be going on? Sorry to bother you with such drearinesses. I hear you are living with Matthew, which some would think enviable. Excuse a rather nontheoretical letter. I am becoming a rather non-theoretical sort of chap. See you.

GARTH

My dear Matthew,

I am sorry to reply so soon to your charming letter, thereby putting you once again in the position of owing me one. I appreciate, and indeed hear on all sides, how extremely busy you are and how beset by urgent and pressing engagements. Naturally you are much in demand. You are quite a public figure, and must have a very different sense of your day from home-keeping small fry who idly pass their solitary hours. I do not want to waste your time. Our chat about the old days can doubtless be postponed indefinitely without too much chagrin. There is not all that much pleasure in talking about the past, even with someone one is fond of. The future, as the poet observed in his cups, is the only "serious matter." Lucky are they who can still boast of one. I write to repeat, tediously perhaps, that I would like to see you. And also to say that I have got some information, or perhaps I should call it a theory, which I should like some time to impart to you. I think it might interest you very much.

Regards,
CHARLOTTE

Dearest Sis,

For heavens sake do not put it around that I disapprove of R. Pargeter! How could such a ridiculous idea gain currency? How *can* one disapprove of a man with a yacht and a plan to visit the Greek islands? Will you now kindly insinuate in all quarters your brother's profound respect for the misunderstood Pargeter, together with your brother's seafaring expertise, handiness with ropes, helpful knowledge of the classics, and all that? The Ralph biz cooketh. I will tell you later. (*I am still very unhappy.*) Thanks for the data re A. Colindale beloved by R. Odmore. I suspected this actually. Thank God she is not fancy free but loves the excellent Pargeter, that sound man. Don't say anything stupid to Ralph, will you, if you see him at that thrash. I may even illicitly come myself. Thanks for the cheque, but when I said money I meant MONEY. Kindly forward fifty pounds. What rotten luck for the Monkley fellow. It shows one shouldn't associate with Austin. Give my love to Matthew. Does he really remember me? He is an old crook in a way but he's a bit larger than the usual pattern in our rotten circle. Are you keeping yourself pure? I mean spiritually of course.

Your confessor and papa in God,

TISBOURNE +

P.S. Re bridesmaids plan, watch out, Henrietta Sayce is a DEVIL.

My dearest Mother,

Your letter has caused me much pain and touched my heart with deep love. I too long to look upon your face, and to see you and my dear father again in amity and peace. I will not write at length. As I have said before, and indeed many times, I cannot truthfully, on any ground, religious or moral, plead pacifism, since I am not a pacifist. I object not to war, but to this war. If I return home now I face a spell in prison, the loss of my Oxford job (which would have to go to someone else), the ruination of my academic prospects in the States, and worst of all the confiscation of my passport. And since I have in all possible seriousness and sincerity decided that it is not my life's work to be a martyr of protest, it is duty as well as common sense to remain here. Please think about it all, Mother, please see *all* the pieces of the problem and see them all together in relation to each other. And please believe me that this would be my conclusion even were I not engaged to be married to an English girl.

I cannot (will not I suppose I should in honesty say) postpone my marriage. The wedding dress is ordered, the bridesmaids' dresses are being made. (We are having a grown-up bridesmaid and a little one.) Everything is fixed. We have already a flat in Oxford and hope to buy furniture for it this weekend. I say these things not in frivolity or to cause you pain, but to make you see and feel the *reality* of this marriage, which will *will*, dearest Mother, take place in August. Please come to it, both of you, please. Gracie will pay the fare. It will complete our happiness, which without you is wounded. *Please*. And forgive your son. He can no other. With so much much love, and also to Father.

LUDWIG

"Austin's here," said Mavis. "Do you want to see him?"

Dorina hastily laid aside her book. She blushed and touched her throat and gave a little gasp. Then she jumped up and closed the drawing-room window as if that made some sort of difference. The sun blazed in onto clean white paint and orange-tawny walls and rather bad water colours executed by Dorina and her father.

"Yes. I was expecting him."

"Oh," said Mavis. "Well, here he is. I won't be far off." She made an ambiguous grimace.

Austin came in, and the door closed behind Mavis.

Austin looked at Dorina and Dorina looked at the floor. She sat down again and motioned him to a seat, still not looking up.

Austin was carefully dressed in the light grey tweed suit, from which the wine stains had been almost entirely removed. He had a new pair of steel-rimmed glasses. He wore a white poplin shirt and a Bellini green tie. He had washed his fair hair, which stood up in an attractive tousled way and rushed back over his head. His eyes looked unusually blue and he appeared young and full of health. But at the moment Dorina could only see his shoes, which had been rubbed clean without being polished.

"Hello," said Austin.

Dorina murmured.

Austin sat down in an upright chair near her, reached across, and lightly touched her knee. Dorina raised her head, brushed her eyes.

278

"Hello, Austin."

"Hello, darling."

"Sorry—"

"What are you being sorry about, silly? What's this book you've been reading?"

"*The Lord of the Rings.*"

"Is it good, funny?"

"Yes."

"Dorina—"

"Oh darling—"

"We are a hopeless pair, aren't we. Don't cry. I'm not worth your precious tears."

"Sorry, I'll be all right in a minute."

"I say, it's so *clean* here. No dust. Round at—where I live now—it's all dust and dirt and awful things in corners. Horrid."

"Mrs. Carberry cleans here. She's very good."

"I wish we had a Mrs. Carberry. I mean— Oh Dorina, I do miss you so."

"Austin, let's be together again. I feel things are sort of closing in. I can't explain. We must try to be somewhere together. Now that I see you I can't understand what went wrong, it's as if I'd forgotten—"

"I know. I've forgotten too. May I touch you?"

"Oh Austin—"

He took her hand.

"Dorina—silly—aren't you?"

"Yes, Austin."

He stared at her, frowning with a kind of amazement. She was wearing a high-necked dress, buff-coloured and sprigged with light pink daisies. Her light brown hair flowed loose to her shoulders, shining and blurred into gold, a young girl's hair. But her face looked thinner, creamy pale and unlined, yet somehow no longer youthful. Could such a face, without seeming to age at all, become suddenly haggard? Her moist hand held his stiffly but hard. Their knees did not touch.

"Look, I'd better just talk," said Austin. "You know I'm a hopeless character, you know me, God knows why you married me, it was your unlucky day when we two met, but here we are, somehow very married, aren't we, other people can't understand that, but we are."

"Yes, Austin."

"I can't think how things have got into this mess, with everyone interfering, if we'd just been left to ourselves— Don't push me away, darling child."

"I'm not pushing you away. Forgive me."

"May I just—touch you so—I'm not so bad, am I? It's only old Austin, you know, your hopeless old husband."

"Dear dear husband."

"That's a new dress."

"It's one of Mavis's. It didn't fit her any more."

"Pretty."

The dress was full-skirted and longish. Austin's right hand nudged at Dorina's knees, his left hand crept a little up her wrist under the lacy cuff. He felt her fast pulse, smelt freshly laundered cotton and flowers.

He went on, "We shouldn't have separated—"

"It was my fault."

"No, it wasn't, but we won't argue that. Maybe it was a good thing in a way, Nature took a hand in the game. You needed a holiday from me."

"No."

"Yes, you did. Anyone would. I need a holiday from myself. And then just lately—well, you know how everything's gone wrong—I left my job—"

"Austin, are you short of money?"

"Well—"

"I wish you'd sell those jewels of mine. They're at the flat, in that little drawer in the bathroom, in a cardboard box. There's a diamond ring and a brooch that goes with it. The diamond ring is quite valuable."

"Oh. Is it?"

"You should get at least fifty pounds for the ring. Daddy gave it to me, but— You will sell them, please? Just to please me? I don't want you to be short of money. You will promise?"

"Well—all right—"

"Dear Austin, thank you. Go on talking, will you. Just to hear you talking to me and to hold your hand is such a relief, it's like when pain suddenly ceases and you can see the world again. You know I can't talk. I've nothing to say somehow, except that I love you."

"Yes, then, I left my job, and there was poor old Charlotte and I felt I had to let her the flat, and Mitzi Ricardo was pressing me and pressing me to come and stay and I thought, when I had to make economies, you know—"

"Is she—does she love you, Austin?"

"Old Mitzi! No! She's just lonely. She's a pathetic figure really, I can't help feeling sorry for her, she's such a broken-down old thing."

"She's hardly older than me, is she—?"

"She seems thirty years older than you. She's lost her looks and got fat and taken to the bottle—"

"Poor thing. You've been so good to her, so good to Charlotte."

"Mitzi just needs company, now that Ludwig's gone—"

"Louis's with—?"

"Yes."

"Austin, Louis has quite stopped coming to see me."

"Has he? Yes. Oh he's tied up with Gracie and that Tisbourne world and Oxford, he's got busy and grand, he's not at all like the old Ludwig any more. He doesn't care about people."

"You care, Austin."

"Dorina, I don't care about anybody but myself and possibly you, please get that clear! You mustn't think I really helped Mitzi or Char out of genuine unselfishness or kindness."

"Well, perhaps there isn't such a thing."

"Perhaps there isn't. That's a very grown-up thought. Perhaps we're both growing up at last."

"It would be about time. Oh Austin, I do wish we had somewhere to go. Clara Tisbourne keeps on asking me to go and stay with them."

"You won't go, will you, Dorina, I couldn't bear it—"

"No, of course I won't go."

"And you won't go on this ghastly cruise they're planning with Richard Pargeter?"

"No, of course not, as if I'd go away on a cruise just when—"

"That's my own dear true wife, my forever and ever girl."

"Oh Austin, we really are sort of together again now, aren't we? It suddenly seems so easy— You will come more now, come every day?"

"Yes, yes."

"And we'll be quiet with each other and talk about the future—"

"The future, yes."

"How we'll be back in our own little place one day soon, among all our own things, our own funny special place, like it used to be, and I'll cook and sew—"

"And we'll make it nicer too, I'll get a job with more money and—"

"Oh dear Austin, I do so much want just to make you happy, I've always wanted that. You've had such a terrible time. I keep thinking of that poor child—"

"That, yes."

"I hardly dared to mention it, it's so awful. I am so sorry for you. And now there's that poor chap who's had the accident, the father."

"Yes. Poor chap."

"How is he?"

"Still unconscious. Yes, well, we'll get back our little home, won't we, Dorina, and—"

"Mavis wants me to move out too now, because, you know—"

"Dorina, is that a serious business?"

"You mean between Mavis and—"

"Yes."

"I think so. She doesn't talk about it. And she hasn't actually asked me to go— And of course they wouldn't—"

"Of course. Oh hell. *Hell.*"

"Austin—"

"Sorry—*hell*—all round me, all inside me— I live in it, I swallow it, I spit it, I am it. *Hell.* Do you know what that is, Dorina? *Hell.*"

"Austin, please—"

282

"I'm sorry, I'd better go. If I stay I'll just start being bad to you. You see, it's no good after all, with us nothing's any good, you're far better off without me, as you really know quite well or you wouldn't have left me like you did——"

"Oh Austin——"

"Sorry. I'll go. You can go on reading your nice novel in peace in this charming well-dusted room. I'll go back to my pigsty and sluttish old Mitzi Ricardo. Oh Dorina, if you knew how heartily I loathe myself at least you'd feel some pity for me."

"I love you."

"If you do you must be mad. Anyway I'd better go before I start tearing our little bit of tapestry to pieces. How you put up with me I can't imagine——"

"Austin, you did mean it about our being together again soon?"

"In *our* little sty, different but still piggy. Yes, though God knows how. If you'll ever forgive me and I ever forgive myself."

"Not yet, but soon."

"Not yet, but soon. That appears to be our motto. It saves us from thinking."

"And you will come now often! I won't go away, you know that."

"Yes, I'll come. You won't go to the Tisbournes', will you, Dorina, you won't go anywhere?"

"No, I won't. And don't be afraid that Mavis and——"

"No, no. But oh God I must get you out of here to somewhere. I must get a job, I must try to get myself functioning somehow."

"Yes, yes. Better go now, Austin."

"Yes. We haven't done too badly, have we, Dorina?"

"No, my darling, we haven't done too badly."

Norman Monkley looked at his wife. He moved his lips and his lower jaw convulsively. It did not look like an attempt either to speak or to smile. He was holding his wife's hand. She was weeping.

"Don't cry now, he'll get better," said the nurse.

"Will he?" said Austin. Austin and Matthew were standing by the window.

"Of course he will," said the nurse.

Norman was conscious and seemed to recognize his wife. He had not yet spoken.

"You've been so kind, you gentlemen, so kind," said Mrs. Monkley. "Norman will be so grateful when he's himself again."

"Well, we must go, I think," said Matthew. "Miss Argyll will come this afternoon, and I'll come again tomorrow."

"And thank you for bringing the flowers and poor Norman's novel."

"Not at all."

"God bless you and reward you, sir."

"Amen," said Austin.

They left the room. Norman's eyes followed them with an expression of puzzlement.

As they came out into the sun in the hospital grounds Austin said, "What did the surgeon say?"

"He said a complete recovery was very unlikely but conceivable."

Austin was silent.

Matthew said, "Why did you hit him, really?"

"I didn't like his novel. It was muck, you know, muck.

284

Of course I didn't mean to hurt him. I just tapped him playfully."

After a silence Matthew said, "I hear you saw Dorina yesterday."

"Yes."

"Was that all right?"

"What do you mean?"

"Well, you know——"

"Your question is impertinent. Dorina is my wife. It's of no conceivable interest or concern of yours."

"It is of *interest*," said Matthew. "Sorry. I know that everything I do and say annoys you."

"Yes. Think that over sometime when you're feeling so bloody superior to everyone."

"I don't feel superior to everyone."

"You do."

"All right, I do. But in a way I can't help it. It's chemical. Just as it is with you."

"Just as it is with me to feel that I'm scum. Yes. You could be right. There's your girl friend waiting."

"Won't you come and talk to her? Let us give you a lift. Come and have a drink somewhere."

"No, thanks. I'm going this way. To the bus stop."

"Austin, don't cut yourself off from people, it's not good. Are you coming to the Odmores' party this evening?"

"Don't be funny. By the way."

"Yes?"

"Thanks for helping me the other day."

"Not at all. Au revoir."

"Good-bye."

Mavis said as Matthew reached her, "How's Norman?"

"Conscious but not talking. The surgeon thinks he probably won't recover his mind."

"He won't remember?"

"No."

They got into the car.

"Poor Norman. Poor Austin. Austin wouldn't see me?"

"No. So Dorina said nothing about yesterday?"

"Nothing."

"No sign of her moving?"

"No. But I hope she will go to the Tisbournes'. We must all just be a little firm with her. I really think it would do her good. It's not just for us."

"I agree. I'm tired of living in the car. Dear Mavis—"

"I know. Did Austin say anything about yesterday?"

"No. I just infuriate him."

"The funny thing is that Austin really loves you. You're the great love of his life."

"Rubbish, my dear. Now where shall we go?"

"Let's go and sit beside that nice quiet parking meter in Onslow Square."

⁂

"Is that Mavis Argyll? She hasn't been to a party in years."

"She's got very grey, but she still has the dewy spiritual look."

"Is it true that she and Matthew—"

"Sssh. Hello, Matthew. I hear you're giving your porcelain to the Fitzwilliam. The Ashmolean is furious."

"My Alma Mater, you know."

"Sebastian has got a job in the Bank of England."

"Gracie Tisbourne has real orchids in her hair."

"More money than sense."

"Hello, Oliver, how are Oldie Bookies?"

"Is that huge lout really Ralph Odmore?"

"Mollie Arbuthnot's boutique is losing a hundred a week."

"The Odmores have invited everybody."

"Even Austin Gibson Grey, I'm told."

"That's going too far."

"Hello Karen, you didn't answer my letter."

"Sebastian darling, one is so busy."

"Gracie and Ludwig have bought a manor house in the Cotswolds."

"Oh Mr. Enstone, how charming of you to come."

"Richard, you know Mr. Enstone."

"Is it true that Matthew and—"

"Sssh. Hello, Mavis, what a stunning dress. I hear you're selling Valmorana?"

"No, I'm not actually, at least I haven't decided."

"Hello Gracie. Shame Patrick couldn't come."

"Hello, Ralph. Yes, Patrick is quite one for the girls now."

"Oh. Girls? What girls?"

"Hester, is Austin coming?"

"I hope so. It would be rather an achievement to have Austin."

"Is it true that Henrietta Sayce has gassed Mollie Arbuthnot's cat?"

"It was in the interests of science."

"Henrietta Sayce is very scientific."

"Such a clever family."

"Ludwig says he's never met Karen."

"Gracie has been keeping them apart."

"Dr. Seldon is discussing hormones with Oliver."

"Patrick Tisbourne is chasing some girl."

"They start so young nowadays."

"Geoffrey Arbuthnot is looking care-worn."

"He's thinking about Mollie's boutique."

"Karen has chucked the pig biz."

"Is it true that Karen and Richard—"

"Sssh. Hello, Richard, I hear everyone is dying to go on your yacht."

"I'm thinking of going commercial, actually."

"Ludwig and Gracie have bought a priory with a swimming pool."

"Henrietta Sayce has been blackmailing her brother for years."

"Is Austin Gibson Grey here? I just want to look at him."

287

"May I fill your glass, sir?"

"Thank you, dear boy."

"Everything Ann Colindale is wearing was bought at Mollie Arbuthnot's boutique."

"Mollie Arbuthnot's boutique is losing five hundred a week."

"Oliver has palmed his ghastly sports car off on Ludwig."

"When does Annapurna Atom set off for foreign climes?"

"What is Annapurna Atom?"

"Richard Pargeter's yacht."

"Richard Pargeter is going commercial."

"He hasn't broken it to the Tisbournes yet."

"George won't go if he has to pay a penny."

"Dear George is the meanest man in the world."

"George once gave us some non-vintage champagne for Christmas."

"How terribly sweet of Ann to wear those ghastly things."

"Ann is an angel."

"She's the only one in our set."

"Matthew and Oliver are discussing Lord Kitchener."

"Mavis, I really am going to come with my motor-car and take Dorina away."

"Is that Charlotte Ledgard over there?"

"By herself in the corner as usual."

"Why does she come if she hates it?"

"Dorina is going to live with the Tisbournes."

"Henrietta Sayce is on LSD."

"Gracie and Ludwig are buying a house in Ireland."

"Please won't somebody go and talk to Mr. Enstone."

"Hester is so worried about Ralph."

"Ann, you look so lovely in white, so pure."

"Thank you, Richard dear. Richard—"

"Richard Pargeter is charging the Tisbournes the earth for that trip to Greece."

"Sebastian has got a job in the Bank of England."

"No wonder we're going to devalue."

"Penny Sayce is having a nervous breakdown."

"No she isn't, she's over there."

"Yes, but she's having a nervous breakdown."

"Penny Sayce is so worried about Henrietta."

"Karen, haven't you ever met Ludwig?"

"I say, Richard, Karen hasn't met Ludwig."

"Ludwig, do struggle over here, there's someone who's dying to meet you."

"I've heard so—"

"I've heard so—"

"Ludwig, I want to talk to you seriously."

"Karen wants to talk to Ludwig seriously."

"Ann, I can't stand this, let's go out to the pub."

"Certainly not, Ralph, you are under eighteen."

"Mollie is so worried about Karen."

"Charles and Geoffrey are discussing the crisis."

"Patrick Tisbourne has won the history prize."

"Henrietta Sayce has been arrested."

"What for? Don't tell me, let me guess."

"Ralph Odmore has become a drop-out."

"Penny Sayce is so worried about Oliver."

"Karen is flirting with Ludwig."

"Char, you know it's fatal to sit down at a party like this."

"Thank you, Clara, I have never been a protagonist in the drama of life."

"Ralph Odmore is going through a rather boorish phase."

"He won't leave poor Ann alone for a minute."

"I hear they've shut Dorina up at last."

"For God's sake someone give Charlotte Ledgard a strong drink."

"Isn't that Dorina over there?"

"They don't let Dorina come to parties."

"Oliver wants Matthew to come to see his incunabula."

"His what?"

"Pinkie darling, I think I'm drunk, I can see two of you."

"Hello, Sebastian."

"Hello, Gracie."

"It's quite sort of private in the middle of the pandemonium, isn't it?"

"Yes, I feel we are alone together at last."

"No one can hear what we say."

"Not even ourselves."

"Sebastian, you do look marvellous with those blue frills."

"Did Ludwig buy you the orchids?"

"No, I got them myself at Moyses Stevens."

"May I send you some flowers tomorrow?"

"Lovely, no one's given me flowers for ages."

"Patrick Tisbourne is in love with some girl."

"It's probably Henrietta Sayce."

"But she's only ten."

"Who is that brutish man with the dirty waistcoat?"

"Is that Austin Gibson Grey?"

"No, it's some Oxford thug that Ludwig brought along."

"He looks terribly drunk."

"He's an Irishman."

"He's the man who cuts Matthew's lawn."

"Don't be silly."

"Do you think Matthew is queer?"

"His name's MacMurphy or something."

"He's pie-eyed."

"So is Clara."

"So am I."

"Karen, I mustn't, I'm getting quite drunk."

"Nonsense, Ludwig, the party is only just beginning."

"I'm delighted you're so interested in Greek vases, Karen. It's such an acquired taste."

"It is, isn't it. Let me fill your glass."

"Matthew is going."

"We shall be able to breathe."

"Oh hello Andrew, I'm so glad you made it."

"I hope I'm not too late, Lady Odmore, it was so kind of you to ask me."

"I so much want you to meet my younger son. By the way, Andrew, who is that stout man? He hasn't made himself known to me."

"Oh dear, that's MacMurraghue. Hasn't he—he's gate-crashing—shall I take him away?"

"Certainly not. Good-bye, Matthew dear, you must come to dinner soon."

"My God, there's Austin."

"No!"

"It can't be, he looks quite distinguished."

"He's had one or two."

"Is that Austin Gibson Grey?"

"Yes, you know, the chap who—"

"Char darling, did you talk to Matthew?"

"No."

"He's gone, I think."

"Yes."

"Andrew, we do hope you'll persuade Ralph—"

"Ludwig and Karen are discussing Greek vases."

"Patrick Tisbourne and Henrietta Sayce are engaged to be married."

"Richard, could you give me a lift home?"

"Sorry, Ann, I'm taking Karen."

"Matthew has brought his Irish valet."

"Matthew is going too far."

"George Tisbourne is removing Clara."

"Clara has passed out in the hall."

"Sebastian, don't."

"Nobody marks us, Gracie."

"Yes, Austin's looking."

"Bugger Austin."

"Ralph, let's go to the pub."

"Oh Ann, how super!"

"Ludwig and Karen are still discussing Greek vases."

"Ralph and Ann have gone to the pub."

"Psst, Oliver."

"Oh Andrew, goodie goodie."

"Could you help me to remove MacMurraghue?"

"Who's MacMurraghue?"

"This chap."

"I see what you mean."

"Matthew's valet is bickering with Austin."

"Matthew's valet seems rather an aggressive chap."

"Now he's shoving his way towards Gracie."

"I say look at Gracie and Sebastian!"

"They are in each other's arms!"

"They are kissing each other!"

"Austin has given the Irishman a push."

"Oliver, just get hold of his other arm."

"A fight is starting!"

"Karen, I am going to take you home."

"No, Richard, I—"

"Karen is in tears."

"Karen, I am going to take you home."

"Matthew's Irish friend has passed out in the hall."

"Austin has called Sebastian a cad."

"Gracie is in tears."

"Oh I *am* enjoying this party!"

❦❦❦

"So you are haunted by that scene," said Ludwig.

"Yes," said Matthew. "I saw this group of people standing in the open space and then I realized that they were demonstrating. It was winter, a dark yellow afternoon with some street lamps on and a little snow falling rather slowly. They were holding a board protesting against the trial of a writer. There were only about eight of them. It looked so odd, almost embarrassing, as if something were trying to happen and not succeeding, this awkward group standing there in the snow with their board, dressed in black, all padded and stocky in their fur hats and boots. They looked so lonely and sort of gratuitous and aslant, if you know what I mean, like something in the corner of a painting. And of course everyone who passed by looked the other way and quickened their step as soon as they saw what was going on. Then I saw a man coming along who looked as if he too would pass by. He hesitated and he looked round, and then he came back and began shaking hands with them. That shaking hands—I can't describe it—it was suddenly as if that place had become the centre of the world. He was still standing there when the police arrived. Four police cars drew up. It was all very quiet, there were no gestures, no raised voices. The police looked weary. They helped the demonstrators into the cars. They were all taken away, including the chap who had joined them. The whole scene was erased and there was nothing left but the snow slowly falling and the day getting darker and people passing by who didn't even know that it had happened at all."

"And later?"

"Later I learnt about some of them. The news gets round somehow. Some went to labour camps, some into mental hospitals, you know."

"Yes. And I suppose that chap too."

"I suppose so."

"So pointless," said Ludwig.

"Yes," said Matthew. "Yes." He went on. "Things that were relative once are absolute now. One feels it's the end of a line. Politics and war used to retain some decencies. Also their power was limited. No nation could destroy another, governments couldn't get at their subjects, and in the interstices of it all human beings could flourish. So tyrannies regularly broke down."

"Won't tyrannies always regularly break down?" asked Ludwig.

Matthew was silent. It was a sunny afternoon, tea-time. The Irishman, whose name was Geraghty, had laid the table and made the tea. He had achieved social advancement by getting inside the house. Now he was outside in the sun dreamily weeding. The walnut tree was translucently golden, absorbed in its own faint trembling. Overhead an aeroplane droned peacefully in fine pitch towards London airport.

"Then," said Matthew, "you could give your life, you

293

could give years of suffering. If you didn't die of it you could probably retain your personality and because of the muddle in which everything was at least you had a chance, and what you did was significant, it couldn't be unmade, you couldn't be unmade. Of course there were brutalities and at a certain point of suffering the mind fails. But that wasn't part of the system. Not because of any virtue in the system, I mean in the bad ones, but because of the muddle. But now—"

"Yes," said Ludwig. "More than to die, the willingness to rot. I would give my life, I think, more willingly than I would give my mind."

"Yes," said Matthew. " 'For who would lose, though full of pain, this intellectual being . . .' One can face suffering and one cannot imagine death. But the destruction or perversion of one's personality, could one face that? And for nothing."

"For nothing. And yet—"

"To live on to regret the just action, to forget the just action, to forget justice itself."

"Anyone might regret acting rightly if the consequences were awful. But aren't you exaggerating the differences? People come out of labour camps. These great actions exist and are known of, even now. You said the news got round. Who knows what deep effect they may not some-how have?"

"Yes, these are the great actions of our century. These are our real heroes. These are the people whose courage and devotion to goodness goes beyond any dream of one's own possibility. Courage is after all, when sufficiently refined, the virtue of the age. It is always perhaps the only name of love which can mean anything to us. We speak of love because we are romantics, and we mean, however hard we try, something romantic by it."

"Yes, yes. But Matthew, not really quite for nothing, their actions I mean."

"Well, maybe in the great web of cause and effect, who knows. But it's not significant any more, it's more like gambling, it's roulette."

"But that doesn't make virtue something different."

"I don't know," said Matthew. "One wants to say 'Of course not,' but what is that 'of course'?"

"All right, perhaps those guys in the snow didn't think they were causing anything, preventing anything."

"That was what made them holy."

"But if they were good, they were good in the same old way. We don't think virtue has changed in ordinary things, so why here?"

"Perhaps only now can we see what it's really like, anywhere."

"Virtue has always had to be its own reward."

"Only in a philosophical sense, dear boy. Fortunately for the human race virtue usually offers many other rewards besides her fair self."

"No, but really, in the end, one is good in order to be good!"

"Where is the end? Where those men stood? I'm not even sure of that any more. One wants things to be better, things ought to be better. There shouldn't be starvation and fear. That's obvious. It's when you try to go deeper than the obvious, when you try to go where God used to be—"

"But we can do without God, I should think!"

"Mmm."

"Better without Him, isn't it?"

"So one feels."

"But isn't one right to feel it?"

"I don't know."

"I don't understand you. Do you mean that behind ordinary decency and duty there's nothing, there's chaos? You were saying things were more absolute now. Then you said because it was all roulette we could see now that virtue was all superficial or conventional or something—"

"There are absolutes where calculation about causality comes up against a brick wall. But these are not moral absolutes. Perhaps indeed they make moral absolutes impossible. When you can't calculate perhaps it doesn't matter so much how you act."

"But that's despair!"

"That's one name for it."

"But do you mean that because of the latest human frightfulness we can see what was invisible before—"

"That there are no categorical imperatives."

"Because in the end we're bound to fail?"

"Not exactly. What is failure, anyway? It's just that at a certain point calculation must break down. It's like Gödel's theorem. It's built into the way things are. Perhaps."

"There's nothing deep?"

"Not that kind of thing. Of course all this is easier to see now because the old religious fogs are blowing away."

"Yet you wanted to become a monk!" said Ludwig.

"Oh that. That was quite different."

"It can't be different," cried Ludwig, "it *can't* be!"

"That is what philosophers always say," said Matthew and smiled. "More tea?"

"There must be a way through."

"A subterranean river? We know where that leads to."

"Another of your beastly absolutes?"

"Yes."

"You do upset me!" said Ludwig. Then he laughed. "This is Gracie's favourite cake. She calls it Tennis Court Cake."

"It's all right with Gracie?"

"Oh yes, perfectly. I'm very glad you didn't see that fracas."

At the party Gracie had been suddenly ferociously jealous because he had spent so long talking to Karen. She had explained it all. Ludwig had understood it all. He felt that his love had been deepened, though the hurt remained. To recognize the hurt and to feel that love was deepened, that was good.

"You and Gracie are just off to Ireland?"

"Yes, we thought we'd get away together before the wedding arrangements get really hotted up."

"Excellent idea."

"So anyway," said Ludwig, "you think I should hang on to what I'm sure of and not worry about the rest?"

"Yes. And not be beguiled by guilt."

"I won't fall into that trap."

"You are by nature a guilty man."

"I worry about my parents."

"They will come round, they'll have to."

"I sometimes feel it's dishonourable to take the easy way."

"Of course you do. And you sometimes feel nervous frenzied impulses to get yourself punished. But these are not your deepest and most serious thoughts."

"I guess you're right."

"You see, we still have a vocabulary."

Ludwig laughed again. "Well—that's something."

"Possibly everything."

"So you think—"

"You are not one of the heroes we spoke of just now. All this adds up to the appropriateness of your continuing your present course of action."

"But appropriateness is not enough."

"So indeed you feel, and this is where guilt and worry about your parents and ridiculous considerations about honour and so forth find a fault through which they can enter. You are discontented. You want to work it out so that you are perfectly justified and absolutely guaranteed. You feel there must be such a structure."

"But there isn't."

"No."

"Ugh-hu," said Ludwig. "I think I'll have some more cake." After munching for a moment he said, "But then, according to you, virtue is an illusion?"

"The idea of it is an inspiration, an important one, in some sense conceivably a necessary one."

"But it is an illusion?"

Matthew looked out of the window at the Irishman, who was asleep under the walnut tree. "What does it matter what we say here? Very few people ever come here. Here language breaks down."

"But those heroes you spoke of?"

"It may cheer them up for a short while to feel that they acted rightly."

Ludwig whistled. "Wow!"

297

"By the way," said Matthew, "have you been to see Dorina?"

"No."

"I think you ought to go."

"What's that funny word you used?"

They laughed.

"Well, you can see her at the Tisbournes'," said Matthew. "It will be all much easier there and much less dramatic."

"Yes, I know." Ludwig was about to say that Garth had written to him about Dorina. He was about to go on to tell Matthew about Garth's man killed in New York. Then he decided he did not want to mention Garth to Matthew just then. He felt ridiculously possessive already about Matthew. Again he had given his heart. How easily it had happened.

"I've brought your supper on a tray," said Mavis.

"I was just coming down," said Dorina.

"Well, dear heart, I'll take it down again. Mrs. Carberry has set the table."

"No, I'll have it here."

"No, please, Dorina. Let me take it down, we'll have supper together."

"No, no, Mavis, I'll have it here, *please* don't argue, I can't bear it, sorry."

"Sorry, darling. I hope you'll like it. I wish you'd eat some meat."

"I hate meat."

298

"I suspect undernourishment may be part of—part of it all."

Dorina's room was powdery dim and yet sunny, obstructed by great shafts of hot evening light which seemed to fill it, making the sisters almost invisible to each other. Sunlight on a window in another street dazzled in Dorina's eyes, and she shifted, shaking her head. She was wearing a short light padded dressing gown, white and a little soiled. Her feet were bare.

Mavis put the tray on the tousled bed. Dorina had been lying down.

"Will you come down after?"

"Maybe."

"Mrs. Carberry is watching telly in the kitchen with Ronald. We could sit with them."

"Ronald upsets me so."

"You said you could get on with Ronald."

"I can't any more."

"Then we'll sit in the drawing-room."

"I know I'm stupid but—"

"We'll sit quietly in the drawing-room. I'll find you another novel."

"I can't read. I didn't really finish the other one. It upset me."

"Well, come down afterwards and we'll talk. Dorina."

"Yes."

"You know Clara's coming for you at eleven tomorrow."

Dorina picked at the button of her dressing gown. "You said something about it yesterday but I thought you were just asking me, I didn't know you'd arranged it all. I said I didn't want to go to Clara's."

"You did agree."

"I don't think I did, I just wanted you to stop talking about it. Mavis, I *can't* go to Clara's, you must know that."

"Dear child, you can't stay on here forever. It's not that I want to send you away, you know that I love you and want to protect you and help you. But just letting you stay on here vaguely from week to week isn't helping you. You're getting—well, it's not doing you good, you're living

299

too much inside yourself and I'm probably the worst person for you to be with because we're so close, in a way it's not like being with another person at all."

"I know."

"You must be forced to make an effort, my darling, you must, before you just forget how, try to do what other human beings do, deal with what's alien, face it, wear a hard surface, live in public. I thought at first this sort of rest would make you stronger, but it's doing the opposite. You're hiding from the world. You need the ordinary compulsory things of social life, having to talk, having to dress. You're becoming a dream figure."

"They'll make me see Dr. Seldon."

"No they won't, they won't make you do anything. They'll just absorb you into their silly busy social goings-on. It'll do you far more good than anything else could at the moment. You need frivolity and gossip, you need Clara. As soon as you find out that you can manage after all, as soon as you see that no one notices you or bothers about you particularly, you'll feel far more brisk and human. Do at least try it, Dorina. If you hate it you can come back here."

"The Tisbournes won't let me be ordinary," said Dorina. "They'll exhibit me. Everyone will come to the house to look at me."

"That's just vanity," said Mavis. "You aren't as interesting as all that, my dearest child, except to those who love you. You won't even be a nine-days' wonder. There, see how bracing I'm being with you!"

"I don't want to go," said Dorina. "It would be the beginning of a bad road. It would hurt Austin, it would divide me from Austin."

"Dorina, you mustn't treat Austin as if he was fragile or insane. He's very tough. You can't hurt him as easily as you imagine. Really, Austin's as tough as an old boot. If you can only get back a little backbone and ordinary stamina, you can manage Austin and make everything good again. It's this drifting on which is so hopeless."

"You want me to go—"

"I want what's best for you."

"I know, but— Oh Mavis, I'm sorry, but I just can't bear the idea of leaving here, except to be with Austin."

The pale wedges and walls of light had dissolved into hazy atoms of obscurity and it was almost dark in the room.

Mavis said after a moment, "Well, you think about it. When you come downstairs we'll talk."

"I think I won't come down, if you don't mind. I feel so tired. I'll go to bed early. I'll put the tray outside."

"Oh dear, your supper's been getting cold. Are you sure—?"

"Yes, yes, I'll go to bed early, we'll talk tomorrow."

"I'll help you to do your packing in the morning," said Mavis. "You know you need only go for a little while. It'll be a holiday. You'll feel so much better. You need a change. You can come back whenever you like."

"Yes, yes, thank you."

"Darling, are you all right?"

"Yes, of course, good night my dearest, yes, all's well, good night."

Mavis went down the stairs. It was hot and dark in the belly of the house. She switched on a light. What would Dorina be like in the morning? But it was true, it was true that Dorina would be better off almost anywhere else. I'm just a part of her mind, thought Mavis. And Austin too, in another way. She needs the company of people who are indifferent to her. It's true that she ought to move. I'm not just being selfish or unkind.

Mrs. Carberry and Ronald were watching telly. It was a ridiculous play about a couple who simply couldn't stop adopting stray dogs. Their house was full of dogs, big dogs, small dogs, shaggy dogs, sleek dogs, sad dignified dogs, and dogs with comical clown faces. Ronald found it all so funny he simply could not stay on his chair but kept falling off it choking with laughter and clutching his mother, who set him upright again. Mrs. Carberry was laughing because the play was so funny and because Ronald was laughing and seemed so happy, but she was also crying. Mavis began to laugh. It really was too absurd, all those

301

dogs. Now they were all trooping down the stairs, it was too absurd. Then Mavis found that she was crying too. In the telly-lit obscurity she and Mrs. Carberry cried and cried.

Tomorrow she would pack Dorina's things and put Dorina into Clara Tisbourne's car. It was the right thing to do. Then at last it would open before her, the ever-after land of Matthew, love, and joy. Mavis wept hot tears of ecstasy at the back of the kitchen in the flickering dark. But Mrs. Carberry wept out of a broken heart to see Ronald so happy and to know what his life would be.

Dorina was sitting on her bed. She had eaten nothing. She was not crying. She had not managed to make Mavis understand, to make her see. Mavis's eyes had been hazy with private happiness. How could Mavis see?

The room was dark now. Dorina covered up the cold scrambled eggs after messing them about a little and put the tray down silently outside the door. Then she lay on her bed.

Tomorrow Mavis would pack her things and put her into Clara Tisbourne's car at eleven. Clara would carry her off in triumph. There would be rejoicing at the Tisbourne house. People would flock to see her. Not unkindly, but with deadly effect.

Austin had said he would come. He had not come. He had sent a note to say that he would soon come. At the Tisbournes' he would never show his face. How energetically the Tisbournes would try to persuade him, try to supervise a reconciliation for which they would take the credit, and how much damage it would all do at this delicate time. Oh why had Mavis suddenly abandoned her and stopped understanding? Mavis was so determined now to see only part of the picture.

There were no presences tonight, only an echoing void which made the dark room seem like an empty concert hall which was somehow full of silent sound. It was as if the sound was really clamouring about her like an electric storm and she had screamed into it. Had she really screamed? Waters of electric sound closed over her head.

She sat up, feeling sick and giddy. If she went to Clara Tisbourne's tomorrow she would not find Austin again ever. There would be a grimacing wall of monkey people between herself and Austin. She would be a traitor to him and in revenge he would kill their love. There was a precious private faithfulness which she must keep whole until the true moment when they were together again. If she went to the Tisbournes' everything there would speak to her of a possible life without Austin. This was what Mavis meant when she talked of healing: treachery and the death of love.

Mavis will pack my bag, thought Dorina, and I shall walk down the stairs in a daze and Clara Tisbourne will take my arm in a firm grip, like a policewoman, and I shall get into the car.

Dorina held her head. The silent storm of sound drummed in the huge hall. Help, she asked, help. *Impossible de trop plier les genoux*. She knelt beside the bed.

Her knee touched her suitcase. She pulled the suitcase out. Then she got up and switched on the light. She took off her dressing gown and put on blouse, skirt, and sandals. She threw things into the suitcase. She plaited her hair and thrust it into an elastic band. She put on a mackintosh. She found her handbag. There was money in it. She listened at the door and then began to glide across the landing and down the stairs. Howls of awful laughter came from the kitchen. Dorina went out of the front door and clicked it behind her.

✳✳✳✳✳

"We might go to Canada," said Mitzi.
"Don't be silly," said Austin.

"Start life anew."

"Impossible. We're both done for. Why not admit it?"

"You're such a cynic," said Mitzi. "Have some more whisky. There, you always get round me, don't you, you always will. You know when I get in a rage it's just because I love you. You know that, don't you?"

"Yes."

"And you forgive me?"

"Yes. I know you love me. We have a lot to forgive each other. Don't think I've just taken your love and your kindness for granted. I'm a sod, but not that much of one."

"I do love you, and it's so nice to talk like this, so cosy, isn't it."

Only one lamp was alight in Mitzi's sitting-room, and Mitzi and Austin were sitting at the table with the bottle of whisky between them. It was a hot close evening and the door stood ajar to give a cool draught. Mitzi's bulgy armchairs were ranged round the table like spectators. Obscure upon the mantelpiece china gnomes and peasant maidens of Germanic origin. Austin feels hot, cosy, sexy. His sleeves are rolled up, his shirt lolls open at the neck, he is sweating. Sweat rolls down his neck through the furry gold of his lengthening shaggy hair. Sweat rolls down his chest through a tunnel full of golden curls. He rubs his sweaty chest with the back of his hand and looks with satisfaction at the dirty smear on his knuckles. He smells his hand furtively. He feels hot and pleasantly restless and slightly drunk. His shirt is widely stained with sweat under the arms. So is Mitzi's light blue dress. She is sweating too. Her dress is open-necked and the dark well of her breasts is visible within, moist and pungent. As they sit at the table and lightly caress each other's bare arms his fingers can explore the tender dew in the crook of her elbow. Her plump arms are covered with long reddish down which glints freshly in the lamplight like young vegetation.

"How blue your veins are and all hot and sort of elastic, I can feel your blood moving." She drew her finger along.

"That tickles."

"But really, about Canada, why shouldn't we go there and have a new life where everything was right? We've both been so unlucky."

"We'd still be our same bad hopeless old selves."

"We could try. They pay well over there. I'd get a typing job, you'd look around—"

"It's a sweet dream and you're a sweet girl. God, how hot it is tonight." He bent down and kissed her at the elbow where the skin was soft and wet and a little stained and tired on the inner side.

Mitzi shuddered and moaned. "Oh Austin, if you knew how much I love you, it shakes me, it does."

Austin looked vaguely at the large head, the round bronzed face glowing with simplicity and health, the short clipped slightly gingery fair hair. And Mitzi's eyes, what colour were they? A light stony greyish greenish blue. Big and adoring. Nice.

"I am a cad," he said, "capable of caddish things. You have been warned."

"That won't do, Austin, talk to me properly, tell me about Dorina."

"No. Never."

"How is she, poor girl, is she really bonkers, you know, binworthy?"

"Do not speak in that coarse way."

"Sorry, but she is awfully odd, isn't she, and she ran away, and she hasn't been much of a wife, I mean you haven't had much of a marriage, have you?"

"No," said Austin. "I haven't had much of a marriage." He caressed the big warm soft hairy arm with even strokes and then passed his damp fingers across his face like that of a sleeper.

"I think you're scared of her. Does she get at you?"

"No, she's an angel."

"But sort of creepy?"

"Creepy, yes."

"God, I'm sorry for her. One does take mental health for granted, doesn't one?"

"Yes."

"You didn't want children?"

305

"Children of hers? God no!"

"Have some more whisky, dear."

"She doesn't support and cherish me," said Austin. "I support and cherish her."

"You need a wife like a carthorse."

Austin laughed. "Be my carthorse, Mitzi. Let me jump on your back and we'll gallop to Winnipeg and live happily ever after!"

"Oh if only you would!"

Austin joggled his chair closer. He leaned his head against the strong warm bouncy flesh of her shoulder. He kissed its warmth through the thin dress and felt in his lips her trembling.

"Oh Austin—"

"Go on talking, Dobbin."

"Yes, I am your Dobbin, aren't I?"

"Dear horsie, I am swinish and you are coarse, we are made for each other."

"I don't think we're swinish and coarse, not now we aren't."

"No, actually now we are rather divine."

"I feel so close to you, I feel we can really talk. Do tell me things. I bet you and Dorina were never any good in bed."

"No. That was part of the trouble."

"We'd be good, you and me. Can't you feel that now?"

"Feel it? Yes. You can feel it too, if you like."

He took her hand and laid it where she could feel it. He took off his glasses. They both sighed and their eyes closed. Austin's knee nuzzled at the hem of the blue dress and his fingers followed. He raised his head and let his lips browse across her cheek.

A few minutes or perhaps longer later on Austin was aroused from a sort of swoon by the sound of somebody falling down the stairs. That clattering bumping sound was unmistakable. Somebody had just fallen down the flight of stairs which led from the landing just outside to the front door. Austin came to, sorted himself out from Mitzi and stood up. He felt damp, drugged, dirty. He hauled at his

306

clothes and said "Oh hell" and went to the door and switched on the landing light.

Dorina was lying at the bottom of the stairs. Her face stared back at him over the heap of her twisted body. Then she kicked, knelt, and was up. Paralysed, Austin saw her convulsed legs, her tossed tail of hair, her frantic hand snatching at her bag, her little foot dabbing for a shoe which had come off. Then there was a flurry, a small explosion, and she had disappeared out of the front door and slammed it after her.

Austin rushed down the stairs. He fell over Dorina's suitcase, which she had left behind on the floor. He tugged at the front door, which seemed to be jammed, then dragged it open. The hot inky night air puffed sullenly into his face. He could hear the high echoing pit-a-pat of her running steps. He reached the pavement, staggered, and began to run after her.

There seemed to be nobody about. He could still hear her steps, but now the orange lamplight dazzled in his eyes and showed him nothing. He choked in the thick air, choked upon her name and found no voice, and his footsteps dragged as if soft rubbery rings enclosed his ankles. He reached a street corner and gripped at railings, swinging himself round. Still the light dancing steps tapped away before him into the distance.

"Dorina! Wait!"

He began to run again.

Then suddenly just above him the darkness congealed. Something huge and awful rushed out of the dark and seemed to sit upon his head. Austin ducked, cried out in fear, stood with uplifted arms staring about him. There was nothing but the purple lamp-dazzled night. Then again an approaching flurry in the air and he was struck violently from above. Pain travelled across his brow and he staggered dazed with the violence of the blow. Terror possessed him. What avenger was this? Was he in nightmare that his own thoughts should haunt him as a night-demon? He began to run, then stopped again as he saw it, a dreadful mask rushing toward him face to face. He saw

307

a pale flat oval visage, a hooked nose, luminous terrifying eyes . . .

Just beside him now, revealed in the sickly light, was a rubbish tip full of bricks and stony fragments. Keeping his right hand before his face, Austin seized a brick and raised it. The creature had wheeled over him and now came at him again, full at his head. Austin swung the brick upward.

A great screeching sound filled the dome of the night. A car, breaking violently, swerved to a halt beside the rubbish tip.

"What is it?" cried a frightened voice.

Suddenly there were people there.

"I hit something."

The driver of the car was standing in the road.

"It's some sort of bird."

"Thank God, I thought it was a child."

"It's a pigeon."

"No it isn't, it's huge, it's an owl."

"Oh Lord, it's our owl, that beautiful tawny."

"You've run over our owl."

"It wasn't his fault, that man killed it with a brick."

"It's whole breast is broken."

"Don't, I can't bear to look."

"That owl was a menace, it attacked a girl."

"They're like that at nesting time."

"That bloody man killed our owl with a brick."

"That man's a murderer."

"Oh look, how beautiful, I can't bear it."

The dead owl lay on the pavement under the lamp. Someone had carefully spread out one wing to display the exquisite glossy feathering.

Austin sat down on some steps and began to sob.

Matthew, just back from a meeting of the Royal Ceramics Society, was arranging his collection. He had mercifully forgotten Norman Monkley, about whom he had been worrying all day. He had bought two large mahogany display cases, into which he was now putting some favourite pieces. He had removed two semicircular tables and fitted the cases into the alcoves in the hall. It did not look too museum-like. The Sung and Ting dishes were all in a crowd on the drawing-room table. He had decided to make a selection of a number of favourites to keep with him and to lend the rest to the Fitzwilliam Museum for the present. The selection was proving very difficult. He stood holding a *famille noire* teapot tenderly by the spout. Of course Ming and Ting were greatest and Sung doubtless greatest of all, but for a weightless charm which was perfect without being sublime it was impossible to better Ching.

Someone was urgently ringing the front-door bell. Matthew frowned and put the vase into the case and closed the case. Who could be ringing in this peremptory manner at this hour of the night? Gracie and Ludwig were away in Ireland, it could not be them.

He went with rather deliberate slowness to the door and opened it just as the fierce ringing was starting up again. He peered out into the dark.

A young woman was standing there. He saw her eyes staring wide with amazed fear. He recognized Dorina.

"Come in, my child."

Matthew had not seen Dorina for a great many years.

He remembered her as a shy thin girl, almost a schoolgirl, with a short plait of light-brown hair. She stood before him now, scarcely changed, with her little plait and her short brown mac and her bare legs, clutching her handbag and staring at him with amazement. Behind her a small quiet rain was falling.

"Dorina, come in, come in out of the rain."

Matthew, like an old soldier, like an old diplomat, was unruffled and smoothly calm.

"Matthew!"

"But of course, why not? Come on in, child." He stretched a hand towards her.

Dorina stepped back as if about to flee, then entered precipitately, glancing behind her and dodging his hand. Then she ran into the drawing-room and turned to stare at him as he followed.

"Matthew."

"Yes, I'm not a ghost am I? I'm so glad you've come to see me."

"But I haven't—"

"Yes you have!"

"I mean, I didn't know you were here."

"Well, I am, as large as life. Gracie let the Villa to me. Sit down. Let me take your coat."

"But where's Charlotte?"

"Didn't you know? Charlotte's over at your place. Austin has rented the flat to Charlotte. Didn't anyone tell you?"

Dorina let her mackintosh fall to the floor. She sat down in an armchair. "Yes," she said. "Austin told me. But—I completely—forgot—I was very—upset—I came here—to find Char—I thought—oh I didn't know you were here—I didn't, I didn't, I didn't—" She rocked her body and began softly and rhythmically to cry.

Matthew sat down and looked at her. Of course she would not know that he was at the Villa, no one would have mentioned his name to her. He felt protective love, pity, fear, terror. She looked older to him now and yet still absurdly childish, her hair coming undone, her little green dress smudged with dirt.

310

"Why, you've cut your knee."

"Yes, I was running and I fell."

Her legs were bare and brown. There was a grimy mess of dirt and blood on one knee.

"I'll wash it for you. Stay where you are."

Matthew went out to the kitchen and filled a bowl with hot water and disinfectant. He found a clean napkin. He stood quiet for a moment at the kitchen window, which was wide open, and listened to the soft hot rain sizzling down. He wondered what he was going to do with Dorina and his heart melted into a vagueness of compassion. Why could no one really help that child? Why had she run out into the night and fallen over and hurt her knee? He went back to the drawing-room, where Dorina was sitting motionless now and still crying with large tears, which she did not wipe but allowed to fall down onto the bosom of her dress which they had stained a darker green.

As Matthew drew up a chair she shrank back. "Now, Dorina," said Matthew, "don't be silly. If I'm to help you you mustn't behave like a child."

"I'm not—"

"I know. I mean, you must try to be rational and see ordinary things as ordinary. I'm going to bathe your knee."

He dabbed at the mass of grit with the napkin. Dorina winced, gazing down fascinated at the reddening linen.

"There, that's quite clean. I've got a clean hankie here. I'll just dry it. Better leave it open to the air."

He withdrew his hand from the smooth warmth of her leg and looked at her. He pulled a chair near. Dorina was staring at him now, very large-eyed, her lower lip trembling in a convulsive and startling manner. He thought, she is going into hysterics, I must do something immediately.

Matthew said, "Look, Dorina, I am going to put my arms round you and you are not going to scream or struggle but just to rest upon me, to rest at last without any fear. Come."

Matthew tried to perch himself on the corner of the armchair. It was too difficult, he was too large.

"Come, get up." He pulled her up, holding her wrists,

311

and settled his bulk squarely into the chair. Then he drew her down again onto his knee and felt her stiffened body relax against him as she buried her wet face in his shoulder and he felt her brow hot against his neck. She was trembling. He held her, not violently but firmly, and waited for the trembling to cease. It ceased at last and she gave a deep sigh.

Dorina seemed asleep. She lay there quite still, her breathing quiet, her head heavy against him, one hand nestling in his. And Matthew sat there and looked away into the room over the tangle of loosened brown hair, looked at hovering ellipses of creamy white where almost invisible flowers meandered in a translucent depth of iridescent milk. He held her as he might have a magic talisman or a sacred relic or the Grail itself. He felt a strange sense of triumph and certainty as if for once in his life an innocent love had imposed upon him its infallible and radiant will.

She stirred and sighed and began to make the motions of sitting up. Her body was still limply relaxed and very warm. Matthew felt, without any alarm, his physical desire for her as he eased himself away and let her slip from him into the chair. He stood up. The room was present to him again, suddenly vivid and detailed, as if he had been entranced or sleeping. He looked down at Dorina. She smiled at him a smile that belonged to the human world, wry, apologetic, humorous. A miraculous smile.

"Good!" said Matthew.

"Thank you, Matthew."

"Look, Dorina, have you eaten anything? What a host I am! Let me give you something to eat and drink."

"No, no. Well, a biscuit or something. I am hungry, now I come to think of it. And yes, a little, all right, brandy with the—soda water—yes."

Matthew ran to the kitchen. He felt boyishly happy and pleased with himself. He ran back with bread and butter and cheese and tomatoes and cherry cake.

"A little milk too?"

"No thanks, I don't like milk."

Dorina was eating the cheese and drinking the brandy. Matthew stood, took a glass himself, and looked down at her with stupefaction.

"That's right, child. Eat and drink. Then we'll talk a bit. And I'll ring Mavis and take you back home in a taxi."

"Oh no," said Dorina. "I can't go back there." She spoke quietly, but with a return of the trembling lip. She thrust her plate away.

Matthew thought, I must keep very calm and make it all seem very ordinary and not at all important. It occurred to him that he did not know how or why she had left Valmorana.

"Mavis will wonder why you're so late. Or will she assume you're staying the night with Charlotte?"

"I didn't tell Mavis I was going."

"But then she'll be worried, won't she? Shouldn't we telephone her to say you're on the way back?"

"She doesn't know I've gone, she won't know till tomorrow morning. I told her I was going to bed early. She won't come to my room."

"But she might," said Matthew, "and she'd find you gone and she'd be upset."

"If she'd found me gone she would have telephoned you," said Dorina with composure.

She can think, she can even be shrewd, thought Matthew, looking at the thin long youthful face, calmer now but still tear-stained.

"I haven't been in long," said Matthew. "I rang her actually on the way home but got no reply."

"She was watching a television play. She and Mrs. Carberry were laughing so much they wouldn't have heard the telephone ring."

There was an air of even precision about it all like a detective story. I must be gentle and calm, he thought.

"I'm not going back there," said Dorina.

"You think it's too late tonight," said Matthew. He looked at his watch. To his surprise it was after midnight.

"I'm not going back there. Mavis arranged for me to stay with the Tisbournes. It's not Mavis's fault. Clara

313

Tisbourne was coming with the car. I can't go to the Tisbournes. I know Mavis wants me to go, to be somewhere else. It's not fair to Mavis if I stay. But I can't go to the Tisbournes. And Mavis had arranged for me to go—"

"Well, don't worry so," said Matthew. "Nobody will make you do anything you don't want. Look, I'll take you over to Charlotte's."

"No, no. I don't want Charlotte to know—I was—with you—"

She is right, thought Matthew. Anyway better not to involve Charlotte. Dorina will want to go back to Valmorana tomorrow. He said, "Would you like to stay here?" He was about to say, After all, why not. Of course you must. But he checked himself and left the question blank.

Dorina's face contracted and she closed her eyes for a moment. She said, "I'll go to a hotel. Only I don't know what hotels cost now and I don't know if I've got enough money."

"Nonsense," said Matthew. "You must stay here. After all, why not. Of course you must."

"No."

"We can't start looking for a hotel for you at this hour of the night in the pouring rain, it's ridiculous. Stay here, Dorina, just tonight, and tomorrow we'll think what's best to do. Ludwig is away. No one will know. You understand me. No one will know."

"I can't decide—"

"Then don't decide yet. Just eat and drink a little more and talk to me a bit. Dorina, there's nothing to be frightened of, you know that, don't you?"

"All right. Yes. Forgive me, Matthew, I'm sorry to be so helpless and spineless. I do feel—better—now—"

Good, he thought. If there was prayer he had prayed for her. But he must not waste what might be a unique chance of making her talk to him.

"Dorina, forgive me and don't answer unless you want to. Do you really want to go back to Austin? If you don't wouldn't it be better to make it clear and go away somewhere? Many people would help you. I'm not suggesting

314

myself, of course, because, well, you know. But I could put you in touch with others who could help, people, perhaps, that you don't know yet, new people."

"You mean doctors, clergymen—?"

"No, no, no, just people! Don't feel yourself so persecuted! There are *other* places in the world, you don't have to sit paralysed in *this* spider's web! But you haven't answered my question."

They were sitting now close to each other. Matthew leaned forward and patted her arm, smiling. How wise he had been to embrace her. If they had not touched each other the tension now would have been unendurable. His desire for her was vague, diffused in benevolence and compassion and the simple liveliness of affection.

Dorina was drinking some more of the brandy and soda. Her rather gaunt cheeks were pinkly flushed. She regarded Matthew with grave deep evasive eyes. How strange it is, he thought, that I have Dorina with me in my house in the middle of the night and no one knows she is here.

"I can't leave Austin," she said. "I am married to him. He must be saved through me, and I through him."

"You are very solemn," said Matthew. "And your decision is probably right. I just thought you should realize and conceive of other possibilities." What a traitor Austin would think me, Matthew reflected, if he could hear these words. Yet all I want is for this hunted creature to feel a little free. No more than that.

"There are none."

"All the same—"

"Have you discussed me a lot with Mavis?"

Matthew hesitated. "Yes."

Dorina was silent a moment. Then she said, "There are things I've never said, even to Mavis."

"Well, say them to me."

"I am afraid of Austin. And I am afraid for him. I can't quite distinguish these."

"I know."

"Matthew, Austin once told me that he murdered Betty, he drowned her."

315

This, thought Matthew. He said at once, as cooly as he could, "He lied, of course."

"Yes," said Dorina. "I knew it wasn't true, of course. He said it to impress me, perhaps to frighten me. That is —what Austin does. Yes."

"Then—don't worry—"

"Yes. Except that I *am* frightened. And—haunted—but it's not Austin's fault— Oh Matthew—I am so tired—" Tears were coming again.

It was no good after all trying to talk to her tonight. "You'd better go to bed," said Matthew, "here. We'll keep you a secret. Just rest now and I'll fix your bedroom."

He ran upstairs, turning lights on. The bed was made up in Ludwig's room. He took off the counterpane and turned back the blanket. He laid out his own best silk pyjamas, pulled the curtains and hurried downstairs again.

Dorina was fast asleep.

Matthew looked down at her as she lay nestled into her spread and tangled hair, her lips parted, her body twisted, one sandal off. He undid and took off the other sandal. She had pretty feet. Then, speaking to her softly, as one might to an animal, he began to pick her up. She murmured faintly and took hold of his hand as he gathered her and jolted her well up into his arms. Her head was on his shoulder, once more. He mounted the stairs slowly and awkwardly, leaning his weight against the banisters. In the bedroom he tilted her carefully onto the bed and then found himself on his knees beside her. He kissed and released the hand that still so confidingly held onto his. He pulled the blanket loose and drew it up over her shoulder. He thought, Dorina, Austin's wife. He remained on his knees a moment longer and directed a wordless prayer to whatever great and powerful heart might yet throb in the universe with some consciousness of good. Then he rose and turned out the light and went downstairs.

Alone in the drawing-room he finished the brandy. He felt excited, surprised, alert and satisfied, as if he had just added another marvelously beautiful object to his collection.

"I'm going to go and see Dorina," said Ludwig, "as soon as we get back."

"Please yourself," said Gracie.

They were alone in the sunshine on a small hemmed-in beach. Sea lapped idly on a strip of pale brown sand. It was low tide. The sand was scattered with tiny creamy-white shells, each one a little masterpiece. Above the sand was a layered pavement of flat smooth faintly striped stones in various shades of lucid grey. Beyond the stones was a coronet of jagged bluish rocks and beyond the rocks an undulation of vivid green hillocks, then the sky, empty, drained of colour, vibrating with light. There was an immense silence.

The sea was golden near to the shore, then a spotty purple, then a glittering blue until at the horizon there was a dark line lightly sketched in to divide sea from sky. Sitting almost upon this line was the sturdy fortress form of Fastnet lighthouse. Never, even in America, had Ludwig felt quite so far away from the ordinary significant world. He had felt elated and a little frightened. He was very very much alone with Gracie.

Gracie was skimming flat stones along the glossy smooth water, making them bounce. She could make them leap even a dozen times upon the watery skin. Ludwig could not do this at all. His stones cut straight into the sea and sank.

They were both dressed for swimming, Gracie in a flowery skirted costume, and Ludwig in black trunks, but only Ludwig had been into the water. Gracie had so far

317

refused to swim at all, maintaining it was too cold. It was, indeed, icy.

"And I'm going to see Charlotte." Ludwig sat down on a rock.

"Did Matthew suggest this?" Gracie skimmed another stone.

"No."

"You've talked an awful lot with Matthew, haven't you?"

"Yes, but not about that."

"All right then, fine, fine."

"But you're mad at me."

"No, no." Gracie came to him, prancing with long sand-encrusted legs. She leaned up against him and licked his shoulder. "Mmm. Salt. Nice."

"But, Gracie, you are mad, you mustn't be." Ludwig had been alarmed to find that it had needed a bit of nerve for him to tell Gracie that he was going to see Dorina and Charlotte. Whatever was his marriage going to be like if he already feared his future wife's opposition to actions which he had concluded to be right?

"I'm not 'mad,' you silly bullikins. And I'm not being bloody-minded either. I just think it's useless and will lead to trouble. You're so clever and yet when it comes to what you do you can't foresee the least thing. If you go to see Char she'll think you're patronizing her, and she'll be right."

'Well—yes—" Garth had said just this about his own visit to Charlotte. This had partly dissuaded Ludwig from going to see her. This, and having other things to think about. "All the same, I think one should go to see people in trouble and take the risk of offending them."

"It's not a risk, it's a certainty. I'll deal with Aunt Char, later on, financially I mean, in a dignified and businesslike way. Which oddly enough she'll perfectly understand and accept. You just don't know what these touchy elderly ladies are like."

"Maybe."

"When you say you want to go and see her you aren't really thinking of her, you're thinking of yourself. You want to have the relieved comfortable feeling that you've done all you can. Then you can relax and forget about her. Aren't I right?"

"Perhaps you are, dearest Poppy. You are such a wise little thing!"

"I'm such a knowing little thing. As for the Dorina biz, you're just no more use there any more. Another two or three visits, and Austin would start being jealous of you. He probably is already. Any build-up of emotion between you and Dorina could only do her harm. Surely you see that."

"Yes— But if everyone argues in this way she'll be left quite alone."

"Married to Austin, I don't see how she can avoid that, it's her destiny."

"I think I'll go and see her all the same."

"It'll end in tears, Ludwig. You don't think I'm jealous, do you?"

"No, of course not, Poppy, how could you be! Anyway you know it's not just personal. I've been thinking, and— I mean, I do want us to be the sort of married couple who help people."

"How ghastly! Like my parents!"

"No, not like that— Sorry—"

"Dear Ludwig. It's just that I hate muddles and scenes and tears and all the *rubbish* that these people imagine is living the spiritual life or something."

"I don't think Austin has any illusions about the spiritual life."

"Austin is a huge fat egoist, as fat as a bull-frog. If I had a long enough pin I'd puncture him. I'd push the pin in until there was nothing left except a flabby grey skin lying in a heap on the ground. I *hate* that man."

"Dear me, you are fierce, Poppy. I'm rather afraid that he loves you."

"He was awful at that party. But oh dear I was even more awful. Ludwig, you have really and truly forgiven me, haven't you?"

"Darling creature, of course!"

Gracie leaned harder against him and toppled him off

the rock. They collapsed onto warm sand and lay holding each other. Their bodies were familiar friends now. They lay thus in each other's arms every night in the little hotel, watching through the window the Fastnet light constantly blinking in the depths of the blue dark, Fastnet speaking of eternity and of the keeping of faith.

Of course Ludwig had forgiven Gracie. Of course he understood. Yet the pain remained curiously clean and undiminished, that picture of Gracie held close in Sebastian's arms. The wound throbbed in him unhealing and somehow separated from his substance like a stigmaton. With this suffering, which he supposed would grow less and finally vanish, he did not burden Gracie, but endured it in silence proudly as a task of love.

"Austin doesn't quite think it's all holy, but he attaches such cosmic importance to everything that concerns himself that it comes to much the same thing. If God was nasty he'd be rather like Austin."

Ludwig laughed. He wanted to make love to her beside the sea. But although the beaches were invariably deserted Gracie would never let him. How wonderful, he thought, to possess her with the sand upon her shoulders. "Gracie —"

"No, please, Ludwig. Someone might come."

"Let's go back then. Quick."

"All right. *Do* you see, Ludwig, about Dorina? They'd make you play a role in their horrible drama. They both enjoy it, you know."

"I don't think Dorina does."

"Oh yes, she enjoys it. Even if she doesn't quite know that she does. She's the sort of woman who really loves showdowns and explanations and confessions and all that. There's a sort of cunning in it. They'd trap you and then pump all sorts of meaning into everything you did and said, *their* meaning, like pumping in poison. Ugh!"

"You do feel it strongly! Come on, Poppy."

"You won't go to see those people, will you?"

"No, I won't. Come on, come on, come on."

The hired car took them back to the tiny hotel which stood in a fringe of golden seaweed, its feet almost in the water, reflecting its pinkly washed walls in the quiet sea.

Ludwig lay exhausted on the bed beside his lovely fiancée. It was evening. The sea was a uniform colour of glowing glossy light blue, the sky a darker bottomlessly absolute blue, the monumental lighthouse etched in clear radiant grey. Soon they would rise, have a bath, dress in fresh light clothes, descend to the bar and sit holding hands and drinking Irish whisky.

"Poppy."

"Yes."

"I'm in paradise."

"Me too."

"Poppy."

"Yes."

"Shall we buy a cottage in Ireland?"

"Mmm."

"Shall we?"

"No, Ludwig. This is lovely, but I don't think I could really live in Ireland. There's too much trouble all the time."

"Trouble, yes." Ludwig had forgotten about trouble.

"Ireland is like Austin. Nice to look at, and one's sorry for it, but it's somehow—awful."

"Poor Austin again!"

"And one would have to know so much history. I hate history. Sorry."

"Yes. I know. Everyone talks history here."

"Ninety-eight and so on. Tell me what ninety-eight was sometime."

"Yes—"

"But not now."

Not now. That night Gracie lay sleeping in Ludwig's arms as he watched the regular endless mysterious message of the lighthouse. Only sometimes, but not now as he blissfully held that naked sleeping form close against his own, did he fleetingly recall that out beyond the blink of Fastnet and over the waves of the horizon there still relentlessly existed, multifarious and dangerous and seething with dreadful life, America.

"Austin hasn't been back?"

"Not since yesterday morning."

"You're sure he believed you?"

"Yes. I was in such a panic, I just said firmly 'She's lying down now, you can't see her,' and then I prayed!"

Matthew was talking to Mavis on the telephone.

"You think he sort of expected that?"

"I suspect he felt he couldn't face her."

"After what she told me happened."

"Yes. He seemed almost relieved. And he'd already written and brought that long letter."

"The one you steamed open."

"Yes. You still think we shouldn't give it to her?"

"Not just yet."

"Another one came by post this morning and I steamed that open too."

"I say, we are going it, Mavis."

"I know. Today's one is just the same, incoherent self-accusation and ramblings about forgiveness."

"Austin is the sort of person who feels he can change the world by writing a letter."

"Yes, he believes in magic."

"Did he say anything about his movements?"

"Only that he was going to see Norman Monkley. He said, 'I'm going to help poor Norman to remember things'!"

"God!"

"I'm so afraid if he doesn't hear from her he'll come round again."

"Let it go another day."

"She still doesn't want to see me?"

"No. It's not that— She's in a charmed state. I can't explain. We've talked a great deal, you know."

"Oh."

"Mavis, I honestly think it's doing her good. And somehow it's the only chance. I didn't want this to happen, I would have shunned it of all things, but now it's happened I've got to go through with it. You understand."

"Yes, my dear, yes."

"It isn't that she doesn't want to see *you*. At the moment she doesn't want to see anybody."

"Except you."

"Except me."

"What about Charlotte?"

"I don't think Charlotte's there. I've telephoned her several times. Of course Charlotte may come in useful. I can't keep Dorina here much longer."

"No. It's too dangerous."

"Quite."

"And if she doesn't want to come back here she might go to Char?"

"Yes. I'll try giving Charlotte another ring."

"Don't say too much, to Char I mean."

"No, no. In fact I'm sure she will want to come back to you, even as soon as tomorrow."

"I hope so. Matthew, I terribly want to see you."

"I terribly want to see you, my darling. But at the moment I've just got my hands full. I've never felt quite so, you know, called upon. It's not that I've actually got to watch her all the time, but I've got to sort of be there."

"Like God!"

"Don't laugh!"

"I'm not laughing."

"She's at peace, I think, for the first time in ages. She's sweating the fear out of herself. Excuse the metaphor. She's got a real sense of security, which I can give her. It's not any merit of mine."

"I know, it's animal magnetism. I've seen you doing it at dinner parties. Sorry, darling, I'm only teasing. I do

323

really believe that you can help her and nobody else can."

"Thank you, Mavis. Hang on till tomorrow. We'll make a plan tomorrow. Today I'll just keep things quietly going here."

"Matthew, supposing Austin turns up at Valmorana and insists on seeing her? What on earth am I to say?"

"Say she's somewhere in the country with Charlotte."

"And I don't know where! Oh God! Or what about Garth? No, I can't say she's with Garth, Austin would hate that."

"We'd better get hold of Garth. We may need him."

"He's moving his digs and he isn't on the telephone."

"Well, write to him, and perhaps you'd write to Charlotte too. Ask them both to telephone you as soon as they get the letter. No need to say much. But we may as well have them both available."

"Yes. Matthew, I'm scared stiff of Austin turning up again. Do persuade Dorina to come back here."

"I will. And I'll keep on ringing Charlotte. Try not to worry too much. I'll see you soon, dear love."

"Dear Matthew—"

"What is it?"

"Keep me safe too. If you really are God."

"Mavis, I love you. That's what that is."

"I know. Bless you. I'll ring again this evening. Look after that poor child."

"Of course. Good-bye, darling."

Matthew put down the telephone and went over to the window. In the enclosed garden outside Dorina was wandering to and fro upon the lawn. She was wearing a clean dress, a little blue stripey affair, which Mrs. Carberry had brought over by taxi in a suitcase together with other things neatly packed up by Mavis. Her light brown hair, carefully combed, was hanging loose, cut off in a level line across her shoulder blades. She was walking to and fro very slowly, looking down intently at the grass. Like a captive, he thought. She had always been a captive. She must have walked rather like that at Valmorana. And in some imaginable way at the flat when Austin was out at the office. She has belonged to Mavis, to Austin, to Mavis, and now to me.

Matthew went down the stairs and out into the sunny shady garden. The garden was large enough not to be entirely shaded by the high brick walls and the walnut tree. The shadow of the walnut tree did not reach the house until the evening. Dorina walked towards him faintly smiling. Here serenity was uncanny.

"You've been talking to Mavis."

"Yes. How did you know?"

"I just knew. Austin hasn't been there?"

"No."

"Good. You and Mavis must feel as if you're holding a hand grenade with the pin out."

"What an image. I assure you we feel nothing of the sort."

"Don't worry, Matthew. I know I can't stay here much longer."

"You can stay as long as you like, my dear."

"Let's sit on the grass. It's so dry. Who cuts the grass? Do you?"

"No. An Irishman called Geraghty from County Kerry. I've given him a week's holiday."

"Because of me. We're all sealed off, aren't we. We might as well be up there travelling through space."

"Do you mind?"

"No. I know it can't last. But while it lasts it's timeless, something rescued absolutely from time. Give me your hand. It's so quiet here. What day of the week is it?"

"Friday."

"Matthew—"

"Yes, my dear child?"

"I think I've told you everything I know, everything I remember, and a great deal more besides."

"I hope you don't regret it."

"No. I feel completely made new. All the fear, all that weird tangled part of my being, you know, seems to have gone out of me and some great blank quiet power has come in. Do you understand?"

"I think so."

"Will it last?"

"Not quite like this. But I do believe that the things that are better will stay better."

"You were so wonderful the way you put your arms around me on the first night."

"I felt then that it had to be."

"This thing between us."

"Yes, what I had to do. Half measures were no good. I had to care for you and talk to you properly."

"You have done so. I don't feel any sort of guilt or worry about having stayed here."

"I'm glad. You know that we can never tell Austin about this."

"I know. Yes, yes. I know."

They were sitting on the grass together underneath the walnut tree. Dorina sighed, pressed Matthew's hand and released it.

"I do really think things will be better, Matthew, things with Austin will be better. Somehow I've stopped being frightened of him, where there was fear once there's now just pity and love. And those other things, you know, have quite gone away."

"There are no final cures, Dorina, don't hope too much. But if you and Austin could come together and be happy I can't think of anything that would make *me* happier."

"I think after all I will go back to Valmorana tomorrow."

"Good—good child."

"I want to start doing things at once, you see. I want to see Austin— You still haven't got in touch with Char?"

"No, she must be away."

"You will help her to move somewhere else soon so that we can have the flat?"

"Yes."

"I feel as if I could make things happen now. Before I was always shut off from life, behind glass, just watching."

"My dear—"

"Matthew, I love you. You know that."

"That's all right. I love you too!"

"Shall we meet afterwards?"

"I don't see that we can, Dorina."

There was silence between them. Matthew took her hand again. They sat like two children.

He saw a tear coming quietly down Dorina's cheek.

"Don't grieve, my child."

"No, I know—how things have got to be—this has been a special enclosed time and can't have any consequences—I mean except in my being better. It's just that when one thinks of—never—never meeting or writing —when there is so much love—it seems like death."

"I know, but—sometimes in life one has to die."

"Yes. And I am brave enough to die. Only never forget that I love you."

"I won't forget, Dorina. The pain is mine too. Don't you forget that."

✥✥✥

Dearest Char,

I rang but no answer so this is just a little note to send love. Why do we never see you? You must come round to dins. I expect you would like some news of us and the children. Let me see. Patrick has won the History Prize. Gracie is blissfully happy with Ludwig in Ireland. George has been promoted (he is now *very* grand). I have been terribly busy with the wedding arrangements. Did I tell you I am designing all the clothes myself? And I am getting the dressmaker to run up quite a trousseau for ME as well! Life is thrilling but *terribly* full. How are you? We really must meet. I will telephone again, but not at once, since the next two or three days are *packed* with jobs, seeing dressmakers, seeing florists, seeing photographers, one is *never* done. We so look forward to the lazy peace of our Greek cruise with Richard immediately after the wedding. George and I will feel it is a second honeymoon for us! I am looking forward to it with such childish glee. Well, that's our news, what's yours? Why do we never see you? You must come round to dins. I will ring again when there's a spot of time. Au revoir, dear, and much love from

CLARA

P.S. George, who has just come in from some jolly drinks with Charles and the boys, bids me send you his *special* love!!

Dear Charlotte,

Just a letter to you not apropos of anything in particular. I would like to have seen you but I have been kept very busy in the East End. The scenes here are depressing beyond words. One sees how little impression the Welfare State has made and how many people are still very poor indeed and desperate, particularly women with strings of children and un-able to cope. The men at least can go to the pub. I am moving very shortly to Notting Hill, where I gather things are just as bad but different. Being able to do so little fills one with sadness. And makes one count one's own blessings. When I'm back on the west side at Notting Hill I'll hope to see you. Maybe I could even enlist your help? Have you seen Ludwig, I wonder? He always speaks of you so warmly. I do hope that you are well and happy. I send sincerest wishes and thoughts.

Yours,
GARTH

My dear Charlotte,

We have been trying to get in touch with you. Matthew and I feel that you could be of great use to us about Dorina. We are rather worried about her.

328

We will tell you when we see you. Probably you are away on holiday. Would you be so kind as to ring us at once when you return? We should be most grateful. With very best of wishes from us both,

MAVIS

P.S. I feel I should say that Austin and Dorina will soon be needing the flat.

Charlotte listened for a while to the telephone ringing. George and Clara had paid the telephone bill. Then she wandered into the kitchen and threw the fragments of the letters into the bin. Her loose tooth was aching. The sun was shining into the kitchen and onto a number of opened and half-emptied tins. There was a smell of decay and a quantity of buzzy blue flies. Charlotte wandered out of the kitchen again and into the bedroom, which faced north. The bed was unmade. The nylon gauze curtains on the window were dark with dirt. She lay down on the bed.

Today's post about summed it up. Clara was too happy to bother except for a hasty note to salve her conscience. Garth was full of pity and felt it might be salutary to think of even less fortunate people. He thought it might do Charlotte good to do social work. Mavis had absorbed Matthew into a final *we*. Matthew didn't care. He had not bothered to write. He had not telephoned. If he was telephoning now it was too late. He only wanted to make use of her to solve Mavis's problems. To make the way plain for him and Mavis. Patrick had got the History Prize. Gracie was blissfully happy in Ireland. George was very grand. *We* were grateful and sent our good wishes. Austin and Dorina were coming home. Mavis thought Charlotte might be of use. George sent his *special* love. Matthew didn't care. The last time she had answered the telephone it was a man who uttered obscenities, having gathered that a maiden lady lived there alone. Perhaps that was him again now. Or perhaps it was Matthew-Mavis, who thought Charlotte might be of use. But it was too late. Charlotte was no use to anybody any more. Even Alison, to whom she had once been of use, had rejected her finally. Therefore she must be worthy of rejection.

Matthew didn't care. Matthew and Mavis were *we,* to have and to hold to love and to cherish till death did them part. They would be rich and joyful. They would live in a grand house and the maid would dust the Chinese vases. Gracie was blissfully happy in Ireland. Clara was so longing for the Greek cruise. Garth was full of pity. So was George, who sent his *special* love. Patrick had won the History Prize. Patrick had written regularly to Alison. He had never once written to Charlotte. Charlotte would be of use. Charlotte would mind the children while Gracie and Ludwig went out to dinner. Austin and Dorina are coming home. Clara's life is thrilling.

Of course Charlotte knew perfectly well, she did not need to be told it in a patronizing communication from Garth, that other people were worse off than she was and she ought to feel lucky. She hadn't got strings of children and a husband who went to the pub. How much she wished that she had, someone like Garth would never know. Of course she had had an easy life, and with a little ingenuity could still have one. She had long ago surrendered the great illusions and the little ones were so much her friends that they had become entirely translucent. She was not the sort of person who would fall out of the bottom of society. She had a good digestion. She could hunger and satisfy her hunger, feel weary and go to a comfortable bed. If she awoke in black misery, as she always did, she had the inductive powers to know that when she had got up she would probably enjoy a cup of tea. A detective story could hold her attention, even the *Times* could. Human beings can keep going and even in some sense enjoy their existence with fewer devices than that. But it somehow remained that she, she Charlotte Ledgard, had been cheated out of her life and survived now as a mere shadow. No wonder Alison had punished her and Matthew thought of her only as an instrument. That she could still be an instrument might have comforted her once, but not now.

So Austin and Dorina were reconciled and would soon be home. Another happy ending. Charlotte would clean the flat for them before she left, buy flowers for them.

They would be grateful, but they would not want to see her again. It would be necessary for Charlotte to take a job, only it was not clear what she could do except look after elderly ladies. Of course she could remind Clara of her kind suggestion and go and live with her and George. Clara and George had a high sense of duty and would never by an eyelid's flicker indicate to Charlotte that she was a burden. Only late at night when Charlotte was in bed and they had returned from a dinner party would they speak of poor old Char and ruefully and kindly wish her at the devil. And then Clara would tease George about Charlotte being in love with him. And Charlotte would lie alone in bed and hear the married couple murmuring below. And everyone would say how generous of the Tisbournes to look after old Charlotte, who was getting on in years and had never been easy to live with even when she was young. She could stick it out with George and Clara until the little Leferriers arrived. Then she would earn her keep, as she had earned it with Alison year after year at the Villa.

Charlotte knew perfectly well too that these vistas were not only fruitless but quite possibly false. In a very abstract way she knew that something unexpected could happen even to her, scarcely something pleasant, but at least something different. She could become ill. Even this might alter things. But she could not change her knowledge of the blankness of the future into any sort of hope, or really conceive of the future at all except as a series of nightmarish rat-run extensions of her present vileness. That she condemned herself in moral terms brought no consoling spring of vitality and even guilt gave her no energy. When this is so one is in extremity indeed.

I hate everybody, she thought, and I hate them not because they are bad or spiteful or because they ignore me or even because they pity me. I hate them in a pure way because they are fortunate and have what I have not, and there is no human being so wretched that my hatred, like the divine mercy, cannot find its way to him. She lay on the wrenched lumpy bed in the twilight, behind the filthy gauze curtains, lying awkwardly, without even the will to

331

make herself comfortable, and she thought about death and whether it made any sense to desire it. No, it made no sense. She was far beyond the truth and its sharp dividings of the world. Whether or not she should kill herself, whether it would seriously matter to anyone or anything if she did, was a question which had no answer, which could not even be properly framed. Why should she kill herself in a fit of envy, and then again why should she not? It was all one. Whether this despair made it easier or harder to act, whether it would finally carry her off, mere chance would decide. She had always been the slave of chance, let it kill her if it would by a random stroke. She would not die gladly, but then she had not lived gladly either. Her swansong would be made of words smashed into nonsense against a cracked world, exploding with it into the chaos upon which everything rested and out of which it was made. And the people who said, as they smiled and sipped their evening drink, "Poor Charlotte killed herself out of spleen," would themselves very soon be dead too.

The morning was wearing away. Soon it would be time to feed herself again, to continue the motions of living. She had certainly been trying to keep herself alive, she had even been to see Dr. Seldon. He had told her there was nothing wrong with her and had given her tranquillizers and sleeping pills. He had troubles of his own. She hated him too all the same. Should she rise up and open another tin of corned beef and another tin of beans? Stoking the machine, keeping the wheels turning for a little bit longer. Should she sit in the kitchen and eat a plateful of stuff with the *Times* propped up in front of her, scanning the Personal Column for an advertisement for a lady companion, cook and housemaid kept? Or should she not? Should she get up and stop the milk and feed herself fifty sleeping pills? She had been so happy once with her father before Clara was born. But that was in a previous existence, that child scarcely a memory, that man not even a ghost.

Charlotte pulled herself off the bed and wandered back into the sitting-room. She could not endure the happiness of Mavis and Matthew, that torture at least she could

332

spare her consciousness. She went to the cupboard where she had put away the items which had once seemed to her so interesting, the swimming certificate, the torn letter. Should she send them to Matthew to trouble his peace? She sat down at the table and began to write. *My dear Matthew, when you receive this I shall be dead* . . . Odd that to face death was really to face nothing. When men said that the spectacle of death could instruct and save they lied. Healthy men said this, men radiant with suffering and guilt, men steely with will and art. Death's real disciples know that there is no face we can turn towards death. Only life stretches away on every hand, hideous and dry and becoming tinier and tinier.

Slowly Charlotte crumpled up the page. She put it together with the swimming certificate and the old torn letter in the empty grate. Betty's words looked up at her: *we'll meet then* . . . *Austin doesn't suspect*. She struck a match and set fire to the papers, poking them until they fell to dust. Then she went to the kitchen and took a glass and filled a jug with water. She went back into the bedroom. She found the sleeping tablets.

Odd that one should so naturally wish to lie upon one's bed to go to sleep forever.

Matthew and Dorina were sitting in the drawing-room looking at each other. It was mid-morning. Dorina's bag was packed. Matthew got up. He said, "I'll ring for a taxi."

"No. Wait a little longer. Please."

"Better get it over."

"Please—"

Matthew dialled the number of the taxi rank. It was engaged.

"I'm sorry," said Dorina. "But after these days with you I don't think I can stand 'never again.' I can't stand it."

"You've got to," said Matthew. He dialled the number again. "Hello. Could you send a taxi at once?" He gave the address.

"I am not going to cry," said Dorina. "I promised I wouldn't." She spoke in a slow precise voice, not looking at him. "That you of all people, to whom I have come closest in all the world, who understand me as if you had made me, that you of all people should be the only one that I can never see again—"

"That's how it is," said Matthew. "Sorry."

He went to the window.

"I am not reproaching you."

"I know."

"There must be some compromise, some second way."

"None. You know that as well as I do."

They had lived an age in three days. He had seen her rise as if from a tomb. Taking her by the hand, he had pulled her up out of the paralysis of fear. She had found her courage like someone remembering her own name. Her love for Austin had been set free into the world. He had seen the joy of resurrection. Only now in the last hours had a sense of horror returned. Like radium, this treatment cures and then begins to destroy. It was time to end it.

"Yes," said Dorina. "Yes. But it's too terrible. I love Austin. Yet I can't help feeling that I belong to you automatically whether you will or no forever. And that this will be so even if we don't meet any more."

"It's meaningless, Dorina," said Matthew. "You are comforting yourself with empty words. I seem brutal now, but I must be. I suffer too. How can one be with someone as I have been with you in these days and not love them? One could do nothing for them unless one did love them. That we must now part absolutely is our bad luck. But only this absolute parting ratifies what went before and

334

makes it other than a sort of crime. If I am to have helped you at all I must abandon you completely."

"After all this—"

"We must make all this as if it had never been."

"Couldn't we at least write occasionally, once a year?"

"No. If you write to me I will not only not answer, I shall tear up the letter unread. Forgive me."

The front-door bell rang.

"There's your taxi."

Matthew left the room and went to the front door. In a moment or two he would be by himself. He knew he could assuage his own pain, there were means. He could not stand much more of this. Bundle her in and away and weep then.

Garth was standing on the doorstep.

As soon as Matthew had opened the door Garth darted into the hall and shut the door again.

"Whatever is it?" said Matthew.

"Sssh. I know Dorina's here. I was coming to see you. Then I saw the Tisbournes parking their car just down the road. They're bound to be coming here too. I ran on first, I thought I'd better warn you."

"Thank you," said Matthew. "Dorina, here's Garth. The Tisbournes are just arriving. Dorina, could you just sit in the dining-room. I'll get rid of them as quickly as possible. Here, take your suitcase and your handbag."

"I'll hide too if you don't mind," said Garth. "I'm no good at acting."

Dorina gave a little moan and crossed the hall, followed by Garth. The door bell rang again. Matthew waited a moment or two, then opened the door.

"Why, George and Clara, what a nice surprise!"

"I do hope you don't abhor the dropper-in," said George.

The taxi drew up behind them.

Matthew said to the taxi driver, "I don't need you after all. Here, let me pay you for coming."

"Oh no!" cried Clara. "Stop him, George. We're spoiling his morning. Matthew, you were just going somewhere."

"No, I wasn't—I mean, it can wait. Do come in."

335

"Taxi, don't go, wait!"

"Clara, I really don't want it. No, go, please. Now do come in, just for a minute. I have got to go somewhere actually, but—"

"Can we just come in for a sec?"

"Yes, yes. Come into the drawing-room. Would you like a drink?"

"Yes, please."

"Clara, medium sherry, George, Scotch and water, that's right, isn't it?"

"Clever old Matthew, you remember everybody's little foibles!"

"He remembers everything, doesn't he. Thank you, dear Matthew."

"Do sit down."

"Thank you."

"It's got quite hot again, hasn't it," said Matthew.

"Yes, it's really a summer for once, like people have in other places. Aren't you drinking, Matthew?"

"Well, yes, but I must go soon."

"We'll take you in our car. Where do you want to go?"

"I must make some telephone calls first, now I come to think of it."

"George, we are being a nuisance."

"No, no, not at all."

"We wanted to ask you something in fact, we are not just on pleasure bent."

"What?"

"It's about Char. Shall I explain, George? We won't keep you a minute. We'll just tell you our little idea and then run off. You know we've been worrying so much about poor Char."

"Naturally."

"Char has got plenty of troubles that we can do nothing about, single and getting old and all those years wasted with Mama, you know. But we felt we could at least help her financially, help her to be miserable in comfort, as they say."

"Gracie—"

"That's just the point. Firstly, I doubt very much if

336

Char would accept money from Gracie, and secondly—"

"Gracie hasn't offered any?"

"Precisely. Our daughter is a mystery, and with Char as she is we just can't wait on mysteries. So we thought we'd start a Charlotte Fund, you know, a sort of *Charlottegesellschaft*."

"Excellent idea."

"And we'd get a lot of people to contribute. There'd be us of course, and Gracie if she wanted to join in, and then we thought of asking you and Mavis and the Odmores and the Arbuthnots—"

"Old Char will be a millionaire at this rate—"

"Be quiet, George. And Penny Sayce and Oliver and—"

"I think we should jolly well start a fund for ourselves while we're about it!"

"But would Charlotte accept it?" said Matthew.

"This is where you come in," said Clara. "Of course George and I have thought of helping her, but she's so difficult and stiff and proud. You know, well I'm not giving away any secrets, that she's in love with George, always has been, be quiet, George, and this makes her awfully touchy, in a way it's the tragedy of her life, and she's always seen us being so happy together and so on. If we ask her she may just go off in a huff and then it'll be that much harder to do *anything* for her. But if *you* ask her and if you tell her it's entirely *your* idea, and that you're running it—you needn't really be, George will run it—you see, she respects you so much, it will make it all much more impersonal and businesslike sort of, you do understand, and please forgive us for hoping, well for assuming, that you'd like to help. Even very small sums, guaranteed every year, from all those people—"

"Of course I'll help," said Matthew, "and do whatever you want."

"Oh *good!* We'll go on now and ask the others. And then you'll explain it to Char when it's all complete?"

"Yes—"

"Thank you so much!"

"It's a very kind idea," said Matthew. "By the way, I've been telephoning Charlotte and got no answer."

"Really? Well, she's—oh she's on holiday I think—"

"Now if you'll forgive me, I must make those phone calls."

"I hope we haven't been a nuisance."

"No, indeed—"

Matthew saw George and Clara to the door. He waved them well away down the street and then turned back into the house.

Garth and Dorina came out of the dining-room like a pair of animals, as shadowy as rats in the darkening hall, and went into the drawing-room, where Dorina sat down and began to cry silently into her hands.

"Please stop it," said Matthew quietly. "You said you wouldn't. Compose yourself. I'm going to ring for the taxi." He dialled again. "The taxi's coming at once. Now, please, Dorina—"

"I'm afraid I upset her," said Garth.

"Shall I get you a handkerchief?"

"I told her that her having come here will absolutely kill my father, it'll kill him."

"Your father will never know," said Matthew. He felt an omen of despair settling on his heart like a big black bird. He wanted to take Dorina in his arms.

"He'll know," said Garth. "He'll find out somehow. He's the sort of man who finds out that sort of thing. Some demon in his destiny will let him know of it. Of course I won't tell him, but he'll find out all the same. Dorina will probably tell him herself, she'll have to."

"I didn't intend to come to Matthew," said Dorina, wiping her eyes with her knuckles. "It was an accident."

"That's perfectly true," said Matthew. "Dorina understands. Leave her to her understanding of the situation. Since it is unthinkable that Austin should know this he simply must not be told it. And the four people who know it will not tell him. That's all. I am very sorry that you arrived at just this moment and I am very sorry that you have upset her."

"So am I, I should have held my tongue."

"Yes. How did you know she was here anyway?"

"Mavis told me. I called about something else. But

338

really, you two must have been living here in some sort of dream world for three days. Three days! My father will run mad. And how can you so coolly put this burden onto Dorina? You put onto her the burden of this silence. It's all very well for you and me and Mavis, we'll be getting on with our own lives elsewhere, but Dorina will be with Austin every day with this dreadful thing kept secret. She's certain to tell him eventually out of sheer anxiety."

"Enough, Garth," said Matthew, "enough. I didn't invite this situation. Dorina came here looking for Charlotte. I talked to her because she was here, I had to."

"You didn't have to keep her for three days—and nights," said Garth.

"You are not suggesting—"

"No, of course not, that's not your style—"

Dorina got up and still concealing her face with crossed hands ran out of the room. The dining-room door closed behind her. The front-door bell rang.

Matthew went out to the door. It was the taxi, the same one. "Sorry, I don't want you just now."

"Make up your mind," said the taximan, as Matthew paid him again.

In the drawing-room Garth was standing rigid in the same position. "As I was saying, that's not your style. You do it by talking. You want to inspire devotion. You want to have people forever. Christ, you might have had me. You've got Ludwig. And now you've got Dorina."

"Garth, please, this is profitless anger."

"Thank God I'm not in your cage—"

"You've upset Dorina terribly."

"And what do you think *he*'ll do to her when he finds out?"

"He won't find out."

"If I hadn't warned you you'd have met the Tisbournes on the doorstep."

"Garth. Stop being angry. *Stop.*"

"All right. Now I suppose I say 'Sorry, sir,' and you say 'Not at all, my dear fellow.' "

"Garth, please."

"I'm sorry. I'm so bloody frightened for Dorina. And you see—I thought of trying to help her too—in my little way—if I'd had less scruple and more nerve I might have done. Maybe you were right to attempt it. People often perish because other people are too meticulous or dignified or something to rush in. One should rush in. But here. It's so dangerous, for both of us, I mean you and me, and the penalty falls on her. Sorry, I'm incoherent—"

"No, you're perfectly clear."

"I'm sorry for what I said about you. I wasn't implying it was all sex."

"Perhaps it is all sex," said Matthew. "But anyway what's done is done."

"If Dorina holds her tongue it'll be for love of you. You realize that? But she'll tell him sooner or later out of sheer death wish."

"No, I don't think she will now—because she is—better—"

"Better! Is that what 'better' is like? God!"

"I didn't invite or want this situation. Now Garth, please go away. This can't be argued about, certainly not in these terms. I must talk to Dorina again and make her calm. I'll get her out of here in the next half hour."

"If you like I'll wait and take her back."

"No."

"You're going to escort her, are you?"

"No. She's going alone in a taxi. She's prepared for that." He added, "I shall not see her again."

Garth lifted his hands and dropped them heavily to his sides. He gave a kind of laugh. "Ah well—"

They had been standing opposite to each other in stiff awkward attitudes. With Garth's gesture they both moved, staring at each other's faces. There was dread and shuddering in the room.

"I'm very sorry," said Garth.

"That's all right. You—I understand."

There was a moment's silence.

"Well, good-bye then," said Garth. "And good luck to all concerned!"

He went out abruptly and had closed the front door

behind him before Matthew could reach it. Matthew went into the dining-room.

The dining-room was empty. He began slowly to climb the stairs. He called "Dorina!" He went into the bedroom which she had occupied. His pyjamas, which Dorina had insisted on wearing although Mavis had sent her night-dress, were lying on the unmade bed. Dorina was not there. "Dorina, where are you?" Matthew searched the other rooms upstairs and downstairs, calling out to her. He even went down into the cellar. He noticed that her suitcase and handbag had gone from the dining-room. There was no sign of Dorina in the house at all.

In fruitless panic he ran out and looked for her in the street. Then he came back and telephoned Mavis. He and Mavis telephoned each other at intervals throughout the day and throughout the night that followed, but there was no news. Dorina had vanished.

❧❧❧

Dear Mitzi,

I am leaving the house early and when you find this I shall be gone for good. Sorry. You were kind to me and I appreciate it but we are not exactly made for each other and I can't forgive you what happened the other night though I know in a sense it wasn't your fault. Some people are sort of automatically the instruments of other people's woe, and you have never brought me luck. (Who has? now I come to think of it.) So let's say good-bye quietly and make a clean break, as they say, with thanks on my part and best wishes to you. Seeing **Dorina** here was a salutary

341

shock actually and I am glad it happened, it was for the best. It made me feel how absolutely above everything else in my life she is. People like you just pull me down. (Sorry.) She is the only person who has ever pulled me up. We needs must love the highest when we see it and all that. It has taken me two or three days to put my mind in order but now it is in order and I know what I must do. I must seek my own good in the honest place and trust myself utterly to that good to overcome all my difficulties: which difficulties lie mainly in my own rottenness. You are better without a chap like me, incidentally. Dorina loves me with a pure love and because she is some sort of angel in my life she can perhaps change me, anyway it is worth trying. And I propose to start as from now and cut out all the shillyshallying diplomacy. I am going to Valmorana to claim my wife. As you will see, I have packed up all my stuff and I shall take (shall have taken) it away by taxi. Sorry, but I think a quick end is better than messing around. Please have the decency and kindness not to try to communicate with me. I shall be trying to live now wholly with and for Dorina and if I am ever to save myself from corruption and chaos I must put my all into that effort now. Please understand and forgive, Mitzi. I couldn't do you much good but I also honestly believe I haven't done you much harm. You'll soon get over yours truly. And all the best, old girl. Good-bye, and I mean it. Please don't reply to this or pursue me ever. You know how bloody I can be. It's no good. This is a moment of vision and I *know*.

Yours,
AUSTIN

P.S. Thanks for everything. *Good-bye*.

Mitzi, standing in her kitchen in her dressing gown, crumpled up the letter which she had found propped up in the hall when she went down to fetch the milk. She turned on the gas stove and lit the gas and filled the kettle and put the kettle on the gas. She walked back into the sitting-room and sat down.

She so little doubted the absolute finality of Austin's letter that some immense time-shift had already occurred between his sojourn with her and the present moment. This was another era. That he should have sat in his room and penned the letter yesterday, even today, was inconceivable. Austin had been lost in some ancient cataclysm. He was utterly gone. A few shattered unconnected things remained. A hurricane had passed removing purpose and future and significant emotion. She sat until the kettle boiled and then made the tea. The house was very silent. She drank a little tea. Then she went up to Austin's room, looked upon its emptiness, and came down again. She wondered whether to get dressed or to go back to bed. She went back into her bedroom and lay down. Ever since Austin's arrival she had lived in a state of vague, often acute, sexual excitement. This too was gone. Her body, which had been large and vague and flabby, like a jelly-fish afloat in warm water, was now shrivelled and hard and small. It was like lying alive in one's coffin, inhabiting a rigid dried contorted frame and looking about with one's eyes.

Despair had shot her down so quickly there had not even been a struggle. She would not try to pursue Austin ever. He had returned to his wife and must be allowed to follow his own good without any hindrance from what was now the far past. He had got cleanly away and now existed elsewhere in the closed circle of his own life, secret and forever gone. Her love for him had grown so fast, love can grow fast. There had been a thousand ties of tenderness, a thousand dreams, from which he had so deftly escaped and fled.

She had a sick old black feeling like the feeling when her parents died. They had both died when Mitzi was in her early twenties. Since then no one had been really kind to her, except Austin. He had been thoughtlessly carelessly kind, he had brought honey-sweetness into her life, but he had never loved her with that special love which makes a person to be, makes them more of a person. Her parents had done that. The weird loved atmosphere of her childhood came back to her now, the shy awkwardness of her proud father, the little drab cosy private formalities of her shabby home. She had shaken it off, cleaned it off like an old smell, though she loved her parents always. In the days of her fame, when she had been a feather-weight bird-swift six-foot-one Etruscan goddess, she had imagined that she had become a different person. But she had never really succeeded. She was her daddy's girl, his Mitzi, the child of that vanished home still. Instead of opening out into wealth and freedom and renown her life had become ever narrower until now it had dwindled to a point.

In the golden days wherever she had travelled in the world she had sent picture postcards back to her parents nearly every day. The postcards were a proud record of achievement, a sort of perpetual fanfare. To search out the gaudiest ones, to stamp them with exotic stamps, had been such a positive pleasure and a cumulative satisfaction. Even now whenever she saw picture postcards for sale in London she felt, in a stale sad way, the old impulse which was a kind of act of love. When her mother died and she sorted out the little house in Poplar, she found all the postcards, hundreds of them, in a big cardboard box. The box was with her now, in fact it was under her bed. Mitzi pulled herself up slowly and edged the box out with her foot. Hanging her head dully down she pulled the lid off and began to turn over the pile of stiff bright cards. The Alps. The Mediterranean. Sydney. San Francisco. Had she really been to all those places? Castles in lands she had forgotten. How little that brightly coloured world had ever entered into her being. She looked at it all now with incredulity. And on the backs, always the same flat message. *Great fun here. Hope you are well. Awfully sunny here. Really hot, lots of wine. Sun shining and swimming marvellous. Much enjoying sea and sun. Much love.* Had the wide world been nothing but sea shores and drink and sun? Those suns were shrunken now in memory and gave little warmth. Had they ever really warmed her at all? What had her life been? She had marvelled when she

344

first saw great mountain peaks with snow. Someone had marvelled. But all was dead now. Even for her dear father she had had no voice really and his love had given her no lasting formation.

I have not achieved myself, thought Mitzi, and I cannot now. I have no money and no job and no Austin. No one is kind to me any more or knows or cares whether I live or die. I could sit in this house forever and nobody would come to me. She continued dully to turn over the cards. One was blank and she picked it up. It was of the glacier at Chamonix and it brought with it a sudden physical sensation of sun and snow and racing on skis. She turned it over and reached for a pencil and addressed the card to Austin. She wrote on it *It's sunny here. Wish you were with me. Good luck.* She propped the card up beside the bed. She thought about her dear father and how his loved being seemed now to be drawing her towards itself. She had seen his coffin lowered into the grave and her life had seemed to end then. Perhaps indeed it had ended. She destroyed her ankle soon after and in doing so destroyed herself. It only remained to complete the process. Mitzi shuffled to the cupboard and found the big bottle of sleeping tablets which the doctor had given her. She had only taken one or two. Now she would take the rest. They would be sorry, Austin would be sorry, this would be the last thing he would expect. At least she could surprise him. He would be sorry. Tears had come and she whimpered quietly. She went and fetched some water and the whisky bottle. She began swallowing the tablets and drinking the whisky, choking every now and then with sobs.

Meanwhile Austin had arrived with his suitcase on the doorstep at Valmorana.

He was in a state of elated self-satisfaction. A great anxiety had been taken from him and he had been led through shame to revelation and certainty. The anxiety concerned Norman. Austin had spent some time at the hospital, where, with a nervous morbid urge to know the worst, he had persistently questioned Norman to find out how much he could remember. Mrs. Monkley could not thank Austin enough for his concern and kindness. Austin peered into Norman's now curiously guileless brown eyes to see if he could discern lurking in those speckled depths any dawning memory of what had actually happened. There seemed to be none. Norman was in many ways much better. He knew his wife and could cope with the present and even talk about the future. He could remember his days in hospital and he could recall his childhood. He had not lost his skills. He could vaguely recall his marriage. Nearer times seemed to have been blotted out. Austin's probing elicited nothing. "Don't you remember giving me your novel to read?" "Novel? No." Norman seemed to think that Austin was a doctor and thanked him warmly for his visits. Austin brought Norman fruit and flowers. The hospital staff now thought that Norman would never fully recover. So that was all very satisfactory.

The shock of having been found by Dorina in Mitzi's arms first prostrated him with such a sense of uncleanness and shame that he could not face his wife. He wrote her two very crawling letters, and then later felt that he ought

346

to have been more manly. Was it really such a terrible crime to hug another girl when one's wife had left one? What struck him now was rather the disparity between the two women. Why was he, the husband of Dorina, stooping to cuddle a fat illiterate landlady? He had been sorry for Mitzi, that was the trouble, and that had led him, as so often, to be far too kind. What a mess it all was. He had endured it, he now saw, only because Dorina had been safely immured and sequestered. She had been, while he developed his thoughts and followed through his phase, in captivity. *She* could have, in this interval, no thought or motion. She was on ice. But now providence had led her, by her sudden brief appearance in his world, to break the spell. This visitation had done all, it had returned him to reality. Whatever demons he and Dorina had engendered between them must be faced together. They had had their holiday from each other and it had produced nothing but misery and muddle. It had also produced the certainty that they belonged together and that, for better or worse, they were chained to each other forever, their minds mutually interdependent down to the last trembling atom of consciousness. People so tied have to live together even if life together is torment since life apart is yet greater torment. So Austin saw. And as he came nearer to Valmorana his determination became more and more radiant with hope. What he felt Dorina must feel too. In the fullness of time they had found each other again, just as they knew they would.

Mrs. Carberry opened the door. She had been away from work for several days. Her youngest child had been ill. And she had had to take Ronald to the hospital for some tests. She said she thought Miss Dorina must be still in bed and would he wait in the drawing-room. Dorina was still "Miss Dorina" at Valmorana and this seemed so appropriate that Austin scarcely noticed it. He stood in the drawing-room now, trembling suddenly with pleasure and desire. He pictured his tenderness. He pictured her joy.

Mavis came in. Mavis was dressed in a blue overall

347

and had tied her slightly fuzzy hair in a ribbon. She looked very tired.

"I'm sorry to come so early," said Austin, "but could I see Dorina, please?"

"Dorina—"

"Mavis, I've decided at last. Please forgive me. I know I'm a hopeless character. See, I've brought my suitcase. If you can bear to have a married couple in the house."

"A married couple—?"

"Me and Dorina! Mr. and Mrs. Gibson Grey happily reunited at last. It's happened, you see, the great moment has come, I knew it would, Dorina knew it would. So can we stay, please? Just till we can get the flat back? You don't mind do you, Mavis? Oh do call her, please. I shall kneel at her feet, I shall. Oh she will be so glad—"

"She isn't here," said Mavis.

"When will she be back?"

"I don't know."

"I'll wait then. Mavis, you aren't angry? I know I've been awful. Has she gone shopping?"

"We've been telephoning your place, only no one answered. We thought she might be with you."

"How do you mean?"

"She's gone. I thought she might be with you. I've been ringing Charlotte too, only she's still away. I don't know where Dorina is."

"But you must know—she can't have gone—she didn't tell me—"

"She didn't tell me. She just packed a suitcase and left. I came back and—"

"She didn't leave a message? Oh Mavis, where can she be, where—?"

"All right, don't panic," said Mavis. "She's with friends somewhere."

"But they would have telephoned you, everyone knows—"

"She's not a child! She can look after herself. She's not a stray dog. She'll communicate, she'll come back, she may turn up at any moment, I'll ring you when she does.

348

Don't worry, Austin, we'll let you know at once, don't worry. Now I must get back to my jobs."

"Mavis, let me stay for the love of God. I must be here, I'd go mad anywhere else. Here is where she'll come back to. Oh what can have happened to her? Please, Mavis, let me stay here, please, until she comes back, I must."

"Austin, honestly, I'll send news—"

"Mavis, I'm so frightened. She will come back, won't she? please, please let me stay here. Oh what can have happened? I know you've got plenty of room at the moment. Any corner will do. I won't need any sheets."

"Oh all right," said Mavis. "All right, all right. You will need sheets, though." She left the room and walked slowly up the stairs.

Dearest Hester,

George and I have been putting our heads together about Charlotte and we've decided to start a sort of FUND to guarantee her so much a year. The situation with Gracie is *delicate* to say the least, and we much doubt if Char would accept *her* help anyway, so as Char just *is* in straitened circs we felt some rallying round of an acceptable kind was indicated. Then I had the brilliant idea of recruiting Matthew as president and nominal head of the whole affair (so respectable!), and he said he would, and now all we need is a *lot* of people to contribute a *little* regularly, and (yes, dear!) we were hoping that you and Charles would stump up. I shall ask all our gang, and then get Matthew to tell Char, and we're sure that if he says he arranged it all she'll say yes! Well, that's my latest bomb. Could you talk it over with Charles and let us know what you think, not just about a contribution but about the whole idea?

We so much enjoyed the party. I have a confused memory of my departure! How tall and handsome Ralph has become.

Ever, with love,

CLARA

P.S. Charlotte seems reasonably okay, in fact she has gone away on holiday. We are doing our best to cheer her along.

Dear Ralph,

I am sorry I have not managed to see you since our

interesting discussion about the dissolution of the monasteries. Thank you for your note about the party. I am sorry you found it so dull. Your parents, in league with mine, are, I am told, hoping that I shall persuade you not to drop out. Do you really need persuading? Does not self-interest unambiguously suggest that a world of order, money, sanity, and cleanliness, together with a roof over one's head, is preferable to being a drugged penniless tramp who cannot even take a bath? And think of the company one would have to keep. The conversation of even a moderately educated stockbroker is more amusing than that of most self-styled "hippies." There is *work* of course, which the dropper-out is presumably shunning. But is not work a blessing? The unoccupied human consciousness naturally becomes a place of torment even without the assistance of LSD. What have I forgotten? Oh well, morality. I suppose we ought to lend our considerable talent to any society which is even halfway decent: how rare they are becoming these days.

I cannot see you tomorrow. I expect we shall meet in public at the Dizzy Club. I shall leave your copy of Toynbee in my desk, and you could pick it up in the afternoon, only I won't be around. I send this as usual by the hand of Williamson minor. What an intelligent and attractive little boy he is.

Yours,
PATRICK

P.S. Would you like to have my paper on the Vikings? We could discuss it later on.

Dearest Gracie,

This is just a routine apology for what happened at the party. I don't flatter myself that my untoward behaviour will have knocked even the smallest apple off your cart. The main hurt is to my own vanity. However. We have known each other all our lives and this momentary rise in temperature prompts me to tell you, what you already know, that in some totally unfrenzied but deep sense of the word I love you and always will and would always help at need, always. There's a lot of alwayses from an unattached young fellow with his life before him, but I know you understand me as you (dear me, here comes that word again) always have. I greatly esteem your fiancé and I am sure you will be very happy; and as for you and me, it was just one of those things. I gather you are still in Ireland, where I trust the customary rain is in abeyance.

Your friend,
SEBASTIAN

P.S. The latest thing is that Patrick is to be a good influence upon Ralph! I am not, however, in my brother's confidence, as I believe you are in yours.

Dear Andrew,

I am so glad that you want to buy Kierkegaard and that we so quickly agreed upon the price! I am sorry I had to leave you with MacMurraghue. I shall never forget your departure into the night with MacM's head weaving about now high now low! What happened thereafter? How I agree with what you said about Ludwig and Gracie. Another good man done for. Let's meet in town when you're next up. I must go now to take my sister to Brands Hatch.

All the best.
OLIVER

My dear,

Austin is installed. There was nothing I could do about it. He walked in! He now occupies the house like a sort of bored mad child. He follows me around. He haunts the drawing-room and the kitchen, starts reading books and then loses them, switches the television on and off and frightens Mrs. Carberry. He nearly has an apoplectic fit every time the telephone or the door bell rings. (So do I.) Ronald saw him yesterday and at once started howling like a dog. I have had enough of this and I urgently want to see you. I'm sorry to sound so peremptory, it's just the nervous strain. Since you now can't come here (it's rather funny really, isn't it) suppose I come over to you? I could pick up the letter you want Dorina to have from you directly she arrives back, I agree we mustn't trust the post, I am out sometimes and Austin snoops about and looks at everything. However I don't really think it's a good idea, your writing to Dorina. She obviously ran away to make a complete break, she must be fed up with all of us. (God, I don't blame her!) I think you'd better keep silent in that quarter from now on. However it's up to you. Matthew darling, let me come and stay with you for a few days. I need this, you need this. You know from experience how easy it is to conceal a girl in your house. (Sorry!) Not that there's any reason for us to be secretive, but at the moment I couldn't bear gossip. I'll send this by the hand of Mrs. C. I can't telephone from here, but will slip out and ring this afternoon. The absolute lack of news is awful. Do you think we should tell the police? I suggested this to Austin and he became almost hysterical. Oh what an awful time. Remember I love you.

Ever, ever,
MAVIS

P.S. For God's sake get Charlotte out so that Austin and Dorina can have the flat as soon as D. turns up.
P.P.S. Of course Mrs. C. can bring that letter for Dorina if you really want to send it. I honestly think it's better not. And letters are such dangerous properties. Please send me at least a little note by return. I miss you agonizingly.

Ralph,

Sorry, sorry, sorry. I can't quite remember the later part of the time. If I hadn't left my handbag behind at the Odmores at least we could have eaten something. I remember somebody crying on a bridge, but I don't know whether it was you or me. It was all a horrible business, sorry. To go off with you was a mean action and my saying so throughout the evening and indeed night didn't make it any less so. I return the pocket-knife which you so sweetly gave me in that pub. I feel my life may easily become a mess, like the mess so many of my friends live in, and I don't want that. I know you are no longer a child and I say to you do not be in love with me—I think you are not really, it is just an idea. There is nothing here. Well, at least we haven't been worse than stupid. I can't write you a clever letter, this is just to say please, in that way, go away, and I am so sorry and I do wish you very well, sorry,

ANN

Dear Karen,

I would like to see you. I am sorry about the tone of my last letter. Naturally your relations with other people are none of my business. I write to you now simply because I am feeling depressed and because you once expressed affection for me, and although much of it may be in the natural course of events have evaporated I trust a residuum of good will may still remain to form the basis of a friendship, for I begin to realize, on mature judgement, that I need friends, including ones of the other sex. No skin off R. Pargeter's nose or anyone's. I think starting on an ordinary job has affected my mind more than I would have expected. I feel old age is imminent and if there are any people at all whom one knows well one should cling to them shamelessly. So could we have lunch next Wednesday? *I will pay*.

LOVE,
SEBASTIAN

My dearest Mavis,

I too am very worried about the lack of news, but there could be so many innocuous reasons for it and I think we may get a telephone call at any moment. It would be premature to alert the police. Waiting is terrible, but will seem as nothing in retrospect. It is indeed ironical that Austin is now in occupation. However, in Dorina's absence we should anyway have had to keep both the Villa and Valmorana manned in case of her return to either. For this reason too I think that, much as I should love to have you here, you should stay where you are for the present. I fear we cannot trust Austin even to stay at his post, and I think you should, at all events, be on the reception committee. I send, along with this, by Mrs. Carberry, the

354

letter for Dorina, which of course you may read. I have left it unsealed—seal it when read. I think it is important for her to have it. Of course you must hand it to her personally at a safe moment, be sure that it is destroyed immediately afterwards, and meanwhile keep it effectively hidden. I agree that letters are dangerous properties. Please burn this one at once. About the flat, Charlotte is still on holiday but I will contact her on her return. I send very much love to you and look forward to seeing you soon when this nightmarish interim shall be over.

Ever, with fondest love,

MATTHEW

My dear Dorina,

We have been very worried about you and this is a little note to welcome you back. It was indeed unfortunate that Garth arrived and that he upset you so much. However he told you in essence nothing which you did not already know about the peculiar difficulties of your situation. Whether you and I acted wisely only an all-knowing Providence could really tell. We acted certainly with a will for the good, and must hope for such blessing as may attend, automatically perhaps, and even in the absence of the above-mentioned Providence, upon such willing. Think back to what was most seriously said and thought between us and hold to that. In respect of any courage and wholeness you have been able to gain I am of course a mere instrument and as such to be cast aside. May you go forward to happiness with Austin. I cannot sufficiently tell you what joy it will bring to me to hear of the renewal of your marriage. As to a certain necessary silence, there are things which even in wedlock must be devoutly buried in the heart, and there is no need to feel guilt or fear about this. I send this little note just to reiterate my goodbye. There can of course be no more communication between us. But simply because our leave-taking was so ragged I take the liberty of thus sending you my good wishes.

Ever your well-wisher,

M.

Destroy this letter at once.

Dear Oliver,

Thanks for helping me with MacMurraghue. He really is a dear man, though not that evening at his best. He was sick in Sloane Square and then felt better and now mercifully cannot remember anything that happened. He is doing penance in his room with the *Parmenides*. I enclose a cheque for Kierkegaard. I am delighted, and will come to London when term ends to pick him up. With Schools imminent and my men all having nervous breakdowns I cannot escape at the moment. I was, I fear, indiscreet about Ludwig's arrangements. The girl has charm and though illiterate is no fool but I am reluctantly concluding that I cannot stand her. A pity, as he is so extremely nice. I look forward to seeing you.

Au revoir.
ANDREW

P.S. My ablest pupil has just attempted suicide. I must go and surround him with affection.

Dear Patrick,

Was your last letter serious? Are you serious? Everything you say now sounds so bloody insincere. You usen't to be like that. You say "What have I forgotten?" I answer "everything that makes life worth living." Are we machines? You sound as if you were becoming one. And you have the cheek to lecture *me*. No, I do not want to read your paper on the Vikings, to hell with the Vikings; and rather than see you in public at the Disraeli Club I would prefer not to see you at all. I want to see you properly alone and soon. I want an explanation of your letter. All right, we might talk about dropping out, I don't know what I feel or think at the moment, I'm a mess, not made of steel like you. Let us meet, I suggest, indeed insist, tomorrow before breakfast near the pavilion. Surely you can make that. I return this note by the hand of snotty dog-faced Williamson minor.

Yours,
RALPH

My dear Ludwig,

You have, as you must realize well, put us into a very difficult and painful position. If only it were possible to discuss this matter with you face to face. Your last letter must, I believe, have been written with the hope that it would at last effect a capitulation on our part and that you would then have all that you want—Oxford, your bride, and complacent parents. But it cannot be. Your mother, I should say at once, does not want me to write to you quite so firmly, but she is (and wishes me to tell you this) in entire agreement with the gist of my statement. If at this point we did what might seem easiest, gave way and blessed your wedding and your plans for leaving permanently this country we would, we seriously believe, be betraying our duty to you in the deepest way. Dear Ludwig, you cannot have any doubt of our love. And we have had till now the blessed felicity of a family life entirely devoid of quarreling, which in this time is unusual. This very fact may in some ways have masked disagreements and divergences which have perhaps existed for some time and are only now making themselves felt. We have never been harsh parents, we have never needed to be, and the appearance of harshness now is simply, under God, the pursuance of our most strict duty and our love. Please read this letter carefully. It is not merely an obstinate repetition of what we have said to you before. About your general attitude to the war, although we do not share it, we will not argue. We understand and respect the view which you have expressed to us in your letter, and earlier too in our frank talks together, and we do not either wish or hope to change it. That is not our question. But now and before it is too late we urge two things. We think that if you are to adopt this position you should adopt it honestly and explicitly and openly in the U.S.A. and not evade the issue by hiding in Europe. The search for good cannot be divided in the way that you propose, it must be a total giving and not a calculation. This is *not* to say that you should seek what you call martyrdom, but that you should at least confront the issue directly when deciding on your policy. (And here, as I said earlier, there are many possibilities.) We also think (and this is a quite different matter) that you should not hasten into a marriage with a young lady who is, we now feel quite certain, *not suited to be your wife*. Please forgive these words which we do not utter lightly. We have in fact felt this from the start, but hesitated to say so because we hoped that you would change your mind of your own accord. Your letter about bridesmaids and such things makes us indeed understand the reality of your plan and prompts us to say that, from our view, we cannot applaud your choice. Unfortunately as you have not brought your intended bride to see us we cannot judge her from first experience. Our impression has been formed from your letter about her and her family, from her own letter to us, and from her photograph. This may seem meagre evidence, but in such an all-important matter an impression *must* without flinching be formed by parents, and the lack of data is not to be ascribed to our fault. We feel that Miss Tisbourne is too young, and that she is insufficiently educated and insufficiently serious to be your *life-long companion*. This is not, my son, the idle prejudice of severe and gloomy parents. You know yourself how much we too care for youth and gaiety and the happier side of life. But a secure future cannot be built simply upon the light-heartedness of youth. You must have a partner to whom you can reveal the deepest of your soul and whose judgements of value are likely to accord with your own. You and your wife should be, in the gravest sense, morally akin. If you are not your union will be a hell of superficiality, loneliness and ultimately deceit. I beg you, Ludwig, to ponder most carefully what I say. You may not agree. But for our sakes, dear child, I beg you at least to postpone this hasty marriage. Please forgive and understand the truly terrible anxiety of two loving parents concerning their only son. In a few days, after you will have had this letter, I may telephone you at about eight or nine in the morning your time at the latest address you gave. Your mother sends her love and kisses. Always, my dearest son, your loving father,

J. P. H. LEFERRIER

358

P.S. Do not misunderstand what I say above. Your mother and I view with horror and misery and a fear which rests upon but too much clear evidence, the consequence, to you of any direct confrontation with the law of this country. In prison here your very life could be in danger. I have, since writing this letter, talked yet again to Mr. Livingstone. He says that it is now becoming a mercifully accepted thing that evidence from a psychiatrist can be offered to a tribunal. This evidence need not be of mental breakdown but may be very various, and can indeed amount simply to a careful restatement of the objector's own opinions.

Little Karen,
  You know how I feel that I feel about you and how I have been feeling that it was about time too, O Lord. But also I now thoroughly intuit and can face that you do not love me and what is more love another. You half told me and the rest I, Richard sleuth, discovered. I don't feel deceived. Your tiny petulant soul has always been open to me really. All which being so I think I cannot bear that yachting trip, can you? In any case it was getting so overrun with Tisbournes and such it was hardly worth having, was it? I am going to pretend the yacht has broken down. Thus we can phase the thing out and save our faces. Why do we both have to live in this blaze of publicity instead of the decent obscurity of marriage? As for marriage, I doubt if I, Pargeter, am made for it. I have been so unhappy for so long I have become resigned. Do not do me the wrong of pitying me. In a way I enjoy it all, and for once am producing, I trust, a conclusion which is not fraught with lies and cries. That it was fun while it lasted is probably the best the likes of me can ever say, and in this case, it scarcely got going at all. I don't think, after our last rather stormy interview and your flight to the country, that this letter will surprise you much, and I doubt if it will distress you much either. What, after all, were you up to? Fate and I are letting you off easily. I myself am a hopeless unworkable human being

designed to be miserable and to cause misery. Better steer clear. Sorry, pretty Karen, sorry.

R.

Dear Andrew,

For reasons which I shall shortly explain to you I return your cheque. You shall not buy Kierkegaard. I may be a businessman but I am not a crook. And especially not in this context, about which I have been thinking. May I come and see you in Oxford on Thursday? Could I stay the night in college? I have something to say to you.

Yours,
OLIVER

Dear Mr. Gibson Grey,

How awfully kind of you it was to spend so much time with poor Norman last week, he greatly appreciated it, or would you know if he could fully realize what you have done for him, I think your visits have done him a lot of good, he is much more alert and looking as if he was trying hard to remember things all the time. He is to leave hospital now and come home. The hospital thinks he may partially recover, anyway he can do some simple work. The welfare people are all very kind and will arrange his training for something. It is a change in our lives. It is a funny thing to say, but he is so much nicer now than he used to be. Do you think his novel could be published, we could use the money. Thank you for helping my poor husband.

Yours truly,
MARY MONKLEY

Ann dear girl,

This is to tell you that such shadowy things as there were between me and Richard have been definitely broken off. I didn't really intend anything, it was the yacht that brought it on! My flirting with R. had a purely Machiavellian purpose, as you know. (I only hope I haven't overdone it.) And I don't think Richard really intended anything either, honestly! It was all so stupid. I felt I

360

should write at once and tell you that that coast was clear again. You've been so sweet about it, you are an ace-girl.

I am still down in the country and propose to stay for the present. I am seeing nobody. I have given up my temp typing job, it was awful. Even the pigs are great. You know you are welcome down here any time. Dad, who is as crazy about you as ever, adds his invitation! Thank God for female friends. All the warmth and sense of the world comes from women, I often think. Let me know your moves!

With much love,

KAREN

Dear Oliver,

Thanks for the cheque back. Yes, do come Thurs. The college guest rooms are full, but you can stay in my rooms. Nice to see you.

Yours,
ANDREW

Dear Sebastian,

Thank you for your letter. Yes, it would be nice to see you. I too value our friendship. I shall hope to have many men friends in my life and in that company you will always, I am sure, have an honoured place. I am rather busy at the moment and cannot manage lunch Wednesday. I think however there is a gap on Friday. Let me know when and where by postcard.

Yours,
KAREN

Dear Richard,

Just a note out of the blue to say why not let's have lunch or a drink one of these days? I suppose we are old friends by now. I seem not to have seen you for ages except at parties. I'll probably ring up some morning.

Love,
ANN

My dear Father,

I begin to despair of our understanding each other. I am not "evading the issue by hiding in Europe." The point is that, given the whole situation, my opinions, my character, my talents, it emerges as being not only my interest but my duty to stay here. Perhaps I have not said this before strongly enough. I leave Gracie out here because she is not a necessary determining factor. Even without her I would stay. Please believe this. You say that the search for good must be total giving and not calculation. But total giving, if it is to be right giving, is not a blind smashing of oneself against fate. If I conceived such self-destruction to be my duty I trust that I would not shirk it. But I do not. To choose such immolation would, in my view, be mere masochism, or the nervous stupid fear of being thought a coward or truant. A dutiful disposal of oneself *must* be based upon calculation, since one is an individual soul, and individual souls have different paths. I have reflected deeply and seriously about my own path and about this I can say no more. What you suggest in your postscript I accept as evidence of the degree of your distress. I cannot imagine that you mean it seriously. How much to this your "harshness" is to be preferred! I know what you have always thought, and what you know I think, about "psychiatrists." I would regard with utter abhorrence the idea of seeking such aid, or feigning mental weakness in relation to what should most of all manifest mental strength.

As for Gracie, there is little point in arguing. You have not met her, and if you do not cross the Atlantic, *which I beg you to do,* you will not meet her. I love her and she loves me and we are both, I assure you, well aware that marriage is a life-long partnership. This is our decision and we have made it. Please, I beg you most humbly and fervently, come to the wedding. Do not think any more that you can dissuade me. In this situation, if we are not to become strangers, which is unthinkable, one of us must yield, and it will not be me. Begging your forgiveness, and with so much love to my mother, ever your loving son,

LUDWIG

Charlotte opened her eyes. She felt pain. Her mind scrabbled in a jolting jigsaw hurly-burly, trying to conceptualize the present, to connect it to some sort of past, even to make out who she was. Something was tied about her neck and shoulders. She was lying on a bed, in a bed, with stiff sheets pulled up to her chin. The sun was shining. Some whiteness dazzled in her vision. The sun was shining horribly and she felt terrible. She closed her eyes. Her throat was hurting, something hurt deep inside her, she felt sick. Her head ached. She fought in the jumble for clarity of mind and for remembrance.

She opened her eyes again and the sun seared them. She peered into the light and saw another bed opposite to her. She was in a room like her dormitory at school and for a moment this memory dazed her. No, it was a hospital ward. There were several beds. There was a young woman in a blue overall and a white cap who was undoubtedly a nurse. Charlotte remembered having taken the tablets, dozens and dozens of them. Why then was she still alive? She tested herself with slight movements. Her limbs, her face, obeyed her will. This was being alive. Thought, surprise, fear made her breathe quickly. She felt sudden overwhelming fear of the death which had evaded her. She had truly wished to die. This awakening brought her life and death as twin terrors.

"I say, you're awake, good! Nurse, look, she's awake."

The nurse became large and near. She was red-headed, snub-nosed, vaguely familiar. "That's right, how are we feeling? Remember me?"

Charlotte remembered nothing except the dormitory at school, the tablets, the fear, and now Nurse Mahoney, and Alison looking through the closing door with one eye open as Charlotte asked the doctor to kill her with a fatal shot.

"I'm Rose Mahoney. I nursed your mother. Remember?"

"Yes." A sound had come.

"You're all right, you're as right as rain, sure. You haven't hurt yourself at all. Just lie quiet now and the doctor'll be coming to you, lie quiet and be good now."

"Isn't it funny that she nursed your mother," said the first voice.

The sun was in Charlotte's eyes. The sun closed her eyes. She drowsed again, trying with little groping movements of thought to discover herself. She hung suspended in water reaching out her thought-limbs like tentacles. Why had she taken the tablets? What awful misery had that been? Vaguely memory was present, the whole of her available self gradually present. Matthew. Yes, she was revived and assembled and ready for more torture. Back again in the old suffering. Tears.

"You remember me?"

"You nursed my mother."

"No, *me*. Not the other one. Sorry, I mustn't fuss you. Would you like some lemonade? I've got some, and real lemons too. We're allowed lemonade. The girl who went out this morning had some sherry, only I think she wasn't supposed to, half a bottle, she kept it in her sponge bag. There's only you and me and Mrs. Baxter in the ward now, and Mrs. Baxter isn't really with us, poor soul."

Charlotte struggled up a little on her pillows. A huge form in a red dressing gown confronted her, casting an even larger shadow. A big smiling face surrounded by short clipped fair hair, now jaggedly tousled. Big arms crossed on the chest.

"Miss Ricardo, I believe," said Charlotte.

"Jolly well done," said Mitzi. "We only met twice, I think. We met in the street. I was with that fool Austin. You were very polite. And we met once ages ago at

364

Austin's flat, just to nod. You brought a basket of goodies from Clara. Austin kicked it down the stairs once you'd gone."

"Why am I here?" said Charlotte. "Why am I still alive?"

"Garth Gibson Grey found you, you must have only just fallen asleep. He listened outside the door and heard you breathing."

"He must have very good hearing."

"You were breathing loudly in a funny way. So he broke open the door."

"Interfering boy."

"I'm so terribly pleased that you remembered me, I didn't think you would. You were so nice that time we met in the street."

"How do you know this?"

"Which?"

"About Garth."

"Oh, they told me."

"They?"

"They all came along at visiting hour to view the body."

"Who came?"

"Oh the lot of them, you know, Sir Matthew and Mr. and Mrs. Tisbourne, and Garth, and Lady Somebody-or-other and some other old party with grey hair. They were thrilled, I can tell you, quite pop-eyed with excitement. Everyone came except Austin."

"You mean they all came and looked at me when I was unconscious."

"Yes. I showed you to them. They weren't half knocked to see me here. I told them not to worry, you'd be all right, the doctor said so."

"Oh God!" said Charlotte. She shrank down in the pillows. Tears of weariness and impotent rage and empty lurking fear overflowed her eyes.

"Oh don't cry now, don't!" said Mitzi. She sat down on the edge of the bed and shyly pawed at Charlotte's limp hand. "You feel jolly funny now I expect, I did when I woke up, but you'll soon feel fine, really, I do. I can't tell you how well I feel, it's like being born again, the world is all wonderful and bright and new, you'll see."

"I hope you're right," said Charlotte. She wiped away the tears with her hand.

"Here, have a paper hanky, I've got lots. I cried awfully when I woke up too. Wouldn't you like some lemonade? I could squeeze real lemons into it."

"No, thank you."

"You haven't asked me why I'm here, why I'm not dead."

"You mean you too—?"

"Yes, I took an overdose. So did the girl who went out this morning. We're quite a little set of delinquents in here. Not Mrs. Baxter, though, she's got something else, she was took bad before you woke, poor old soul. The milkman found me. He wanted his bill paid and he came up. I hadn't taken too much, you know, not like you. I got dizzy and stopped taking them. You really did it properly, they had an awful time with you, Rose told me."

"Rose?"

"Rose Mahoney, the nurse. I say, it's nearly visiting hours again, they'll all be trooping back, I wonder if Austin will come this time, of course he wouldn't know about me, unless they told him, would he."

"Can one refuse to be visited?" said Charlotte.

"Visitors, Miss Ledgard," said Nurse Mahoney, opening the door.

"Charlotte, don't *worry*," said Matthew. He was sitting on her bed, weighing one side of it down considerably. Clara and George had drawn up chairs. Garth was standing. Hester was arranging the flowers.

"What have I got to worry about?" said Charlotte. She lay back relaxed and floppy, conscious of her unkempt hair and naked face, yet suddenly not caring.

"Exactly," said Clara.

"I mean, don't worry about what you did," said Matthew. "It's nothing to feel ashamed of and it may even be a good thing, it may lead you to—"

"I'm not ashamed of it," said Charlotte. She was very

366

present to the scene yet giddy with detachment. They were all so solemn, yet of course enjoying themselves like mad, one could see the muted glow in their faces, curiosity, superiority, joy. How she had delighted them.

"It was very naughty of you, of course," said Clara.

"You gave us an awful fright," said George. "You did, you know. *Dear* Charlotte!" He impetuously squeezed her hand and dropped it again. He wore an anguished sentimental smile intended as a special private communication to Charlotte.

"It had nothing to do with you," said Charlotte, "with any of you. It was a private action of mine, of my own."

"But you belong to us!" cried Clara.

"They'll probably want you to see a psychiatrist," said Matthew, "and if—"

"A psychiatrist? *Pouf!* Any psychiatrist I ever met would have done well to see me."

"My dear Charlotte, indeed," said Matthew, "I thought you would feel like this. But if later on you should want to talk things over with anyone, I should be very glad to—"

"Why ever did you do it, Char?" said Clara. "We were flabbergasted."

"Talk to *you*," said Charlotte to Matthew. "But I scarcely know you. This is the first time we've met for years."

"All the same—"

"I regard your suggestion as an impertinence."

"I'm sorry—"

"Char, don't be cross—"

"I am not cross. Hester, it is kind of *you* to have come. And Garth, I suppose I should thank you for what you did."

"I see no reason why you should," said Garth.

"Dear, dear Charlotte," said Hester.

"We all realize it's a way of drawing attention to oneself," said Clara, "but all the same—"

"Why isn't Austin here!" said Charlotte.

"Austin?"

"He ought to be visiting Miss Ricardo."

"Oh, Miss Ricardo, yes. Er, Austin, I don't know, I expect he'll come— Matthew, should we tell—?"

"No."

"I'm tired," said Charlotte. "Would you mind going? Thanks for the flowers. Now please go."

"Miss Ledgard should rest," said Nurse Mahoney.

"We'll come again tomorrow," said Clara.

"I won't be here."

"I liked what you said about the psychiatrist," said Mitzi, when they had gone. She had sat demurely in her bed during the visitation, sedately and silently bowing over Clara's polite wishes. Now she had bounced up again. "Oh Rose, there you are. Rose, I'm worried about poor Mrs. Baxter, she's still asleep and she's got that rather funny look, do you see what I mean? Oh well, doctor will soon be here."

"I'm sorry Austin didn't come," said Charlotte, "it would have completed the picture. I expect he will."

"Oh bother Austin, never mind him. What lovely flowers you've got. Rose, do you think we could have another vase, those ones are all bunched up?"

"You have them," said Charlotte.

"No, no, they're yours. Rose is getting married next week, aren't you, Rose? She's marrying a petty officer in the Navy. 'Every nice girl loves a sailor.' Look at her blushing!"

"Do have the flowers," said Charlotte.

"No, no—"

"Why did you do it, Miss Ricardo?"

"Do call me Mitzi."

"Mitzi."

"Do you really want to know?"

"Yes."

"Well," said Mitzi, settling down on Charlotte's bed, "it was like this, Charlotte. I was born in the East India Dock Road, you see, and my father was in the old clothes business, but *his* father had been a docker, and my mother's father was a ship's chandler, if you know what that is, and . . . ."

In these days Austin set out every morning to look for Dorina. He had quite settled in at Valmorana. Mrs. Carberry made his breakfast and at about ten o'clock he set off as if he were going to work. Sometimes he went a little earlier and travelled on the tube in the rush hour with the people who were really going to their offices. He made no special plan for his search. He went every day at random to different places, to places which he knew Dorina liked, to places which they had visited together. He went to the big picture galleries and the royal parks. He hung about the Festival Hall and the Embankment and lingered on the bridges. He looked into restaurants and teashops. He usually had a quiet lunch in a pub, reading the newspapers, and sometimes spent the afternoon at the cinema. Rooting in a cupboard in Dorina's room at Valmorana he discovered a small water colour in the style of the Norwich School which he removed and sold, receiving to his surprise fifty pounds. He felt rich, but spent carefully, taking only sandwiches and beer for lunch, or occasionally a salad and a glass or two of wine, and occupying the cheaper seats in the cinema. He ate heartily at breakfast time and in the evening when Mrs. Carberry left his supper ready for him in the kitchen. He saw little of Mavis, though they were not on bad terms. They exchanged silent and sympathetic smiles when they met on the stairs. He had not communicated further with Mitzi and thought very little about her, though he had heard some vague story about a farce with sleeping pills. He felt curiously enclosed and almost contented. The occupation suited him. He had a little money to spend, he had an objective, and he felt free. He did not doubt at all that Dorina was alive and well and that she would soon reappear. Meanwhile she was safe, she was away, she was elsewhere, and none of the others knew where she was. She was even more safely stored for him now than when she had been incarcerated at Valmorana. There were moments of panic, but those concerned himself really more than her. About her he felt, when he was alone, strangely little anxiety. He avoided Mavis, so as not to be touched by her fear or by the notion that there was really anyone else involved in the matter at all besides himself and Dorina. He loved his wife and expressed his love naturally and easily in his wanderings round London. He enjoyed searching for her, being preoccupied with her all day in a vague manner; and feeling that he was doing something necessary and good and was not supposed to be doing anything else. Sometimes he forgot her entirely.

Garth searched more scientifically. He wrote, after consultation with Matthew and Mavis, a large number of letters to people who might have heard of her or to whom she might have gone. Often these were quite remote people, elderly family connections or old school friends whose addresses Mavis had found in Dorina's diaries. He visited small hotels, methodically taking one area and then the next and combing it through. He questioned taxi drivers and guards on stations and assistants in big shops in Oxford Street. The police had by now been informed, though no one had told Austin this. The police were sympathetic, but politely unwilling to mobilize their resources in order to look for an eccentric lady who was obviously staying with friends in a fit of pique. They took Dorina's description and promised to let the family know if she turned up drowned. Garth too felt occupied but profoundly unhappy. He was working part time in Notting Hill and devoting the other half of the day to the search. No one at Notting Hill bothered about him very much or questioned him about his views or his ideals, and it did not seem to him to make much difference to the sum of human welfare whether he worked or not. Though he felt no desire to return to philosophy, he felt that his brain was rotting. He worried intensely about Dorina, imagining her miserable or mad or dead. He regretted bitterly that he had not "done something" about Dorina earlier, somehow secured for himself a place in her mind, in her, yes, heart, which he could easily and harmlessly have, with a little cunning, done. So he might now have held her, saved her. A thread would have connected them. He had let her pass by not so much because he was scrupulous as because he was afraid. With more courage he could have prevented whatever awful thing might be impending. He felt a vacuous possessive love for her which tormented him with restless physical aches. Of his father he saw nothing. With Matthew and Mavis he was brief and businesslike. They wanted him to move into Valmorana, but he refused. He lived now in a single room in a shabby road off Ladbroke Grove, in a noisy house full of West Indian busmen. He knew that Matthew wanted to talk to him, wanted even some kind of reassurance from him, but he took a grim pleasure in treating Matthew very correctly but blankly. He knew that this time was an interim however. He knew that until Dorina should be found he himself was a dedicated man, a wandering man under a curse.

Matthew did not search, he waited. He organized, as he could, the searching of others. He and Mavis briefed Garth, briefed the police, even put a discreet notice in the *Times*. The Tisbournes, who had perforce been told and who had told everyone else, had to be restrained and placated. People rang up with theories. Mavis made little darting visits to the Villa occasionally when Mrs. Carberry was at Valmorana, and sometimes she and Matthew met somewhere for a quick lunch or a drink, but they always felt guilty and hurried back to their posts. If ever Matthew left the Villa he would leave the door unfastened, in the evening all the lights were left on, and the door was never locked even when he went to bed. At night he would start up often, thinking he heard a soft foot on the stairs. He was quiet and easy with Mavis and they comforted each other, but there was, for the moment, no intensity between them. Their feelings and their fears were concentrated upon Dorina. Matthew was alone a lot of this time, keeping the Villa in readiness for her return, and thinking immensely about her and bending his will upon her. He also thought with puzzlement about himself, amazed to find how, after so many years of reflection, he remained baffling to himself. Occasionally at night he found himself reliving that scene with Norman on the landing, his own calm lies to the police, the awful doomed smoothness of it all. He would have liked to talk to Garth, but Garth was cold. Ludwig was still away. Charlotte, who had left hospital and returned to the flat, had not communicated with him. He thought that she would probably do so before long, in spite of her ferocity to him, but he felt no keen interest in seeing her, only a sort of hurt guilt. He experienced a vague fretful desire to change his life utterly, but could see no way in which this could be done. Mavis's quietness and sweetness consoled him very much and he laid up in her constancy all his hopes of future joy.

On the evening in question Matthew had been out to have a quick drink with Mavis. She had been tearful, and he had felt, as he held her hand in a dark cocktail bar, deprived of eloquence. The extension of time had affected them both. Too many days had now passed, each one like the last, and why should not such days go on succeeding each other until they should seem no longer like an interim? The postponement of life could not go on much longer but it was not clear how it could be ended. Hope was living through change and on and on into fear. So Mavis wept with fright and bafflement and Matthew told her that he loved her, not so much feeling the words as using them as a talisman. He did not any more know how to live through this time either, or to relate himself to its peculiar future.

Later than he intended Matthew was now walking along the road towards the Villa. He had had to park his car quite a long way off in another street. It was evening and

372

the lamps had just been lighted up against a sky of throbbing dark blue with very high corkscrew towers of brilliant pink cloud. It was a sky such as he had often seen in southern Japan, but which was rare in England. The sky held his gaze and the street below it was dark, until he had nearly reached the Villa. Then, blinking into the sudden obscurity, he looked down and saw that the front door of the Villa stood wide open.

Matthew was suddenly breathless with apprehension and joy. His heart accelerated violently and he went gasping along by the railings and up the stars and in through the open door. It was murky in the hall and his eyes were still darkened after the light above. He called out "Dorina! Dorina!" Then he stumbled upon something on the floor, threw out his hands, and stopped. There was something whitish spread all about on the floor of the hall, and now he could see into the drawing-room, whose floor was also strangely pale, the carpet strewn with pieces of—something. There was something hard and clinking underfoot as now he moved to turn the light on.

As soon as Matthew saw what it was he also knew what had happened. He leaned down and picked up a handful of small fragments. Blue and white Ming this, *famille verte,* amber-yellow Tang, pallid creamy Sung, celadon Sung, ash-grey Sung. He looked about the drawing-room, moved again into the hall, looked into the dining-room. The glass display cases were empty. Everything had been smashed, every single thing.

"Where is she?" said Austin.

Austin was standing on the stairs. He was panting and had pulled his shirt open almost to the waist. His blond hair stood out stiffly in every direction. His face glowed. It seemed a brazen head crowned with spikes.

It was difficult for Matthew to turn his back upon his brother, but he did so and walked as slowly as he could into the drawing-room, turning on more lights. Austin followed.

"Shut the door, would you," said Matthew.

Austin kicked the door to behind him with his foot.

Matthew began to get out the whisky decanter and

glasses, shuffling his feet through the fragments of porcelain. His hands were shaking violently.

"I said *where is she?*"

"If you mean Dorina," said Matthew, and his voice was shaky too, "I don't know." He felt sick and frightened and very sorry for himself indeed.

"You called her name as you came in."

"I thought she might have come back here."

"Come *back?*"

Oh God, thought Matthew. But he must know anyway. Yet how, and what can I say to him, and what is going to happen?

"She *was* here," said Austin. "It's true. I could hardly believe it. Where is she now? *Where is she now?*" He came close to Matthew.

"I don't know," said Matthew. He looked into the glaring eyes. "Have a drink."

Austin knocked the glass out of his hand and it joined the fragments upon the floor.

"Do you mind if I have a drink?" said Matthew. "This is all rather a shock." He poured some whisky into the other glass.

"Where is she?" Austin repeated. His voice was thick and bubbling with anger and he could hardly gasp out the words.

"I've told you," said Matthew. "I don't know where she is. I swear to you that I do not know where she is. That is true."

"You're hiding her somewhere," said Austin. "You've got her somewhere, somewhere secret. I've looked all through the house. I can't see her. I thought she might be here. I found one of her things, oh God—she left a —handkerchief—in one of the—bedrooms—I knew it was hers—it had a—ladybird on it— Where is she—is she here—are you expecting her—now—why was the door open—why did you call her name—?"

"Austin, I don't know where she is," said Matthew. "I thought—I thought she might call on me if she came back. But I had no special reason to think this. You know how we've all been looking for her. I don't know any more about her going away than you do."

"But she was here— You had her here when I called to see her at—and they told me she was lying down—then they told me she was gone—and all the time—she was here—with you—oh God I'll—" Austin's voice broke on a sob.

"No, no, everything they told you at Valmorana was true, I promise, I swear."

"Your false—words—how can I listen—lying swine—she was here, you said so yourself—and her little handkerchief—in a bedroom—"

"Dorina was here," said Matthew, "just for one night—I'll explain—" What was the best lie to tell now? Whatever was said Austin would believe more than the truth. It hardly mattered now what was said.

"Three nights—they said—but I knew more—all that time—she was here—"

"Who told you?" said Matthew.

"Never mind, I always find out about you, you can't hide from me, you kept her here, upstairs, while I was in torment—"

"Stop it, Austin," said Matthew. "I'll tell you exactly what happened, *listen,* will you. Dorina came here looking for Charlotte. She didn't even know I was here. It was a night when there was a rainstorm and as it was quite late she stayed here overnight and went back to Valmorana in the morning. Then later on she left Valmorana and disappeared. That was how it was. I promise you, honestly."

"Do you swear on your very deepest honour that every word of this is true?"

"Yes."

"I can tell you're lying. I can always tell when people are lying. And especially you, you have such a rotten—look. What you say can't be true. Why didn't Dorina answer my letters? And she knew where Charlotte was, I told her myself—"

"She'd forgotten."

"Forgotten! You got her here, you kept her here, you made love to her, you—"

375

"Austin, I did not make love to Dorina, nor even conceive of it, I swear on my knees, how can I make you believe the truth, look—" Matthew picked up a sharp fragment of cut-glass tumbler from the floor and squeezed it violently into the palm of his right hand. He let the glass fall. Blood streamed over his fingers.

Austin, who had been standing close to him, bent forward swaying from the waist and gave a long shuddering breath. He stared at the blood as if examining it and then sat down heavily in one of the armchairs. Matthew, almost crying with the sudden pain, fumbled for a handkerchief. He wrapped the hand in the white handkerchief and watched the bright red stain spreading.

"Austin, I didn't—"

Austin leaned back in the chair. He let something fall with a crack onto the carpet beside him. It was a piece of cast iron, part of the leg of a cast-iron table, something which might have been seen in a nearby rubbish tip.

"You made love to Betty," said Austin.

"I did not," said Matthew. He felt a little faint. He sat down too and found that his eyes were swimming with tears.

"You did. I have the proof."

"Austin," said Matthew, and he had now to control a whimper in his voice, "when will you and I find the truth? I did not ever make love to Betty or dream of such a thing, or Dorina either."

"You used to meet Betty secretly in London. People saw you together. And I found a letter—torn up—in your flat—"

Matthew gave a long sigh. "Let us get rid of this anyway," he said, "at last. I met Betty secretly once because we were going to buy you a birthday present. It was her idea, and her present. We were going to buy a tennis racket. You remember that time when you got so keen on tennis. Betty wanted to give you a new racket, but as she didn't really know about tennis rackets she asked me to come with her to Lillywhites to choose one. That's all *that* was. It was a secret because she wanted to surprise you. She loved you. Dorina loves you. God knows why."

"I don't believe you," said Austin. "You've just invented that." He was leaning forward now, drooping his head, mopping his mouth, his hair flopping before his face.

"Would you like some evidence?" said Matthew. "I can give it to you." He got up and went to the desk. He returned with a piece of folder paper which he gave to Austin.

It was an old faded letter. Austin stared at it, his lips trembling. Betty's writing.

> Dearest Matthew, about our tennis racket plot, could we meet not Piccadilly station after all but Café Royal? I have told Austin I am meeting a school friend! He is very credible really, though he is so nervy and anxious about things. I believe he's going to forget his birthday this year just like he did last! I'm longing to see how surprised he'll be when he sees an enormous package!! I promise I won't mention you. Thank you very much for helping with this, I couldn't poss have managed alone, would have made a bloomer! Won't A. be surprised!
>
> With love from
> BET

Austin crumpled the letter and threw it on the ground. "Why did you keep this?"

"Because—because I thought you might need to see it —one day."

"So you were carrying on with Betty all the same. This is an alibi which you arranged between you. You go round the world, but you have this all ready to show me. Why else did you keep the letter except to get yourself out of trouble?"

"I knew your insane suspicious nature," said Matthew. "Of course I shouldn't have helped Betty to buy the racket, but she was always so open, I didn't want to be the one to suggest that she was married to a— I somehow couldn't get out of it—anyway I was just going abroad again— Your wife loved you, she never imagined you'd seriously think those sort of thoughts about her—she was—you know how she laughed at everything—she was a simple open person—"

"Why did you keep the letter?"

"At first by accident. Later because I—thought you might be—"

"It's all a lie," said Austin, throwing back his hair. "What happened to the tennis racket?"

"I cancelled the order. Because Betty was dead."

"What kind was it?"

"Slazenger."

"I don't believe you," said Austin. "It doesn't ring true. You were carrying on with Betty just as you have been with Dorina. You're a lying adulterer."

"I have never made love to either of your wives, Austin. This is all in your mind."

"Your sort don't need to. You held their hands and fondled them and stole them. You discussed me with them. 'Nervy and anxious' and so on. Poor Austin. They came to you about poor Austin. Isn't that as bad as anything? Are you so stupid that you can't see that? Do you really deny before heaven that when Dorina was here you held her hand and talked to her about me?"

Matthew was silent.

"Where is Dorina?" said Austin.

"I don't know."

"I came here to kill you. It's just as well you weren't in when I arrived." Austin picked up the piece of cast iron and slung it across the room, where it smashed the leg of a chair.

"Have some whisky," said Matthew.

"All right." Austin was hanging his head again. He kept sweeping back his hair and letting it fall. He took the glass without looking up. He gave a dry sob and began to drink the whisky. Matthew could hear his teeth knocking against the glass.

"I'm sorry, Austin," said Matthew. "I have never meant you any ill. One day you'll just have to forgive me."

"Or kill you. Could I have some more whisky? Is it Scotch?"

"Bourbon."

"I thought it tasted funny."

As Matthew sat down he brought out his note case and began writing.

"What are you writing there?" said Austin, regarding him from under his hair.

"A cheque. For a hundred pounds. For you. I imagine you're short of money."

Matthew reached the cheque over. Austin took it with the tips of his fingers, examined it, and pocketed it. "Thanks."

There was silence for a while. Matthew drank his whisky greedily with closed eyes. Then Austin said, "Well, I must be off."

"Shall I ring for a taxi?"

"No, don't bother. Well, thanks for the cheque. Good night."

"Good night."

Austin paused at the door. "Was this stuff insured, by the way?"

"Only for the journey," said Matthew. "Not otherwise."

"Too bad. Well, good night."

Austin went away through the hall, kicking through the sea of brittle fragments as he went. The front door still stood wide open. It closed behind him.

Matthew reached for the soda siphon. Inside the cupboard he saw a white shape. It was one of the Sung bowls which, because it had a slight chip on the rim, he had put away out of sight. The soda siphon was empty.

Matthew went out into the kitchen and put his right hand under the cold tap. It was still bleeding and very painful. He began to cry.

"So you talked to your papa on the telephone?" said Gracie.

"Yes," said Ludwig.

They were in the drawing-room at Pitt's Lodge. Clara and George had just gone into the country to spend the weekend with the Arbuthnots.

"Did you have a good line, could you hear clearly?"

"Very clearly."

"Isn't the telephone extraordinary. Someone rings up from America and it sounds as if they're in the next room."

"Yes."

"What time was it in America when he rang?"

"Two o'clock in the morning."

"What a funny time to ring."

"He wanted to be sure of catching me before I went out."

"I never can understand that time thing and which way round it goes. What was the weather like there?"

"We didn't talk about the weather."

Ludwig was sitting stiffly on the sofa, his hands folded on his knees, staring very hard at a pink lustre cup on the mantelpiece. Gracie was arranging some purple and white dahlias which Karen, looking very cheerful, had brought up from the Arbuthnots' country garden and delivered briefly in person that morning.

"Sweet of Karen to bring these, wasn't it."

"Yes."

"Karen looks marvellous in her bridesmaid's dress. Did

380

I tell you Henrietta Sayce wants to be dressed as a page? She's such a comical little girl."

Ludwig said nothing. Gracie glanced carefully at her fiancé and then stood back from her vase with tilted head. "Any news of Dorina?"

"Of course not."

"Why of course not?"

"Do you imagine," said Ludwig, "that if I had any news of Dorina I would not impart it to you at once?" He turned a tense face upon her.

"All right, all right, I just asked. Why are you so cross with me, Ludwig?"

"Sorry, Poppy. I'm not cross with you. I'm just—"

"You are cross with me, I think. I believe you often are but you suppress it. You shouldn't do that."

"Sorry, darling."

"Your papa has upset you. Bother him."

"Yes."

"Well, never mind. What shall we do now? I know, we'll go and have a drink in that new pub in the High Street. We could have sandwiches there too if you like. Then we take a train to Charing Cross and walk across Hungerford Bridge to the Hayward Gallery. There's that exibish of what's-his-name we haven't seen yet. Then you can go on to the B.M. and work for a little bit, or I could tuck you up here if you like—and then—"

"Poppy—sorry I—I feel I don't talk to you enough—"

"Talk then. What stops you?"

"You do. You're stopping me now."

"Really, Ludwig, I don't know what you mean."

"If I want to talk about anything that really matters you become all sort of cold and vague and change the subject. You can't stand any sort of seriousness—"

"That's most unfair," said Gracie. "I'm just as serious as you are. I have my manner just as you have your manner. If I sound sort of—off-hand—that's the way I talk. You know I'm serious. Don't be so unjust."

"Yes, yes, I know, I'm sorry— But you do shut me up."

"Shut you up, a big man like you!"

"Yes. You know perfectly well what I mean. You won't

381

talk about— You evade things— You don't help me—"

"What on earth are you saying, dearest Ludwig? What won't I talk about or let you talk about?"

"Dorina, for instance."

"But what's the *use* of our talking about Dorina? We can't help Dorina by endlessly chatting her over the way my parents do. You don't want us to be like them, do you?"

"No, but— You're so—casual about it—and anything could have happened to Dorina—it's *awful,* her disappearing like that, just *awful.*"

"I agree it's awful if anything's happened to her, but I bet it hasn't. She's staying with someone or staying somewhere just to alarm us. She always was a tease."

"A tease. That doesn't describe Dorina, at all."

"I know you're very fond of her."

"Don't bring stupid jealousy in."

"I am not jealous! Why in God's name should I be! Or should I?" Gracie threw the secateurs down onto the table with a crack.

It was a cloudy day and a small cold rain was falling onto the little courtyard outside.

"No, of course not! Please, Poppy! But you seem so determined not to see anything that's really frightening in the world."

"I can see frightening things," said Gracie. "More than you imagine evidently. I just keep my mouth shut."

"Well, maybe— It's just that— I'm not explaining properly—in Ireland—you wouldn't even talk about Charlotte and you didn't want me to go and see her."

"Oh not that again. Charlotte's perfectly all right. There's nothing like a sham suicide to make everybody love you. Now she's the belle of the ball, except that Dorina's stealing some of the limelight by having so very inconsiderately vanished!"

"Poppy, you're so hard on everyone. Charlotte really did try to kill herself."

"Pooh!"

"It was only accident, Garth turning up like that, that saved her."

382

"You wish you'd found her."

"I ought to have gone to see her."

"You're not really thinking about Char at all. If you were you'd just be relieved and forget it. You're thinking about yourself. You feel guilty, not even that, you feel that some sort of satisfaction has been taken from you."

"No," said Ludwig slowly. "I know what you mean. But it isn't like that."

"You're supposed to be an intellectual but you're very bad at explaining yourself, aren't you."

"Well, these things are difficult, I guess. And one must be able to talk about them—"

"Talk away, then!"

"I was saying, one must be able to talk about them— with one's wife—without being shut up. I feel I'm not telling you all the deep things that I think, and—"

"I know you imagine I have no deep things, being only a woman."

"No, women can be deep too, of course—"

"How splendid! But not me. You're wishing you had a deep woman and not stupid me."

"Poppy—"

"I know I'm uneducated. I know your father's against me."

"He isn't—"

"He is. I read his letter."

"Oh—Poppy—"

"It was sticking out of your jacket. Do you think it was easy for me to say nothing about that? Husbands and wives don't have to scream to each other about every hurt, especially if it's an unavoidable one. Often it's better to keep quiet."

"*Dear* Poppy—"

"I expect now that you've talked to your father you've decided to go home to America after all."

"No, of course not!"

"I've never felt really secure with you. And then you say I evade frightening things! I live with frightening things, I live and breathe them."

"I know, I'm sorry—"

383

"You don't know. You've never tried to imagine what I feel. I'm sure all those men in Oxford despise me."

"Nonsense, Poppy! It's just that—you seem to want us to live such a selfish shut-in sort of life—"

"I want us to live an ordinary life. I love you. We've got money. I want to have children and live in a nice house and send our children to decent schools and have proper clothes and holidays and—"

"Never bother about anybody else."

"I don't want to live in a slum and be miserable, why should I? the idea of marrying you is a vision of happiness. Do you object? I have a talent for happiness. Do you mind? You've got what you want, Oxford and so on. Why shouldn't I have what I want, it's innocent enough, without being accused of selfishness?"

"I'm not accusing you of selfishness and I'm not suggesting we should live in a slum! We can live what you call an ordinary life, which for most people is a pretty extraordinary one, without refusing to think about anything difficult or unpleasant! You seem to think it's a simple thing for me to decide to live here and marry you and abandon my parents and my country—"

"Well, you don't have to marry me!"

"But it's been bloody difficult and terrible and of course I'm upset when my father tells me I'm acting wrongly."

"Do you have to be your father's slave? You're grown up, aren't you? He can be wrong, can't he? Mine can, why can't yours? Or is he God?"

"No, but he's got something. Oh Poppy, if you could only see the sort of cage I'm in— I don't want to fight in that vile war, but neither do I want to waste my life and talents going home and protesting—and then the gods send me the job at Oxford and you and it's all so easy and I don't see into my motivation any more and—"

"What does your motivation as you call it matter so long as you're doing the right thing? As soon as a few things go well for you you feel guilty instead of grateful. Surely you'll have enough trouble in your life, any human being does, not to fret because you're lucky now? You seem quite cross that you've got a nice job and we're rich."

"I've got to think it out, to think it through, to see exactly what I'm doing and why. You may dispense with thinking, but I can't."

"Of course I'm just a mindless cow."

"Please—"

"And if you've made up your mind why bother with all the thinking through—that's just to make you feel comfortable doing what you've decided to do anyway. It's a sort of self-indulgence, like endlessly discussing Charlotte and Dorina and how awful it all is and feeling superior and so on—"

"Poppy—"

"Anyway perhaps you haven't made up your mind if you're so shaken by a scolding from your father. I know I'm the trouble, it's all because of me—"

"Poppy, don't make every damn thing so personal—"

"Marriage is rather personal, I should have thought. You feel uncertain about me and that makes you feel uncertain about everything. Your father thinks I'm too young and too stupid and too frivolous to be your wife. Well, perhaps he's right."

"Please let us stop this argument," said Ludwig. "I can't discuss these things with you, you just get emotional and personal, I suppose all women do. I'm sorry. It's my fault. I shouldn't have brought the matter up. I'll hold my tongue in future as you suggest."

"I didn't suggest anything of the sort."

"You did. But please let's stop this fruitless bickering. I'm going to the B.M. now. I'll feel better when I've done some work. I'll come back here this evening. Please forgive me. And let's regard the matter as closed."

"Ludwig, don't be so cross—"

"I'm not 'cross.' It's—it's more serious than that. But also it doesn't matter. I mean as between us. Now I'm going to collect my books and go."

Ludwig marched out of the room. He collected his things and paused by the front door. There was no sound or movement from the drawing-room. He called out "Well,

good-bye honey, see you about six." There was no reply.
He went out and closed the door behind him.

Some twenty-five minutes later as he was walking along
Great Russell Street in the rain he saw Dorina. She was
wrapped up in a mackintosh with a scarf tied round her
head and her hands deep in her pockets, walking along
slowly on the other side of the road. He half paused, then
walked on. She had not seen him. He thought, well, she's
all right then. His own confusion and misery were so
great that he felt unable to cope with Dorina, he felt no
spring of interest in her, he almost felt resentment at
seeing her now. To walk by was an expression of his own
despair. His spirit was too tired, too troubled. He could
not at this moment lift a finger for anybody. He went into
the Reading Room and sat there in a daze of unhappiness,
the dripping sleeves of his coat spread out damply over
his books.

Dorina returned to the little hotel where she was staying in Woburn Place. Louis had seen her and had passed
her by. What could it mean? The unexpectedness and
mystery of the happening made her feel sick with fear as
she sat now on her bed, her teeth chattering with cold. The
room was unheated except for a weak one-bar electric
fire which had to be continually fed with tenpenny pieces.
Louis had been told something, told to avoid her, ignore
her. She had been condemned. She was cast out as if she
were a criminal, shunned as if she were invisible. Louis's
passing by had been a new and ghastly portent. She had
stood still looking after him, but although he had certainly

seen her and had passed he did not now look back. This was the final proof that she was lost, that she was rejected, that she had fallen out of the world altogether.

When Dorina had run away from the Villa on the day when Garth came there she had walked about the streets for a long time indulging her misery and her sense of aimlessness. She sat on a seat in a square with people passing her by and waited, almost as if she expected someone who knew her to come along and quietly lead her home. At first she vaguely intended to return to Valmorana. Then she realized that she could not do so. She had done something—but what was it?—which made it impossible for her to return to Mavis. Why she had originally left Valmorana she had by now forgotten. She had committed the crime of leaving and the even greater crime of staying with Matthew, and Valmorana could not receive her again.

By now it appeared to be afternoon, and Dorina was feeling faint with hunger. It was difficult to leave the seat where she was sitting, but she was afraid that she might actually lose consciousness there and be carried back to Valmorana without being able to help herself. She got up and went to a tea shop and had some coffee and a sandwich. To return to Valmorana still seemed to her like death. To go back there now would be to climb into her coffin. She had been there indeed as an animated corpse. The time spent there after her parting from Austin now seemed ghoulish, filthy with ghosts. It must be simple, she said to herself, it must be simple. She must stay out in the open now, do simple and ordinary things, not be stared at or thought odd for what she did or where she was. She decided to go to Charlotte, and she did in fact take a taxi to the flat and knock on the door. At this moment Charlotte was lying inside on the bed in a deep coma. It was an hour later that Garth found her.

Dorina did not like to linger at the flat upon the stairs in case some neighbour saw her or in case Austin should come. The thought of Austin had hovered over her like a contraption of black gauze ever since Garth had terrified her by his warning. During the spellbound days with

Matthew she had of course thought about Austin all the time, but Matthew's presence had so completely banished fear that she had seemed to see her husband conjured up as a heavenly apparition, bathed in a radiance of compassion and understanding. She could really think about Austin at last, and realized that she had never, since the days of courtship, really been able to think about him at all. Rather he had thought her, had possessed her with fear and love, had raced through her being like blood. Now there was distance and clarity and sense. She could, with Matthew's help, experience love without suffocating in it.

Only now that bright atmosphere had vanished utterly, blotted with darkness and fear and crime. She stood on the stairs outside the closed door of the flat and trembled with the old terror, only now it was worse and she felt guiltier, for Austin would find out, or else she would tell him, she would have to. She ran down the stairs and at first simply wanted somewhere to hide. She had a little money with her. She also had her cheque book. Some tiny mean instinct of self-preservation had once led her to conceal from Austin that she had some money of her own, though not much, in a bank account of which he knew nothing. He had taken all her other money. This was just a remnant, representing perhaps the little grain of selfish mistrust which still remained in Dorina's poor shuddering soul after its exposure to Austin. She deceived him about it and then forgot it. It came back to memory now, not with any special significance except that she could, at this moment, afford to go to a hotel.

She went to one at random, was greatly stared at by the clerk, but was given a room and treated as if she were an ordinary person. When signing the register she wrote her name as Dora Friedlander, and gave as her address the address of an old school friend in Manchester. To invent an address seemed to her criminal, while it was no crime to invent a name for this jelly of being which had never really had much identity even before its troubles. She was given a key, went upstairs, and lay on the bed and cried. She took no supper and fell into sleep as into the arms of some vague all-healing illness.

388

The next morning, awakening and not knowing at first where she was, she was overwhelmed with misery and fear as she remembered herself and her situation. She drank some coffee, said she would stay another night, and retired to her room to think. Only thinking had already become impossible. She felt, as one who tentatively explores the first symptoms of a grave ailment, the gathering of spirits about her. She stared at her handbag and it immediately fell off the dressing table onto the floor. She experienced a frightening sense of connection with her environment which she had not had since she was eighteen. Then a picture fell down. Dorina put on her coat and hurried out. She went to Hyde Park and wandered about. It was a sunny day. She felt in an urgent way that she ought to hand herself over to somebody. But whom?

She went to a telephone box and tried to telephone Charlotte, but there was no answer. She bought a sandwich and went back into the park. She thought of old friends, she even thought of going to Manchester, but since her marriage she had cut all ties, and who could be expected to receive the stranger and the ghost that she had become? At some more lucid moments she told herself that there were only two possibilities. Either she must return to Valmorana or she must go straight to Austin. It was then that she remembered, what she had since leaving the Villa entirely forgotten, the scene which she had witnessed between Austin and Mitzi. This memory came to her with a shock of gratuitous extra horror. After thinking about it for a while however this thought resolved itself into pure pain and puzzled her no more. If she was now to go back to Austin it must be as a slave without will, and if Austin loved Mitzi too then this also must be endured. Austin's love for herself she never doubted.

She could go to Valmorana, she could go to Mitzi's house and seek Austin. And yet could she really, after what had happened, do either of these things? She had given herself to Matthew just as surely as if they had lain in bed together. He had spoken to her with the voice of truth, he had exorcised her fears, he had helped her to love her husband better, so it had seemed. Or had he

389

merely enchanted her with a particular and strange love for himself? The idea of returning now to Matthew did not occur to Dorina for a second. Already he belonged to the past, to a time outside time, to a place she had visited in a dream. What remained were the blackness, the crime, the impossibility.

She went back to the hotel. The room looked odd, as a room might look to someone terrified or mad. She took tablets and fell into fiery dreams. The next day she hurried out and wandered again. She walked in St. James's Park. She went to the National Gallery. In the afternoon she went to the cinema and cried for two hours in the dark. Austin's intuitions were good, but temporally confused. He was often upon her track or in places which she visited on the next day. He too walked along the Serpentine, but too late. He went to the Tate Gallery, but too early. Once they were both in the same cinema at the same time, but arrived and left at different moments. A day and another day and another day passed. She changed her hotel. Garth had been right. The certainty grew upon her that she must tell Austin, and not tell him after a while, compelled by nervous terror, but tell him at once and ride the consequences into whatever smash or chaos might ensue. She started to write a letter but the sight of the words upon the page made her faint with terror. Must he know *that?* Her vision became troubled. Whenever she looked away a little child appeared in the chamber pot. Lurid dreams like waking visions crowded all her sleep.

I must see a doctor, thought Dorina. She thought this not so much because of what she saw as because of her bodily state. She felt hungry but could not eat, weary but could not rest. She had a dull pain in her back and a throbbing pain in her knee. She was running short of sleeping pills. Yet in order to consult a doctor she would have to have an identity, which she had not got. She thought of Mavis, kindly gentle Mavis, her motherland, forgiving all. Mavis would put her to bed, as she had done so often in the past, and sit beside her until she fell asleep. Perhaps that could be. But if she crawled back to Valmorana now she would surely die there like an old dog upon the doorstep. There could be no peace there for her now. Austin would enter like a black bolt and shiver the house to pieces. There was only one place for her to go now, and it drew her more and more like an awful doom-laden magnet, and that was back to her husband. This she increasingly felt, and with it, at a particular time, was joined the certainty that Austin already knew about the secret crime of the three days.

But there was no moment when it was possible to return to Austin or to ring him up or to write to him. The barrier of real action was too difficult. So she passed her days in wandering about London and waiting for a sign. She felt that if she wandered for long enough she would simply meet Austin somewhere. She walked and stood and sat and the sun shone upon her and the rain rained upon her and she grew weary and thin and cold. When she returned to her hotel at night her bedroom was like a waxwork show. Sometimes the apparitions were so palpable that she tried to touch their dead surfaces.

Then on the morning in Great Russell Street she saw Louis. When she recognized him she felt a great shock and a flood of relief. She had thought about him, but without purpose. And here was her sign. Here at least was the thing that would change the awful succession of these powerless dream days. But Louis saw her, paused, and then walked on. He did not even look back. I must be changed, thought Dorina, into some awful effigy of myself, something like the things which I spawn here in my bedroom. So they had all rejected her, condemned her, forgotten her. Perhaps they all knew about the three days. Perhaps in what seemed to her like a short time years and years had passed. Austin thought she was dead. Austin thought her dead and his thought had made her invisible to Louis. Austin had always meant death to her, he was her death and it was that in him which she loved. This was perhaps a reason why, even in this extremity, it never occurred to her to take her own life. Her life was Austin's and he would take it from her in his own ripening of time.

Tears were in Dorina's eyes. In these days tears lived

391

there, like hot slimy creatures in a hole. She got up heavily
and put a coin into the electric meter. The room was gaunt
and cold. Automatically she took off her dress and then
remembered that it was morning not evening. The rain
had made everything so dark. She was really ill now.
Tomorrow there might be fever, delirium, ordinary sickness, doctors. She decided to warm herself with a hot bath
and to get into bed. Shivering, she went into the bathroom
and turned on the hot tap. Then she took two sleeping
pills. The bathroom filled with steam. Yet still she felt
so cold, only her face was warmed a little by her crying.

She thought, if only there were some recourse, somewhere I could go to out of the mess and nightmare of my
failed life, somewhere where I could rest and drop the
burden of my sin, as I used to imagine when I prayed when
I was a child. Is there any prayer or place of gaze still
left which is not a mere enchantment? There should be
such, even now, even without God, some gesture which
would bring automatic world-changing wisdom and peace.
*Pliez les genoux, pliez les genoux, c'est impossible de trop
plier les genoux.* Who had said those beautiful words to
her and what did they mean? Then suddenly she remembered. It had been her skiing instructor at Davos. Not a
holy man after all. So that was all that was, another
senseless fragment of ownerless memory drifting about like
a dead leaf.

She took off her clothes and stood trembling with cold
in front of the little electric fire. Then she picked up the
fire and moved it into the bathroom. In spite of the steamy
bath the room was murky and chill. She balanced the
electric fire on top of the lavatory, turning it so that its
ray was towards her as she stepped gingerly into the bath.
As she did so a vibration from the traffic outside made
the electric fire shift and quiver. In a moment it was
sliding towards her. It fell into the bath with a loud splash
which mingled with Dorina's shriek. She shrieked and the
surging water closed over her head.

"Oh do stop crying, Clara," said George Tisbourne wearily.

It was nearly two o'clock in the morning and they had finished the bottle of whisky.

"Clara, let's go to bed. Enough, enough."

Outside in the night it was raining quietly. They were in their little cramped drawing-room, Clara sprawled on the tiny settee, George restless, moving from upright chair to upright chair, examining the bottle. The uncurtained night windows contained their distracted elongated reflections.

"It's not your fault about Dorina," said George.

Dorina had at last sufficiently identified herself by her death. Dead, she was soon found.

"I know," said Clara, sitting up a bit and controlling her voice. "I even know that. It's the pure pity of it. It suddenly lets in on you—you know—all the awful things, all of them, that one's usually unconscious of."

"I know," said George. He thought, I am growing old. I love Clara, but we don't talk any more, we know each other too well, there are no surprises, we have grown together into some sort of single ageing bundle. And everything one strove for and which seemed an achievement is touched already by mortality and seen to be dust. The children despise us. I have had my final promotion.

"Oh if only we'd found her—"

"She was a doomed girl."

"So we say now."

"I can't understand," said George, "why she ran off in the first place. What was it all about?"

"She was frightened of Austin."

"So you keep saying, but I can't see it. Austin seems to me pathetic."

"Women are often frightened of men. It's like cat and dog."

"Nonsense. You aren't frightened of me, are you?"

"No," said Clara, after a moment of staring at the window, her mouth red and wet and slightly open. Prolonged crying had altered her face so that she was scarcely recognizable.

"No, nobody would be frightened of me," George said aloud to himself.

"Oh if only she'd come here. I did suggest we should go round with the car and sort of kidnap her, only you wouldn't. Oh if only, if only—"

If only I had had the courage to stick to mathematics, thought George. He pressed his forehead against the cool slightly sticky glass of the window. I could at least have tried. I could have lived in a world of pure thought and left something beautiful behind me. A life in administration is a diminishing wasting life. And now mine is nearly completed and what remains is just idling.

"Is that Gracie moving about?" said Clara. "Why isn't she sleeping? I gave her some sleeping pills."

"She didn't take them. She said she didn't want to sleep. She said she'd sit and listen to the rain."

"She's in such pain and she won't talk. I can't bear it."

"It'll blow over—"

"I don't know what to think. Ludwig going off to Oxford like that, and Gracie suddenly turning into a deaf mute. She's been going round like a zombie for the last two days."

"It's just a tiff, Clara. They've got to find out what quarrelling is like some time."

"We've never found it out," said Clara.

No, thought George. We might have been better off if we had. We've never fought each other for a principle, we've always preferred peace. We've each surrendered our

394

soul to please the other. Perhaps this doesn't matter. Perhaps this is what love is.

"You don't think it's all going to break down between Ludwig and Gracie? His parents still haven't answered my letter. And you know Gracie wouldn't go for that fitting of the wedding dress yesterday."

"Gracie's a petulant girl."

"I blame Ludwig. I've never really liked him."

"Clara, be careful."

"Oh, we're always being careful. We don't say what we think even to each other, though we know each other's thoughts like an open book. Ludwig's a prig. He's too priggish to love genuinely and really give himself. He's a cautious man. At Oxford he'll be a dry old stick before he's thirty-five, fussing about college business and his latest article."

"You don't really think this, Clara."

"If they are going to break it off—"

"They aren't."

"I hope they do it in time for Gracie to get Sebastian after all. Do you think the Odmores would mind if we used the same wedding dress?"

"I must look after Austin," said Mavis. "I can do it."

"He hates almost everybody," said Matthew.

"He's got used to me."

"He knows we meet?"

"It's not mentioned."

"And he shows no sign of moving out of Valmorana?"

"No."

"Austin knows when he's onto a good thing," said Matthew.

"It isn't like that at all," said Mavis. "It's not anything like that. He is terribly stricken, he is scarcely sane."

"When others take refuge in insanity it's too bad for those of us who are incurably sane," said Matthew. "I am terribly stricken too."

"She was my sister."

"I'm not accusing *you* of taking it lightly."

"In a way, having Austin to deal with has helped, it has given me an immediate purpose, something compulsory."

"We must avoid guilt. You mustn't worry about his having found that fragment of letter—"

"I feel far beyond guilt. Dorina and I—we were closer than I've ever made you understand—there's a sort of timelessness in our relation—somehow while I live she can't die—and now she is dead, I am dead."

"Don't speak so," said Matthew. "After all this, perhaps a long way after, there will be a new time. You and I have a life to live, Mavis."

"I know. But at the moment I am dead to it. I am possessed by Dorina. And because of her, Austin means something. In an odd way, I can *see* Austin now, it's as if, just for this, I am God."

"What does he look like?" said Matthew.

"I'm sorry," said Mavis. "I can't respond, I can't talk that language. I can hardly talk at all. Except perhaps I could talk about her, like a very long poem going on and on."

"You are in better case than I," said Matthew. "You live with her, you die with her. I am left with the tangled end of good intentions that went wrong. I shall never know the extent of my responsibility. I loved her."

"Yes," said Mavis. "And perhaps that will be between us always."

"Do you mean dividing us? Because you blame me?"

"No, no, no."

"Or because you're jealous?"

"No. The pain I'm in kills structures like jealousy. I was jealous. But not now."

"Why then?"

"Her death is an absolute. One comes to places where one has to stay. Perhaps I shall have to stay here."

"So you think. But death is recovered from. All deaths are. This one will be. And this is right."

"I don't know," said Mavis. "I can't really see the future. But I feel like a prophetess. I feel like Cassandra. I feel hollow. Silence is best or else a scream. I feel fatal and curiously eloquent."

"Yes. You are speaking a strange language. Even your voice sounds strange."

"I am possessed. I can't talk ordinary language any more. I'm sorry. I feel hollow and clean. In a dead sort of way. Sterile. A vacuum. All the ordinary sort of—life germs—have been killed."

"I know what you mean," said Matthew.

"I can't even grieve for myself. They say all lamentation over death is lamentation over one's own death. This is not so."

"Yet you said you died with her."

"The dead don't grieve."

"I almost envy you," said Matthew. "You have made her into a goddess. I cannot. But however great the tragedy, you are still subject to truth and time. You are alive and you have a future. Your mind is a living thing which will alter. You even have duties. It is strange to appeal to you now in the name of duty. For myself, I mean. But I need you too. I need you for the forgiveness and healing which only you can give me."

"I hear your words," said Mavis. "I must go now."

"It was an accident. Not doom, not fate, accident. We must keep this before us too."

"I shall scream, Matthew. Better not to. I must go."

"May I kiss you?"

"No. Please don't touch me. It's still impossible. I'm sorry."

"I'll ring up."

"Yes. Good-bye."

397

Mavis was white and her eyes did not look upon the ordinary things of the world. The skin of her face was so taut and drawn that even the bone structure seemed to be giving way to the pressure of an enormous force. She looked much older, but beautiful in a dreadful way. Gazing elsewhere, she walked past him.

Matthew, alone, gave himself up to a luxury of grief which Mavis was without and beyond. He felt misery, regret, remorse, guilt. He loved Dorina, and his love, now set free and made pure forever, battered upon that last impenetrable wall. He saw her, he heard her, he imagined all manner of cherishing of her, and he knew that she was dead. Later Mavis would console him, would hold his hand and hear him accuse himself. But that time of consolation was not yet.

⁂

Her funeral had been like the Triumph of Flora. Austin had never seen so many flowers all heaped together. They had made her into a flower maiden. So she might suddenly rise again, resurrected, a maiden composed anew out of flowers. There was magic there. Austin had persuaded the priest to read the *Dies Irae*. Clara Tisbourne had caught hold of Austin's sleeve afterwards but he had pulled it away. "Quick, get Austin!" Clara had said, but Austin had pulled away.

Dorina was a sort of full-time occupation now, as she had been in the days before her death, only differently. Austin sat a lot with Mavis in the drawing-room. They sat together often in silence, stiff and upright, not as people usually sit together, but more as if each were alone. Sometimes, like Quakers in a meeting, one of them would feel moved to speak about Dorina. The other seemed not to listen, did not reply. Yet in this way they comforted one another.

Sometimes softness came and tears. Austin wondered what it would be like to believe that Dorina was with God. *Mihi quoque spem dedisti.* Could there be, after all, pure tears for sin and the certainty of redemption into another world? Only his tears were impure and he wept not because he had failed her, but because he had lost her, not even that, because she was so overwhelmingly no longer there, she whom he had petted and bossed and feared about so much. He had feared really more for himself than for her, had feared prophetically how terribly she would hurt him one day. That fear had made him into a tyrant. And now she had gone and taken the fear with her and he felt utterly undone.

Mavis fed Austin regularly but did not eat with him. Mrs. Carberry went about on tiptoe. Austin sometimes went for walks by himself, wandering about in a daze so that he seemed to forget that Dorina was dead and kept looking for her still, on buses, in trains, among the crowds of London. He kept searching for her face. The feeling that she was *somewhere* persisted in him, although he knew that really she was not anywhere any more, least of all in the deep hole into which they had lowered that ridiculously small coffin.

Austin knew that Mavis went to see Matthew. But he also knew that there could at this time be no communication between those two. Austin thought about Matthew occasionally, but not much. It was as if, for the time, Matthew was mercifully dead too. He was out of this, he was an outsider. The present emptiness of everything was a sort of comfort. The elegiac sadness of the desolate world was without joy but also strangely without horror. Dorina had taken her ghosts with her into the grave. It was a very complete ending.

But it left Austin without any purpose. This absolute absorption in another was, he supposed, love. He mused about love. He had spent, wasted, such a quantity of spirit in wondering whether Dorina really loved him and whether

399

she would go on loving him or murder him by loving someone else. But what was this thing that had seemed so all-important? Could he not simply have willed Dorina, as if he had been God, not greedily desiring a return? Yet did not God always want a return, had He not specifically created us to glorify Him, and did not the word "jealous" make its first appearance in literature as applied to Him? Then must we be better than our creator, could this be done in logic? But there was no creator, and indeed no logic.

What was clear was that he and Dorina had somehow lived wrongly, unable to use except for mutual destruction the spirit of love which inhabited them both. Now spirit has gone out of my life forever, he thought. I am mere animated earth. I shall live on as if in sleep, jerked here and there a little by those automatic purposes with which nature provides this kind of animal. But for the time even these purposes seemed absent and the days passed in a series of blank futureless presents. Only sometimes, with a presage of possible recovery, there was a small spring of satisfaction which oozed and dried up at intervals. It was a tiny impulse of pleasure but it came from a potent source. It was the thought that after all perhaps this death was a felicitous solution. He had wanted Dorina to be held prisoner from the world, to be held secure for him. Now she was shut up forever in the most final of all prisons. Now at last she was absolutely safe, and could never hurt him any more.

❊❊❊❊❊

Ludwig sat alone in his college room in Oxford. The blurry golden leaves of an unclipped wistaria made the window into a Gothic arch. Beyond were towers, elm trees in the sun. Merton clock spoke the half hour with a mournful cadence. The afternoon was a pale vain expanse of profitless time.

Ludwig sat holding a diamond ring in the palm of his hand. The ring which Gracie had bought in Bond Street and which he had slipped onto her finger in the shop, dazed with happiness. As he looked at it the atmosphere of that day came back, that particular echoing dusty brightness of sunny London, crazed and rattling and gay.

Gracie's letter ran as follows.

Dearest, when you said you wanted to be by yourself for a few days I thought it possible that you wanted simply to nerve yourself to break things off. So I am helping you by making you feel free. I am not breaking things off, but I want you now to feel free, to begin again or go away properly. I know that the death of Dorina has seemed to you like a symbol or sign. You blame me because you didn't go to her earlier. You feel that I lessen you in some way. Oh Ludwig, I love you more now than ever before, because fear makes one love more I think. This is the most awful thing that has ever come to me. To say these things is so hard. I don't know if you love me enough. I love you absolutely but you love me only partly. I thought it didn't matter because perhaps men always love only partly, while love fills a woman's whole life. But now it is agony. I didn't talk to you about your "great decision" partly because I thought I'd just sound shallow and stupid and partly because I don't like moral fuss. You know what I mean. I *felt* about it but I couldn't talk it. Another sort of girl would have talked it endlessly with you. Perhaps you need that other sort of girl, and one who is educated. Your father's letter was terrible to me. I feel you must partly agree with your father about me only you didn't let yourself know it. And when you talked to him on the telephone you were different after. I love you, I love you. We have never been

401

quite at ease with each other though and that is my fault. Perhaps you might come to treat me as an inferior and I would play the part too. But if you really love me none of this matters. Oh God I am sorry to be so stupid and I write this with *tears, tears.* Of course nothing here is fixed or has happened at all. I have talked to nobody, not even my parents. Let us just think a while. When you went away I felt it was some sort of real parting. Now I don't know. I wanted to run after you screaming. You said "Good-bye." Was it good-bye? Is it because of Dorina or that you feel I am not educated enough? I send the ring as a way of sending my love. Keep it safe. Nothing is fixed or final, is it? I am just *so unhappy, so unhappy, so unhappy.* What did it mean, your going away like that? *I love you.*

GRACIE

Ludwig put the ring away in a drawer. Gracie's letter caused him terrible pain. But his going away had meant something, and perhaps it would have been yet more agonizing if Gracie had decided not to understand. His way of life with Gracie had, for the moment at any rate, broken down. He had to take flight into loneliness. A sense of absolute confusion about the deep bases of his life had rendered him almost mad with misery. Only solitude itself, in a blank way, though it brought no solutions, brought a very small measure of relief.

That Dorina should have electrocuted herself with an electric fire on a rainy morning in a small hotel in Blooms-bury made Ludwig feel a disgust with himself and the world which was almost mysterious in its intensity. He did not blame Gracie. He did not think that Dorina had done it on purpose. The thing was pure chance and yet weighted with a significance of horror which he could not bear to contemplate. That he had actually seen Dorina on the day that she died and had passed her by was so nightmarish that he felt he would never be able to tell anybody about it. It was something to brood upon forever or to whip oneself with into some frenzy of new desperate

402

action or flight. So he had run to Oxford. And now every-thing seemed at stake, everything in doubt, every issue once more wide open. Hearing his father's quiet slow authoritative voice on the telephone had shaken him so much. His identity rocked, he had to rethink the world.

He had written to Matthew but had had no reply. He had a nervous desire to see Matthew and to try to explain himself to him, but he hesitated to intrude at this time upon Matthew and Mavis, who would now be more than ever in each other's company. Ludwig felt sad that Matthew's special lonely availability seemed now to be a thing of the past. Also he felt a suspicion that, after all, Matthew's spell might prove to be broken. Ludwig now intuited muddle, even despair, where previously he had revered experience and wisdom. Matthew was on the rocks too, perhaps, and Ludwig would have to struggle on by himself.

But where to? The college was empty now, except for a few servants, as everyone was on holiday. Oxford, deserted by its academics, full of troops of marching tourists, seemed now unreal and unconvincing. Its dreadful old beauty appalled him. He tried to work but found with terror that he had not the will. He sat in the Bodleian and drowsed away into terrible dreams. How could he become complete, could he ever be, or was he a man doomed to kill half of himself to let the other half live?

One torment was that it was every hour possible to take a bus to the station and get on a train to London. Tonight he could lie in Gracie's arms. In constantly deciding not to return to London he was constantly obeying some obscure imperative which somehow seemed to him to be on the side of his salvation. Was this paralysed muddling on from moment to moment what moral thinking at its most difficult was really like?

Merton clock struck the three-quarters, casting down the last hollow note into a trough of everlasting incom-pleteness. Human life perches always on the brink of dissolution, and that makes all achievement empty. Ludwig felt his youth, he experienced it physically as if the whole of his body surface had been fused into some charged and glowing material. He stirred and twitched inside it. Decisions which he made now would affect his whole life, not only in its circumstances, but in its quality, in its very deepest texture. According to what he chose now he would become a totally different person later. Various forty-year-old, fifty-year-old Ludwigs regarded him from the shores of possibility with sad and perhaps cynical eyes. To which of these shadowy forms should he give the spark of life? Who did he want to be?

Such precious things had been granted to him, sources of happiness, sources of good. Was it that he was unworthy of them, since he now conceived of surrendering them out of what seemed at moments a stupid guilt-ridden petulance? For any good that lay beyond, elsewhere, his eyes were dim. It seemed unthinkable that he should sacrifice his whole career now because of some idle nervous intuition. Or because his father thought that he was evading the truth. Or because he imagined this or that about his future self on no evidence at all. And meanwhile he had given one of the gravest of all promises to a young girl. And he loved her. And he wanted now more than anything else in the world to be in her arms. He groaned, darkening his face, hiding it from the golden time-ridden light of the leafy window. If only delay itself could have no consequences. If only all could stand still and the relentless procession of the hours be checked so that he could rest quietly in a real interim. Oh was it not even now somehow possible that everything could be well?

❊❊❊❊❊

"Excuse me, sir," said the police officer. "I am looking for a Mr. Gibson Grey."

"That's me," said Garth, who had opened the door.

The sudden sight of the policeman made Garth flush with fear and a whirling sense of guilt. What had he done, or what had happened? Immediately he thought, my father is dead. Then he thought, my father has committed some terrible crime.

"Could I come in, sir, and talk to you for a moment?" said the policeman. He followed Garth in and up the stairs.

Garth's room had a large square uncurtained window opaque with dirt through which the sun mercilessly shone to reveal a dance of moving dust particles, bare gritty floorboards, Garth's grey sheetless unmade bed, a chest of drawers with all the drawers open, a ruck-sack, a toppled pile of books, and a vague sea of underwear. There was a sweaty smell of old socks and a darker smell of filth and rats.

Garth went every morning to the emergency housing centre. What he did there was beginning to feel a little bit more like a profession and a little bit less like doing odd jobs. There was a certain primitive satisfaction in the evident importance of the work. And it was nice, sometimes, to occasion a look of relief in the eyes of those who were at their wits' end. All the same Garth felt dissatisfied and unhappy and even, to his surprise, lonely. He had never, in what now seemed his tougher and more hopeful days, imagined that solitude would be other than a welcome friend. Now he yearned vaguely for more mundane relationships.

That he had saved Charlotte's life, which he had undoubtedly done, had given him an almost childish sort of pleasure, it was like an unexpected present or a treat. Oh *good,* he felt whenever he thought of it. He did not expect Charlotte to be grateful and he did not even think that it was likely to constitute any sort of bond between them, he felt it rather as a little private achievement of his own, something he had felicitously pulled off. Also he wondered if he should perhaps regard it as a sign that he was after all upon the right road. But then Dorina had died.

When his mother was drowned Garth had been ten. He

was away at school at the time. The shock of it sliced several years out of his life. He could remember his earlier childhood, his jumbled home, his gipsy mother's sweetness, his father's emotions. Austin had been a tempestuous father, affectionate, permissive, suddenly harsh, often lachrymose. There was a good deal of quarrelling and shouting. Childen can manage storms of emotion provided there is love. A sturdy precocious little figure, he fought his father and bossed his mother. He was the centre of the world. Then suddenly there was no mother and no father and no world, only a blackness covering years now inaccessible to memory. And when he emerged his father was much older and a stranger.

The shock of Dorina's death produced a phantasm of being in love with her. Had there really been a pent-up passion behind that taboo? A woman paced his dreams who was half Betty and half Dorina. And he began to remember. He remembered his mother's funeral, Austin crying, Austin jerking his hand away. He remembered that appalling distress, his own defeated grief, the beginning of estrangement, the beginning of real fear. So in those years, which he could now dimly see, his emotional loving bullying young father had become the changeling of today. Dorina had somehow been a product of those years of misery, a sort of alleviation and yet a sort of embodiment of all those awful thoughts, a wounded grounded angel, a piece of spirit lost and crazed, no longer connected with its source and centre, but spirit still. Garth now saw a little into the mystery of his father's passion, and her death had this use for him, that a stream flowed again between himself and the past and after being dry-eyed for many years he was able to weep again.

After this, so swift is spirit, though still in sadness, he began to feel a new interest in himself.

Garth stood in the dusty sunlight in the stained room and faced the officer of the law. If it should be his father's death, or worse. Love for his father possessed his body like memory.

"Well now, sir," said the policeman, "I wonder if you recognize this bag here?"

Garth looked down at a blue leather suitcase which the officer was carrying and which he now dumped on the bed. It looked familiar. Then Garth recognized it as the bag which had been stolen from him at the Air Terminal when he returned from America.

"Why, yes, it's mine! So it's turned up!"

"Perhaps for identification purposes you would be so kind as to name some items which might be found inside it?"

"I'm glad to hear there's anything inside it!" said Garth. "Well—there is—or was—a dark green sponge bag, with a sort of silver-coloured toothbrush in it—"

"Yes, sir?"

"And—I hope—there's a—er—novel—called—er— *The Life Blood of the Night.*" Garth blushed.

"That's right, sir. What have we here? A novel entitled *The Life Blood of the Night.* Not much doubt about that, is there, I mean there can't be many of them knocking around! Here we find also a few articles of clothing and toilet articles. What else was in the bag, sir?"

"Oh an electric shaver, a camera, they're gone, and some of the clothes. Nothing that matters, really. How did you find it?"

"We found it abandoned, sir, on a building site. Lucky you put your London address inside. The ladies who now occupy the flat told us where to find you."

"The ladies—? Oh yes, well, I'm so glad. I never thought I'd see it again."

"Never give up hope, sir. Now perhaps you would just sign here? That'll be all then, good day. And may I express the hope that your novel will be a best seller?"

When the policeman had gone Garth eagerly pulled the novel out. He leafed it through. It was all there. He pulled the bed together and settled down. He was soon absorbed, spellbound. The novel really was rather good.

"I should think it over if I were you, Charlotte," said Matthew wearily. He unfolded a clean handkerchief and drew it down the side of his face and inspected the dirty damp smear. The weather was stupidly hot again.

"Really, Matthew," said Charlotte, "how can you imagine that I need to reflect? Why ever should I consent to be the grateful pensioner of such a ghastly band of well-wishers? Even if it is your idea. Which I doubt, naturally. Now be honest, wasn't it really Clara's idea?"

"Yes," said Matthew, "it was Clara's idea."

"And you were to be the front. I thought so. It has the Clara stamp."

"Clara is a very kind woman. It's a very kind idea. There's no need to swear at me about it."

"I'm not swearing at you. Dear me, you do look hot. You also, if I may say so, need a shave."

"But you are short of money, Charlotte."

"If I'm desperate I'll borrow from you. As it is, I propose to get a job."

"Oh. What kind?"

"I'm not sure yet. After all, I'm not a dolt."

Charlotte, looking radiant and full of vitality, was striding up and down the drawing-room at the Villa. Matthew lay stretched out in an easy chair. Charlotte was wearing a rather long dress of coarse linen with wide blue and white stripes and a wide belt. She had a very good figure. Her grey hair had been newly set and slightly tinted with mauve. Her blue eyes blazed with life and purpose. Matthew watched her puzzled, exhausted.

"Well, all right," he said. "I'll tell Clara. Have another drink."

"Thank you. There's something I wanted to tell you."

"Oh yes, you said in a letter—"

"Need you look so bloody limp? When I was young, men didn't loll about like that in the presence of a woman."

"Sorry—"

"I'm sorry to be so abrupt, but as I hardly ever have the pleasure of seeing you I have to make the best of my time. It's about Austin."

"Austin—" Matthew rocked his bulk in the chair in an attempt to lean forward.

"Austin and Betty."

"Oh no, not that."

"You mean you know?"

"I don't know what you're going to say. I just don't feel in the mood for Austin and Betty just now. Could you shove the decanter along?"

"Matthew, please. How did Betty die?"

"What are you talking about?" said Matthew.

"How did Betty die?"

"She fell into a deep lock on the river near my cottage. She couldn't swim. She was drowned. What are you at, Charlotte?"

"She could swim," said Charlotte. "I found a swimming certificate of hers at Austin's flat. She could swim very well."

"All right," said Matthew, wiping his face with his hand. He was somehow sitting on the handkerchief. "She could swim. Swimmers can drown too. She knocked her head on something."

"But Austin said she couldn't swim. He said so at the inquest."

"Did he? I can't remember."

"You *must* remember, you're lying, I can see you are. And another thing. You were meeting Betty secretly."

"How do you know?" said Matthew. He rocked himself again to try to extract the handkerchief.

"I've seen a letter of Betty's to you, making a secret

409

appointment. Austin must have found it. It was torn and stuck together again."

"That's right," said Matthew. "I was meeting Betty secretly so as to help her buy a tennis racket for Austin's birthday. It was to be a surprise. I've told Austin this since. So there's no drama there, Charlotte, sorry."

"But why did Austin say she couldn't swim? And why did he go round later on hinting that she'd committed suicide? You know he did that. He can't work it both ways. If she could swim she was unlikely to get drowned by accident in a river on a summer's day. And if she could swim she was even more unlikely to have chosen drowning as a method of suicide. Nor would she have been able to kill herself by drowning unless she'd tied on weights or something. And nothing of that sort came up at the inquest. And if it really was an accident and she fell and hit her head and so drowned why was this never said, and what were Austin's motives for saying that she couldn't swim and then for hinting later that she killed herself?"

"Well, what do you think happened?" said Matthew. He hauled out the handkerchief, now a stringy rag. He noticed that the seat of the chair was damp with his perspiration. Perhaps it would make a permanent stain.

"I think Austin killed her," said Charlotte, "and I think he did it because he believed rightly or wrongly that she was carrying on with you."

"I've explained," said Matthew, "that we were going to buy a tennis racket for Austin's birthday. That was the only secret meeting I ever had with Betty."

"Well, never mind that. I'm not accusing you. I'm accusing Austin."

"Oh, let it go, Charlotte," said Matthew. "Austin never killed or tried to kill anybody except in his imagination."

"He might kill you."

"I know how it all was, Austin is no murderer—"

"Matthew, he might kill you."

"Only he won't. And now, dear Charlotte, since we've had our talk and I now know what to tell Clara let us call it a day. I've got to see the Monkleys and then give Mavis dinner and then I've promised to call on Charles

410

Odmore since Hester, as you probably know, is down at the Arbuthnots for the pig festival or whatever it is—"

"Matthew, I simply don't understand you," said Charlotte. "No, don't try to get up, I've got you cornered and I'm not going to let you go. I have accused your brother of murder of his first wife. You seem quite unmoved and you don't even answer the charge."

"I know he didn't, that's all," said Matthew. "I know him better than you do. You're just thinking all this up to make an exciting drama and a thrilling secret between us and so on."

"You swine," said Charlotte quietly. "And I didn't invent the swimming certificate and—"

"Oh let it go, Char."

"Are you going to marry Mavis?" said Charlotte.

"I hope so."

"Matthew, I am not amusing myself. Sit still and listen! I seriously want to warn you, you could be in serious danger—"

"Oh stop it, Charlotte. And do stop playing amateur detective."

"Do you know that I've loved you all my life?" said Charlotte. She stood in front of him.

"You haven't known me all your life."

"Don't be a fool. I've loved you ever since I've known you. Ever since George introduced us. I've been in love with you."

"I thought you loved George."

"Clara invented that myth in order to humiliate me."

"Come, come, Charlotte—"

"Matthew, I love you. You are the one, the only one. I love you and it relieves my heart so much now to tell you so. I have remained single because of you. I have lived all these year in the thought of you, in the lack of you, in the hopeless hope of you—"

"Char, this won't do," said Matthew. "I'm sure you feel something now, but I can't believe this and I'm sure you don't really. I know one has to account for one's sufferings somehow—"

"How can you be so cruel!" said Charlotte. Tears started

suddenly into her eyes, and she turned away, brushing them roughly.

Matthew leaned forward and managed to get up out of the chair. "I'm sorry, but I just don't believe that you have wasted your life because of me."

"Don't believe it, then. I don't interest you enough for you to work up any guilt about me, that's what it comes to."

"If you've thought about me, I'm grateful—"

"You set up in business as a sort of sage. All right, you probably don't do it on purpose, it's an instinct. But all it means is that you're prepared to muddle about with people you feel connected with, where the connection is amusing or flattering. It's a sort of sexual drive, really. You want power where it's interesting. Where you could use it to some decent purpose, but the interest's lacking, you put on the other act, frankness and simplicity and not saying more than you really feel and so on. All right, I'm just on the wrong side of the barrier. But I should have thought that even politeness, to say nothing of gallantry, might have made you behave a little less cynically to me."

"Oh God, Char, I'm sorry," said Matthew. "I won't argue with you. I'm just so tired out with emotion at the moment. Please forgive me and let's be friends."

"You never came near me, even when I wrote to you. You wrote me a smarmy hypocritical letter."

"I'm sorry—"

"Thank God I've got the dignity of real love to support me. I haven't got anything else. I doubt if you really know how to love at all."

"You should never say that to anybody," said Matthew.

"Well, I'm going," said Charlotte, picking up her handbag. "I won't bother you any more. I came to warn you about Austin. I really think he's capable of killing you. I didn't intend the declaration of love. But as you don't believe it it won't worry you. Good-bye."

"Charlotte, wait a minute—"

With a swing of blue and white skirt she was gone and the front door banged as Matthew reached the hall.

He returned to the drawing-room. The chipped white

412

Sung bowl with the peony pattern was sitting in the middle of the mantelpiece. He picked it up and looked down into the creamy white ocean of its depth. He saw again the scene in the Square, the black gawky group of protesters and the man walking across to join them and the miraculous shaking of hands and the trodden snow and the empty scene after the police had taken them all away.

❧❧❧❧

"It must have been accidental," said Mavis.

She and Austin were sitting over tea in the drawing-room.

"Oh God, it haunts my dreams so," said Austin.

"Yes. Have some more cake."

"I blame myself—"

"I don't see that you should."

"Oh I do. I think—some people—think I blame everyone except myself, but it's not so."

"For this, no one was to blame."

"Oh well, who know how networks of causes can make one blameworthy. I expect that every time we do anything even slightly bad it sets up a sort of wave which ends with someone committing suicide or murder or something."

"That could be," said Mavis. "That was the sort of thing which when I believed in God I handed over to Him."

"But now—"

"There's nothing to be done. Except to try as usual. One can't see the network."

"Still, one is haunted."

"But I can't see how it can really be your fault."

"Well, I was showing off. He was so fat, you see."

"Fat?"

"Yes, even then. He wasn't as agile as I was and he was afraid to do the climb down. The pool looked so attractive at the bottom of the quarry, all turquoise blue, you know, among golden rocks, and the day was so hot. I got down there and paddled and splashed around and sort of taunted him and he sat up at the top in the heat. He must have hated it. I meant him to."

"And then—"

"Then I took off all my clothes and swam. I can remember it now. One of those hot days when one's body remains warm inside the cool water and the water is like a sort of silver skin. Strange. That must have been about the last happy moment of my life."

"Surely not. And then—"

"I thought he'd come down then, he must have been so envious. I could see him casting around, trying to find an easy way down, but he funked it. Then I got my clothes on and started to climb up, and he threw stones down at me as I was climbing and I fell."

"Wait a moment, Austin. Are you sure he threw the stones? Perhaps you loosened the stones yourself."

"I'm sure he threw one stone at least—it doesn't matter —I can't remember."

"But, Austin, it does matter. You say you've always blamed him for this— But if he didn't really do anything at all—"

"He laughed—"

"But only before you fell."

"He saw that I was in difficulties and he laughed."

"But that's not bad. You'd been mocking him just before—"

"I'm sure he threw a stone—anyway—it doesn't matter —it was terribly much harder to get up than to get down—I got into a panic—then lots of stones started rolling down on top of me—a sort of avalanche—and I couldn't hold on—and I fell all the way down to the bottom and—there it was."

Austin, who had been sitting stiffly staring at the wall

414

as he spoke, put his cup down with a clack, gasped, and was suddenly breathless. He panted, lowering his head and supporting his brow, then half sidled half slipped out of his chair onto the carpet beside the window. He pushed the sash up a little and sat there, leaning his head against the bottom of the window, panting and gasping.

Mavis thought, he is going to have hysterics, in a moment he will be screaming. She ran to the door, ran back again, stared down at him. His face was contorted and he drew long slow shuddering breaths. Then she saw that he was trying to smile.

"Sorry," said Austin, "it's just the pollen."

"The what?"

"The pollen. Asthma, you know. I'll take a tablet in a minute or two. Funny thing, I know the garden's full of beastly pollen, but it does help to breathe fresh air. When one gets a fit any room seems too airless. Of course it's worse for other people, it must look as if I'm dying or something."

"Can I get you anything?"

"A little milk—perhaps I could have the milk jug—thanks—milk helps—don't know why—probably psychological—"

Mavis watched Austin sitting on the floor beside the window drinking milk in gulps out of the Crown Derby milk jug. She felt very odd herself, suddenly breathless and weird. Austin smiled up at her, almost perkily. His golden hair was brushed up, his handsome face scarcely wrinkled, bronzed and glowing. He had left off his spectacles. He looked like a successful actor. She sat down on the floor opposite to him on the other side of the window, tucking her dress in under her knees.

"Better now?"

"Better now. Sorry if I startled you."

"Not at all."

"Where was I? Oh yes. Well, there it was. I broke my right wrist—I fell like that, you see, stretching out my arm—and I broke a lot of little bones in the hand, rather unusual—and it all went stiff—then I couldn't write for

415

ages and ages—and that was, well that was really the end of me."

"Oh nonsense, Austin, you're a fighter, there's a huge will inside you."

"I've got to survive—that's what my will's been for—it's been all used upon that—it's always been touch and go."

"Anyway it wasn't his fault. Even if he threw a stone it wasn't. He didn't mean to hurt you. And you aren't even sure he did throw a stone."

"Oh well—if it wasn't this it was something else—he would have—it's done now—"

"You're so vague. You mustn't be."

"One can be vague about the details. The main thing is overwhelming."

"But if all the details are wrong the main thing may be just in your imagination."

"Well, the imagination is real too."

"But Austin, think, it may be real to you, but that doesn't mean anything is somebody else's fault. I mean, there is a rather important difference between an awful thing and an imaginary awful thing!"

"There's always fault in such cases. Imagination sniffs out what's real. It's a good diagnostician."

"This sounds to me like madness," said Mavis.

"No, no. There's too much proof. Look at my poor old hand. That's real enough. Stiff as a branch of a tree. I can bend it this way and that, but I can't close my fingers. See. No wonder people shun me. It's like a claw, a beastly witch mark."

"There's nothing repulsive about it," said Mavis.

"But you notice it?"

"Well—yes—but only because I know you."

"Oddly enough I don't think it's ever made me unattractive to women. Rather the opposite in fact."

"You've had treatment for it?"

"Then. Not now. Not for years. It's hopeless."

"You might try again," said Mavis. "They find out things. Let me look at it."

Austin stretched out his right hand, revealing a grubby

frayed shirt cuff. Mavis took his hand in both of hers. Austin's fingers were red and plump at the end from continual nail-biting. Mavis moved the stiff fingers a little to and fro. "Does that hurt?"

"No."

"It doesn't seem too stiff. I'm sure you should see a specialist. I'll inquire about people."

She went on gently fingering the stiff hand and moving it about.

"Funny thing," said Austin.

"What?"

"It never occurred—to any other woman—to do that—to my hand."

∗∗∗∗∗

"What about this one, darling?" said Mitzi. She was reading out from the evening paper. *"Charming unfurnished cottage to let, Surrey-Sussex border, unspoilt village, suit writer or artist."*

"I don't like *suit writer or artist.*"

"Why?"

"It means it's damp and has a hole in the roof and no proper kitchen."

"Well, we could mend the hole and warm away the damp, it's quite cheap— Or this, this sounds lovely: *Old Mill freehold for sale. Mill wheel in working order. Trout stream.*"

"But we don't fish. And the mill wheel would make a dreadful noise."

"Or this. *Excellent subject for development—*"

"I refuse to develop."

417

"Well then, *Small Georgian House*—"

"Too big."

"Wait, you silly creature! *Small Georgian House in village divided into four flats. Large garden.*"

"It'll be on a main road. And there'd be quarrels about the garden."

"*Converted barn with paddock*— That's better. The dog can run about in the paddock."

"Mitzi darling, these are dreams."

"Well, I like dreaming," said Mitzi, "especially with you. There must be somewhere for the dog to run about, mustn't there."

It was late in the evening at Mitzi's house. Mitzi pretended that the evening was chilly and had lit a fire in her sitting-room for cosiness. They were eating sandwiches and drinking white wine. Charlotte, trying to persuade her friend to drink less, had prescribed a regime of sherry and wine and no spirits.

"What sort of dog shall we have, Char?" said Mitzi. "A collie? A retriever?"

Charlotte stared into the fire, into a deep crumbling golden shaft that was white and blinding at the end. She blinked her eyes.

"We can't afford any of these places, Mitzi."

"We can if I sell this house. And I'm going to apply for that sports journalism job. Of course that means we must be near a station so that I can commute. Somewhere on the Dorking or Guildford line, or in Kent—"

"But—I must contribute—"

"Don't keep fussing about that. Just let me arrange everything. What shall we call the dog?"

"I'll get a job," said Charlotte. "I suppose I can learn to type. Or I could work in a library—"

"Rover. Fido. Bonzo."

"Certainly not. A dog should be called something like —Ganymede—or Pyrrhus—or—"

"All right. Pirrus. I like that. Pirrus! Come here at once, sir!"

"You mustn't be in a hurry to sell this house, Mitzi—"

"I've made up my mind. Have you written to Austin yet about how he can have the flat back?"

"Not yet. Are you sure—?"

"I'm sure. Are you?"

Charlotte looked into the deep glowing shaft with the invisible end. "Yes."

"And you'll move in here soon?"

"Yes. But I must pay rent."

"Of course not. And you won't be ashamed of me?"

"Don't be a damned fool."

"Come soon then," said Mitzi. "I'm so terrified you'll change your mind."

"All right. I'll write to Austin. I'll come here."

"You don't feel I'm just pressurizing you? You don't feel sort of cornered or—doomed—about it?"

"I feel fine about it," said Charlotte and leaned back in her chair and regarded her companion.

Mitzi, in a black trouser suit with a white shirt and a black velvet bow tie, looked ridiculously and charmingly chubby, like some plump eighteenth-century beau. She had had her hair carefully cut in receding layers. Her round face was shiny with health and pleasure. She grinned and grabbed a sandwich.

At first Charlotte had just drifted along. In the hospital Mitzi had laid claims of ownership to her. Mitzi had stood beside her bed while she was unconscious. Mitzi had welcomed her back into life. And so henceforth somehow she was Mitzi's property.

Charlotte had vaguely noticed these claims. It was Mitzi who arranged the taxi to take her back to the flat. When Clara arrived Charlotte was already gone. It was Mitzi who, it turned out, had ordered the milk and filled the fridge with goodies. Mitzi who cooked her lunch on that day. It was very kind, very kind indeed. Charlotte thanked her and said good-bye and shut the door. Clara rang up. Garth rang up. Clara said Charlotte ought not to be alone and would— Charlotte said she was fine and no, she did not want to visit or be visited. Matthew rang up and said he would ring again and suggest a meeting. Clara rang up and said did she know Dorina was dead, she had elec-

trocuted herself with an electric fire in a hotel in Blooms-
bury. No, Charlotte did not know. Clara felt that Charlotte
ought to know. Would Charlotte like to come—? No.
Charlotte went to bed and thought about Dorina. It was
a shock but Charlotte felt curiously detached and less
upset than she would have expected. Now of course
Matthew would be comforting Mavis. Charlotte thought
about her own death and how she had survived it and now
lived in limbo. She looked for sleeping tablets to send her
to sleep. There were none. She cried for some time.

The next day it was rather difficult to get up. She made
some tea and went back to bed. The door bell rang but
it was only Clara. Charlotte talked to her in the hall in
her dressing gown. How—? Fine. Would she—? No. The
tea was cold, Matthew did not ring. Charlotte went to
bed again. She cried some more. Then Mitzi arrived laden
with all sorts of things, food and drink and flowers and
terrible magazines, and whisked around the flat with dreadful energy while Charlotte lay back and watched. Would
Charlotte come out to lunch at that new Greek restaurant?
Why not. Would she please wear *this* dress? (Mitzi rooting
in wardrobe.) All right.

Over lunch Mitzi talked about Austin. Othello is said to
have won Desdemona's love by telling her about his army
career. Mitzi won at least Charlotte's interest by the directness and vigour of her view of Austin. Mitzi's "attack" was
refreshing. Austin was a cad because he was really frightened of women. Austin had been afraid of his father, of
course. Then he had been afraid of Matthew. Austin had
wanted to get back at his father because his father wouldn't
let his mother spoil him, but then he took it out of the
women instead. Austin liked to have a dramatic relationship with a woman, he could never be cosy. He liked weird
witchy women whom he could bully because he was afraid
of them. He would have liked a mad wife whom he could
keep in chains. What he wanted was to see the woman
acting what he really felt. But then it all got too intense
and he had to run away. Of course he couldn't make head
or tail of *me,* said Mitzi, because I wouldn't play this game

420

at all. Then she started to cry. She said, one must have somebody to look after.

How Mitzi had then become a habit Charlotte could not quite say. Just, perhaps, because she was so delightfully unlike Clara. Mitzi had helped too because she was a simplifier. When Charlotte complained about Matthew's neglect, Mitzi said, go and see him, and Charlotte went. That Charlotte was then able to qualify Matthew as disappointing was partly because to explain Matthew to Mitzi was inevitably to diminish him. Charlotte felt a kind of sadness in doing this, but a certain satisfaction as well. "He's too big for his boots," said Mitzi. "Why can't he just be friendly and loving without making such a fuss? There's little enough love around. He's conceited and mean."

Matthew *was* disappointing. He *was* conceited and mean. He had taken the wrong tone. He could have had Charlotte's love for nothing. Did he imagine that she would somehow reduce his value if he permitted friendship on these terms? Did he think she would boast about a "relationship"? Why did he have to cut everything up into little pieces and classify it and introduce ideas of truth and exactness where they had no place at all? Who could say precisely what Charlotte had done or not done, suffered or not suffered, for love of Matthew? She had loved him always, thought of him always. Love is not time's fool and rejects notions of exact measurement. How many hours per day of thinking about the beloved counts as being in love? Such ideas are absurd. Love laughs at locksmiths and also at Locke. Love belongs to the ideal.

Such things, which she might have said to Matthew and could not say to Mitzi, Charlotte thought of afterwards. Of course I idealized him, thought Charlotte. How much smaller he seems in reality. Vain and touching and full of his little pretensions. He's just a Teddy bear after all. I suppose I shall go on caring about him, little as he deserves it. But from now on he is Mavis's. And I am not going to wear that agony. Let him go now, I shall not trouble him again. She wept all the same, not only because of a bleak loss, but because a certain occupation of dream-

ing was gone forever. About Austin she occasionally reflected with an almost cold curiosity. But her interest in
Austin had always derived from her interest in Matthew,
and in a new concern for herself she now almost forgot
him.

Meanwhile Charlotte realized that Mitzi loved her. She
was grateful. At first she had been Mitzi's plaything, her
little property. Now she was more than that. Charlotte
felt no alarm. She had never particularly either liked or
disliked the company of women. She had never really
know a woman well, not even her sister, not even Alison.
But then she had never hitherto met a woman like Mitzi.
Mitzi crossed barriers and borders uncrossed before because she was oblivious of their existence. Mitzi looked
after Charlotte and bossed her around. She also admired
and revered Charlotte and deferred to her and wanted to
be instructed by her. They found it quite uncannily easy
to talk to each other. Mitzi could make Charlotte even
chatter. She could make Charlotte laugh. Charlotte became
increasingly conscious of the charm of her large handsome
honest artless companion. She laughed at Mitzi and in a
prescient way was made happy by her. She looked forward
to her company. She let herself be made happy. A younger
Charlotte would have analysed and considered and taken
fright. The old grey Charlotte just smiled.

One must have somebody to look after. To get out of
Austin's flat, to shake off all those messy smelly connections and horrible memories, was suddenly dreadfully
necessary. Where should she go? Why, to Mitzi's house of
course. Charlotte stayed there one night, then two nights.
Charlotte said she had always wanted a dog. Mitzi said
she had always wanted a dog. Charlotte said one can't
keep a dog in London. Mitzi said then why not let's live
in the country. Mitzi had always wanted to live in the
country. So, it turned out, had Charlotte. Life was suddenly full of simple pleasant animating possibilities. Charlotte looked at it all and laughed.

"What are you laughing at, love?" said Mitzi.

"Nothing, little one. Yes, sandwich, thanks."

Charlotte was thinking, how astounded they'll all be

when it turns out I'm living in a cottage in Sussex with an Amazon and a big dog!

⁂

"May I fill your glass?"

"Thank you, dear boy."

Garth went on. "And I felt that Ludwig had cut me out with you."

"Quite."

"I kissed Dorina, you know, one day, behind the hedge, in the garden at Valmorana."

"What sort of kiss?"

"Hard to describe. Passionate but noncommittal. Sealed off. I don't know what she thought about it. I felt pleased with myself at the time. Did she tell you this?"

"Yes."

"What did she say?"

"It made her wish you were really her son."

"Odd. That never occurred to me. I so absolutely can't see Dorina as a mother."

"It's a pity she never became one."

"My father would never have—"

"No."

"If I could ever have seen her as a mother, even a substitute one— But she was always special, taboo, young."

"Special, haunted."

"Haunted by my father? I wonder."

"I think Dorina was always a wanderer on the face of the earth, a sort of stray."

"From where? Aah— How well did you know my mother?"

"Fairly well."

"You know she was really a gipsy? She didn't just look like a gipsy, she was a gipsy. Only she kept it secret. I don't know why."

"She told me."

"Everyone tells you everything in the end. Even I do."

"I've told you quite a few things this evening."

"Yes. And thank you. You didn't mind my just turning up?"

"I would have summoned you."

They both smiled.

"So you see it was partly vindictiveness. I wanted to help Dorina, to make her talk. And I could have done."

"Yes."

"Only of course I was terrified, it was so dangerous. It may seem quaint to you, but I am a bit afraid of my father."

"Did you fear him as a child?"

"No, not really. But since—well, since my mother's death, I suppose. I fear him now."

"He is to be feared."

"I'm interested that you think so. Anyway, when I found that you'd just walked in—"

"I explained."

"Yes, yes. When I found you'd grabbed Dorina and were putting her through it, I felt you were taking away something that was mine. Also I was annoyed that you hadn't 'summoned' me, as you put it, earlier. You didn't seem interested."

"Sorry."

"Not at all. I scared Dorina really on that evening because I was furious with you."

"I know."

"Well, that's it, and thanks for listening. Uncle Matthew."

"Call me Matthew."

"I'll try. It'll take a bit of time."

The telephone rang and Matthew pulled himself up.

Garth, who was sitting near the window, turned his chair and blinked into the golden evening light. A soft breeze was swaying the walnut tree in graceful play. The Irishman, with a long shadow, was clipping the edges of the lawn.

Matthew was saying into the telephone, "Yes . . . yes . . . yes . . . I see. . . . Could I ring you back? . . . I'm going out to dinner. . . . How late can I ring you? . . . Wait, I'll just write down the college number. . . . Good . . . Absolutely . . . Good-bye, then."

Matthew returned to his seat. "That was Ludwig."

"About Gracie?"

"Yes. So you mean to shut yourself up and rewrite the novel?"

"Yes."

"And you'll accept my little donation? You can pay it back if the novel's a success."

"Yes. And thanks."

"Now I must throw you out. I'm having dinner with Mavis."

"How's my father?"

"Still dazed. He'll be all right."

"Oh, I know *that*."

"He'll come to look on it all as a kind of achievement."

"You know, you're much more sort of cynical than I expected. I always thought of you as— You were going into a monastery or something, weren't you? Why didn't that come off?"

"I'll tell you another time. Can I give you a lift anywhere?"

The front-door bell rang.

"Could you go and see who it is?" said Matthew, who was writing a cheque.

In a moment or two Garth returned, closing the door behind him.

"It's Gracie. I told her to wait in the dining-room. I say, your clients do queue up."

Matthew thought for a moment. Then he said, "I'm going to funk Gracie. You can deal with her."

"*Me?*"

"Yes. You've got the tricks of the trade. I'm tired. And Mavis is waiting. I'm going out through the garden. Good-bye, and thanks for coming. See you again soon."

Matthew handed Garth the cheque and went out through the glass door and disappeared.

Garth stood for a moment or two in the radiantly lit evening room. Then he returned to the dining-room, opened the door, and stood in the doorway.

"I'm sorry," he said. "Matthew's gone. He had an appointment."

Gracie came out into the hall. Garth had not seen her since his departure to America and he contemplated her now, a little woman, thinking how changed she was in her evident unhappiness. She was small and pale and somehow determined, no trace of tears; the wispy colour-less hair banded the little head like steel and her face against her upturned coat collar was almost grim with sadness. He wondered now how he had recognized her.

"I see. Garth, can I talk to you for a bit? I won't stay long."

Garth hesitated. Then he said, "Sorry, I've got an appointment too." Enough was enough. He would not employ the tricks of the trade on Gracie. He said, "Would you like to ring Ludwig? He's in his room in Oxford. The number's beside the telephone. I'm just going away." He moved past her towards the front door and opened it.

Gracie moved after him. She murmured, "I won't ring. He's coming back." She followed him out into the street. Garth closed the door.

"Which way are you going, Gracie?"

"This way."

"I'm going the other way. Good night then, and— Good night."

Gracie walked slowly away and Garth set off in the opposite direction. He turned two corners back to the Kings Road so as to give her plenty of time to get ahead, and then started walking at a leisurely pace toward Sloane Square station. He saw her in front of him again, a significant little figure in the vivid light, wandering along as if even her steps were uncertain, pausing when people jostled

426

her, then creeping onward like a piece of wood in a sluggish stream. With her hands in her pockets and her air of pensive dejection she looked like an actress cast as a prostitute. At one point she paused and looked back and saw him. She gave no sign of recognition, but walked on a little faster until she came to the station. When Garth reached the station and descended to the platform she was gone.

It was rush hour. He pushed his way into a crowded train to return to Notting Hill. He felt pleased with himself yet sad. His fellow beings pressed him with their bodies and fanned him with their breath. The swaying carriage smelt of sweat and pneumatic darkness and ordinary life. Garth felt drained and sad but somehow pleased. He felt complete in himself, whole, competent, young, and full of will. Matthew's cheque was in his pocket. He studied the surrounding faces with interest. He began to think about his novel.

My dear Ludwig,

You will be glad to receive this letter from us to say that Mom and I have decided after all to see it your way. I am sorry that I was not able to talk to you properly on the telephone. I cannot speak with any power on that instrument and you too seemed unable to explain yourself upon it. We must see each other and as you have declared yourself so inflexible we have no choice but to give way. We think in any case after yet further reflection and after a long talk with Mr. Livingstone that it would now be inadvisable for you to return. As Mr. Livingstone put it, as far as the U.S.A. is concerned you are finished. Having in view the lapse of time and your determination not to avail yourself of the suggested expedients, your return here would almost certainly involve you in a court case, prison, and all the subsequent misery of being an outsider in this society. Your chances of further study would probably be nil. We spoke with Mr. Livingstone about the parable of the talents, and we think now that you are acting certainly wisely and possible rightly in staying at Oxford. We have all prayed about this. (In fact the whole congregation prayed for you last Sunday, though without having been given any details.) And I trust and believe that we have reached a just decision. This is not what your mother and I would have wished for you, as you know, but I hope that you will feel that your parents are able to face new and alien facts without a failure of their love for you—and that love now unambiguously dictates a surrender of our former position. Equally we have come to feel that we cannot further oppose your marriage. I trust you have not communicated our misgivings to your pretty bride. Parents should not withhold their countenance on such an occasion except in extreme circumstances, which we feel do not obtain here. Our instincts were to caution you. But that done, we have done our duty and are now resolved to accede cheerfully to your firm and declared wishes in this matter. After all, as you say, we cannot judge the young lady without meeting her and this we are determined to do very shortly. We had decided that we would attend the wedding, but now feel it unnecessary and undesirable to wait for so long. So we are booking a passage on the boat, tourist class, for the end of next week or the beginning of the week following. We will send details by another post. We trust you will make bookings for us in a modest hotel. It will be a great joy and blessing to see your face and to meet your no doubt charming wife-to-be. Your mother joins with me in sending our most cordial love.

Your loving father,
J. P. H. LEFERRIER

My dearest Gracie,

I cannot go through with it. I am sending the ring back to you not to put upon your finger but because you paid for it and it is yours. I have been in hell these days and I hope you will—yet how can you—forgive me for my failure to communicate—and for what I communicate now. I cannot marry you. The deepest sources of my spirit, the most sacred things I know, simply forbid it. I love you and perhaps I shall always love you—but that makes no sense. If I leave you now, as I must, it will be my duty, as well as the order of nature, to forget you. Of course I cannot forget you, but I mean that my feelings must cool, must cease to be love, love must die, my love and your love, which seemed the greatest thing in the world. At least it seemed to be a monument which nothing outtopped. I had never loved so before, and I think you had not, and there was, alas there is, a glory which can never be again. I love you more at this moment as I write than I have ever done in all our happy times. But it cannot be, Gracie. What makes it so bitter is that there is not, I believe, any fault in our love. It is just that I am not in my right place in the universe. And if I married you I would be increasingly not in my right place, and this would be true to eternity however happy we were together. There is a completeness I must seek elsewhere or else fail utterly as a man. Perhaps it is not in my stars to marry at all. I know now that you would come anywhere with me and share my fate, and this knowledge is precious. But where-ever I now go in life I must go alone. To marry now would be to enter a realm of compromise which I am commanded not to enter. And since I am not a gentleman volunteer I have no choice but to obey. When I think of your sweet-ness and your perfect love for me and your grief my will faints. But I must speak truth now or become everlastingly corrupt. Please do not try to see me, it would only increase the pain. Pardon me. Please tell your parents. If there is lost expense over the wedding clothes I will pay— Oh Gracie—

LUDWIG

Dearest Hester,

Gracie has definitely broken with Ludwig. I don't know the details, but she came to the conclusion (which of course I knew all along) that he was simply not the right man. I must say I am very relieved indeed. In fact he has behaved very oddly and irresponsibly, just clearing off to Oxford and shutting himself up with his books. Well, let him stay there, say I. I always thought him a conceited priggish humourless young man, and he is after all a foreigner. I doubt if we should have got on at all well with his family, and there would always have been the threat of his taking her back to America hanging over our heads. Gracie is very relieved too at having had the courage to terminate this situation and to be *free* once more. She is delighted to be back again in her own world. She is quite restored and gay. I wonder if you and Charles and Sebas-tian could come to dinner next Tuesday? Gracie will be here and she joins with me in looking forward *very much* to that. I will telephone. You and I must meet soon to discuss things.

With love,
CLARA

Funny old Char is still being stiff and proud about our scheme, but she'll come round!

Dear Dr. Seldon,

Thank you very much for seeing Gracie and for, partially at least, reassuring us. I did not realize it took such a long time for somebody to die of starvation. She still refuses to eat and lies all day on her bed crying and talks a good deal about suicide. We have done all we can and hope that she will recover soon or we shall have to cancel all sorts of arrangements. I am glad that you think she is not a suicidal type. But when you send the prescription for the sleeping pills please be sure they are not the kind you can kill yourself with. We do not leave her alone. Thank you so much for coming. I am sorry that she refused to talk to you.

Yours sincerely,
CLARA TISBOURNE

Dearest Hester,

Is it true that Gracie and the Leferrier boy have broken it off? Someone told me this at a party, but I could hardly believe it, after the dresses are made and everything. What a blow to poor Clara. But perhaps it is just a rumour. I hope so. And what on earth is this about Charlotte living in a lodging house at Shepherds Bush with a drunken women who beats her? Surely Charlotte is too old for games of this sort, but really one can expect anything these days.

The boutique is closing down. It was doing very well and I am quite sorry, but I just find I am too busy. Geoffrey is selling the pigs and thinking of setting up a market garden, and I can see I shall have to help him, as I am the only business head in the family! I wonder would you and Charles and Sebastian like to come down to the Mill House next weekend? Karen will be there and she joins with me in looking forward *very much* to that. Please come for dinner on Friday if you can. The garden is a dream and the young people can splash in the pool. Tell Sebastian to bring his swimming gear.

With love,
MOLLIE

Dear Ludwig,

Just to say that Oliver and I are having a super hol in Greece and even Kierkegaard is enjoying it, although a policeman did hit him yesterday with his truncheon because he was parked in a naughty place. I got a card, by the way, from MacMurraghue, who says he will do us a paper on the Aristophanic Socrates, so now our glorious programme is complete. For once I almost look forward to term! (MacM. is back with his old ma and full of Irish gloom. He requests us to kick the Pope on our return journey. Always a bad sign.) Meanwhile Oliver and self, just leaving for darkest Peloponnese, are having, in every respect, a thoroughly Grecian time. (I know you are a tolerant fellow.) The ancients had the root of the matter in them, don't you think? Though I suppose I shouldn't say so to a man about to marry the sweetest girl in the world! Looking at the great Artemision Zeus in the museum today I was somehow reminded of you! That beautiful stern brow spoke of relentless things and absolutes. What has that either to do with the sweets of marriage? ἤ τοι Κύπρις ὀυ Κύπρις μόνον, and even Zeus, etc. Excuse this letter, am drunk with ouzo and retsina. Oh the bright awful air of this country! No wonder the ancient Greeks were, contrary to what is popularly supposed, such a truly appalling lot.

With love to you,
ANDREW

P.S. Oliver, who is writing his daily report to his sister, sends love.

P.P.S. Guess who we saw down by the Piraeus tucking into their avgolemono? Richard Pargeter and Ann Colindale! They blushed a bit when they saw us. Old Annapurna Atom was tied up by the quay. They must have sneaked off by themselves! Sorry, retsina bottle upset at this point. Drunk.

Dearest dear Gracie,

I am very sorry indeed to hear about the demise of your engagement. What happened exactly? What rotten luck. Though better not repent at leisure, etc. I am personally sorry too, as I respect Ludwig. I do see though that perhaps after all he isn't quite our sort? I mean, definitely not a funny man. Ma implies telephonewise that you are prostrated; I trust she exaggerates as usual. What kind of philosophy can I offer you? One recovers from love. The echoes are faint at last. (At least I personally do not recover, but it is established that other people do.) Also, at your age you ought to recover. One must not weep upon the shore. The best cure for love I'm told is falling in love again. So lift your beautiful head up and look about you. (Seen anything of young Sebastian lately?)

I won't tell you about me. It might make you feel even sadder! Much much love from

yrs (glorified)
PATRICIUS

P.S. Henrietta Sayce sent me a *large* stink bomb through the post. It has soaked my desk and person. I fear her sports are yet but childish.

Cheer up, Sis

Dearest Matthew,

You are being very kind (but of course you would be) and I am so deeply glad that you understand. To cope with Austin now is the least I can do for Dorina. It seems mad to say it, but I cannot help feeling that she somehow died for us, for you and me, taking herself away, clearing herself away, so that our world should be easier and simpler. And not to profit at once and grossly by that simplicity is our penance. It is, after all, a long way round and a long way through. But we will find the path, my darling. I cannot ask Austin to move at the moment. I honestly think that my concern stands between him and breakdown. For the present, I have to be absolutely available and absolutely there. I cannot ask about "plans." We live from day to day in a denuded world the atmosphere of which I cannot quite convey to you, but some great Renaissance Italian could have painted it. I have never felt so *sorry* for anybody. (It isn't exactly pity and it isn't exactly compassion.) And being able to feel this empty aching sorriness does me good too as perhaps nothing else could. I know you will understand, and wait lovingly for this strange time to be over. If you can pray, pray for Austin now.

Ever, with so much love, your utterly devoted

MAVIS

Dearest,

Love is time's fool, one knows, however much in bliss. Having achieved the universe I am all anxiety. Love lives with dread. In the instant I undo all, see myself, in the first moments of happiness, undone. We are young. Let us be cunning, O my love, to keep somehow what we have. This is the thing itself, or else it does not exist. Let us cozen it with a golden shrewdness. This is for a lifetime surely? Oh we are young, we are young. I have never felt this before as such an agony. We are pure in heart but cannot stay so. We are fine but will be made coarse, free but will be bound. If there are gods for this, I pray to them and embrace their knees. Be ingenious, my very dear, and keep with me our present in our future, keep our great love forever, growing, changing, overlaid, besieged, surrounded, ageing, and yet in its heart utterly uncontaminated and clear as Grail crystal.

I'll see you this evening. This comes as usual by Williamson minor.

My dear Ludwig,

I am sorry to hear of the final termination of your engagement. Yet also I confess I am, for your sake, relieved. I am sure you have done right. There are moments when one must choose spirit rather than joy or be forever diminished. You are young and the choice for you is meaningful. When one is older distinctions become unclear and this perhaps is damnation. Thank you for telephoning me and for speaking so frankly. May I come and see you in Oxford? I will ring tomorrow morning.

Yours,

MATTHEW

FATHER PLEASE CANCEL YOUR SAILING I AM COMING HOME LUDWIG

434

Gracie lay back in the boat, limp, her light dress of papery thin cotton tacky with sweat, gently plucking the warm flesh at her thighs, at her neck. The trees were green, were black, floated and swayed dizzily and were taken away. Now there was only sky, almost colourless with its brightness, quiet and empty and sizzling with light. Hollow sounds of distant voices came over the water, weightless wooden balls of sound bouncing lightly on the azure ripples, skipping and echoing away into the slumbrous afternoon. A coolness crept upon the water, concentrated now in her trailing hand as it silently broke the surface. A hand made of peppermint, made of coconut ice. Gracie's eyes closed and she existed floating in the midst of a warm pink sphere, lying limp and boneless, her body light and extended and drooping like a plucked tossed flower. The hollow sounds boomed far distantly, buzzed and droned.

Gracie was in a woody glade. Her mother's white dress had mingled with green leaves and faded. Her mother, leading Patrick by the hand, had gone away down another vista. This was Gracie's place and she was alone in it and suddenly panting with a sense of significance and fear. Before her, across a little lawn of cropped velvety grass, there was standing all by itself a single tree with a smooth shaft of light grey close-textured trunk of a glowing colour between silver and pewter. Above the high shaft a thick cloud of leaves moved, though there was no wind, with intricate tiny curtsying movements, and seemed to wink noiselessly, turning dark and pale sides alternately in the

435

absorbed still complex light. The dim leafy cone swelled and diminished, its fine top thinning into an extremity of pure sky. Gracie knew of the leaves, of the pencil-thin peak and of the void beyond, but she gazed at the trunk of the tree, at its perfect smoothness and roundness and she felt a shudder of urgency pin her to the earth as if an arrow from directly above her had passed through her body and her feet and pierced the earth below with a long thin electrical thrill.

She was conscious of herself with a fullness she had never known before, and yet also she was absent, or something was absent, there was no anxiety, no thought even, just this thrilling sense of full and absolute being. She stood quite still for a while breathing deeply and staring at the tree. There was fear but now it was uninhabited, impersonal. She kicked off her shoes and stood barefoot, feeling the cool grass creasing the soles of her feet with little precious patterns. She thought, I must walk to the tree, and in doing so I shall make a vow which will dedicate me and alter my whole life, so that I will be given and will never belong to myself again ever. I have to do this. And yet at the same time I am free, I can stay here, I can run back into the wood. I can break the spell which I know I am in some way weaving myself. I can make the tree cease to glow and shimmer, make my flesh cease from trembling, unbind my eyes and disavow this vision. Or I can walk to the tree and make everything different forever.

She began to take off her clothes, her dress fell from her. She stood there white and lithe as a boy, compact and dense, an arrow, a flame. Still in the midst of fear, she began to walk springily across the grass. If she could but keep this visitation pure and whole some greatness would come to be, if she could but cover this precarious space and lay her hands upon the tree she would be filled with angelic power, the world would be filled with it. She moved without sound or sensation upon the grass. She reached the tree and knelt, circling it with her arms, laying her lips upon its cool close-textured silvery bark, a little pitted and dimpled to the touch. As she knelt upright now, pressing her whole body against the shaft, she felt an agony of shame, impossibility, achievement, joy. She lost consciousness.

Something was rubbing softly against her ankle. She stirred and groaned, tried to sit up but seemed to fall, her head rolling away into the dark. She opened her eyes and saw slowly moving green branches above her, saw blue sky, heard hollow sounds of voices over water. She began to pull herself up.

Garth's bare foot, which had been pressing upon her leg, withdrew. He sat resting on the oars, smiling, blinking.

"Oh dear, I fell asleep!" said Gracie. "Was I asleep for long?" She pulled down her skirt.

"Only a few minutes. You'd got into such a funny position, I thought you might hurt your arm. And you were squashing your pretty hat."

"My arm does feel stiff—ooh—pins and needles. Fancy my going to sleep like that."

Gracie streaked back her loose hair, tugged at the neck of her dress, patted a little dew of sweat from her temples. "I'm all hot and crumpled. Oh how strange, I had a dream, just in that little time, so vivid."

"What was it?"

"Well, it wasn't really a dream, it was a memory, something which really happened, one doesn't dream real things, does one."

"I think one does sometimes—one sort of embroiders them—and then one doesn't know what one's remembering and what one's imagining."

"Perhaps it was like that—but no, I do remember it quite clearly, not just as dream. It was something that happened to me when I was about eleven, a sort of mystical experience."

"What happened?"

"Oh, it's nothing to tell. And I can't convey the atmosphere. I was alone in a wood and I took my clothes off and kissed a tree. It was a sort of sustained vision. It was like being released into another world, as if I'd never ever

437

be the same again. Yet it wasn't religion really, it was nothing to do with God or Jesus Christ."

"And were you the same again?"

"I—don't—know. It seems silly not to know, but— It comes back to me sometimes with a sense of being reserved—sort of—"

"Reserved for—?"

"I don't know. It's sometimes made me disappointed with things as they are. Then occasionally it would all come back in a sort of *feeling* about a particular thing, as if that thing partook of *it*, came from that world—"

"I think I—yes—"

"What does it mean?"

Garth said nothing. He moved the boat onward very slowly, lipping the glossy surface delicately with the light oars.

"It was odd, dreaming it suddenly like that. I have dreamt about it—sometimes—I think—only unless one tells one's dream one forgets it. Do you find that? So I was never certain. And now—oh yes—in this dream I ended up by fainting. That was rather marvellous actually. Do you ever faint in dreams?"

"But in real life—if you remember—you didn't faint?"

"Oh no. I held onto the tree for a while, and even then it was all fading. And then I put on my clothes and ran after my mother and Patrick. I never told anybody, *anybody*."

"Not even—?"

"No."

The boat glided into a bower of willows and Gracie gently arrested its movement, letting the lanky green streamers pull through her hands.

"And—so strange—you know we often went back to that wood afterwards but I could never find that special tree again, though I looked for it and looked for it. Wasn't that odd? And it wasn't any kind of tree that I knew at all."

"Where was it? Somewhere in Scotland?"

"No, in Gerrards Cross."

"Well, there are gods even in Gerrards Cross."

438

"Then you think it was religious?"

"There are gods and gods."

"You know, I had that feeling, *that* feeling, and almost that sort of faintness, when—"

"When?"

"Oh well—nothing— I'm making too much of it. I usually don't think about it at all."

They were silent, Garth regarding the girl, Gracie edging herself up a little more and trying to pull her pink sun hat back into shape. It was hot and green in the domed willow arbour but there was a coolness of watery smells muddled in the air. Gracie looked up.

Garth propelled the boat quietly out into the open and London was distantly lucidly hazily present, smudged with trees, the Serpentine bridge, the Hilton hotel, Knightsbridge barracks, and tiny and far away the towers of Westminster.

"Did you ever have anything like that?" said Gracie. She punched her hat.

"Yes."

"Well, what *is* it?"

"You'll be cross if I tell you."

"No, I won't— Oh you don't mean—"

"Yes."

"Just sex?"

"You needn't say 'just.' Intellect is sexless, but spirit is almost all sex. In fact, it is all sex, only it sounds misleading to say so."

"It sounds horrid."

"Not horrid. Consider Shakespeare. All sex, all spirit."

The boat glided a little faster now towards the bridge. Gracie looked at Garth. He was looking thin and fit and sunburnt, his face hard and shiny. The sun had made golden tints in his flowing dark hair and he looked a little like his handsome father only—what?—grimmer. She turned her head aside and said, "There's Peter Pan. I met Matthew there once."

"Matthew—"

"I feel I've lost Matthew."

"I feel I've lost him too. It doesn't matter."

439

"I know. It doesn't matter. Now I feel almost sorry for him somehow—and I think that's a bit awful—a sort of sacrilege—and yet—"

"One must relax one's grip on people. Your pity doesn't harm him, you know. It doesn't even touch him. It doesn't even reach him."

"I know what you mean." She sighed, and with the sigh all her sorrow came flooding back, not after all diminished by one merciful iota. The boat moved into a cool echoing cave in the shadow of the bridge. Dim watery lights wanly flickered overhead. Obscurity at once brought tears into her eyes, like the blank undiverted relaxation of the night-time.

Her days were dreadful now. She lived inside a maimed wreck of herself. Insane hopes still survived in scattered parts of her being, and there were terrible encounters with little separated minds which did not yet know that all was lost. A blind stupid idea of consolation, dying but refusing to perish, was her chief torment: the idea of being consoled by Ludwig for all this suffering. She would take it, where else should she take it, to him. His sweetness, his absurdity, his pure strength, his absolute devotion, were present in every detail to all her thoughts, and he was sovereign over her misery. There was no question of there being anything else in the world at all. Love rolled her and tossed her and trampled her. She had wept more than all her childhood's tears, and such bitter unrelieving tears those were now, tears of hopeless regret and defeat and the rending tenderness of a rejected heart. If she could only hold him in her arms and all be well again. Oh if only if only if only.

"I'll take you back and get you a taxi," said Garth.

"Sorry—"

"That's all right, Gracie. Old friends must help. And I did know you when we were both children."

"You're so kind, Garth, you help everybody."

"One does one's best."

"And I meant to ask you about your novel. Did you hear from the publisher?"

"Yes. They're going to publish it in the autumn."

440

"I'm so glad."

It is odd, thought Gracie. I am still alive. I have put a pretty dress on. I cannot remember putting it on, but here it is. Though I am screaming mad in my heart I can converse. I can even check my tears. I am here in a rowing boat on the Serpentine. I can feel the sun.

"Garth."

"Yes."

"This will sound silly and I don't mean it that way but—"

"Go on."

"You know I said I sometimes had *that* feeling, that special feeling, about things—on some occasions—you know—"

"Yes."

"Well, I had it that day in the Kings Road, when you followed me and wouldn't come to me."

"Really."

"I don't quite know why I call it that feeling, because it was different too—and yet it was that, it sort of shook me, I suppose it's a kind of fear, a sense of the world being quite without order and of other things looking through. I mean, when you went away and then I turned round and saw you walking behind me along the road."

"And you pretended not to notice."

"And I pretended not to notice—that was part of *it*—but I knew that you knew—"

"Yes."

"I felt quite frightened on the station platform, as if I were afraid that you would arrive before the train."

"Sorry."

"No, no, it wasn't bad at all. Then we met again by accident. Wasn't that odd?"

"Yes."

"And you asked me for a drink. Would you have got in touch with me if we hadn't met in the street on that evening? I suppose you wouldn't. I've never asked you why you wouldn't talk to me at Matthew's?"

"It would have been all false."

"But this isn't false."

"This is—nothing, Gracie. I help you to pass the time. That is really all you have got to do just now. This is a little enclosed moment. You will move out of it and forget even its atmosphere. You will remember nothing of this time. You will recover. You have many friends who are waiting for that. One friend perhaps in particular."

"You mean—yes. I must try to—believe in the future. You are so kind, Garth. You are a kind helper and a kind person."

"An instrument. All's well here at least. Let me help you out."

Gracie took his warm hard hand in hers. With a slight shock she stepped from the rocky yielding surface of the boat onto dry land.

❈❈❈

"Are you thinking of taking a holiday?" said Austin.

"A holiday?" said Matthew. "What from?"

"Oh I don't know. All one's moneyed friends run off at this time of year. I supposed you might be thinking of Scotland or a trip to the Med."

"No."

"You're looking tired. I'm sure you need a change of air."

"In fact I've been idling."

"I daresay that's what's tired you. Why don't you do some government work? A chap like you can always pick up the threads. I'm told Charles Odmore is dying to rope you in for something or other."

"I might."

"Well, I must run. It's very kind of you to have asked

me for a drink."

"Not at all."

"I've got to beetle over to the flat to pick up some warmer clothes now the weather's changed."

"One can get a touch of autumn at this time of year in London."

"You know Garth's living at the flat now? He's done some redecorating. The place looks quite something. Even the bathroom."

"That's good."

"It's amazing what a lick of paint and some Regency wallpaper can do."

"I'm sure."

"Oh I forgot to tell you. Garth's publishing a novel in the autumn. He wrote it in America."

"Good for him."

"Crazy *avant-garde* stuff I imagine, I haven't read it. He's awfully busy. He's just started another novel. And he's revising that thing of Norman Monkley's. You remember that chap Norman Monkley wrote a novel?"

"Yes."

"Well, Garth's revising it and it might be published too. Garth's going to let the Monkleys have all the royalties."

"That's good of him."

"Well, he could hardly do less. I went to see the Monkleys last week. Norman was doing some sort of basket work. He's quite a sweet character now."

"Good."

"I must fly. I've got to get over to the flat, and I said I'd cook supper for Mavis. She'll be exhausted. She's been spending today carting the char's idiot child to an institution."

"Mavis is very kind."

"Yes, isn't she. You know, her kindness to me has been an absolute revelation. I felt such a miserable wreck and she's quite put me on my feet again. I must say I had a rotten time. But now I feel like a reconstituted Humpty Dumpty."

"She's good at helping."

"You can say that again. You know, she's awfully like

443

Dorina in a way, she's got that concentrated sweetness, but without any of the feyness and the fear. I don't think Mavis is afraid of anything."

"No, indeed."

"Poor old Dorina was just a sort of half person really, a maimed creature, she had to die, like certain kinds of cripples have to. They can't last."

"Maybe."

"That idiot child will probably die in its teens, the doctor told Mavis. A good thing too. Mavis didn't tell the mother, of course."

"Naturally—"

"Mavis has certainly helped me to see the world in perspective."

"I'm glad."

"One must have a sense of proportion. I used to be a bundle of nerves. I used to worry about every damn thing."

"One shouldn't do that."

"Well, ta ta."

"Wait a minute," said Matthew. They had both risen. A darkish evening brooded like mist in the unlighted room. A wet chill wind had plastered a few translucent stocking-coloured leaves from the walnut tree upon the window pane.

"Yes?"

"Can I ask you something?"

"Anything. Anything in the world."

"You said once," said Matthew, "you said it to several people, that Betty committed suicide. But that wasn't true, was it?"

"Of course it wasn't true," said Austin.

"You said it out of resentment against me?"

"Yes."

"So that you could blame me and make me feel guilt?"

"Yes."

"I see."

"Anything else you'd like to know?"

"Why did you say at the inquest that Betty couldn't swim?"

444

"I didn't say it," said Austin. "Betty was quite a good swimmer. She just hit her head in falling."

"You did say it. I distinctly remember."

"I didn't."

"Oh well," said Matthew, "maybe my memory is at fault. Anyway, what does it matter now."

"You seem depressed," said Austin. "You mustn't give way to depression. You need a week or so at the seaside."

"Maybe."

"Well, I really *must* dash now, I've got to buy frozen peas and all sorts on the way back. Good-bye, then, and chin up."

"Good-bye, Austin."

Alone, Matthew sat down and poured himself another stiff whisky. He was drinking too hard these days.

When a man has reflected much he is tempted to imagine himself as the prime author of change. Perhaps in such a mood God actually succeeded in creating the world. But for man such moods are times of illusion. What we have deeply imagined we feign to control, often with what seems to be the best of motives. But the reality is huge and dark which lies beyond the lighted area of our intentions.

I came to set him free, thought Matthew. I came to change magic into spirit. It was all to be brought about by me. Now when it appears that somehow or other, by means which I do not even understand, he has got out, I ought to be glad. Did I really want to be his mentor and to set up as his judge? No. He has his desolation as I have mine, and let him be free of it. I wanted that bond to be cut, but I did want to cut it myself. And now I am sad as if I had lost a beloved.

"Pinkie," said Clara, coming into the dining-room, where her husband was reading *The Times* over breakfast, "that was Hester on the telephone. She says that Henrietta Sayce has been killed in an accident."

"My God!"

"Oh dear, oh dear——" said Clara. She sat down at the table and dissolved into a speechless rigmarole of whimpering whining tears. Her face looked haggard, wrinkled, smaller, older. Inside her crumpled housecoat with its frayed collar she clung to herself and swayed with the sudden mourning of those who realize that they are old. George watched her with compassion, with fear.

"Oh dear," said Clara, mopping her eyes with her sleeve and shuddering anew, "it's so unbearable. Poor little girl. I know she was a difficult child but she was so sweet and so awfully clever, I can hardly believe it, it sounds idiotic but I used to think sometimes she might make a wife for Patrick when she grew up, they were so fond of each other, and there's all that money on Penny's side, and now she's dead, oh dear, dear, dear——"

"Poor little wretch. What happened?"

"It was last night. She was climbing on some scaffolding and she fell off and broke her skull. She never regained consciousness."

"Poor Penny."

"Yes. Poor Penny. Martin dying of cancer for two years and now this."

"Is Oliver with her?"

"That's another thing. Oliver's incommunicado somewhere in Greece with that Oxford—you know, that Hilton boy. They don't know where he is."

"You'd better go to Penny."

"Hester says Mollie's with her. Mollie know her better than I do, but I'll call over just in case. Oh dear— And it will upset Gracie so. Everything upsets her now. She cries so over the television."

"You'd better ring up Patrick and tell him."

"Oh— I *can't*—"

"Well, I will. Do compose yourself, Clara. After all it isn't one of our children."

"Yes, but it might be. Patrick is so rash and Gracie is wasting away."

"Charles says Matthew told him that Ludwig is going back to America. That's one good thing. Gracie will feel better when he's gone."

"I hope so. I hope he won't get himself killed in the war just so as to upset her more."

"She needs distractions. Perhaps she'll interest herself in the Villa now Matthew's moving out."

"Why is Matthew moving out, I wonder?"

"So as to make a love nest for himself and Mavis, I imagine."

"I gather Mavis is having an awful time with Austin. I think she's a saint."

"Austin is exploiting her. He always exploits women. He's the sort of man who always manages to find the right woman for the sort of trouble he's in."

"You sound envious."

"I'm not. I manage it too. Only in my case she's always the same."

"Darling—"

"Matthew will rescue Mavis at the appropriate moment."

"Oh Pinkie, I must get dressed. Do you think I should ring Penny now? Oh how awful it is! What can I say?"

"Leave it till after ten. Here, have some more coffee. Would you like some brandy?"

"No, no. I'm glad about the Villa."

"So am I, especially if Gracie really means it."

"About our all going to live there together? Oh I'm sure she does. She needs the family terribly just now. We all need each other. We must close our ranks. At least we've still got each other, not like poor Penny, oh dear I can't bear to think of it—"

"Clara, please, coffee."

"Pinkie, it will be good, won't it, when we're all together in that lovely house. It's the only thing that cheers me a little, that and hoping that now Gracie and—"

"She said she wanted Charlotte to come too?"

"Yes, she wants Char too. You know, I think we weren't bossy enough with Gracie when she inherited from Mama. We should have told her firmly to let us deal. She'd have been happier. Children don't really like freedom."

"Maybe. Would Char come though? Isn't she still staying with Mitzi Ricardo?"

"She's only doing it to annoy us, to show us how little she needs us. She'll get over her pique. When we're all together she'll come. She did it for Mama, she'll do it for us. After all, she loves us and family matters to her, though she pretends not. You and me and Gracie and Patrick and Char. We'll put a brave face on the world—"

"You'd better go and see Charlotte."

"I know. I've been so upset about Gracie and so busy and now there's Penny—oh God, I must get dressed— Pinkie, it's too awful, what *can* I say to Penny? I think I won't telephone, I'll just go round. And I've got so much to do today, with the Odmores coming to dinner, at least that's something, isn't it, I do so hope—"

"Hmmm, yes. Rather unfortunate. You haven't seen *The Times*."

"No. What?"

" 'The engagement is announced between Sebastian Robert, elder son of Sir Charles and Lady Odmore and Karen Janice, daughter of Mr. and the Hon. Mrs. Geoffrey Arbuthnot—' Now, Clara, please, *please*—"

"You're a snob, that's why," said Mitzi.

Charlotte was silent. She was slowly putting her clothes into a suitcase.

"You haven't got what it takes," said Mitzi. "You aren't capable of real relationships. People like you just aren't. You've always lived in a polite little world. Nobody ever really meets anybody else in your world. How many people have you ever really met in your life? You became all dead and frozen years ago. You're the real old maid type. You get frightened if anybody looks at you. You've just lived by the conventions. You've always been protected and looked after and spoilt and dressed up in hats and beads and kid gloves. You don't know what real people smell like."

Charlotte was silent.

"I don't know what I'm making these eggs for," said Mitzi. "What's the use of eggs when everything's gone to pieces and died on us? I can't eat. I feel sick with misery. Little you care." She spooned the eggs into the bin.

Charlotte was silent.

The kitchen communicated directly with Charlotte's room. The cottage was tiny. The garden was tiny, pretty, with a pebbled path. There was a fir wood on one side. On the other there were red brick bungalows. Charlotte had already planted a beech hedge to screen them.

"You've never loved anyone in your life. I don't think you really know how to love at all."

"You should never say that to anybody," said Charlotte.

"Well, go on, who have you loved, tell me."

Charlotte looked down into the suitcase where her clothes were carefully folded. Neat packing did not fail when life failed. She bit the inside of her lower lip and breathed deeply. She was determined not to shed any more tears. Mitzi had been hysterical twice, and her own tears had flowed too often. Mitzi was angry and tearless now, but if Charlotte wept there would be more screams. Charlotte forced back the tears, but could not speak.

"Cat got your tongue, dear?"

"Please don't nag me," said Charlotte.

"Nag, nag! It's you who nag, throwing that word at me all the time. When you argue it's reasoning. When I argue it's nagging."

"I'm sorry, Mitzi."

"You're not sorry. If you were you wouldn't wreck everything. You're such a bloody coward."

"It's better to go sooner than later," said Charlotte. "It would be even more awful later."

"That's a stupid argument. Why go at all? You haven't even given it a try."

"It's no use."

"Why not?"

"We're just not compatible."

"Compatible! That's a silly newspaper word. God, and I thought you were so intelligent! We're different. But that's what love's about."

"It's no good, it's just a mistake."

"Just a mistake, she announces calmly. Pity you didn't find that out before we acquired a cottage and a mortgage and a dog, isn't it. Pirrus thinks you're horrible, don't you, Pirrus?"

Pyrrhus, a large black Labrador, rescued, not for the first time, from the Battersea Dogs' Home, looked up anxiously from his place by the stove and wagged his tail. Pyrrhus's lot had always been cast with couples who fought and parted, abandoning him on motorways, on lonely moors, on city street corners. He had been called Sammy and then Raffles and then Bobo. He had only just learnt his new name. He had been happy for a little while in the snug cottage and the rabbity wood with his new

450

humans. Now perhaps it was starting up all over again. He heard the familiar sounds of dispute, the cries, the tears, and he wagged his tail with entreaty. A virtuous affectionate nature and the generous nobility of his race had preserved him from neurosis despite his sufferings. He had not a scrap of spite in his temperament. He thought of anger as a disease of the human race and as a dread sign for himself.

"I'm sorry," said Charlotte.

"What do you think you're going to do anyway? You can't go anywhere tonight. You've missed the last bus. *And* it's raining."

"When I've finished packing I'll go out to the telephone box and get a taxi to take me to the station."

"And where will you go then?"

"To my sister's house."

"To be their pet dog. Sorry, Pirrus. Pirrus has far more spirit and independence than you have. You hate them all. You told me so."

"They're my family. Whether I love them or hate them is irrelevant."

"That's right, deny love. Deny, deny, deny."

"It isn't like that—"

"Thank God I've got the dignity of real love to support me, I haven't got anything else."

"I want love," said Charlotte. She sat down on the bed. "I want it more than I want anything in the world. But you and I just don't get on, we can't manage it. You bully and I sulk."

"I'm not grand enough. I grew up in a house with twenty-five people and one lavatory."

"You're not educated enough," said Charlotte. She snapped the suitcase shut and pushed it to the floor.

"Oh Christ! Well, I can learn, can't I?"

"It isn't just that, Mitzi. We're different animals, we're set at different speeds, everything that's natural to one irritates the other."

"You don't like my table manners."

"Manners are modes of being—"

"I see what you mean about irritating. If you could just hear youself saying that—"

"It's all my fault, I admit—"

"I ought to have a tape recorder."

"I should have had the sheer intellect to see that it wouldn't work. You were very kind to me when I was very sorry for myself and you were a blessed change—"

"Then why not stay with your old blessed change."

"It was all a novelty. I agree we shouldn't have got the cottage and Pyrrhus. We were in far too much of a hurry. There was a sort of excitement and a sort of new world. But it was too good to be true. And as soon as there was any strain it came to pieces."

"What you call excitement I call love. I love you, Charlotte. You've made me love you and you've let me love you and you can't just walk out now."

"It'll be harder later."

"Don't keep saying that."

"Even love doesn't matter all that much," said Charlotte.

"What on earth do you mean? What matters more than love?"

"Reality."

"What are you talking about in that horrible cold way?"

"You and I are just dreaming of love together and we're dreaming private dreams. But reality wins in the end. Reality is family life, duty, everything that's hard and compulsory and not a matter of the caprices of the will."

"Maybe it does win," said Mitzi, "but I don't see why it should win." She picked up the spoon and began slowly to wash the egg off it under the tap. As she turned away her head two tears were rolling down her cheeks. The zip at the back of her dress gaped at the top. She had put on more weight during the honeymoon.

"And what am I supposed to do," said Mitzi in a controlled voice, "while you go crawling back to family and duty?"

"You can stay here. I've told you I'll give you my half—"

"I can't stay here alone, I'd be frightened. And what

about Pirrus. I suppose he goes back to the Dogs' Home. The Dogs' Home man said they'd had him in three times already—"

"Don't bring Pyrrhus into it," said Charlotte. "It's all bad enough without Pyrrhus."

"You just want your feelings to be spared."

"I want to get away," said Charlotte.

"Well, what are we going to do with Pirrus?"

"If you don't want him I could take him to Clara's."

"I do want him. I love him. He's my dog just as much as yours, I should think! He's my dog more than yours since you're going to go away and leave us both."

"Oh stop it," said Charlotte. She put on her coat. "I'm going," she said. "I'll write from London. If you want to sell the cottage I'll arrange it."

Mitzi came out of the kitchen. Tears were quietly coursing down her face. Pyrrhus followed her with a hesitantly wagging tail.

"Please don't go," said Mitzi. "Try it a little longer. I'll be good. I won't nag. I'll learn things. Anything you like. I'll be different. Just give me time. I love you so much. I'll make myself what you want, whatever you want."

Charlotte stared past Mitzi with unfocused eyes, hard and vague. The door of the trap, still ajar, was closing, and it was the moment to dart through, to escape. Later on escape might be much harder or even impossible. Later there would be far more to destroy, more ties to cut, more pain to cause, less of life remaining in which to become, however meanly and modestly, something else. If she did not get out now she would be condemned to mediocrity, assenting to be diminished. Now was the moment to dart through, if necessary to batter through, not into freedom, for freedom could not ever be hers, but into what she had called reality. It was not snobbishness to prefer the austerity of that truth and whatever hope it held, not of happiness, but of some final bitter wit. It was impossible to explain to Mitzi why all this was a mistake, a fantasy, an illusion, why it could never never work. Mitzi always spoke of particular things as if they could be changed. But everything needed changing, they were the wrong people, it was all a charade, or rather two charades, since each of them was performing alone. It was all false and sickening and ultimately frightening.

"I'm going," said Charlotte.

"Don't go. *Don't go.*"

"Good-bye."

"Nobody loves you as I love you. Nobody needs you as I need you."

I suppose that's true, thought Charlotte. Only nothing follows from it.

"I'm sorry."

"You can't go. You just can't go out of that door and leave me and Pirrus behind in this house forever."

If I don't go now, thought Charlotte, I shall have lost a chance which I shall eternally regret and yearn after. I shall look back and see how easy and how painless it would have been now to break a bond which will by then have become a chain. All I have to do is to walk out of that door. These tears will cease. I will walk.

"You can't," said Mitzi.

Charlotte sat down on the bed. Tears covered her face as with a veil and filled her vision. She could feel Mitzi pulling to get her coat off and she allowed her arms to be dragged from the sleeves. Love, even fake love, even dream love, was something after all. After all she loved Mitzi, though it was with a fake dream love. And Mitzi loved her and needed her. And what would become of Pyrrhus? And they had paid money and got a mortgage and planted a beech hedge. Perhaps in the end reality would win, smashing it all to pieces. But oh not yet, not yet, while there could still be reconciliation and scrambled eggs and late night whisky and the shutters to be closed and Pyrrhus's bed to be made. Perhaps it would be worse later, but then perhaps later would never come, perhaps she would die, and it was terrible now and she could not walk through that door and refuse comfort and relief and weary shuttered sleep to herself and to Mitzi that night. Charlotte shed defeated tears, and her tears were already like those of married people who love each other, cannot stand each other, and know that they can never now have any other destiny.

⁂

"He never even talks now, poor mite," said Mrs. Carberry. "When I came to see him he just turned away his head. Who knows what goes on in his mind, what he suffers and thinks there, poor little boy, all shut up inside himself."

"I'm sure he doesn't suffer," said Mavis. But she wasn't sure.

"Still, Walter and the other children are happier," said Mrs. Carberry, "so we must look on the bright side, mustn't we. Ronald was such a burden to them really. I think he frightened them in some sort of way. It is scary when people aren't quite right."

You bore the burden, thought Mavis. Women do.

"What will Mr. Gibson Grey fancy for his supper now?" said Mrs. Carberry. "I've got all the list except that. What about lamb chops and kidneys? I know he's partial to kidneys." Mrs. Carberry was devoted to Austin.

"Yes, that will do very well," said Mavis, "and get some runner beans, he likes those."

"And that Italian ice cream he likes—"

"Yes, a cassata. Thank you, Mrs. Carberry. Wrap up well. It's raining again."

Mavis returned to the drawing-room. The room was dusky with yellow afternoon rain. She kicked her shoes off and lay down on the sofa. She felt desperately tired these days. Matthew was still in Oxford.

She allowed her mind to become vague. She often drifted into vagueness now, bidden by nature to rest out of an

455

almost chemical self-defence. From this vagueness later certainties would come perhaps without too much pain. She feared pain terribly just now, senses of loss and failure which might maim her mind with their horror. She lived in many worlds.

She talked to Matthew on the telephone. He was loving, he was waiting, he understood perfectly. For a long time she had told herself, I am suffering from shock. After Dorina's death how can I live as an ordinary person, make decisions, be held responsible? I am permitted to drift, to perform simple tasks, Mrs. Carberry, Austin. The care of Austin was after all Dorina's legacy.

The resting and the vagueness had made already some things clearer. There was no question of reanimating the hostel. That era of her life seemed not only closed but distant. From that service she had been definitely de-mobbed. The will for it was gone. God was dead at last. The decision itself, thus quietly formed for her by drifting time, was clear enough, but its significance was still some-how obscure. Was she now different because some of her had died with Dorina? Or was this newness a still dormant seed of life which she had gained from Matthew? Drifting time would doubtless answer these questions too. She had only to rest and to wait. Should she sell Valmorana? Matthew would decide.

Meanwhile Austin was still there and showed no im-mediate sign of moving. Garth was occupying the flat, busy with his new novel, and Austin, who attached great importance to Garth's novel, did not want yet to intrude. Austin had no money and no job. Sometimes he went out and looked for a job. Sometimes he just went out. He was omnipresent and yet not burdensome. He was charming to Mrs. Carberry. Her great treat was when he helped her to wash up. Mavis chastely kissed him good night when he went off to bed. He was like a child or a younger brother. Mavis had always so much wanted a brother, not a sister.

She and Austin had stopped talking about anything important. The great storm of talk had passed over and gone. They had said everything to each other. They had

456

talked Dorina through and through. They had talked about their childhoods. They had even talked about Betty. The only subject on which they were silent was Matthew. Now they only chatted.

I am still wearied out by that death, thought Mavis. And I am aged by it. It sets me in the midst of some new truth which I have yet to recognize. The fiercer agony of it had abated sooner than she would have expected. It was as if Dorina's shade had deliberately withdrawn so as to cause her less pain. She had died for me, Mavis thought. But the thought remained vague. She was somehow selfless, she thought, she was somehow good. Now it was as if Dorina had been merely a stage of herself, a phase which she was growing out of. Dorina's departure had released her into some sort of vast beyond.

Changes were taking place, there was no doubt, within the haze. Austin had quietly ceased to be an emergency and was becoming something else, she was not sure what. She had said and thought, and she still said to Matthew on the telephone, that she was helping Austin, saving him from collapse, saving him from misery and mad-making shame. She had helped him, certainly, with help which only she could have given and which his marvellous instinct had led him even relentlessly to seek. Misery and shame she still apprehended in his atmosphere, demonic familiars which could no doubt never be entirely exorcised. Yet now they seemed at last domestic, tiny as flies.

Austin had been to see Matthew, setting off and returning with at least apparent jauntiness. He spoke of Matthew with airs of responsible sympathy, Matthew was not looking well, not looking at all well. "Matthew is a spent storm," he then said. Mavis had not commented on the phrase, but it haunted her. On the telephone she asked Matthew about the meeting. "We talked, it was quite relaxed." "What did you talk about?" "Oh, many things. Betty." "He talked to me about Betty too. It must have been a relief." "Yes. He seems rather better, wouldn't you say?" "Much better. He said you looked tired." "Yes. He said I needed a change. In fact I think I'll go to Oxford for a bit." "Darling—then I won't see you—" "I'll be back soon, don't worry." "Are you going to persuade Louis to stay here?" "Yes, we'll talk of that." "I'm sure you'll persuade him if anyone can. Don't be long away, my darling."

Austin was better. Matthew would be back soon. Mavis longed for Matthew but she could not yet properly run to him, could not yet hurt Austin or lie to him or ask him to leave. Matthew, moving quietly in the background, understood it all, controlled it all. She felt in him already the security of a husband. Whatever happened Matthew would be there. And soon they would be together in that way again. Of course there had been imperfections. He had been so sweet and droll about them. She loved him more for that. They would soon get used to each other and then all would be complete. Matthew was leaving the Villa, he was finding a flat, he would come at the right time and carry her away from all worries and all problems to his secret privacy. When and how he should decide it, she would slip her burden at last.

Of course Austin's sojourn at Valmorana was causing comment, mainly, Mavis imagined, of the kind purveyed by Clara Tisbourne, who constantly adjured her not to be victimized. "Mavis, stop being saintly, that man is a *vampire!*" Clara cried. "I know," said Mavis, and her eyes became huge and hollow with consciousness. "Clara dear, I can't just kick him out, he's so unhappy." "He knows when he's well off," said Clara, "I never saw a man with a clearer idea of which side his bread was buttered." "You don't realize he's a wreck, he lives with terrors." "He appears to thrive on them! Oh well, I expect Matthew will arrange something soon, won't he." "Yes," said Mavis. "Matthew will deal."

Mavis, limp and relaxed upon her sofa, found that she was smiling a little and wondered how on earth she could find anything to smile at in a situation which was potentially so awful. Suppose Austin just wouldn't go? Would Matthew have to induce some sort of showdown? Austin would be defeated again, on the run again. Mavis had been by now thoroughly initiated into Austin's view of himself as a victim. "I am an accidental man," Austin had

458

once said to her. "What do you mean, Austin? Aren't we all accidental? Isn't conception accidental?" "With me it's gone on and on." "We are all like you." Yet he has been unlucky, she thought. If only it could all come right and be peaceful now, if only what had been so precariously healed could be kept safe and whole. Austin and Matthew had chatted amicably. Need there be any more drama?

Of course he *is* a vampire, she thought. And this, she realized, had been somehow why she had smiled. And he knows it and he knows we know it. She pictured Austin's handsome cunning face, radiant with complicity. After all he had accepted his accidents and if he always tried to turn them to account who could altogether blame him? Didn't we all do this? In a way, she thought, he is without vanity and he doesn't even try to deceive. He has got his own kind of truth. What will happen to him, I wonder? Must he be crushed again?

Mavis, almost slumbering now, was roused by a sudden loud report. Something near to her had crashed or exploded with a loud crack and a shattering clang. She sat up in horror. Then she saw that one of the pictures had fallen off the wall. Nothing but that. Nothing to be alarmed about. Nothing to worry about at all. Mavis rose and picked up the shattered picture, a little seascape by Dorina, and turned its face to the wainscot. She was trembling with shock and memory. What strange and terrible things lay ahead?

⁂

Ludwig leaned on the rail of the ship and looked at the sea. The immense undulating grey faintly luminous expanse was soothed and pitted with a light rain whose glittering curtain faded into a still translucent haze through which the horizon cut a hard iron-dark line. Just below the line the clouded sun had laid a streak of icy silver upon the water. Above the line huge bundles of coffee-brown cloudlets marched in fast disorder.

Ludwig's mackintosh was glistening with wet and his head was bare, his short hair rain-darkened and plastered to his head like a cap. Water drops stood and ran upon his face unhindered as upon a rock as he gazed steadily out upon the water. He was going home.

He felt very miserable, very frightened, and very elated. During the days and days of talk with Matthew at Oxford he had taken his world of beliefs and principles entirely to pieces. It had seemed doubtful to him, it still seemed doubtful, whether it could ever be reassembled. All the machinery which provided important reasons for doing anything seemed to have been, in these discussions, dismantled. This was something which had apparently happened before when he talked to Matthew. Only this time it had really happened. Yet why were the cases different? Or was it only that they had led to different conclusions?

It did not seem to him that Matthew had influenced him. Matthew had simply provided the firm surface against which to place the destructive lever. Yes, it had seemed a work of unmitigated destruction. And Matthew's face, especially late at night, for they had talked every night away, had glowed like that of a saint with something too pure to be called cynicism or even nihilism: something which was perhaps more dreadful than either. Yet Matthew himself had seemed untouched, like a holy man whose form is seen to burn but is not consumed.

"Of course," said Matthew, wearily, rather near the end, "if you decide to go back you will at least satisfy a nervous urge not to have missed anything." "But I will have missed something," said Ludwig. "I shall have missed Oxford." "Oh well, you may get that later on. This you can only have now." "But I'm not just collecting experiences," Ludwig shouted. "Of course not. I am," said Matthew, yawning and looking at his watch.

At one stage it had seemed easiest simply to decide what he most wanted to do and do it, since duty and history and love had all turned out to be hollow contraptions, through which one looked into some awful white space. But the examination of this problem only gave an even more primitive form of life to the questions it had seemed to dispose of. What *did* he want to do? He was far too contaminated by those old ideas of which he could make so little sense even to pose the question in a pure way. Sometimes this purity itself seemed the most desirable thing of all. "Oh, toss a coin!" said Matthew, departing to bed.

"If you want to get away from Gracie," said Matthew, "that's one way of solving it by making it into a simpler problem. On the other hand, if you are dreaming of a reconciliation with Gracie then you will at least in that sense want to stay. It could need courage to stay if you aren't." Ludwig clutched his head. Was *that* it? Was he just running away from the shame of staying on after breaking Gracie's heart? "Do you conceive of yourself as having behaved like a cad?" asked Matthew. Ludwig had never put the question. He did now. It opened vistas. And did he dream of reconciliation with Gracie? Yes. Sometimes he dreamed of nothing else. "Try to find a few small things which are clear," said Matthew.

Of course he had in some superficial sense "decided" to go home before Matthew's arrival in Oxford. But he had, after sending the cable to stop his parents' journey, told nobody else, and almost felt that he had merely established a further interim for reflection. He dreaded the return of Andrew Hilton, who would bring with him such a breath of the reality and dearness of what, here, he would be losing. And Ludwig weighed that loss very fully, to the point of anguish. Then the more he thought of it, the more it seemed that the two great halves of his former decision remained solid. He was not to fight in the war and he was not to waste his talents and that added up to staying put. What had changed? Perhaps only his relations with Gracie.

"Get Gracie out of the way if you can," said Matthew

patiently. Ludwig struggled. And it did seem to him at last that his decision about Gracie was something separate, and probably more certain than the other matters with which it had come to seem so mixed up. "Be ruthless," said Matthew. Ludwig tried. He had rejected Gracie, and that was indeed the word, for reasons which were, if any reasons were good, good reasons. He loved Gracie and he wanted her and she could make him very happy but he knew too that in tying himself now to this young girl he would lessen himself and diminish his possibilities in a way for which this love could not compensate. There was, after all, an ineradicable doubt. They could not really be of one mind and he would grow away from her. She would be just a part of his world. He had no clear ideal of marriage but he could now see this as less than perfect. And it was too early to accept a compromise. These things, when he could force himself to eschew the language of love, became clear. His daemon said "no," and when he had yielded to it he had felt, amid his wretchedness, a tiny grain of relief which was made of the deepest stuff of his being.

So he came to see this at least plainly. Nor was he in any doubt about his parents. "Do they come in?" said Matthew. "No," said Ludwig. "I mean I love and I care, but I can't take them as a measure." "Has your father influenced you?" "No—or only in so far as he is myself." "And you aren't afraid of being thought a coward?" "No. That least of all." Why then was he here on this ship moving hourly closer to the United States of America? He knew he was not just solving the problem of Gracie by running away from it. That problem, however agonizingly it still remained with him staining the tissues of his imagination and his thought, was solved. He did not even trouble now to probe and doubt his feelings. This was a great love, but a great love is not the measure of all things. Of course, he suffered, of course Gracie suffered. It did not matter absolutely. He could sustain the parting from Gracie in the end, either in America or in Europe, since sustained it had to be. Oh God, she was sweet, sweet he felt at every hour and his body mourned for her. The pain was pure and devoid of dubiety. But then, with that at least made clear and set aside the solid diptych of his former decision faced him still. Was he after all returning, as Matthew had at one point hinted, just out of a nervous desire to have the experience of martyrdom merely because it proposed itself? And even if that was so did it matter? And if it did not matter why did it not matter?

One thing which was evident was that Ludwig's certainty that he must return grew somehow with the days. If this was simply the clarification of the desire to return, the "do what you want" which he had yearned for earlier, that would indeed be something. The particular comfort of Oxford filled him at times with a sort of aesthetic distaste, but that was partly a nervous defensive affectation, in so far as it was not a product of deeper movements of a different kind. Oxford was solid enough, and what he was abandoning was a reality of wonderful value in a world in which few values were anything like as pure and clear. That much he knew, as he struggled to understand why he was doing what he now seemed to have no doubt that he had to do. "It is important to understand it *now*," he said to Matthew. "Later it will be blurred, I shall have forgotten."

"Try to stop looking at yourself and look at the issue," said Matthew, exhausted. "Stop worrying about your motives. All right, you'll have to come back to your motives, being you, but give them a rest, for Christ's sake." Ludwig looked. It occurred to him then with some shame that in the hot hurlyburly of his own motivation he had almost forgotten the cause. He thought about the war. He recited the facts, the history of it, like a litany, to Matthew, who remained silent. He thought about justice and about man's inhumanity to man and about how there are things one cannot be a party to. Here it stood outside him and before him with a plainness which made even the desire for virtue seem like a frivolous personal whim. "Does that work?" said Matthew. "Not quite," said Ludwig. "I can't quite do it that way. That's not all." "What remains then?"

Ludwig felt that, for him, what remained was a small

463

pure undoctrined need to bear witness. Not even perhaps to do battle for a view, except in the sense that bearing witness was doing battle. And since there was this need the thing itself demanded that it be done unambiguously and fully. The requirement was, when it came to it, wonderfully impersonal in quality and seemed to come cleanly away from the mess of his motives like a fossil coming out of the cliff. This was how the world was, so this was what a man must do. "That's it!" he said to Matthew, explaining it at last. "What does 'so' mean?" said Matthew. "What do you mean, what does 'so' mean?" "What does 'so' mean in 'This is how the world is, so this is what a man must do'?" Ludwig thought, and said, "Am I back at the beginning again?" "Not necessarily." "Perhaps I am thinking about myself after all," said Ludwig. "Perhaps I am thinking about myself in the future and how much less complete a person I'll be if I pass this up. But if this is my thought how does it differ from just wanting an experience?" "I think it differs." "It's hard to see just now, my eyes are blurring." "One's eyes always blur," said Matthew.

It didn't seem to come from myself, thought Ludwig, it seemed to come out of the issue, and that's what made it so clean. But Matthew is right. Why should it come out of the issue and attach itself to *me*? What's the link? He put the question thus to Matthew and Matthew did not answer for a long time. Then he said, "Well, one could generate the whole argument again out of that question." "So we *are* back at the beginning?" "No, or if we are it's with a difference." "What difference?" "We've got two very pure items here." "You mean—to be joined? I feel that too. But perhaps it's all just psychology." "If anything isn't just psychology this isn't." "Well, or refined self-interest or—" "God would live here if God existed." "Where?" "Inside your link." "And if He doesn't exist there's no link?" "He doesn't exist but your argument is not faulty." "So there is a link?" "There are two pure things juxtaposed." "Simply juxtaposed?" "Simply pure." After that, since it was four o'clock in the morning, they went to bed. The following day Matthew returned to London.

It had stopped raining. The streak of silver light had closed up and the sea was more ponderously grey, choppier now that the calm rain had ceased to stroke it, throwing up little fragments of white foam which left the wave crests and were whipped up into the coldly driving air. Ludwig thought about Oxford and the pain brought tears into his eyes and the sudden tears warmed his cold damp face. He had no books with him on the ship, for the first time no books. He had sacrificed something of immense value, something very particularly his, and which he would now almost certainly never find again. Would he in later years detest the Ludwig who had made that sacrifice and would his life be soured by hatred for that feckless person? Perhaps that bitter disfiguring regret, and not the human completeness of which he had spoken to Matthew, would be his reward for this decision. Not wholeness, but to be devoured by obsessive remorse. Perhaps. Well, it was done. He had let the college down, of course. They would be without an ancient history tutor for the Michaelmas term. He wondered if Andrew would cancel the Aristophanes class. Perhaps he would do it with MacMurraghue. At the thought of the Aristophanes class he closed his eyes. He had wanted that Aristophanes class more than he had ever wanted anything in his life, more than he had wanted Gracie.

He fumbled in the pocket of his raincoat for something which he had brought with him for a purpose. He drew it out. Gracie's engagement ring. She had sent it back to him for the second time with a sweet tragic note, which Ludwig had read through once and then destroyed in case he should be tempted to read it again. He remembered it by heart nevertheless and he knew that it would remain with him for his torment. *I am so unhappy I think I shall die of it. I want nothing in the world except what I can't have, you, you. . . .* Ludwig looked at the ring and remembered the scene in the jeweller's shop and how he had kissed Gracie in the taxi afterwards. He recalled the rather crinkly striped dress she was wearing and how he had smelt the fresh smell of the material mingled with the faint scent of her make-up and her sweat when he laid his head down on her breast and felt her heart beating against his cheek. How appallingly clear memory could be. Would these pictures ever mercifully fade? He looked at the ring. Then with a quick motion he threw it into the Atlantic. Eight hundred pounds' worth of Bond Street diamond flashed away from him to vanish into the brightening air. He did not see it hit the water. And as he saw it go he thought, a greater man would have kept it.

✠✠✠✠

Matthew was doing his meditating in the upstairs passenger lounge. It was not yet time for him to meet Ludwig in the bar. They had talked so much at Oxford, there was a slight shyness and by tacit agreement they let each other alone during parts of the day. Then there were the regular rendezvous to be looked forward to. Matthew wished that the voyage might never end.

While Matthew had been helping Ludwig to clarify his motives for leaving, he had hoped somehow at the same time to clarify his own; for he had realized, a day or two before he went to Oxford, that he would probably have to go. He had not of course discussed his own situation with Ludwig, and Ludwig with the sweet egoism of youth had not inquired or, Matthew believed, even wondered. When Matthew announced that, if Ludwig had no objection, he would accompany him, Ludwig had cried, "Gee, that's great of you!" and seemed to imagine that the pleasure of his company would be quite a good enough reason for Matthew to take the trip. And in a way, thought Matthew,

466

he was right, even righter than he dreamed. But of course there were other things. And he had not told Ludwig that he was going away forever.

His departure had come to seem to him inevitable. But what did that mean? Had Austin, with unerring instinct, made the one move which would render his brother powerless? Had he not only broken the spell but turned the tables? Matthew's quaint sadness at having been unable to be the instrument of his brother's salvation seemed something puny now when there was so much more to regret. Had he lived all these years with himself to find himself at the end still so unpredictable? Was he now just running away out of chagrin?

Something or other had, in however ghastly a sense, done Austin "good." Perhaps it was simply Dorina's death. And perhaps the "good" was temporary, a prelude to some new and different phase of obsession. If Austin now seemed "free" without going through any of the procedures of spiritual reconciliation and liberation recognized by Matthew, could it still be that he was, in this respect at least, really free? Was it genuinely the case that Austin didn't care any more? It almost seemed to Matthew at one point that Austin had simply forgotten, as if some banal almost impersonal relationship had been slipped into the place where the horror had been. The fear seemed to have gone and the hatred was changed. To say that the hatred was gone would be to say too much. But again, in some way quite outside Matthew's calculations, it had changed.

At that stage, and when that was clear, that change of some quite unauthorized kind was taking place, had taken place, Matthew felt with a blessed simplicity that it was time for him to leave off. Any further close interest or concern from him would be not only fruitless but intrusive and improper. Nature could now take its course in some soothingly vulgar way. There could be drifting apart. He could even allow himself to come, and he laughed suddenly at this, to detest Austin heartily. That was where his high purposes had got him, and the best they could apparently do. Oddly enough, Taigu would have appreciated this. So it would drift on, London was quite large enough now to contain them both, and the quality of this failure would be the quality of his own final acceptance of an utter ordinariness of life.

But then, with the inner gasp of a man told by his doctor that he has a serious illness, Matthew realized how very much more awful the situation really was. Of course he had not minded Mavis looking after Austin, of course he had waited and understood. Of course Mavis was in some harmoniously inevitable way Matthew's future. This was the resting place and this the end. Time had circled to this point. And when Matthew had swallowed the knowledge that there was nothing more he could ever do for Austin except let him alone, and that this would be quite adequate, he associated Mavis instinctively with this sense of defeat and the inception of a humbler, more domestic sort of life quite devoid of the drama which he realized he had with a certain eagerness returned to England to find. The unexpected simplicity of his love for Mavis had even seemed to symbolize the modest enlightenment which he had achieved.

But at a certain moment, with the sudden alteration of quantity into quality which dialecticians speak of, he saw. One way of putting it was that Austin had simply stayed with Mavis too long and had contaminated her. Matthew felt stirrings of a sudden blind painful rage which made him feel, for the first time in his life, that he resembled his brother. With a strange precision Austin had taken his revenge for the pollution of Dorina. Of course Austin had not really done this "on purpose." It had all been, like so many other things in the story, accidental. But it was too beautiful not to have been also the product of instinct. Of course too they were not, he supposed, in love with each other. They did not need to be in love with each other, any more than he and Dorina had needed to be. Nor had Mavis's love for him swerved or faded. It did not need to fade, for everything to have become suddenly so dreadful. Naturally, Mavis had become fond of Austin, as women so often did become fond of Austin, sorry for him, maternal, and so on. As Matthew had sincerely said in a letter, such plain affection was just what Austin

468

needed at this juncture in his life. But then what? Mavis's affection could not be treated like a sticking plaster and pulled off when the wound had healed.

Austin was cunning. And Mavis, it became increasingly clear, expected Matthew somehow to "deal." She could not manage without an initiative from Matthew which would inevitably seem like a re-enactment of the past. Of course Austin was not "cured," Matthew could now see, of course the deep things were exactly as they had always been, and exactly as they would always be, whatever pious hopes the self-styled good might have about the matter. Mavis must be claimed or lost. Austin must be allowed once more to play the role of victim. This he expected and perhaps even wanted. The stage had been set again by whatever deep mythological forces control the destinies of men.

I am simply jealous, Matthew told himself, trying to find a simple brutal way to make sense of the misery he felt. He went to see Ludwig in Oxford to find distraction and to see if a look at someone else's mess could enlighten him about his own. In a curious separated way he had thoroughly enjoyed talking to Ludwig. It was, he told himself with bitter jocularity, his most satisfying sexual experience since the boy in the Osaka airport bookshop. As their discussion battered on he had sometimes almost panted with emotion. His affection for Ludwig blossomed to an extent which surprised him. So, in the midst of horrors, there could after all be something new. And as he listened to Ludwig and replied to his arguments, and as he studied the dear head, so grave and beautiful in debate, he rehearsed what he would do, how at a certain point he would simply take Mavis away, take her for a while out of England, how he would again enact the fake murder of his brother, and how absolutely fake it would be, and how Austin would enjoy shedding his crocodile tears and rolling in his humiliation and hating his brother and sobbing out to the fates that it was all as it had ever been. Only as, once again, listening to Ludwig Matthew imagined it, he realized that he would never do it. Ludwig was godsent. He would go away with him.

And when it came to it he did not even care too much whether Mavis understood or not. People could not always be understanding everything. He wrote her a sad ambiguous letter. Let her read between the lines if she could. He recognized that he felt resentment against Mavis and that this helped. Her carelessness and then her sentimentality had brought about the whole thing. She had acted stupidly, she had acted like a woman. And after all he had never needed women in his life. It had been so ephemeral mischance that he had failed her in a crucial way. She had been sweet about it, almost as if she was pleased. Perhaps she was pleased. Perhaps it makes a woman feel maternal. It matters less to a woman, women are vague. It had made him feel very sad and mortal. And remembering that failure now he thought how many awful irrevocable things had happened. He thought about the child lying dead in the roadway, Norman lying unconscious on the landing. These moments would be forever in his nightmares. And he thought about Austin and he felt horror and hatred and a desire to get away. He wrote a rather abstract account of the whole matter to Taigu. *Perhaps this is my ultimate spitefulness against my brother,* he said in the letter. Taigu did not reply. Taigu never wrote letters. Leaving, when it came to leaving, was suddenly quite easy. Later, he would feel tenderness and regret and loss. Later still he might feel that he had done the right thing. Now he simply felt that he was escaping.

As for Ludwig's troubles, he found them thoroughly exhilarating. He did not now at all try to analyse, as he would have done even a few years earlier, his love for the boy. It was enough that it was love and that its light fell a little way into the future. He would stick by Ludwig through whatever unpredictable trials lay immediately ahead. "I'll be asked what I represent." "Yourself." "They'll ask me about pacifism, they'll ask me about God." "Deny everything." "What am I then?" "A solitary conscientious American." And a very good travelling companion to have, thought Matthew. He felt at the moment that he would willingly spend the rest of his life with the young man. But he was too old to worry himself with looking ahead and at least wise enough to know that it was useless. What would be would be. There was America to come and beyond America lay Japan. Perhaps he would end his days sweeping up azalea leaves after all.

Matthew, ensconced in an armchair in the upper lounge, was not in fact now thinking about the past or the future. He was reflecting that he had not really answered Ludwig's crucial question. Or was what he had said the answer? It was no use asking Taigu. Taigu would only laugh and offer him a cup of tea. Of course Ludwig did not need to know. It was marvellous how little Ludwig needed now that he was launched. Matthew felt that he was lucky to be with him even as a spectator. And then he recalled, with a poignant sense of connection, the scene in the Red Square, and the solitary conscientious Russian who had walked over to join the protesters and to shake their hands and who had possibly in that one instant wrecked his entire life. Was it not enough to have these as one's heroes, and to recognize and imitate them without otherwise knowing why? What Taigu thought about it all he would never really know. He would never be able to share in Taigu's mind. From the good good actions spring with a spontaneity which must remain to the mediocre forever mysterious. Matthew knew with a sigh that he would never be a hero. Nor would he ever achieve the true enlightenment. Neither the longer way nor the shorter way was for him. He would be until the end of his life a man looking forward to his next drink. He looked at his watch and drifted down to the bar.

❧❦❧❦❧

"Darling, our very first party!" said Gracie, now nearly two months pregnant, to her husband.

The drawing-room in the Villa was looking charming. Mrs. Monkley, who came to do, had been cleaning and polishing all day, and everything glowed and shone. The creamy Sung vase which Matthew had given them for a wedding present occupied the centre of the mantelpiece. The room was full of small fat William Morris cushions, some placed upon the floor in case guests subsided. The many lamps were soft. It was already dark outside. On the table dozens of glasses glittered beside dozens of bottles. It was the moment of quietness before a big party when the host and hostess survey their lovely home and wonder why they have been such fools as to invite all those people.

Garth was wearing a dark suit of silkily light tweed. His hair was shorter and sleeker. Gracie was in peacock blue Thai silk. They were a handsome pair. Garth looked proudly at his bright little wife. "Moggie, you look lovely."

"New dress."

"That's right. I want everything you wear to be new. I want to feel that I invented you the day before yesterday."

"You did."

"And you don't mind?"

"Are you sure *you* don't? I might be your Frankenstein."

"I saw happiness passing and grabbed it."

"And you don't feel that you ought to be having a destiny of deprivation and struggle?"

"No."

"And you don't mind our being rich?"

"No."

"And you think being happy is a proper occupation for a lifetime?"

"Yes."

The bell rang. It was their first guests.

"I conveyed Ma and Austin in Kierkegaard," said Patrick. "Hello, love birds."

"Gracie, darling girl," said Austin, kissing her.

"Dearest Austin—"

"Mavis is coming later."

"Darlings, you've got the new curtains up," said Clara.

"What a manly little fellow your brother is!" said Garth.

"Don't tease him!"

"I think you are three very handsome men," said Clara.

"We are all handsome," said Austin. "We are beautiful. We are a very good-looking family."

Patrick, blond, fluffy-haired, plump, smooth, rosy-complexioned and six foot tall, punched his brother-in-law amicably.

Clara was now wearing her hair straight and rather short. She looked radiantly juvenile. So did Austin, his copious golden locks flowing down onto his collar. He never wore glasses now. His contact lenses were a great success.

The door bell began to ring again and the hired butler went to attend to it. Outside in the kitchen Mary Monkley kicked off her shoes and sipped a tiny sherry. Norman was so kind to her these days, like a nice child. But she missed the bad old Norman whom she would now never see again. Funny, wasn't it. And if she had been still alive Rosalind would have been eight today.

"Gracie, such a pretty room."

"Garth, what super reviews of your book."

"What a lovely idea with the cushions."

"Wasn't that Kierkegaard parked outside?"

"Gracie, what a pretty dress."

"I was saying to Gracie, what a lovely idea with the cushions."

"Oliver has sold Kierkegaard to Patrick."

"There's one born every minute."

"Clara dear, my spies tell me you will soon be Lady Tisbourne."

"Ralph, how nice to see you. Patrick is in the kitchen doing the ice."

"Karen and Sebastian have brought a Spaniard back from their honeymoon."

"Not *ménage à trois?*"

"No, no, he's a cook or something."

"Gracie has got a treasure."

"Isn't she the mother of that child who——"

"Sssh. Hello, Austin. You're looking a picture. Where's Mavis?"

"She's coping with the decorators."

"Garth, what marvellous reviews of your book."

"Here come Mr. and Mrs. Pargeter."

"Ann, how delicious you look."

"I say, have you seen the reviews of Garth's book?"

"Sure to be a best seller."

"Mollie Arbuthnot is crazy about Karen's Spaniard."

"Geoffrey is furious."

"Oliver Sayce is buying a bookshop in Oxford."

"Charlotte Ledgard is living with a weight-lifter."

"I can't quite see Char reposing on a hairy bosom."

"My dear, it's a female weight-lifter."

"What a charming idea with the cushions."

"Isn't it a charming idea."

"Patrick is going to read history at Balliol."

"George and Geoffrey are discussing the crisis."

"Isn't Austin gorgeous."

"He nestles in the bosom of the Tisbourne family."

"He always was a friendly little viper."

"Gracie adores him."

"Mavis is furious."

"Oliver and Andrew have borrowed Richard's yacht."

"Richard is charging them the earth."

"Isn't Ann looking happy."

"How long for though."

"Andrew is spending his sabbatical term studying Oliver."

"Matthew is making another million in New York."

"Mollie Arbuthnot has paella for breakfast every day."

"Ralph is going to read history at Balliol."

"There's Dr. Seldon."

"He looks as if he's got something."

"Doctors are so infectious."

"People ought not to invite doctors."

"I hear that chap's in prison."

"What chap?"

"That American chap."

"What was his name? Lucas Leferrier or something."

"Where is he in prison?"

"In America."

"Oh, in America."

"Wasn't he the chap that used to dangle after Gracie?"

"Sssh. Hello, Gracie, what a lovely party."

"What lovely reviews of Garth's book."

"There isn't any ice."

"Patrick and Ralph are still out in the kitchen."

"Do you think Austin is wearing a wig?"

"I wouldn't blame anyone for wearing a wig these days."

"What's he in prison for?"

"Drugs or something."

"I do hope they don't take drugs at Balliol."

"Matthew has gone into a monastery in Kyoto."

"Where's that?"

"Mollie Arbuthnot is learning the guitar."

"Charlotte has gone native near Midhurst with a female acrobat."

"Clara will soon be Lady Tisbourne."

"Mollie will soon be Lady Arbuthnot."

"Aren't we all getting grand."

"Anyway, we're still socialists."

"That fat man must be a gatecrasher."

"No, his name's MacMurraghue, he's Gracie's pet."

"Richard is buying a house in Eaton Square with an indoor swimming pool."

"Matthew is staying with the parents of that chap."

"What chap?"

"That American chap."

"Hello, Karen darling."

"Hello, Gracie darling."

"Hello, Sebastian darling."

"Look at Gracie and Karen locked in each other's arms."

"Patrick has visited Charlotte, he says it's a hoot."

"Won't somebody go and talk to Mr. Enstone?"

"I don't think people should invite clergymen."

"Matthew is opening a Protest Bookshop in New York."

"How ghastly."

"My dear, he's coining money."

"Oliver has gone into partnership with Matthew."

"There's big money in Protest."

"Look at Gracie and Sebastian locked in each other's arms."

"Garth is a cool customer."

"Garth is a great man."

"Like father like son."

"Mavis and Austin are turning Valmorana into a hotel."

"Mavis will do all the work."

"Austin will chat with the guests in the bar."

"Austin is a caution."

"One can't help admiring him."

"Austin is like all of us only more so."

"He gets away with it."

"We'd all like to."

"Everybody is justified somehow."

"Mollie Arbuthnot is discussing Spanish tummy with Dr. Seldon."

"Patrick has visited Charlotte, he said it's awfully touching."

"Matthew has gone to Hollywood."

"Where's that?"

"Have you seen the super reviews of Garth's book?"

"Garth is going to write best sellers under the name of Norman Monkley."

"Where's Mavis?"

"She isn't coming."

"She looks just like Dorina these days."

"She's got that pale haunted look."

"Austin would give anybody a pale haunted look."

"George and Geoffrey are still discussing the crisis."

"Patrick and Ralph are still out in the kitchen."

"MacMurraghue is sloshed."

"Penny Sayce has cancer."

"My dear, she can't have, it's impossible."

"Gracie's expecting."

"So is Karen."

"So is Ann."

"Hester and Clara are matchmaking for their grandchildren."

"Everything is moving into a new phase."

"MacMurraghue has passed out in the hall."

"There's still no ice."

"It doesn't matter, everyone's too drunk to notice."

"What did you say?"

"Don't you feel that everything is moving into a new phase?"

"Gracie, it's so lovely to partake in your happiness."

"I say, look at Austin."

"What do you mean?"

"Look at his right hand."

"He's holding his glass."

"He can move his fingers."

"I was telling Gracie it was so lovely to partake in her happiness."

"Yes, lovely."

"A privilege."

"I say, look at the time, we must be off."

"So must we."

"So must we."

"Such a lovely party."

"Such a marvellous evening."

"Such super reviews."

"Our revels now are ended."

"Good night, darling."

"Good night, darling."

"Good night."

"Good night."

"Good night."

#1

BLOCKBUSTER OF THE YEAR!

THE TRADE

by

H. B. GILMOUR

Meet Daniel Shorer . . .

The slum kid who wrote—and slept—his way out of the ghetto; whose name is on every bestseller list, whose body warms the best beds in town . . . The literary superstar whose bold novels and lusty life-style made him a generational hero—until he became obsessed with a woman who was too young, too beautiful and too lost . . .

The explosive behind-the-scenes novel that explores and exposes the World of the Bestseller! A shattering insider's look at the passions, politics and people who make and break the books that become #1! "AUTHENTIC . . . A SEXY, ABSORBING BOOK!"—*Publishers Weekly*

(78-009, $1.50)

available wherever paperbacks are sold

OUTSTANDING FICTION FROM
WARNER PAPERBACK LIBRARY!

☐ **THE SHERMANS OF MANNERVILLE** by Jack Ansell

"The novel of the year. The best novel of Jewish-American life since *Call It Sleep*."—Stephen Longstreet   (66-801, $1.25)

☐ **57TH STREET** by George Selcamm

An intimate, revealing novel of "the very private lives of people in the New York music scene."—*The New York Times*   (66-818, $1.25)

☐ **DIRTY MONEY** by Norm Rudman and Ernie Sheldon

Myron Gendelman, veteran of a thousand hours of computer dating and still a virgin. Sexual fantasist supreme. And engraver at the U.S. Mint. Is he responsible for the absolutely filthy $5 bills that are flooding the country?   (65-831, 95c)

☐ **NEIGHBORS** by Russell O'Neil

Meet the neighbors. Tom and Ethel. Cynthia and Herb. Joe and Peg. In their lush corner of suburbia life is good. Not for them the violence of the city. Pot is out, bourbon in. Even their adulteries are discreet. They have the good life—if you don't look too closely.
                    (66-851, $1.25)

☐ **THE AMERICAN PRINCESS** by Edward Kuhn, Jr.

"A richly readable and exciting story of an American girl married to a prince of a tiny Himalayan mountain kingdom."—*Saturday Review*   (68-865, $1.50)